The Last Raider

DOUGLAS REEMAN

The Last Raider

HUTCHINSON OF LONDON

Hutchinson & Co (Publishers) Ltd
3 Fitzroy Square, London W 1 P 6 JD

London Melbourne Sydney Auckland
Wellington Johannesburg and agencies
throughout the world

First published 1963
Second impression 1970
Third impression 1972
Fourth impression 1974
Fifth impression 1976
Sixth impression 1979
© Douglas Reeman 1963

Printed in Great Britain by The Anchor Press Ltd
and bound by Wm Brendon & Son Ltd
both of Tiptree, Essex

ISBN 0 09 105640 3

*For Winifred
with my love*

Contents

'And God shall wipe away all tears from their eyes; and there shall be no more death, neither sorrow, nor crying, neither shall there be any more pain: for the former things are passed away.'

Revelation
Chapter xxi
Verse 4

Part One

'. . . a gesture of defiance.'

I

THE great sprawling mass of Kiel dockyard and its crowded harbour seemed to stagger as the late December gale swept down from the Baltic and lashed the grey water into a wild turmoil of whitecaps. The rain, which had been falling heavily for three days, hissed across the sheds and low dockside buildings, and moved in sudden flurries through the deep puddles with each fierce squall. It was early afternoon, yet already the visibility was poor, and shaded lights gleamed faintly from the offices of the German Naval Headquarters.

The Admiral flinched as an extra savage squall sent a flurry of rain crashing against the tall windows of his office, and made his lofty view of the dockyard below even more distorted. The packed assembly of moored vessels, battle-cruisers, destroyers and supply ships was merged into one jagged panorama of rain-washed steel, broken here and there by a glittering pattern of dancing spray.

Behind him he could hear the subdued and respectful murmurings of his staff, and he could see their figures reflected in the black glass of the windows, their uniforms gleaming beneath the harsh gas lighting which hung above the giant map-table. The table filled almost a quarter of the room, and at a glance showed the sprawling wastes of the North Atlantic, the North Sea and the narrow gauntlet of the English Channel. Hundreds of small flags and coloured counters represented ships, both friendly and hostile, recent losses and the long black barriers of the minefields.

The Admiral frowned, and plucked impatiently at the gilt buttons on his frock-coat. His staff were all waiting. They were always waiting nowadays it seemed. Gone was the excitement and eagerness of the early days, and after three years of war, with 1918 only five days ahead, they seemed to have become as stale and entangled as the counters on the chart.

13

He forced himself to turn and face them once more. He saw them stiffen automatically, their faces empty and waiting to record his own mood.

He cleared his throat. As he moved his heavy body nearer the rectangle of officers, the light shone down on his massive silver head so that it appeared too heavy for his short, thick-set figure, resplendent nevertheless in an impeccable uniform with its display of forgotten decorations.

'Gentlemen!' His deep-set eyes moved along their faces, hard and yet sad. 'I have called you together once again to tell you the news you have all been waiting to hear.' He waited, sensing the new interest which seemed to move through the oak-panelled room. 'We of the High Sea Fleet Staff know better than most of the stalemate which has existed in the war at sea for some time. On land it is no better, but perhaps there it is less important. At sea there can be only one victor. The British hope to crush us with their blockade.' He paused to wave his hand towards the streaming windows. 'The rusty mooring-cables of our major war vessels are proof of their success, and we have tried repeatedly to bring the enemy to his knees by similar methods. The newest arm of the Navy, the U-boats,' he paused again, as if the very mention of submarines was distasteful to him, 'have attacked enemy foodships and supply vessels of every kind, while our cruisers have been forced to shelter behind the booms and nets of our harbours. The result has been, of course, that the enemy has brought in the convoy system, and the barbarism of this unrestricted type of warfare has also lost us our friends and sympathizers overseas, and may even have forced the Americans to make their final decision to attack the Fatherland!' He was speaking more openly than usual, but he knew his staff extremely well. He pointed at the long red lines which marked the trade and convoy routes in and out of the British Isles. 'In the past we have sent out single raiders to harass the enemy shipping lanes. Good ships, commanded by dedicated and fearless captains. Pause for a moment, gentlemen, and think back to some of those raiders. *Dresden*, *Moewe*, *Seeadler* and others, all of which did more to upset the balance of sea power than any major fleet action!' His voice rose to a shout, and he leaned on his hands, his shadow across the chart like retribution itself. 'With the loss of our colonies and bases overseas many said that the days of the commerce raider were over. How could such a vessel exist? they asked. For months I have been advocating such a raider, one more glorious episode to be added to the name of the Imperial German Navy!' He had their full attention now, and for some reason they had all risen to their feet, their faces fixed on his.

'I do not have to tell you, the members of my staff, that the war has become bogged down with pessimism, and even despondency. The Western Front is at a standstill. Rain and mud have done as much as the casualties to cause a stalemate there. In the Navy morale is low, dangerously so! Our men need a symbol, a gesture of defiance which will rock the enemy to his foundations. A single raider, which can come and go as it pleases, which will sink, burn and destroy enemy ships wherever they can be found. Huge enemy forces must be deployed to search for it. Sailings will be cancelled, and desperately needed cargoes will lie rotting in New York and Sydney.'

The Admiral lifted his massive head from the chart, his eyes clouded with emotion. 'At last, gentlemen, I have been heard! The Grand Admiral, even the Emperor, has given his consent! The work which you and I have done to this end will at last be rewarded!'

He paused as the room came alive with excited cries and even handclaps. The Staff Operations Officer, a tall, dignified captain, saw the Admiral nod in his direction, and rapped on the table for silence. Unlike his superior, he was unemotional, and his cool precise voice brought them all back to reality.

'The *Vulkan*, as you know, is stored and provisioned for her voyage. We have merely been waiting for permission to put this plan into operation. All the past experience of our commerce raiders has been put into her conversion. She is a comparatively new ship; well armed, economical to run, and as a merchant ship will excite as little attention as possible. There has been much consultation and argument about which captain will have the honour to command her. I myself was in no doubt. Korvetten Kapitän Felix von Steiger is the only man.' He was rewarded by the mutter of approval which flowed round the table.

Von Steiger, the man who had already in the war carried out one of the most daredevil and rewarding raids of all time. In his converted merchant ship *Isar* he had returned to Kiel through the blockade, his masts and yards festooned with the house-flags of his prizes. For six months he had moved like a will-o'-the-wisp through the South

Atlantic and even to the Pacific, causing chaos and terror wherever he went.

'In a few moments von Steiger will be here. I will give him his sealed orders, and you can get any additional information which your respective departments require.' He cleared his throat. 'But never underestimate the importance of this cruise. Never let it from your minds for an instant. A success at sea at this moment could be the very hinge upon which the door to victory could be opened!'

The Admiral had returned to the darkening window. He half listened to the voices of his officers behind him, while his eyes brooded over the storm-lashed shapes of the fleet. Soon now, he thought. A setback in their sea lanes, hundreds—even thousands—of miles from the combat areas, and the enemy would be forced to cut down his naval patrols. The steel ring which encircled the approaches to Germany would be weakened, and then the trap would be sprung! The might of the High Sea Fleet would be out again. A brief picture of Jutland crossed his thoughts, and he saw again the streaming battle-ensigns, the long grey muzzles roaring defiance at the Grand Fleet, and, above all, the proud battle-cruisers causing ruin amongst Admiral Sir David Beatty's squadron.

A brief gust of cool air moved across his neck as the tall double doors were opened by the marine orderlies.

He forced himself to wait a little longer before turning, allowing his staff time to study the neat, slight figure which stood facing them.

Korvetten Kapitän Felix von Steiger stared back at the semicircle of flushed, excited faces, his own expression calm and outwardly relaxed. His short, dark hair was glossy beneath the lights, and the neat beard, beloved of newspaper artists and photographers, jutted almost impudently above the black cross which hung about his neck. But there was nothing calm or relaxed about his eyes. The eyes, which had earned him the nickname 'Tiger of the Seas', were gold-flecked, even yellow, in the harsh light, and as he stood waiting for the Admiral to turn they flashed momentarily with something like hatred.

The Admiral was speaking again. Introductions were being made, heads bobbed in formal acceptance of his presence and importance. He hardly listened, and started slightly as the Admiral guided him across the room towards the fire which blazed beneath the great carved mantel, above which the Emperor's picture glared fixedly at the rain-lashed windows.

As he moved von Steiger felt something grate beneath his polished boots, and as he glanced down at the rich carpet his stomach seemed to contract to a tight ball. There was a trace of sand gravel where he had been standing. He felt the pain of loss and longing once more, and turned to hide his eyes from the others. He had travelled directly from the graveyard by carriage to this conference, so that the gravel must have been from his wife's graveside. Through the flames in the grate he saw the bowed heads, the sweeping, relentless rain and the despair which had risen to a climax as the earth had fallen on the polished coffin. He still could not grasp it completely. Freda, laughing, beautiful and, above all, part of himself. Now there was nothing.

He heard the Admiral say in his thick voice, 'Perhaps you would care to add your own comments, Captain?'

Von Steiger nodded. His voice was surprisingly firm and controlled, and he realized that he was listening to himself, like a spectator watching someone else playing a part.

He looked at the expectant faces. Faces smooth and plump with good living. How would they feel, he wondered, if instead of the dockyard beyond that window there was only the grey waste of the Atlantic, and the horizon a shelter for the enemy, the hunters? As he looked towards the well-planned chart and the neat counters he wondered if they realized just how much pain and misery each sinking represented, how little hope there was left amongst those who still had the strength to think.

'I shall sail tomorrow night as arranged. I shall pass through the Skagerrak on the twenty-ninth and sail northwards, hugging the Norwegian coast.'

Their eyes were fixed on the chart, following his invisible voyage.

'The nights are long now, so my chances are good for breaking through the blockade. If we are lucky we should be able to pass south of Iceland. If not we shall go through the Denmark Strait.' He spoke as if it was of no importance. As if the Denmark Strait was not the worst and most hazardous passage at the height of winter. In fact, von Steiger knew it was pointless to explain the difference. How could he describe the agony of the ice, or permanent darkness and shrieking storms, to men who fought their war from behind desks?

The Admiral said suddenly: 'We were all very sorry to hear of your tragic loss, Captain. It was very sad.' He flushed as the gold-flecked eyes scanned his face. He had almost said 'inconvenient', and the look in von Steiger's cold eyes showed that he had realized the fact.

Von Steiger took the heavy, red-sealed envelope and tucked it inside his jacket. Sealed orders were always the same, he thought briefly. They gave credit to others, but the onus was on the man who carried them.

'We shall be thinking of you, Captain!' The Admiral drew himself up stiffly. 'The Imperial Navy depends on this voyage for more than just a gesture. You will have the loneliest command of all time, but the proudest! May God go with you!'

Von Steiger clicked his heels and moved towards the door. He realized that they had expected him to make a speech. Inspire them with wild promises perhaps. It was too late for that now. They all thought that his new command, the *Vulkan*, was a challenge to him, but it was a haven. A freedom from the land and all that it now represented to him. Once in this ship he could try to purge himself clean from the misery which surrounded him. He smiled slightly. To purge myself, he thought, that is more than appropriate. Vulkan was the God of Fire!

The others, seeing him smile, were humbled, and as they watched the doors close behind him imagined that von Steiger was already planning some new deed, which they themselves would share.

Only the Admiral still pondered, and felt uneasy.

. . . . . .

As von Steiger left the headquarters building he realized that the rain had stopped. Overhead, the clouds, full-bellied and menacing, still moved with purpose, and he thought that before long the rain would return. He hunched his shoulders inside his long greatcoat and pulled the black fur collar about his ears. The wind moaned across the dockyard, and the air was ice-cold and damp. Here and there the mobile cranes stood abandoned and forlorn in the deep puddles, and occasionally von Steiger caught a brief glimpse of dockyard workers moving listlessly through the deepening shadows.

He thought of the Admiral and his staff, and some of his anger returned. He had been surprised at the Admiral's calm welcome, especially in view of their previous meeting three days earlier.

It had been in the same room, and von Steiger had stood beside the great chart while the Admiral had expounded his theories on strategy and surprise. Von Steiger had argued that the cruise planned for the *Vulkan* was a waste of time. It might be a brave gesture, it might even be moderately successful, but viewed against the backcloth of war it was unlikely to change any succession of events.

He had been surprised at the Admiral's anger. It was almost as if the cruise had been planned for *his* salvation. Then the Admiral had become more conciliatory, almost affable.

'I realize, Captain, that the loss of your dear wife has made you confused. I understand that very well. But Germany needs you, even more than she did. . . .'

Von Steiger sickened at the memory of the smooth words. He tried to shut his mind to the Admiral and to concentrate on the stark series of events which overnight had changed—no, ended—his life.

But as usual he obtained only a disjointed set of pictures. Freda waiting to greet him at the big house on the edge of the Plöner See, anxious, soothing and loving. The pictures flashed through his mind as his feet trod carelessly through the trapped rain-water and instinct took him towards the waiting ship.

She always wanted to help others, he reflected. It was a cruel twist of fate that she should have been killed while helping the enemy. There was a hospital for wounded French prisoners near von Steiger's estate, and Freda spent much of her spare time helping to nurse them back to health.

That last night had been rough and stormy like today, he recalled. Rudi, the coachman, had told him how he had been driving her back from the hospital. She had shouted to him through the rain: 'Drive fast, Rudi! The Captain will be home on leave before us unless we gallop!' She had laughed as old Rudi whipped the two horses into a fast trot. Then there had been the fallen tree, a confused jumble of screaming horses and splintering coachwork. Then silence but for the hiss of rain across the empty road.

Rudi had dragged himself more than a mile to a cottage to get help, but it had been too late.

Von Steiger had arrived home a few hours later. More pictures flashed across his tired mind. The goodness and strength of his home had come crashing down as he mounted the steps. Tear-stained faces, hands plucking at his arms as he pushed them all aside and ran up to her room. Then, behind the locked door, silence once more. He had sat all night just looking at her white, composed face and at her dark hair, still damp from the wet road.

He found that he had halted and was staring up at the high bows of the *Vulkan*.

Against the sombre warships her white bridge superstructure and jaunty funnel made a splash of colour, and her tall, black sides looked well cared for compared with the rust-streaked vessels alongside.

Although he had been aboard for hardly more than an hour at a time since he had assumed command, he already knew every detail of her. He had immersed himself completely in the ship, if only to control the agony of mind which held him like madness.

The *Vulkan* had been built just before the war as a quick-passage banana ship, and was blessed with all the latest equipment. She had large refrigeration spaces, electric light throughout and a fair turn of speed. Although to all outward appearances she was a typical ocean-going steamer with a high fo'c'sle and poop and all the main super-structure grouped amidships behind the bridge, she had been cunningly converted into a deadly ship of war. Deep in her bowels, silent and gleaming on a miniature railway, three hundred mines were stowed in readiness to be dropped from her poop. Below the bridge, screened by painted canvas, were the torpedo tubes, and on the poop was a long twenty-two pounder, camouflaged with an imitation hand-steering position. But up forward were the *Vulkan*'s main teeth. Two great five-point-nines were mounted beneath the fo'c'sle, their muzzles concealed by steel shutters cut in the ship's sides, which could be dropped within seconds, and two more similar guns were mounted just a little farther aft, concealed by a false deckhouse. With that forbidding armament and two hundred and twenty-five officers and men, she could speak loudly, and with confidence.

A few heavy drops of rain heralded the next downpour, and he walked slowly towards the main gangway. As he did so he caught sight of the officer-of-the-watch and side-party standing to greet him. It was strange that he had hardly spoken to any of his officers or men. Before, when he had commanded the *Isar*, he had been given the pick of the German Navy. It had been a voyage of adventure, excitement and ultimate glory. Now that side of warfare had been turned away for ever. With the first million men to die on the Western Front, and with the mounting savagery of the unrestricted sea warfare, there was little room left for such ideals as honour and glory. To survive was the fighting man's only prayer.

He sighed as he flicked open his fur collar, the motion automatic and arrogant, and marched up the gangway. He paused at the top, his gloved hand raised to the peak of his cap as the pipes twittered in greeting.

He did not look back at the land. He no longer needed it.

.   .   .   .   .

Lieutenant Emil Heuss pushed back his chair from the table and stretched his legs. Around him the café was alive with noise and laughter, and the air was already heavy with cigar smoke and the smell of pork fat. At the far end, distorted by the blue haze, three elderly musicians bent their heads wearily across their violins as if to listen to their Strauss waltz, whilst on either side of them the service doors to the kitchen swung repeatedly to a stream of perspiring waiters, their laden trays of beer held high to avoid collision and the clutching hands of the officers who were already the worse for drink.

Heuss stared at the littered table with distaste, and pulled a cigar from his pocket. His two companions were doing likewise, and Heuss could feel a sense of failure, as if this last dinner ashore had become yet another anticlimax. His serious face was pale and finely made, sensitive yet stubborn, and he felt in some way excluded from the drunken merriment around him, even from the conversation of his companions.

Lieutenant Karl Ebert, the *Vulkan*'s gunnery officer, his round pink face flushed and unusually cheerful, grinned at Heuss and stuck his cigar between his teeth. 'Cheer up, Emil! This time I think we are really going to sail! Soon we shall be away from all this.' He waved his arm vaguely and sent a glass skittering on to the floor. 'I can almost smell the deep water again!'

Lieutenant Paul Kohler, torpedo officer, and a member of the *Vulkan*'s ship's company for less than a week, frowned and raised his hand reprovingly. 'Keep your voice down, Ebert! Have you no thought for security?' His pale, slightly protruding eyes were cold and hard, and as Heuss watched him from across the table he thought he looked completely without pity.

But then, nothing seemed to be real any more. Even this ritualistic 'last dinner' was beginning to get on his nerves. There had been repeated rumours and preparations, and each time the sailing date had been put off. There had been three temporary captains during his six months aboard, and now they had von Steiger, although even he had hardly made an appearance. But today he had been to see the naval staff. That at least had seemed significant. Heuss signalled towards a passing waiter, who nodded vacantly and hurried on towards some senior officers.

Ebert was talking about guns again. 'With the layout of fire control which I have at my disposal I can tackle two or more targets at once! We will show the world a thing or two when we get out there!'

Kohler pursed his thin lips. 'Torpedoes are the ultimate weapon, my friend! See what the U-boats have done so far! They have taken the war right into the enemy's camp!'

Heuss stirred, the old irritation growing within him. 'Ach, you sicken me! We have a ship which according to you has everything we need! But think! Over half the crew have never been to sea before, and those who have have probably forgotten what it is like!'

'At Jutland——' began Kohler patiently.

'No, not again!' Heuss threw up his hands in mock despair. 'That is all I hear nowadays! That battle was nearly two years ago, yet still people rant about it as if it solved the problems of the world! Well, it did not! It only proved that the naval staffs of the two nations involved were fools!'

Ebert shifted uneasily. 'Steady, Emil! Keep your voice down!'

Kohler twisted his handsome features into a mask of disapproval. 'Were you at Jutland, Heuss?'

'Yes. Were you?' He glared rudely at the other officer until he dropped his eyes.

Heuss spoke more softly, his eyes far away. 'Yes, I was there, in the old battle-cruiser *Seydlitz*.' The café seemed to fade, and he saw again that vision of sea power as he had watched it that far-off May afternoon. From his armoured position high on the battle-cruiser's bridge he had watched the battle take shape, a glittering display of naval power and strength the like of which the world had never seen before.

Line upon line of battleships and cruisers, wheeling and re-forming like ponderous prehistoric monsters until the moment of clash was unavoidable. There had been actions in plenty before, tip-and-run raids on the English coasts, skirmishes in the Channel and the battles of Coronel and Falkland, but this was quite different. Never before in the history of man had two such great fleets been drawn up to meet each other in the open sea.

Through his observation slit Heuss had seen the lithe shapes of Beatty's squadron drawing closer, while out of sight from each other the two main fleets had waited with agonizing suspense for their scouting battle-cruisers to engage. He remembered the giant British *Queen Mary* as she blew up and broke in two. His own ship and her consort, the *Derfflinger*, had been concentrating their fire on her when a plunging salvo had ignited her magazines and blasted her apart. One moment there had been a proud and beautiful ship tearing through the grey water with every gun firing; then there was an orange flash which defied every description and a pall of smoke which rose to a thousand feet, and when it subsided there was nothing. Not even a spar.

The two fleets had struck, parried and separated. A great victory was proclaimed by the British. The German Fleet had retired to its base and had not dared to test the might of the Royal Navy again! The German Admiralty also proclaimed a major victory. They had sunk more British ships than they themselves had lost, and had out-manœuvred the enemy at every phase of the battle! Who was right? The argument raged without cease in every wardroom and on every messdeck in the Navy, and to Heuss the arguments had seemed empty and pointless.

In anger he said: 'It was a damned waste of life and ships! They fought in a way which would have made a soldier sick!'

The beer arrived and he drank deeply, aware that his head was beginning to ache. He had volunteered immediately he had heard of the proposed use of a new commerce raider. He frowned, trying again to fathom out the reason for his eagerness. As a regular officer he had always been rather on the outside of the Navy's close-knit, un-imaginative circle. He had enjoyed the companionship more as an onlooker than a participant, his cynical humour being a self-made barrier between himself and the others. Jutland had changed him in some way. He glanced at Ebert's round, cheerful face and smiled in spite of his uneasiness. It will be the Eberts of this war who survive, he thought. The thinkers and the idealists like myself will go to the wall.

There was a slight commotion at the door, and through the smoke he saw the swaying shapes of three soldiers in field-grey being pushed back into the street by an enraged waiter. The door swung cosily into place, but not before Heuss had seen the soldiers' bandages and the one who had walked with crutches.

A red-tabbed staff major at the next table exploded angrily. 'Could they not see this is for officers only, eh? The swine must be mad!'

Heuss swivelled unsteadily in his chair and stared at the angry little major with hatred. 'They were back from the front, Major! Probably looking for their officers?' His voice was mild, and a sudden hush fell in the café.

'What the devil do you mean, sir?' The soldier was purple with rage.

'I have heard that there are no officers at the front, Major. That they are all on the staff!' He stood up and eyed the man with contempt. 'You're not fit to wear that uniform, and if I was not so drunk I'd have it off your back!'

The Major scrambled to his feet, his chin level with Heuss's shoulder. He suddenly seemed to realize that there were half a dozen blue uniforms to every field-grey one in the café, and some of his courage failed him. He said stiffly, 'I shall report this to the Commander-in-Chief!'

'Yes, and I shall report you to the Major-General commanding this district! He is my brother!' Heuss added wildly.

The musicians struck up another waltz, the beer began to flow again and Heuss staggered out into the street and the steady rain. Ebert took his elbow, and together they moved along the deserted pavements.

'Where is Kohler?' asked Heuss vaguely.

'He decided we were too crude for the likes of him!' Ebert laughed, relieved to be free from a threatening scene. After a while he added: 'Is your brother *really* the Major-General here?'

'As a matter of fact, Karl, my brother, once a very good lawyer, is now a very bad corporal in the artillery!'

They roared with laughter, so that some old women gathering sticks for their fires from beneath the dripping trees stopped to peer at the two naval officers who clasped each other's shoulders.

Ebert wiped his eyes. 'Well, Emil, at least your brother had the sense to be a gunner, eh?'

.   .   .   .   .   .

The long, overcrowded train ground to a final halt at the Kiel terminus, and with a last convulsion the engine deluged the wet platform with steam which then hung motionless in the damp air.

In a small luggage-van at the rear of the train the four blue-clad seamen scrambled to their feet and tried to peer through the tiny barred windows. A feeble glow penetrated in from the shaded station lights and played on the unshaven faces of the three men and on the pale exhausted one of the fourth, who was little more than a boy. For three days they had lived in the tiny van, locked up like animals, and made to manage as best they could with an evil-smelling bucket propped in one corner, and a pile of loose, dirty straw thrown in as an afterthought by the military police when they had left Cuxhaven.

The boy, Willi Pieck, ground his teeth together to stop them from chattering. His uniform was thin and smelled of damp and sweat, and he clasped his arms round his slim body to drive away the cramped numbness from his bones. His companions were silent, and he wondered if they were thinking about their new ship or if, like himself, they were dreading what new humiliation would be thrown at them.

Pieck had joined the Imperial Navy a year earlier at the age of sixteen, and the past six months of his young life had been spent in the dreaded Cuxhaven Detention Barracks. Try as he might, he could not believe that he was out of the place, nor had he the experience and understanding which maturity might have given him to free himself of what he believed was a permanent scar on his mind.

One of four brothers, he had been raised in a small village just outside Flensburg. He had helped his invalid father to run the bakery after the others had left to fight in the Army. It had been a great event in the village as the three young men, self-conscious in their field-grey uniforms and smart spiked helmets, had waved a final farewell from the train window. That had been three years ago. One brother lay somewhere outside Ypres, another had disappeared on the Dardanelles, and the third had merely been posted missing.

Willi Pieck had watched his mother grow older and more shrunken with each devastating piece of news, and tried to pluck up the courage to say that he, too, wanted to go and fight for the Fatherland. At last he had made up his mind to go. It would be difficult, he knew, and he would have to lie about his age, but he had heard of others who had managed it well enough. Surprisingly, his mother had said very little. It was as if she thought such a decision was inevitable. But it was to be the Navy for him, and because his father had once served as a cook in the High Sea Fleet, and knew the recruiting petty officer, it was all arranged.

Like a man inspired he had thrown himself into the business of learning to be a seaman, and had strained his frail body to the utmost so as not to fall behind the others in his squad, all of whom seemed to be quite old and in their middle twenties. The rifle drill and endless hours on the sun-baked barrack square that had left his shoulders aching and feet swollen to twice their size merely made him more determined, and at the completion of his training even his petty officer had to admit that he might make a man in the end.

Looking back, perhaps that petty officer had been trying to warn him. Willi had led a quiet village life, and apart from the fact that he had always known that he was not so tough and strong as his brothers, he had never thought of himself as being different from anyone else.

At the barracks some of his friends had pulled his leg about his appearance, and had said more than once that he would make a better girl than a boy. But he had laughed it off, and had set himself a task to prove that he was better than they.

He closed his eyes and leaned his forehead against the damp wall of the van. If only someone had explained these matters to him earlier. He was only a country boy, and when the divisional officer had shown an interest in him he had been proud and flattered. He had planned to write to his parents and tell them that a real naval officer was helping him with his studies and was going to speak to people in the right quarters about him.

And then that night when he had been summoned to the Lieutenant's cabin. At first he had not understood what the man was asking him to do, and as he relived the nightmare in his memory he could picture the young officer's face, flushed with drink, and his hands hot and unsteady on his shoulders, the lust making his eyes blaze with a kind of madness.

Willi had run terrified from the room, and had lain shivering in his bunk, unable to wipe away the revulsion from his mind. He did not report the incident, and next day was charged with stealing money from the Lieutenant. The money was found in Willi's bunk, where it had been carefully planted while he was on the parade ground, and the case was complete. Too late he had tried to ask advice from the officer-of-the-guard, and had even tried to explain what had really happened. But the officer had looked uncomfortable, and had advised him to plead guilty to the larceny. 'It will seem better for your parents, you know,' he explained.

The detention barracks; grey stone, barbed wire. Permanently damp and hungry. The guards had used every humiliation they knew to break his spirit, and several times had made him stand naked on the parade ground while they jeered and threw insults at him.

It was there that he had met his present companions. When the time of their sentences had almost expired they had been told that they were to be drafted to the *Vulkan*. It was hinted that it was to be commanded by the famous von Steiger, but even that comfort had been denied to Willi Pieck. A provost officer had slapped him across the mouth and bellowed in his face: 'You useless little pig! Von Steiger will break you in pieces the first week you are aboard!'

He jumped as Schiller dug him roughly in the ribs. He was a great hulking mass of man, who made even his tight-fitting uniform seem shapeless. Convicted of getting drunk and assaulting the military police who came to arrest him, he seemed little changed by his recent experiences.

'Come on, Willi, wake up!' His voice was rough and nasal, his nose having been broken several times in his long naval career. He had been drunk in every port which mattered, and many which did not. He was content to remain a common seaman for the rest of the war and, if necessary, until the end of his days.

Apart from the lack of drink and poor food, he had remained unimpressed by the prison life. Having seen it all before, he knew that in the small world of the Navy it was merely a matter of time before he came in contact with some of those guards. He mentally rubbed his thick hands at the thought. He had once crippled a provost petty officer

27

by pushing him into a dry-dock. At the enquiry it had been found that it was an accident. Schiller often smiled at the memory.

He peered at Pieck again and gestured with his thumb towards the thin, scarecrow shape of Seaman Alder, who still stood staring at the barred window. 'Give me a hand with him, he doesn't seem too well.'

The authorities alleged that Alder was a coward, and therefore a menace to the morale of the Navy. It was also said that he was saved from the firing squad only by his past record. The clemency of the court martial had moved everyone almost to tears. Except Alder, and the doctor who tried to explain that the man was mentally ill, shocked almost to a point of insanity.

Alder had been the last survivor from a torpedo boat which had blown up on a mine near the Dogger Bank. They had found him frozen to the tiller of a small boat with eight dead men for companions. An Iron Cross had been recommended, but he had broken out of the hospital and had run away.

Such crass ingratitude should have been punished by death, said the President of the Court. It was an insult to the Emperor, and a betrayal of his dead comrades.

Alder rarely spoke, and seemed indifferent to the small acts of kindness which Pieck and Schiller had shown him.

The fourth man, Hahn, was a convicted thief. He was a small, sullen-mouthed seaman who had been caught selling blankets and clothing to civilians. He said suddenly, 'What do you think of our chances aboard the *Vulkan*?'

Schiller eyed him with open belligerence. 'Shut your mouth, and get our things together!' And to the van at large he added: 'Listen, the lot of you. *Vulkan* is just a ship and von Steiger is an officer, see? Whether he is a big bastard or a little one, I do not know . . . yet! When I find out I'll tell you what I think. Until then, keep yourselves out of trouble. They'll be watching us!' Suddenly he grinned, his white teeth brightening his battered face. 'Still, it could be much worse, they might have sent us to the Western Front!'

·   ·   ·   ·   ·

Lieutenant Heuss stretched his cold fingers towards the glowing wardroom stove and winced as the feeling returned to his limbs. From first light that morning he had been on the *Vulkan*'s maindeck supervising the loading of additional stores, his eyes watering in the relentless north wind, his teeth gritted against the nausea of the previous night's beer. Ebert had been working with him, but unlike Heuss had managed to stomach a good breakfast, and now stood staring into the fire at his side.

The wardroom had originally been used exclusively for the ship's passengers, and was a large rectangular space which ran the full width of the vessel. A long green curtain divided it in two and separated the recreation space from the dining compartment. The curtain swayed gently to the slow roll of the ship, and Heuss listened to the rattle of loose gear as the hull lifted to the unaccustomed motion. That morning the paddle-wheeled tugs had warped the *Vulkan* from her berth, and she now lay alone at a buoy, well out in the harbour. He could sense the new urgency about him, the whine of dynamos, the steady whirr of fans and the noisy movement of seamen about the upper deck, constantly harried and goaded by the hoarse shouts of the petty officers.

He eyed the other officers with interest. They had all been summoned to the wardroom to meet the Captain. To be told their orders. He shivered in spite of himself. This time there was no doubt about the signs.

Lieutenant Kohler paced restlessly across the worn carpet, his pale eyes watching the small door through which the Captain would come from his quarters. A dangerous man, Heuss mused thoughtfully. Eager, dedicated and cruel. There were the two elderly Reserve sub-lieutenants, Wildermuth and Seebohm, who were being carried as boarding officers to supervise the unloading of possible prize ships and, if necessary, to sail them independently back to Germany. Both ex-merchant navy mates, they seemed uneasy about their new companions and rarely left each other's side. Of the Chief Engineer, Niklas, and his assistant, Schuman, there was no sign, and the growing plume of smoke from the *Vulkan*'s tall funnel told their story for them. Below, in the bowels of the hull, they were making their last checks on the maze of machinery which would be their salvation throughout the voyage. Heuss sighed. How like the High Command in all their wisdom to choose a single-screwed ship for such a hazardous cruise. No margin for error.

Another officer joined him by the fire. Sub-Lieutenant Max Damrosch was tall and slim, with an open, boyish face. At twenty-two he was the youngest officer aboard, and had joined the ship only the previous day. He had already been detailed to assist Heuss in the Captain's Attack Team on the bridge, and bombarded him with questions at every opportunity. Heuss liked him for it, and enjoyed his open enthusiasm. Heuss glanced at the brass clock. 'We shall soon know now, Max. Our fate for a month or two!'

Damrosch rubbed his hands over the fire and frowned thoughtfully. 'The First Lieutenant told me last night that with luck we might be down in the sunshine within a month.'

Heuss replied with a non-committal grunt. He did not like the First Lieutenant. His name was Erich Dehler, a man of forty-five, old for his rank, and a Reserve officer to boot. During his six months aboard the *Vulkan* Heuss had crossed swords repeatedly with Dehler, for as the next senior officer aboard Heuss had to consult him on every irritating matter of routine and preparation. Dehler was an ex-merchant navy officer like the boarding officers, but unlike any other man aboard had actually served in this ship in peacetime as second mate. His knowledge of the vessel, his undisputed efficiency as a navigator and his qualifications as a seaman had won him the coveted post of second in command. But as a man he was hard to get on with. He was poorly educated, and showed his resentment by blaming the regular officers and the snobbery of the Navy for his own lack of advancement. Several times he had cornered Heuss, his heavy red face angry and bitter. '*I* should have had this command, Heuss! Just because I don't belong to the right clubs and haven't the right accent is no reason for this bloody unfairness!' If he speaks in that line to von Steiger he had better watch out, he thought.

The door opened and von Steiger entered the wardroom, followed by Dehler, whose heavy, broad shoulders seemed to tower over the Captain's slight figure.

Von Steiger gestured for them all to sit down, and threw his cap carelessly on the table. He was still wearing his immaculate shore-going uniform and decorations, and Heuss had the impression that he had not slept the previous night.

Von Steiger stood for some moments as if deep in thought, his eyes on the polished table. He seemed to shake himself free from his inner distraction, and ran a brief glance along their waiting faces. 'I will not keep you long. You have a great deal to do, and there will I hope be much more time later on for getting better acquainted.'

Heuss watched him from beneath lowered lashes. He took in the bright decorations on von Steiger's tunic, the Iron Cross, First and Second Class, the Order Pour le Mérite, the three gold bands encircling his sleeves which to the Navy and to the world symbolized his complete hold over the ship and all who sailed in her. He stood as if completely relaxed, yet Heuss's sensitive appraisal told him that, like the calm expression on the Captain's face, this appearance of self-control was a mask, even a guard, against some new force which he was only just holding under control. Heuss knew of von Steiger's recent loss, and yet it did not seem to fit the pattern of such a man that he should be turned from his set path by a personal disaster. He watched the neat brown hands which rested on the table; capable, competent hands. There was a latent power about the man, mixed with arrogance, and yet was there not humility? He frowned, and concentrated on what von Steiger was saying.

'We shall sail tonight on the tide. By this time tomorrow we shall pass through the Skagerrak and keep close inshore to Norway. Absolute vigilance is essential at all times, and for that reason I want the best lookouts available. They are among the most important men in the ship.' The gold-flecked eyes moved slowly along their faces. 'I have had a copy of my new Standing Orders printed for each officer. Read them, they are important. This is no ordinary warship, gentlemen. Once clear of the minefields we shall be completely alone. Every ship we meet will be hostile in one way or another. Our colonies are gone, even the neutrals are fewer and less willing to help than in earlier days. Nevertheless, we shall behave like part of the Imperial Navy, which we are, so long as we are alive. We will be branded as pirates perhaps, but let no stain on our actions and characters add to a mere reputation. The men are largely untried and untrained. You must rectify that as soon as possible. With a ship fighting alone, the discipline must be regulated to suit the occasion. The men are human beings, not useless cannon-fodder, as some people believe!'

Heuss stiffened at the sharpness of these words. There was bitterness unconcealed in von Steiger's tone.

'Over the last years, even months, we have seen great strides in our

31

war machine. When I joined the Navy I was trained in sail, yet that was only twenty years ago. . . .'

Heuss made a rapid calculation. Von Steiger was thirty-nine, or soon would be, yet the mark of command was clearly etched on his tanned face. There was a youthfulness, too, about his trim figure which clashed with the authority invested in him.

'Now the war is fought with weapons which were only dreams in those days. However,' his eyes flashed with sudden anger, 'many changes are not for the good. Humanity and honour have been shelved. Poison gas and unrestricted submarine warfare have seen to that! Men have been struck down not by valour and unity of effort, but by the weapons of loathsome cowardice and human degradation!' He became suddenly calm. 'In this ship there will be no additional burden to that shame. We will fight with honour. That at least we can do.' He halted, and Heuss saw a small bead of sweat on his brow. Von Steiger thrust his hands into his pockets. 'Any questions?'

Kohler stood up, his heels clicking together. 'Yes, Captain! With the might of Germany behind us, how can we fail?'

Von Steiger was unmoved. He looked at Kohler with cold eyes. 'I will answer that question, Lieutenant, when we are safely back in Germany!'

Heuss grinned, and stood up to cover Kohler's confusion. 'Captain, I should like to thank you for your confidence. After this war it will be remembered how it was won rather than who won it. To tarnish the record of the Navy would only——' He faltered as von Steiger lifted his hand.

'Thank you, Lieutenant! Some other time I should be delighted to hear your views, but now I have signals to dictate!' He ignored the flush which spread across Heuss's face. 'That will be all, gentlemen! Lieutenant Dehler will give you your watchkeeping duties and other extra appointments. Let me just say this. This is not a mere escapade, this is *real* war. Those of you who were at Jutland or in the Dogger Bank battles may have thought you had seen war at first hand. Forget it all! Those battles were planned by amateurs for an occasion which can never arise. They rank with the folly of sending cavalry to charge into machine guns and barbed wire, or of sending half-trained soldiers to attack tanks. Those episodes may be well remembered by the historians, but *our* war is the one which will count!' He picked up his cap and nodded to Dehler.

Heuss watched von Steiger lift his foot to step over the door coaming and then pause. He turned. 'If any of you wish to send a last letter, my steward will take them ashore in an hour. I expect those of you who are married would like to——' He stopped and bit his lip, and then hurried through the door.

In spite of von Steiger's earlier curtness and brusque interruption, Heuss clearly saw the anguish on the Captain's face. My God, he thought, he is being torn apart. He is like a man being driven to the edge of despair.

Damrosch said quietly: 'He is a really great man, Heuss! I have never seen anybody like him!'

Heuss arose from his thoughts, confused and angry, but at the sight of the young officer's serious face he relented. 'Yes, Max, our Captain is a man.' He grinned ruefully. 'I think he has *really* taken a liking to me!'

At that moment the deck started to vibrate with slow insistence beneath their feet. Eighty feet below them the great engine began to rumble with steady confidence.

Ebert seized them by the shoulders, his pink face shining. 'Hear that? She is alive! Tonight we sail for Germany! For the Fatherland!'

Then they were all shouting and cheering, their voices echoing around the spray-soaked decks outside. Only Dehler did not smile or cheer. As he watched their excitement he felt the weight of his age and the incessant smouldering of his own failure.

. . . .

The wind, which had gone round to the east, was mounting in force, and the open expanse of the main harbour was lined with fast-moving cream-coloured crests which contrasted with the angry grey water and the dark evening sky.

Von Steiger stepped from his sea cabin at the rear of the bridge to look briefly at the bustling decks below him. Seamen in oilskins shining like beetles scurried to and fro in orderly confusion, and here and there an officer stood aloof and watchful, his voice whipped away by the wind. The harbour was in shadow, the moored and anchored fleet silent and brooding. He could almost sense the invisible binoculars and telescopes trained on his lonely ship, just as he knew the hopes that rode with his journey.

He readjusted the strap of the binoculars about his neck and pulled his cap tighter on to his head, then stepped into the wide wheelhouse.

He ignored the formal salutes, the quick, darting stares of the men who thronged the place, and walked to his tall, scrubbed, wooden chair which he had caused to be bolted on the port side. He knew from hard experience that it was unlikely he would be far from either the chair or his tiny sea cabin throughout the voyage. His spacious quarters were deserted now, he would not need them.

He sat on the chair and stared down at the wide foredeck beneath him. His vision was split in two by the tall foremast with its tiny black pod from where the masthead lookout would keep constant watch. The lookout could see five miles farther than anyone else aboard. That could be a margin of life or death for friend and foe alike.

The decks looked neat and secure, and only the carpenter and his mates still moved about the two forward holds, checking the lashings on the covers and hammering in a few more wedges to make sure.

He thought of the precious coal stored in those holds. The most valuable stuff aboard. Full holds and bunkers, and even the passageways and unused cabins were filled with the gleaming material of power.

He watched the small group of seamen in the high bows. He could see the bulky shape of Lieutenant Dehler as he supervised the last preparations for letting go from the buoy. The cable had been unshackled, and only a slender slipwire held them to the last link with the land.

A few traces of blown spume floated across the thick bridge windows, and he half turned to watch the busy scene around him. Heuss stood by the rank of brass voice-pipes at the rear, whilst Damrosch waited out on the open starboard wing of the bridge, his face glowing in the ice-fingered air. The Coxswain, a giant Berliner called Lehr, stood heavily behind the polished wheel, his chin resting on his chest as his eyes dreamily watched the compass in its bowl. A seaman waited by the big-dialled telegraph, his fingers on the handle, his eyes nervously avoiding his captain. Petty Officer Heiser watched over his signalmen, his long telescope open and tucked under his arm in readiness. They all stood and waited, their bodies swaying and staggering to the uneven motion, surrounded by a vapour-cloud of their own breath. The varnished woodwork glistened with condensation, and a constant light spray drifted over the front of the bridge like fine rain, so that the lookouts on either wing had to shield their powerful Zeiss glasses and wipe their streaming faces before the ice rime could form.

An eery green light flickered through the gloom, and von Steiger heard a young signalman draw in his breath.

Petty Officer Heiser snapped his telescope shut and said quickly: 'Signal from flagship, Captain! Proceed when ready!'

Von Steiger heard Heuss say, half to himself: 'They certainly believe in letting the whole world know! A brass band on the jetty would have been the thing!'

Von Steiger smiled without humour and sat up in his chair. 'Stand by!'

The telegraph jangled, the noise making them all start.

Far below, the old Chief Engineer, Niklas, looked at the repeater dial as the demanding needle jerked from its long sleep. He grinned at his young assistant through the steam and noise, and felt something like relief. Below his high catwalk the naked stokers toiled and sweated with their shovels and trimmers, their eyes blinded with dust, their ears deaf but to the hungry roar of the furnace doors.

Von Steiger sighed. The open sea again, and God alone knew what danger lay beyond the *Vulkan*'s corkscrewing bows. 'Slow ahead!'

The ship shuddered, and a mounting white froth surged from beneath her high counter. Damrosch dropped his arm, and the distant fo'c'sle party were galvanized into action. The wire hawser was slipped from one side, and as the men hauled like demons, the long snaking halter flashed through the ring on the buoy and emerged dripping through the fairleads. They were free.

'Half ahead! Coxswain, steer straight for the boom gate! When we pass through the boom, bring her round to the north-east!'

'Very good, Captain!' Lehr's thick legs were straddled as if he was riding the ship, and his deep eyes glowed softly in the binnacle light.

The revolutions mounted, and the land began to slide into the darkness until it was merged into one purple shadow. A small harbour launch curtsied past, and they saw upturned faces and waving hands.

The boom-defence vessel drew abeam, and a light began to stammer across the black water. Heiser read the message, his lips moving with practised ease. 'Good luck, Captain!'

Von Steiger nodded absently. 'Make to them, "We will do our best!"'

The *Vulkan* passed from the harbour approaches and thrust her stem into the first angry roller. The ship shuddered and plunged forward to meet her natural adversary. A seaman messenger clamped his hand across his mouth and turned green, whilst from all around came the clatter and creak of loose gear. The ship was coming awake again from her long rest, and threw off her fetters with contempt, so that men were running across the streaming decks once more to lash down the gear which threatened to throw itself into the creaming wake.

Von Steiger glanced at the door as Lieutenant Dehler clumped into the wheelhouse in his gleaming oilskins.

'Ship secured for sea, Captain!'

Von Steiger's voice was unruffled and cold. How easy it was to play the role of captain again, he thought vaguely. 'Very well, Dehler. Double the lookouts, and close up the hands at Defence Stations. Check that the ship is properly darkened, and then set the watch below to altering the ship's appearance. Just as I told you today. We will become the S.S. *Gripsholm* of Sweden!'

Dehler sighed and hurried away again, his face lined and tired.

Heuss stood at von Steiger's elbow. 'Wireless message from the Commander-in-Chief, Captain. He says that the Emperor prays for our victory and safe return.' He handed the signal sheet to von Steiger, who glanced at it and crumpled it into a ball.

He stared hard at Heuss. 'Prayers are for preventing war, Heuss, *not* fighting it!'

He turned away from Heuss's look of surprise and settled himself in the chair. Against the panorama of spray-slashed glass and the open expanse of black water beyond, von Steiger looked like part of the ship. Unmoving, invincible and ruthless.

2

THE Forenoon Watch of New Year's Day, 1918, found the *Vulkan*
one hundred miles to the north-east of the Faeroes, that desolate group
of islands which, swept by the elements all the year round, lie north of
the last Scottish islands and four hundred miles south-east of Iceland.
The wind still blew strongly from the east, but after nearly four days
of slinking along the Scandinavian coastline and then butting into the
sullen fury of the North Sea, it seemed to have less effect on the deeper
water, which shone in the pale sunlight like green glass and rolled in
long, even banks, broken only occasionally into angry white crests.
The clouds had rolled away the previous night, but the pale sky was
masked in vapour, which denied the sun its strength and seemed to
accentuate the harsh brittle cold which nipped at the skin and made the
breath catch in the throat.

Von Steiger sat silently in his chair on the port side of the wheelhouse, his leather bridge-coat turned up to his ears. In his hands he
cradled a cup of scalding coffee brought by Reeder, his personal
steward. The excitement which had shown itself as the ship had left
harbour had vanished. They were through the protective minefields,
clear of the neutral coasts and were at this moment moving north of
enemy territory. The ship seemed tense and nervy rather than alert.
Overhead the wind moaned and rattled through the rigging, and from
behind von Steiger's chair came the crackle and distorted murmur of
Morse through the open door of the wireless-room. It reminded him of
the latest signal from the Admiralty. To lay mines to the north-west
of the Irish coast. No reason was given, just a bald statement. He
fumed inwardly as he glanced at the crumpled signal. Now that they
had him on the high seas it appeared as if he was expected to respond
to their every whim without explanation.

The wheel-spokes creaked back and forth as the helmsman, muffled to his eyes, fought to keep the ship on course. Lieutenant Dehler stood swaying beside the chart-table, while his assistant, Damrosch, paced the bridge wing, his breath pouring like steam from his reddened face.

In the harsh light the ship looked different, even gay. She now had a bright-yellow star painted on a white funnel, and the blue flag with its yellow cross was painted on the side of the hull. The Swedish flag streamed from the poop, and the new name *Gripsholm* was displayed in several places around the ship.

Von Steiger drained the coffee and put the cup on the screen, where it vibrated to the engine's steady tune. New Year's Day, he thought moodily. The men moved about the ship with neither spirit nor energy. Years of bad food and harsh discipline had taken their toll, so that now they were at sea again they seemed lost and ill at ease. The feel of the engine reminded him of the fuel accounts which lay in his sea cabin. Every minute of the day, every turn of the screw, meant that the black hoard of coal was falling. As soon as we break south, he thought, I must try to capture a collier. As coal makes up seventy-five per cent of England's exports, it might not be too difficult.

As the *Vulkan* lifted her four and a half thousand tons over the next roller, von Steiger felt the pressure of first one arm of the chair and then the other against his ribs. She was taking it quite well, and the weather would get worse yet.

He stared steadily at the barren sea and felt the smallness of the ship. No patrols, no fishing boats, not even a swooping gull broke the hard, restless panorama.

I must try to get some sleep. I cannot sit here for ever. He stirred uneasily at the thought of his neat bunk, and dismissed the idea instantly. He could feel Dehler's eyes on his back, and wondered how a man could nurse so much hatred. He had tried to draw Dehler's resentment into the open, and had even attempted to take him into his confidence. It was useless. Dehler either said nothing but the minimum comment, or started a long tirade about his subordinates, blaming them for their faults, lack of ability or the like.

He ticked off his officers mentally, and came back to Heuss. He was by far the most competent and also took a great interest in the crew's welfare. The seamen, wretched in their damp, overcrowded quarters, harried and bullied by their petty officers, had little enough to look forward to. Heuss's watchful eye might make all the difference. Ebert was a good reliable gunner, and that was enough. Kohler was equally efficient, but lacked any sort of tolerance or warmth. Most of all he lacked charm. Von Steiger had long ago decided that an officer with charm could be excused many other faults. The two boarding officers and the engineers were all right, and young Damrosch, who now froze on the open wing because he thought his captain would expect it of a junior officer, was very likeable and willing. By and large they were a fair cross-section. They had good training, and experience would come also, given time.

He gazed bleakly at his reflection in the salt-caked glass. Time. An easy word. He remembered Heinz, his brother-in-law, tall yet stooped in his field-grey uniform as he had stood at his side by Freda's grave. One sleeve empty and pinned to his tunic made it hard to visualize him as an officer of a crack infantry regiment. In that slashing rain they had waited for Heinz's driver to collect him and take him to the station. He was going straight back to France, to the Front.

Von Steiger explored the memory uneasily, like a man will touch an old wound. They had always been firm friends, and when Freda had died the importance of that link seemed all the more vulnerable.

Heinz had said impetuously: 'What went wrong with Germany, Felix? What happened to bring us down like this?' His grey eyes had hungrily explored the dripping churchyard and sodden grass. 'Look at me, Felix! I am going back to that hell! To the mud and wire, and to that horror they call war!' He hurried on, unaware of von Steiger's shocked eyes. 'I have to lead my men to their deaths!' He laughed, a despairing, bitter sound. 'Men, did I call them? Boys more like, to be led by a one-armed officer who knows the war is already lost!'

Even now von Steiger flinched at the words. Lost. Of course he had known it, too, and yet there had always been hope with Freda to wait for him. When his father had been alive, and they had all lived in the great house on the edge of the Plöner See, with its long avenue of trees and smooth lawns, Freda had laughed at such black thoughts. 'Never mind,' she had said, 'I will look after you all!'

The old Admiral von Steiger had died, and now Freda had followed him. Heinz had been the last link, and even he was condemned to

39

certain death. For over three years the great armies had swayed back and forth over fields and towns, villages and hamlets, which had become a battleground, then a place where only wreckage abounded, and finally a sea of mud where shell-hole overlapped shell-hole and the trenches had been blasted to reeking gullies of pain, mutilation and despair.

Von Steiger closed his eyes tightly and excluded the roar of the sea and the wind's mad song, and tried to remember the other days. How was it, he wondered, that they had no inkling of what it would be like? Perhaps like Damrosch he had relied too much on his superiors. He thought of the grand overseas cruises, the revues, displays of naval might and the slow, exhilarating climb up the ladder of promotion. With such a family tradition behind him it had been difficult, for the Dehlers of the world were plentiful, and jealousy was rife within every service.

He thought, too, of his son Rudolf, a serious six-year-old with a face so like his mother's that it hurt even to think of him. He had been packed away to Dresden to the care of a distant cousin, a good, kindly, stupid man, who was free of the notions of glory and the tradition of the Imperial Navy.

The brass telephone at his side jangled with sudden insistence, and he had it to his ear before Dehler could move from the chart-table. Far away, his voice whipped and distorted by the wind, came the voice of the masthead lookout:

'Smoke, sir! Bearing red four-five!'

Von Steiger stared at the swaying black pod on the foremast. So it had happened at last. There was no escape. Like Heinz, he was committed.

'Very well.' He kept his voice calm. He could sense the tautness in the man's far-off voice. 'Keep passing your reports, and try to see her masts. Warships have heavier masts, fighting tops, tripod masts and the like. When you can, report on her funnels, too.' He held the telephone out for Dehler. 'Report every scrap of information. He has just sighted a ship!'

He slipped from the chair and beckoned Damrosch into the wheelhouse. He saw the unspoken question on his face and said evenly, 'Have the men piped to quarters, but do not clear for action yet.'

He opened a slim leather case and selected a black cheroot.

'Will we fight, Captain?' Damrosch looked suddenly pale.

Von Steiger's teeth showed white momentarily against his beard.

'Agonizing, is it not? Like two insects meeting in a rosebush. Does he eat me? Or do I eat him?' Then in a sharper tone: 'Lively now! And close all watertight doors immediately!'

. . . . .

In one of the small forward messdecks Willi Pieck sat on a padded bench, his knees drawn up to his chin to steady his thin body against the ship's plunging motion which was felt so acutely in the bows. As the raider ploughed into each successive roller the small dimly lighted space seemed to drop from beneath the men who were off watch, and every stomach-shaking lurch brought groans and curses from the huddled figures around the scrubbed table, where a game of skat was in progress. The scuttles were sealed with thick steel deadlights, and the light from the small bulb above the table was yellow and weak.

The card-players concentrated on their cards, heedless of the rattle of loose gear, mugs, seaboots, plates and various articles of clothing which rolled and clattered back and forth across the deck, tangled together in a mixture of salt-water and vomit.

Pieck stared at the men at the table with wide, unblinking eyes. Schiller dominated the group, his cap tilted over his eyes, a black cheroot-butt protruding from his mouth. It was amazing how easy it had been for Schiller to fit in and make himself at home. He had become the senior rating of the mess, thus deposing a mean-looking man called Lukaschek. He now had the best bunk beside the steampipe, and his face was cheerful and at ease.

At Pieck's side Alder swayed vaguely with the motion of each wave, his troubled, vacant eyes staring at his hands. Occasionally he spoke aloud as he fumbled hopelessly with his shattered memory and disordered mind.

'Two hands,' he whispered, staring at the two pale shapes in his lap. 'Two hands. My name is Emil Alder. I come from Brunswick.' Something wet fell on his knees, and he realized with sudden shame that some spittle had fallen from his open mouth. 'Must try again.

41

Two hands. My name is Emil Alder. . . .' His voice trailed away into a meaningless mumble.

Schiller glanced across the table in his direction and frowned thoughtfully, then turned his attention back to the cards.

A mouth-organ's plaintive notes ebbed and flowed from another mess, and occasionally they heard the powerful thunder of water breaking over the fo'c'sle and flooding along the upper deck.

Pieck closed his eyes, and relived the nightmare which dogged every new happening, and killed the hope which he had held so fervently when he had stepped aboard. How he wanted to belong, to be part of these men who cursed and joked over their soiled cards and broken-match bets.

The shame of the barracks, the feeling that he had been made different from other men and the final degradation of the detention quarters had done their work well. But the chance to get aboard a ship which was not only to strike a blow for Germany, but was also commanded by the pick of the country's sea-raiders, that surely was enough? The chance to lose himself in the comradeship for which he had always craved, and cleanse the guilt from his name, so that his parents would again be proud of their last son.

But the previous day Pieck had been working on the twenty-two pounder on the poop, which was to be his action station. In spite of the wind and the cold, he was happy. The gunlayer, a stocky seaman named Hellwege, had been explaining the parts of the gun and showing him how to clean away the salt which gathered in the mechanism like sand. This was the life, nothing else mattered.

Hellwege was a cheerful man, and was amused by the boy's keenness. He was also a kind man, and wondered how anyone could send such a frail-looking boy to sea, on a raider at that. A great wave surged against the *Vulkan*'s hull so that she reeled, caught off guard for an instant.

Hellwege laughed, and gestured with his thumb towards the bridge. 'I bet that made the pigs up there jump, eh, Willi?' He nudged the boy roughly in the ribs, but Pieck only stared at the open wing of the bridge, his face ashen.

There was no escape, after all. Lieutenant Kohler stood outlined against the angry sky, his handsome face disdainful and irritable as he stared after the receding wave. Lieutenant Kohler, the divisional officer who had promised to help Pieck. Who had instead opened his eyes to shame and fear.

Pieck stared across to Schiller, wanting to tell him, wondering how he could begin. A tear formed in a corner of his eye. He dare not speak of it to anyone. He could not risk losing his last friends.

A bell jangled like a mad thing overhead, and simultaneously the bosun's mates ran through the ship, their pipes trilling.

'All hands! All hands! Hands to quarters! Close all watertight doors, enemy in sight!'

The figures sat like statues. Then there was one concerted rush, in which Schiller's guttural voice could be heard hurling advice and curses at all and sundry. As the men clambered up the small ladder which joined the mess to the maindeck, Schiller turned and grabbed Alder by the sleeve. 'Come on, comrade! Here, Willi, give me a hand! We don't want that bastard Petty Officer Brandt chasing us up again!'

Then the mess was empty. The cards lay forgotten on the table, the mouth-organ lovingly wedged in an empty bunk. Overhead, the thunder of running feet died away, and a great, deathly silence seemed to fall over the ship.

.   .   .   .   .

His Majesty's Boarding Steamer *Vole* was making heavy weather of the big rollers, and the officers clinging to her small bridge had to struggle to keep their glasses trained on the distant ship.

The little steamer had originally been used for carrying freight, livestock and a few passengers between the Scottish islands and the mainland, but like most of her consorts had been taken over by the Royal Navy for use as a boarding steamer. They carried out limited patrols, and stopped and searched neutral ships to ensure that war material useful to the enemy was not being carried, or exports from Germany were not being smuggled through the tightening blockade. The boarding steamers were equipped with wireless, and reported all suspicious vessels, if necessary, to the lurking cruisers which made the bulk of the British patrols.

The *Vole*'s captain, a grey-haired Reservist, wiped his streaming face and shouted above the whine of the wind. 'Swedish ship! Signal her to heave to! They won't like that in this weather!'

Flags soared to the yard, and a lamp stammered across the tossing water.

The Yeoman of Signals read the slow reply. 'S.S. *Gripsholm*. Sweden. On passage to Reykjavik, Iceland.' The light flashed again. 'Have you . a doctor on board?'

The Captain frowned, and glanced at his gunners who clung to the four-point-seven on the fo'c'sle. So the Swede had some injury or illness aboard.

The First Lieutenant shouted, 'Shall I clear for action, sir?'

The Captain lifted his glasses again. The tall black ship was nearer now. Decks deserted but for two or three oilskinned figures and two heads on her high bridge. Harmless enough, but might be worth a search.

'Stop engines! Stand by to lower boats with boarding party! And tell the doctor to go across with them!'

The little steamer idled to a halt, her deck heaving in the deep troughs. The other ship loomed nearer, her bow wave dying in response to the *Vole's* signal.

As the first boat was lowered and the First Lieutenant clattered down the bridge ladder, the Captain lifted his glasses again.

The Swedish flag had gone. Even as he stared in disbelief and horror, a white ball soared to the ship's gaff and broke stiffly in the breeze. The black cross with its spread eagle, arrogant and final.

The Captain yelled: 'Clear away the gun! Open fire! Get that boat back on board!' But it was too late. It had been too late from the moment the British captain had failed to train his gun on his enemy.

A shutter fell away on the stranger's bow, and the long muzzle which appeared flashed fire immediately.

The *Vole's* captain saw other guns, and was blinded by the salvo which screamed down on his ship, the shells blasting into her sturdy hull and turning it into an inferno. He tried to crawl to the wireless-room, but realized that the ship was already keeling over. His fingers slipped on the riveted deck as it rolled on to its beam ends. He was still shouting his orders as another shell fell on the shattered bridge and blasted him to oblivion.

44

The *Vulkan* steamed slowly past and then gathered speed, her powerful bow wave surging and gurgling amongst the pathetic broken spars and upturned lifeboat.

Then she was gone, stealthily and guiltily, like an assassin, the wet mist closing in around her, so that the sea was once again empty.

3

THE rising wind shrieked around the *Vulkan*'s superstructure and found every crack and slit in its defences. As the ship steamed steadily northwards towards the Denmark Strait the darkness enfolded her like a cloak, and the sea, which had been at first grey-green, appeared as white-capped pewter, the crests crumbling with each savage gust.

In the Captain's small sea cabin the air was stale with smoke, and unmoving behind the sealed scuttle. Von Steiger sat at the small table which was littered with rolled charts, intelligence diaries and coal returns. His jacket was undone, and he looked strained and tired. He glanced briefly at the officers who were crammed into the small space. Dehler perched uncomfortably on the bunk; Niklas, the engineer, who squatted on the other chair, and Ebert, whose round face looked strange with a layer of stubble. Heuss stood leaning against the closed door. Reeder, the steward, had left a plentiful supply of coffee, and there was also a silver flask of brandy, propped for safety in the waste-paper basket.

Von Steiger's eyes narrowed as he drew in on a fresh cheroot. 'Good, you are all here now.' He leaned back, his hands in his lap. 'I have called you together as heads of departments to discuss a few points which I think want clearing up. Yesterday we sank that boarding steamer. It is essential that we put a good distance between us and the scene as soon as possible. I do not think that the British will worry unduly about the ship's loss, but they will search the area. That rules out our taking a short passage north of Scotland, as I intended. The detour around Iceland will cost us several hundred miles, and a great deal of coal. It also means that we shall have to steam a long way in order to reach the Irish coast and get rid of the mines. I want to do that as soon as possible for they are always an additional hazard. We will have to move some of the coal aft to compensate for the loss of weight there when we have laid the mines.' He paused, watching their faces, gauging their reactions. He could hear the officer-of-the-watch, Kohler, yelling orders at one of the lookouts. He drank some of his brandy, and felt its warmth move like a soothing hand over his aching body.

'Now, yesterday's action. The gunnery was very good, Ebert. But I think in future we will dispense with the twenty-two pounder unless it is a major action. It takes too long to clear away, and does not compare with the main armament. All the same, it was good shooting. The masthead lookout, too, is to be congratulated.' He frowned. 'Fischer is his name. See that all these men are rewarded, Dehler.'

Dehler stirred. 'Rewarded? I don't see what you mean.'

'Give them a pot of jam, some little luxury, anything! Show them we appreciate their efforts. Morale is low. We cannot afford any lethargy.'

Dehler persisted. 'We are wasting time by going through the Strait, Captain. Why can't we just make a dash for it?'

Von Steiger sighed. 'We cannot afford the luxury of chances. Our job is to sink ships, not to go down in glory in the first week of the cruise! Use your head, man!' He saw the man flush, and continued evenly: 'We must really *train* our men. Work at it, keep on to them, even if it means letting some ordinary routine drop out. Recognition is the thing. Two funnels or more means a large merchantman, a liner or something of the sort. We must avoid them at all costs. Full of passengers we cannot accommodate, and no worthwhile cargo. Or they might be armed merchant cruisers.'

'We can manage them, Captain!' Ebert stuck out his jaw.

Von Steiger smiled faintly. 'Maybe, but they could pin us down with damage and casualties until bigger warships arrived. Remember, the enemy is all around us. Do not forget this. He is everywhere, maybe even now a cruiser is shadowing us!' He ticked off the points on his fingers. 'Neutral ships usually have pale funnels and may be showing lights. The real prizes will most likely have black funnels. British freighters and colliers, they are our real aim!'

Niklas grunted. 'When will we get more coal, Captain? At this speed we are getting through it too fast.'

Von Steiger shrugged. 'Soon, I hope. We will catch a collier and put a prize crew aboard. Then we can take what we want, and send her away again to meet us at another rendezvous.' He glanced at Heuss, who seemed to be breathing heavily, as if he was only just holding himself under control. 'You are quiet, Heuss! Any questions?'

Dehler laughed harshly. 'Poor Heuss is still enraged by the way you polished off that little ship, Captain!' He glared triumphantly at Heuss. 'Too much for his poor little stomach!'

'Is that true, Heuss?' Von Steiger's voice was quiet, and he was conscious of the tension between them.

Heuss pushed himself away from the door, his eyes flashing with anger. 'Since my personal views are to be bandied about before my colleagues, I can freely say that I was sickened by the episode! I know that we are fighting a dangerous game, but to slaughter those men like that! It was sheer butchery!' He turned to face the Captain squarely, all caution gone. 'And I thought we were going to fight with honour, Captain!'

Von Steiger blew out a thin stream of blue smoke. 'Go on, Heuss, I am interested.'

Dehler laughed, and Ebert looked uneasily from one to the other.

Heuss waved his slender hands helplessly. 'I am no coward, and I am not squeamish! But to attack and destroy those men, without giving them a chance! We could have beaten them with just our machine guns!' He looked at Dehler with hatred. 'And you only laugh *because* they were small and defenceless! You have not got the guts for real fighting!'

Dehler was on his feet with surprising agility. 'Why, you little swine! You overbred apology for an officer!' He recoiled as von Steiger's voice rang like a whiplash across the cabin.

'Silence! Both of you! How dare you behave like this!' His eyes were yellow and seemed to dominate all of them. 'I do not have to explain my reasons, but I thought you were men to be treated as intelligent beings! Since you are evidently the opposite, I *will* explain, just this once!' His face suddenly became calm again, but without taking his eyes off them he stood up and poured another glass of brandy.

'That ship was as great a menace as any cruiser. We had to destroy her, and at once! If we had waited she would have wirelessed for help, and that would have put paid to all of us, to you, too, Heuss! Even asking them for a doctor gave us time to close the range . . . that is war! God, surely you don't imagine I enjoy killing unprepared men? But I intend to sail and fight this ship for as long as I can!' He dropped his voice to a mere whisper. 'But if I cannot rely on your assistance, Heuss, because of your unbalanced ideals and your apparent disregard for the facts, then I will do it without you!'

He stopped, his hands drumming on the table. 'You may return to your duties.'

He watched them go. Heuss, humiliated but defiant, followed by Niklas, whose old grey head was bent with worry—or was it shame?—for all of them. Ebert clicked his heels and hurried away; he at least had come out of the conflict unscathed, but looked taut and shaken. Dehler faltered by the door, his heavy face expressionless. He could hardly hide the triumph in his eyes. In one blow he had driven a wedge between his two enemies. He would show all of them, he thought. He should have been given the command, yet von Steiger treated him like a peasant and Heuss hated to serve under him because of his poor background.

Von Steiger eyed him coldly. 'Well?'

'Thank you for upholding me, Captain. These others should be taught a lesson!'

Von Steiger sat down and rubbed his eyes with his knuckles. At length he said: 'I will always back you, Dehler, because you are my First Lieutenant. But my respect you have still to earn! Now get out and leave me to think!'

He stared at the empty cabin, and then closed his eyes. I am to blame, he thought. Because my heart is not in this voyage they react to my uncertainty. They have no confidence in each other, because I have none in myself!

His head fell across the waiting charts, and he was asleep.

．　　．　　．　　．　　．　　．

Lieutenant Paul Kohler winced as a sheet of spray rose lazily over the bows and dashed itself against the bridge windows. He stared stolidly ahead although the visibility was non-existent and the ship's roll was growing more pronounced, so that he had difficulty in maintaining his stance of aloof watchfulness. It was a quarter sea, and the ship was taking it badly. The long black rollers cruised effortlessly out of the darkness and piled up against her hull, until beneath the great weight of water she laid over to one side and hung, it seemed, for several minutes before she laboured upright again to meet the next onslaught. Even in the wheelhouse it was bitterly cold, and the wind screamed and hummed through the rigging like a thousand mad violins.

Kohler wondered what the other officers were doing in the cosy warmth of their cabins. But von Steiger was the only one who counted, and it was up to him to see that Kohler received all the merits he deserved. It was quite useless to go through a naval career without planning each detail in advance. He smiled. With luck he might be allowed to take a prize ship for himself and drive it back to Germany. If he got home before the *Vulkan*, or if indeed he was the only one to reach Germany again, his future would be assured.

Sub-Lieutenant Wildermuth banged his hands together, and Kohler frowned with annoyance. Of course, Wildermuth was a prize officer. *He* would be given the task of taking over any worthwhile capture. What could an unimaginative old fool like him know about the presentation of an honourable deed, or making his efforts appreciated in the right quarter? Old enough to be my father, Kohler thought. He shuddered. Old, fat and ugly. How could they make such a man an officer? Some people at home had no idea of the damage they were doing to the Navy by such acts of stupidity. No doubt some fat civilian in his steam-heated office had made the decision.

The rage, which was always ready to be fanned into a flame, blazed within him. Germany, the Fatherland, was being betrayed by such people! Filthy merchants, who bribed and wheedled their way into the confidence of staff officers who had become soft, so that they could wax fat on the profits of war. Kohler's eyes smarted with sudden emotion. While at sea and on the battlefields the true sons of Germany were laying down their lives in steadily mounting numbers. Let these others wait, he thought savagely. After the war they will be winkled out and exterminated. The Emperor will have to abide by the will of the élite of his officer corps. In time of peace the country will be led by those who won her a victory.

Wildermuth moved towards him, his face worried. 'Sea's not breaking. Just a damned great swell.'

'I can see that. What about it?'

Wildermuth rubbed his nose and blinked at the chart. 'Could be ice about. This time of the year usually brings down a lot from Greenland. It calves from the big glaciers up north and makes its way down to the Atlantic.' He shook his head. 'Bad stuff, ice.'

Kohler lowered his voice so that the men on watch could not hear. 'I know that, man! The sea always remains unbroken when there's ice about!' There was contempt in his tone. 'It keeps like that because of the shelter afforded by the icebergs!'

Wildermuth still fidgeted. 'That's right. I don't like it.'

'Ach! We are in the Denmark Strait, and such hazards must be expected. But while there is a good wind the lookouts will be able to see any ice if it comes our way.'

He realized that Wildermuth was staring at him, his mouth hanging open.

'What in hell's name is the matter now? Try to look like an officer, even if——' His words stopped in mid-sentence, and he realized with a sudden chill that there was no longer any sound but that of the sea and the muffled beat of the engine. Even as they had been speaking the wind had vanished. He reassembled his thoughts with difficulty, still expecting to hear the moan and shriek outside the bridge. But there was nothing.

Wildermuth stared round with alarm. 'See? What did I tell you? Ice!' He walked nervously to the side of the wheelhouse, his professional seaman's instinct crying a warning. He peered out into the darkness. But instead of the sea he saw only his reflection in the glass. He thought fleetingly of his invalid wife in Hamburg, and how much the prize money could mean to her comfort. How could he convey his fears to a man like Kohler?

The ship heaved over on her side once more, and a pencil rolled noisily across the chart-table. On the port wing of the bridge a lookout stamped his booted feet to restore the circulation, and Wildermuth jumped at the sudden sounds. He swallowed hard. 'Shall I call the Captain?'

Kohler eyed him angrily. 'What for? To tell him there is ice about? God, he knows that, man! He only wants to be disturbed if anything unusual happens! Haven't you read his Standing Orders?'

Kohler watched Wildermuth walk back to the windows. As the

51

other man passed the brass telephone it buzzed noisily, and Kohler pushed him rudely out of the way to answer it.

'Bridge?'

'Officer-of-the-watch speaking!' Kohler stared at his reflection in the salt-caked windows. He made a handsome picture with his clean-cut features and pale eyes beneath the polished peak of his cap. Unconsciously, he adjusted the silk scarf about his neck.

'Masthead lookout reporting, sir.'

'I know that, you fool! Just tell me what you see!'

The man sounded confused. 'Sir, I've been up here for three hours. My relief hasn't arrived. I am so cold I can hardly move my arms!'

Kohler gripped the telephone viciously. God in heaven, I am surrounded by a watch of maniacs! 'Is that *all* you wanted to tell me?' He struggled to control his voice. 'Do you realize you are supposed to be keeping a sharp lookout? There may be ice about, and all you can do is whine about the cold! Who is that?'

A mere whisper answered. 'Braun, sir.'

Kohler bit his lip. He remembered Braun. A tall, good-looking boy with a weak mouth. He had already considered him as a possible convert, but this was *too* much.

'Report to me when you come off watch!' he barked.

'But, sir!' He was cut short by the hand-set being slammed into its cradle.

Kohler dismissed him from his thoughts, and to cover his irritation began to snap out orders at his weary watchkeepers.

High overhead in his tiny crow's-nest Braun, the lookout, swayed his head from side to side, the agony in his legs making him moan with pain. As he moved his head, as if in some way to alleviate this suffering, he felt the ice forming on his muffler where his breath froze with each short gasp.

He put his hands on the lip of the canopy and tried to jump up and down, but his clothing, stiffened by salt and ice, held him firm, and he knew that he was near to collapse. With sudden desperation he peered down at the deck below. As it swayed eerily from side to side, its pale planking white against the black water, he tried to see someone he could call or send for that swine Hahn who was supposed to relieve him. No man was supposed to do more than two hours aloft in this weather, and he had arranged for Hahn to be the one to take his place.

He stared wretchedly at the deserted deck and tried to control his chattering teeth. At least he *thought* he had arranged with Hahn. He was so dazed by exposure and numb with cold that he could no longer think properly He was nineteen years old and reasonably healthy, but he knew that unless he could get warm within the next few moments he would collapse, and if he did that he would never recover consciousness. He peered at the telephone in its leather case. It was no good, Lieutenant Kohler was already after his blood, he could not risk asking him again for help.

With fumbling hands he lifted his powerful Zeiss glasses and swept the area directly ahead. He cursed weakly and wiped the thin film which had formed on the lenses and tried again. He got the usual jumbled picture. The dark arrowhead of the bows, the streaming white wave on either side, and the occasional gleam of broken crests beyond. Apart from that the water was too dark to have any shape at all, and a light mist, pale and indefinable, seemed to surround the ship.

With mounting desperation he hung the glasses on their hook and began to lever himself out of the pod, his numbed fingers impeding every movement. He had made up his mind. He could be on deck in a few moments, and get Hahn or somebody else in his place before the bridge realized he had gone. The foremast was too far from the bridge for anyone there to see him descend, and Kohler was not in the habit of using the telephone unnecessarily. He sobbed aloud as he began to drag his thighs over the edge, every move starting a fresh flood of pain through his frozen limbs. Blindly he groped for the steel ladder which ran straight down the rear of the mast, his gloves slipping on the smooth sheen of ice. He had to look down to see if his feet were on the rungs, for he could no longer feel anything below the knee. He bit his lip and tried the next two rungs.

Soon be all right. A little shelter, and cocoa from the galley. Perhaps someone had some schnapps he could buy.

He opened his eyes wide as an extra-bad pain jarred his leg, and as he did so something beyond the mast took his attention. He blinked, and looked again.

That damned mist. He cursed with mounting frustration and pain. Below and behind him he could see the tall square shape of the bridge. He was still well above it and had hardly covered any distance at all. He peered forward again and gurgled with horror.

The mist was still there, but it had more body to it. A long sliver of white, which grew even as he stared, until it resembled a jagged, phantom cliff. An iceberg! He twisted his head from side to side but could not see either end of it. It lay across the *Vulkan*'s course in an unbroken line.

He shouted, his voice cracked, but nobody could hear. He stared back at the bridge calling like a maniac, but even the lookouts were too deaf to hear him. Braun was too frozen and terrified to realize that he was hardly making any noise and his voice was too weak to carry. 'The telephone! Must try to get back!' Mumbling and whimpering in turn he started to drag himself back up the glittering, treacherous rungs.

．　　　．　　　．　　　．　　　．

Above the swaying wheelhouse, Willi Pieck crouched beside the camouflaged range-finder. He pulled the frozen canvas canopy around his body to protect himself from the intense cold as he bent over the mechanism to ensure that the oil was free from ice.

Petty Officer Brandt, the most unpopular N.C.O. aboard, a man who would make trouble when it was not easily found, had ordered Pieck to carry out this additional duty although the boy should have been off watch and below in the warmth of his mess.

Brandt had hounded and chased the four new seamen from the detention barracks from the moment they had stepped aboard, but, shaken by Schiller's indifference and Hahn's cunning, he had concentrated his wrath upon Pieck and the defenceless Alder.

Pieck was still wearing only his thin uniform and oilskin, the petty officer having refused him permission to get his watch-coat. He clenched his fists like a child and rested his head against the range-finder. One way or the other, there was always someone who tried to extinguish his small spark of hope.

With a sigh like that of an old man he lifted his head. It was then that he saw the iceberg.

Afterwards he tried to remember how it had looked, but could recall only its ghostly gleam through the mist and its terrible menace. For a long moment he could not drag his eyes away. The iceberg was getting sharper in outline, and the ship appeared to be dashing towards it with something like eagerness.

Then all at once he was up and running for the ladder, heedless of his own safety and conscious only of the realization that the lookout for some reason had not seen the danger.

He fell the last few rungs, but picking himself up with the resilience of a rubber ball, he burst into the quiet calm of the wheelhouse.

'Sir! Sir!' Pieck was tongue-tied with the urgency of his news.

Kohler spun round. 'How dare you come in here like that!' But the reprimand died on his lips as the boy stepped into the small circle of light. For a moment Kohler was completely off balance and could only stare at Pieck's stricken face.

Making a tremendous effort he snapped, 'Well now, Seaman Pieck is it not?'

The boy swayed, and would have fallen but for Wildermuth, who said, not unkindly, 'Make your report, lad!'

Pieck still stared at Kohler, but his lips moved mechanically as if he was mesmerized by those opaque eyes.

'Iceberg, sir! Dead ahead!' The words dropped like grenades in a sleeping trench.

As Wildermuth dashed to the forward window calling: 'What did you say? Where is it?' Kohler strode to the telephone and cranked vigorously at the handle. Excluding everyone else on the bridge but Pieck he said, 'If you are lying, I'll——'

He paused, the lifeless telephone still in his hand, as the starboard lookout screamed out: 'Ice! Dead Ahead!'

Wildermuth gasped and jumped back from the window as if he had been scalded. He had seen the white wall for himself. It rose over the ship with contemptuous majesty, maybe a hundred feet higher than the foremast itself.

Kohler, still caught off balance by Pieck's appearance on the bridge, felt panic rising within him.

'Hard a-port!' His voice was toneless, his eyes fixed on the ice.

The helmsman had taken one turn of the wheel when a sharp voice cut across the bridge like the bite of a whip.

'Wheel amidships! Full speed astern!' Von Steiger walked slowly to the front of the bridge as a man would walk to a window to see a passing parade. 'Bosun's Mate, pipe the watch below on deck! Close all watertight doors and swing out the boats!'

As the frightened seaman ran from the bridge von Steiger added,

55

almost conversationally: 'Never put the helm over, Lieutenant! You might slit open her belly on an ice ledge!'

Von Steiger listened to the clang of the telegraph and waited for the increasing tremble beneath his feet which would tell him that the great screw was fighting to stop the ship's relentless dash to destruction. He controlled the raging fury of anxiety and anger which made him want to scream at Kohler's stupid mask of a face.

With great care he took a cheroot from his case and lit it with enforced slowness. He could hear the twitter of the bosun's pipes from up forward, followed instantaneously by the trample of running feet and orders shouted hoarsely in the darkness. It seemed an age since he had entered the wheelhouse, although it was only seconds. He had recognized immediately the seeds of demoralized chaos, and had been sickened by it. From his position he could see the iceberg quite clearly now, and he knew that to a less experienced eye it would appear as if it was already touching the stem. He stared along the deck at this silent adversary and waited. He could hear the helmsman's uneven breathing, and one of the lookouts muttering to himself as if in prayer. He stiffened as a small piece of ice detached itself from the top of the berg and seemed to float down to the sea like a feather. There was no sound, but he guessed that the piece of ice weighed many tons.

Dehler arrived breathless on the bridge, and von Steiger said softly: 'Ring the masthead lookout, Dehler. There seems to have been a fault somewhere!'

Dehler licked his lips, fascinated by the iceberg. 'Can we get clear?'

'I think so. We have had good warning, thanks to this man.' He spoke over his shoulder. 'What is your name?'

The reply was subdued, even frightened. 'Pieck, sir. I—I was on top of the wheelhouse, sir!'

Von Steiger clenched his fists inside his pockets. Was it his imagination, or was the ship beginning to go astern? He waited, not trusting himself to speak. A few more seconds might have been too much for the ship. Her four and a half thousand tons, with a following sea to help the thrust of her screw, would have been hurled against the foot of the berg, and that would have been the end, if they were lucky. If they were not, the ship would have slit open her round bilge on a razor-billed ledge, deep below the surface, and then sunk slowly. To die up here in these bitter wastes would have been too terrible to contemplate.

The thought made him angry, and he hardly looked up when a lookout reported wildly: 'We're going astern, sir! She's pulling clear!'

So I have done it again. His lips curled as if with contempt for himself. The iron captain who is always beyond criticism.

He whirled round with sudden impatience. 'Take over the ship, Dehler. Put her ahead and steer south-west until you are clear of this ice. Reduce speed for an hour, and we will see what happens.'

He looked from Kohler to Wildermuth, his eyes bleak. 'What happened, Kohler? Why was there no report? Was the masthead lookout asleep?' He waited, tapping his foot.

Kohler stood rigidly at attention. 'He deserted his post, Captain!'

Von Steiger turned his face away and watched the pale mist, which now hid the iceberg completely. 'Deserted?' Soft, half disbelieving.

Kohler nodded vigorously, some confidence returning to his voice. 'Yes, sir. The duty petty officer has just found him lying on the maindeck. He has broken his leg, and says that he was going below to get warm, sir.' He licked his lips, his voice ingratiating. 'I had no idea this could happen, Captain. I have a bad watch to work with. I have to carry all of them, sir.'

Von Steiger turned to Wildermuth. 'And is that *your* explanation also?'

Wildermuth hung his head. 'It is as Lieutenant Kohler has said, sir.' What was the point of bringing up about the telephone message? he thought heavily. It was hard enough working with Lieutenant Kohler without adding to the unpleasantness. After all, he thought, it would not do the lookout, Braun, any harm to spend a few days in the cells because of his stupidity.

Von Steiger felt the raw edge of the air for the first time. Until this moment he had not noticed that he was without his bridge-coat. They are both lying, he thought wearily. Something else happened, but I shall never know the truth. The one thing I must be sure of is that it will never happen again.

Sharply he said: 'I see. I trust that you will learn by this mistake, and control your watch in future!'

Kohler nodded eagerly. 'It will not happen again, sir!'

'That is true!' He eyed them coldly, hating them both. 'I have already told you the importance of eternal vigilance. In this war only the dead can afford the luxury of carelessness.'

57

Kohler showed his teeth. 'I will put him in the deepest cell, Captain. It will help to improve his memory!'

As if he had not heard, von Steiger continued, his tone flat and remorseless, 'By the authority vested in me by the Emperor and the Admiralty, I hereby sentence this man, Braun, to death by shooting!' He saw the horror forming on their faces and continued, 'The sentence will be carried out at dawn tomorrow, the firing party to consist of all the masthead lookouts not on watch!' He turned on his heel, adding harshly, 'You and Wildermuth will supervise the execution!'

Wildermuth took half a step forward, his hands outstretched. 'But, sir . . .'

In the doorway the yellow eyes glowed like a cat's. 'My men will respect their obligations, whatever the cost! You will all do well to remember that in future!'

4

FOR six days and nights the *Vulkan* drove west and south round the bleak coast of Iceland. There was neither light during the day, nor even a glimpse of a star at night, and throughout that incredible journey the weather reached such a pitch of fury and destructive vehemence that the ship seemed to have been condemned to a nightmare of wind and mountainous seas. Since that first encounter with the solitary iceberg the weather had steadily worsened, so that as they battled blindly round Iceland's North Cape the wind which screamed down from the Arctic reached over one hundred knots, and the waves towered over the weather side and curled their overhanging crests in readiness to strike her open decks and send her yawing on to her beam.

The men had stopped wondering at each mounting onslaught, and were no longer capable of thought of any kind. They went on watch, clinging together like frightened children, and waited for their spell of duty to end. Then, sapped of all resistance, they fell into their sodden bunks, or lay without feeling on the canting decks. Even then they were not safe from the urgent whistle from the Deck Watch. One of the boats was torn free of its davits and flung like matchwood across the bulwarks. Wires parted, and canvas dodgers were blown to nothing, seconds after replacement. Numb and senseless, the seamen spliced, and struggled across the treacherous decks with new ropes and stays, while all the time their tiny, isolated world swung on a giddy pendulum, and tried to trip their tired feet and send them spinning away into the great patches of streaky foam which seethed around the ship like steam.

Sometimes they were dragged on deck to face the weather when the ever-present menace of ice made itself felt in the shape of huge patches of trapped sea-water freezing into fantastic blocks of immovable proportions. With axes and hammers, steam hoses and iron bars, they worked like fiends, sweating beneath their oilskins in spite of the cold which held the ship in its remorseless grip.

After nearly a week of this torment they had at last reached the North Atlantic, and as the waves thundered against the hull they ploughed their way slowly yet steadily eastwards, every turn of the screw taking them nearer and nearer to an alien shore.

The mine stood on the small slipway which overhung the *Vulkan's* poop, its dull black sphere stark against the white creaming wake, which, straight and clean, disappeared into the night astern of the racing screw. Heuss stared through the darkness at the mine, fascinated by its long horns, which gave it the appearance of an obscene creature from another world. The last of the mines, he thought. The last of a long field which the raider had laid during the previous four hours, throughout which time the nerves of every man aboard had been stretched to breaking point as the ship steamed along its set course, lookouts peering into the night, and each man gritting his teeth as a fresh mine plummeted down from the stern. Each one would splash into the wake, and instantly vanish. When the water calmed and the raider had gone on her way, the black eggs with their sensitive horns would be floating below the surface, held captive by their sinkers and long cables, to wait with the same terrible patience they had shown since they had been loaded at Kiel.

Lieutenant Kohler held a small shaded lamp against his wrist, peering at his stopwatch and counting the seconds. He staggered against the poop's swooping, sickening movement, and then said sharply: 'Right! Release!'

The seamen heaved at their jacks, and the mine trundled on its trolley along the slipway. It faltered, staggered and plunged over the edge.

Heuss gritted his teeth again, but the men who had converted the banana-boat to a raider knew their job. The mine vanished into the gloom. The slipway was empty, and Heuss turned away, suddenly sickened.

The muttering of the seamen about him faded, and even the roar and hiss of the sea seemed to disappear.

He had been on watch the morning when the lookout, Braun, had been shot. I shall never forget that moment! He stared down into the water, his hands gripping the guardrail.

There had been endless preparations, and all the time the wretched Braun had sat propped on the mine slipway, his broken leg sticking out in front of him, neat in its splints and bandages. Opposite him, barely yards away, the firing party stood in a swaying line, their heavy Mauser rifles gripped in gloved hands. Two petty officers tied Braun's hands behind him and took away his cap, so that he looked even more defenceless than before. Kohler and Wildermuth had stood side by side, the latter sick and grey-faced, but Kohler upright and expressionless.

The petty officers dragged a length of rusty chain and tied it quickly to the victim's waist. His own sinker for the final journey.

It was then that Braun recovered from his state of shocked silence and began to scream. Heuss's blood turned cold as he relived each agonizing second.

'Don't let them do it! Tell them I tried to get help, sir!' His eyes rolled white in his ashen face. 'For God's sake help me!'

Kohler drew his sword and raised it above his head. Eight rifles swayed, and then steadied on the writhing figure before them.

There was a ragged volley as Kohler's sword sliced downwards, and when the wind whipped away the smoke, the slipway was empty. Not even a drop of blood to mark the murder. Only the man's cap in a petty officer's hand to show what had happened.

Heuss had pushed into the wheelhouse and then halted. Von Steiger still sat in his chair, his eyes fixed on some invisible point ahead of the bows. Heuss had said, 'Execution carried out, Captain!' He could not keep the tremble from his voice.

Von Steiger answered slowly: 'I could not escape my responsibilities, Lieutenant. And neither, I fear, can you!'

Heuss walked away, and then on impulse returned to stand behind the Captain. 'Was it absolutely necessary to kill that man, Captain? Haven't we enough to stomach already?'

'It became necessary. My officers must be upheld, right or wrong.'

Heuss clenched his fists, conscious of Ebert's worried glance through the side window. 'How do you think the men will feel about this, sir?'

'The men?' Von Steiger sounded distant. 'Whatever they feel, they will do as I say!' He twisted round to face Heuss, who was shocked to see the pain on his tired face. 'Because, Heuss, we are not playing a game any more! Forget your misplaced sentiment, and you will begin to understand! Of course I want victory with honour! But most of all I want victory! War in itself is evil, and we cannot disguise it by our own stupidity!'

Heuss had continued to stare at him, shocked still more by von Steiger's calm tone. Inwardly he cursed himself. What was the use of trying to fight this man? He was without a soul. You need none of us, he thought, and our admiration and hate affects you as little as rain upon a stone. He heard himself persist, 'But, Captain, if we lose our belief in humanity, what else is there?'

Von Steiger had regarded him for several seconds. 'Nothing, Lieutenant! Nothing at all!'

Heuss shook himself, and once more the sea's roar intruded on his racing thoughts. He heard the seamen chattering as they scampered back to their messdecks. Perhaps they do not care after all, he thought. Von Steiger seemed to know even the inner thoughts of his men, although he never left the bridge. He was uncanny, like an unravelled legend.

It was a week since they had sunk the little steamer, and they had covered nearly eighteen hundred sea miles in their detour around Iceland. Because of the unbroken cloud they had been unable to use a sextant, and watchkeeping and navigation had become mere guess-work. The ship had made endless alterations of course and speed in the maelstrom of storm and noise, yet here they were, and somewhere across the plunging bows lay Ireland and the northern approaches to England. How did von Steiger do it? Bluff, or some supreme power which made them all so small in his hands?

The ship gathered way and swung on to her new course. A smell of boiled cabbage floated from the galley, and as he passed Heuss heard a seaman describing the minelaying to a cook. '. . . a terrible death!' the voice said.

Heuss faltered, and heard the cook answer with derision: 'Death? Who the hell cares about that? You would do better to worry about piles or rheumatism in this damned ship!' The philosophy of the lower deck!

· · · · ·

Von Steiger sat in his tall chair, his hands leafing through the Chief Engineer's latest reports. The ship moved in slow, labouring rolls across the empty grey Atlantic, and beyond the bows, which pointed unwaveringly to the south-west, the horizon was a clear, hard line.

He could hear Niklas breathing heavily at his side, and could smell the coal-dust on his overalls. A good man, he thought. Nearly sixty, and a lifetime afloat in ocean liners, warships and dirty tramp steamers. Now a key man in a commerce raider. He frowned at the neat figures on the soiled paper. They had steamed another one hundred and eighty miles from the place where they had dropped the mines. Coal was being consumed at a terrible speed, and already he felt the sluggish buoyancy of the ship as she devoured her own ballast. The mines, too, had made a difference of some ninety tons aft, and for twenty-four hours the sweating, cursing seamen had shovelled and dragged some of the coal supply to the stern to compensate the loss.

Von Steiger's head drooped and he shook himself awake angrily. It was strange how easily he had dropped back into his role. There was no escaping it. The ship was not to be a sanctuary after all. In spite of all his hopes he was being made to force his men on, to drive them to the very mission he despised.

Niklas said quietly: 'You have a lonely command, Captain. I would not take your responsibility for the world!'

'It is what I was trained for.'

'It is hard to take a man's life, Captain!' The old man looked at von Steiger sadly.

'Do you think I did wrong?'

Niklas shrugged. 'I am told that on the Western Front a general or even a colonel can sacrifice a thousand men. Even ten thousand if that is not sufficient! And all for a whim! To test the enemy's strength perhaps, to hold a position which cannot be held or to fight overwhelming odds!'

'But was *I* wrong?'

Niklas picked up his blackened cap. 'You were committed, Captain. What is one man's life when we all depend on your strength and instant obedience of your orders? You lead us. You have become part of the ship!' He shook his head slowly. 'Only God can give you the final answer to your question.'

Von Steiger dozed and brooded in silence as the ship thrust her way across the deserted ocean. The shipboard noises lulled him like distant music, and the wind sighed around the pitching bridge. He heard the stammer of Morse from the wireless-room and the rattle of shovels from the forward hold.

Suddenly Heuss burst into the wheelhouse, a signal-pad grasped in his hand. His eyes were wild, and von Steiger's tired brain instinctively flashed a warning.

'We have just intercepted a signal, Captain!' Heuss's voice was flat and hard. 'Two neutral ships were talking to each other.'

The atmosphere was tense in the wheelhouse, and von Steiger's eyes flickered as Heuss added, 'It seems that our mines have had an effect already!'

Ebert gasped aloud, 'By God, that was quick!'

Von Steiger ignored the interruption. 'Read it, Heuss!' He felt that he knew what was coming, yet Heuss's tone made his stomach contract.

Heuss read from the pad. 'The S.S. *Isle of Cuba* was sunk this morning, whilst making the north-west passage to England. She struck a mine and sank immediately!'

Von Steiger kept his voice even. 'That is war, Heuss.'

Heuss lifted his eyes, his face white. 'The *Isle of Cuba* was a hospital ship, Captain! She was returning from Europe full to the deck-seams with helpless wounded men!' He shouted at the bridge at large, 'Is that war?' Then he laid the signal by von Steiger and walked on to the open bridge-wing. But the cold wind no longer helped him, and he felt unclean.

. . . . . .

Von Steiger groaned and stirred in his tall chair. His body was stiff and cold, and he had to rub his hands sharply across his eyes before he could remember what had awakened him. Kohler was peering down at him, his face grey and unshaven in the morning light. Makes him look almost human, he thought vaguely.

'Ship, Captain! Bearing red four-five!' Kohler repeated his message, his eyes searching von Steiger's face.

He jerked out of his weariness, his joints protesting as he levered himself down from the chair. 'Any details?'

'Masthead reports that it might well be a freighter, sir. She's hard to see because there seems to be a lot of rain-squalls around her. But he did get one good bearing on her at the time, and now he has reported that she's holding her course!'

The telephone buzzed and von Steiger massaged his numb thighs, as Kohler nodded and talked into the mouthpiece.

'Yes, sir. Freighter. Seems to be steering north-east by north. One funnel, and low in the water.'

Von Steiger bit his lip. The two ships were approaching each other on almost parallel courses. It will make the approach seem all the more natural, he thought quickly.

'Sound Action Stations, Lieutenant!' He waited until the bells had begun to jangle, and added, 'You go to your station now, we may need the torpedoes!' Into the telephone he said evenly, 'Let me know instantly she alters course, or shows any sign of alarm.'

'Ship bearing red five-oh!' The port lookout could see her already.

He made rapid calculations, ignoring the clatter of feet through the ship and the distant squeak of ammunition hoists. The attack team arrived panting on the bridge, but he hardly gave them a glance. She is probably doing about eight knots, and we are doing a steady fourteen. She will be up to us in a quarter of an hour perhaps. He could hear Ebert barking through his telephone on the deck overhead. He would be already swinging his range-finder on to the target, and passing the ranges and bearings to his hidden guns. Heuss and Damrosch were in the wheelhouse at their stations, and he noted briefly that Heuss looked red-eyed, as if he had not slept for days. Damrosch looked fresh and a little dazed, and was watching him like a hawk. A tame hawk, he thought, but strangely reliable.

Heuss was the ship's signals officer, and was giving his orders in a low voice to his small staff at the rear of the bridge. The signalmen had stripped the canvas covers from the flag lockers and had spilled some of their colourful contents on to the deck, the halyards already in their eager hands.

Von Steiger remembered what the Chief Engineer had said. Not like the other command he had held; they had been the cream of the Navy. Well, we shall see, he thought calmly.

How easy it was to drop into this slot. It was as if he had spent all his life on this damned bridge.

He heard Heuss catch his breath, and saw that he had his binoculars trained. With a start he realized that he had not yet looked at the enemy ship. He was getting careless, and that could be fatal.

He rested the powerful glasses against the open door and watched the ship move ponderously across the lenses. About five thousand tons, British by the look of her businesslike outline. She was making heavy weather of the blustering sea, and seemed unable to ride out of the deep troughs which deluged her decks with spray. Well laden, he mused. Probably a straggler from some convoy or other. Making a lot of black smoke from her spindly funnel. That would make her very unwelcome in any convoy, for this was U-boat territory.

Over his shoulder he asked distantly, 'Is the ship closed up at Action Stations?'

'Yes, Captain!' Heuss sounded strained.

'Well, report it in future, Lieutenant, I am not a mind-reader!'

Lehr, the Coxswain, who had taken the wheel from the quarter-master, shifted his huge bulk and smiled a secret smile. Tension on the bridge already. That was good, he thought. Showed that they were alert for once.

Von Steiger watched the other ship with great concentration. She was close enough now for him to see her high bridge and the small splash of colour beyond, probably the red ensign. British, as he had imagined she would be.

'Make a signal, Heuss! Ask her name.' His eyes never wavered from the slow-moving freighter.

The Morse lamp on the wing of the bridge began to clatter noisily. Not too fast, he noted with satisfaction. Merchant ships rarely had a really proficient signalman, and fast naval Morse would be an immediate give-away.

'What is the name of your ship?'

There was a long pause, and they began to think that the stranger was not keeping a lookout. Then the uneven wink of a powerful lamp stabbed back across the heaving water.

'What is the name of your ship?'

Von Steiger smiled grimly. A cautious one, this. He was not taking any chances. The lamp began again.

'*Gripsholm*, Swedish!'

A long pause, and then: '*Cardiff Maid.*'

There could be no doubt now of her nationality, and von Steiger signalled with his hand towards Damrosch, who licked his lips and then blew a long blast on his whistle.

The Morse lamp began again. 'Stop immediately! This is a German cruiser!'

Von Steiger could well imagine the consternation on the other vessel's bridge. The unexpected meeting with another ship after crossing the Atlantic, and almost within sight of home. Then the curt order to heave to, and the German ensign breaking out at the gaff for all to see, and wonder no more.

Damrosch, his eyes wide with excitement, pointed with disbelief. 'Look, they're turning away!'

Von Steiger pressed the button by his elbow and overhead a bell rang with brief authority.

A nerve in Heuss's cheek jumped uncontrollably as one of the big five-point-nines roared out from its sheltered mounting beneath the fo'c'sle. His eyes followed the direction of the invisible shell, and as he watched he saw a tall column of water rise straight out of the sea less than half a cable from the freighter's bows. He tore his eyes away to watch his signalmen, who, with deft fingers, had shackled on their flags and hoisted them above the bridge, to stand out stiffly in the keen breeze.

'Stop immediately! Abandon ship!' Von Steiger had obviously decided not to waste time over this one. Too near the enemy patrols, no doubt.

Heuss licked his lips, suddenly nervous. What was the matter with that fool of a British captain? He was still trying to swing away, and the frothy tail beneath her high counter indicated that his ship was increasing speed and showed no sign at all of complying with von Steiger's signal. 'For God's sake, what's he doing?' His voice sounded unnatural. He can't possibly hope to get away now.

Von Steiger ignored him and bent quickly over the bell mouthpiece of one of his voice-pipes. 'Ebert? Captain speaking. Open fire with everything you have. As quick as you can!'

Heuss found himself at von Steiger's side. 'She may not understand your signal, sir! Is it necessary to murder everyone on board? She can't escape now!'

Von Steiger lowered his glasses momentarily and turned to face him.

His cold eyes gave him a brief but searching appraisal, and then he resumed his study of the *Cardiff Maid*, which was now practically end on to the *Vulkan*. Her stern was swaying steeply as she heeled bravely in response to maximum rudder. Von Steiger's eyes narrowed as he followed the movements of the ant-like figures grouped on her poop. His voice was quiet but cutting.

'I put down your impertinence to inexperience, Lieutenant! I have no wish to kill helpless men, whatever you may imagine, but I have my duty to consider first!' Overhead Ebert's harsh voice could be heard rapping out orders, and from forward the two guns which would bear swung their slender barrels straight on to their target. 'Use your eyes, Heuss! He is not running away!'

Heuss lifted his glasses dazedly and peered across the tumbling green water. As his eyes focused on the other ship, he flinched as an orange flash lit up her stern, followed immediately by a loud crack. A shell whined over the raider's bridge and ricocheted across the wave-tops before exploding in a brown puff of smoke.

'She has a gun apparently!' The voice cut into Heuss's reeling thoughts. 'The gallant captain intends to——' The rest of the sentence was cut short by the double explosion from the forward guns. Like an echo, the twenty-two pounder barked out from the poop, and as the freighter's gun-crew laboured around their puny weapon, the complete salvo tore into the ship's side and exploded with a deafening roar.

Von Steiger watched carefully as the second salvo left the guns and screamed straight into the other ship. The rear of her bridge erupted in smoke and flame, and, as if sheared off by a giant knife, the tall funnel staggered and then pitched over the side, sweeping away two of the lifeboats as it passed.

There was another crack, and the deck beneath their feet lurched slightly, and Heuss's nostrils twitched at the pungent smell of cordite.

'She's hit us!' Von Steiger's face hardened. 'Damrosch, pass the word to ascertain the damage! Heuss, ring down full speed ahead. I'm going to close with this maniac!' He spoke into the voice-pipe again. 'Ebert, shoot for her waterline! This may be excellent target practice for you, but even one of her little shells could do us a real injury at this stage!'

With steady, remorseless fury the raider's guns fired again and again. The freighter seemed all at once to have changed from a trim, sturdy merchantman to a floating wreck. She was listing slightly to starboard, and both her masts had been shot from her decks. The bridge was little more than a tangle of twisted metal, and from her erratic course it seemed likely that the steering had been destroyed. A shell punctured her poop, and with a sullen roar her ammunition locker exploded and flung the defiant little gun high into the air, complete with the pieces of its crew.

'She's signalling, sir!' The petty officer sucked his teeth and read the erratic light through his brass telescope. 'I am stopped. Am abandoning ship!'

'About time too!' Von Steiger pressed the button again, and with one final shot the guns fell silent.

Sub-Lieutenant Seebohm scrambled panting on to the bridge. With a nervous glance over his shoulder at the stricken ship, he saluted. 'The shell hit us on the starboard bow, sir. Passed right through into the forward hold before exploding. No damage, sir. That hold is full of coal, so there was no harm done.' He faltered. 'One of the men was killed, though. Must have touched him as it passed.' There was wonder in his voice. 'Hardly a mark on him, sir!'

Von Steiger looked up sharply as a ragged cheer rippled along the forward deck. He snorted, and watched the *Cardiff Maid* begin to fall heavier into the eager waves. She was quite still now. Heavy and useless. He could see a lifeboat being lowered jerkily down her canting side and some figures already jumping into the water.

'Muster the first-aid party in the waist. Get all the rope ladders over the side and stand by to pick up every man. I don't want a single one left behind.'

The raider slackened speed, and glided slowly towards the solitary lifeboat and the cluster of bobbing heads. The surface of the sea was thick with coal-dust and oil, and sprinkled with splintered woodwork, torn spars and the remains of the other boats.

They were very close to the other ship now, and from his bridge von Steiger could see straight down into one of her shattered holds. The grey light gleamed dully on the jumbled shapes of closely packed vehicles, their new khaki paint torn and blistered by the searing heat of the raider's shells. A good victim. All army transport on its way to the Western Front.

There was a heavy rumble as some huge piece of machinery tore itself loose and crashed through the heeling vessel. She leaned still farther on her side, fragments of her shattered superstructure pitching into the water dangerously near one of the swimmers.

'Not many survivors.' He spoke to the bridge at large, his eyes studying the white upturned faces in the lifeboat. 'That second salvo must have seen to them!'

Heuss leaned limply on the bridge screen, looking across at the sinking ship. It looked so big and helpless now. No defiance, no beauty. Just a broken ship, trying to hide man's cruelty in the waves.

The lifeboat scraped alongside, and he saw some of the seamen pulling the shocked and dazed survivors up the swaying ladders. Several of the men had jumped down into the boat itself and were tying lines around the shoulders of some of the wounded and motionless figures who could no longer help themselves. Dehler was leaning over the rail, pointing at the other men who were swimming slowly towards the tethered lifeboat. 'Get those men next! Get a move on, you lazy swine!'

Heuss noticed that the rescued men no longer seemed to have any personality or shape. They merely stared listlessly at the busy German sailors, and allowed themselves to be helped, cajoled or pushed, like so many puppets.

As one man was being hoisted up the side, the *Vulkan* swayed heavily in a steep roller, and he swung helplessly against the rough plating. He gave a thin scream, and as he swung clear again Heuss noticed that he had left a red smear on the black paintwork. A cruel splash of colour, which faded and ran in the salt spray even as he watched.

Wildermuth stood at the foot of the bridge ladder, his face tense with excitement. 'Captain, sir? Shall I bring the Master up to you?'

Von Steiger nodded, and there was a silence in the wheelhouse as the small, grey-headed figure in the sodden blue uniform appeared at the top of the ladder. The gold lace on his sleeves was faded and torn, and his old, weathered face was lined with shock, which made him seem older than time.

Wildermuth snapped at him to move on to the bridge, and the English captain swayed slightly, his face uncomprehending.

Von Steiger stepped forward from his officers and saluted gravely. Heuss remembered the incident for a long time afterwards.

The silence on the bridge, whilst from the deck below came the urgent shouts of the men and the clang of metal as the guns slid into their housings. From beyond the bridge rail he could hear the agony of tortured steel as the sinking ship began to break in two. But inside the shelter of the bridge screen the small tableau held his attention so that he could hear his own heart beating.

His brother officers. Damrosch, young, eager and too dazed by the brief but savage engagement to control his elation. Wildermuth, self-important, and still scowling because the prisoner did not understand him. Seebohm, anxious and watchful, trying to gauge von Steiger's mood.

And the Captain. Had they all been dressed in sacking, Heuss knew that von Steiger would have looked every inch a leader. With his fur jacket and black gloves, his cap tilted at a slightly rakish angle where he had caught it with his binoculars, and above all his calm, impassive face, he stepped forward and saluted the vanquished enemy.

In perfect English he said: 'I am sorry I had to sink your ship, Captain. You fought a brave but hopeless battle. I pity you for your loss, but admire you for your courage. I should like to shake your hand.' He held it out, his eyes shaded and expressionless.

He had spoken simply, and without emotion. Perhaps, Heuss thought, merely as one seaman speaking to another.

The British captain took the proffered hand and nodded vaguely. 'It's a bit of a shock, y'see.' Had the others realized it, he was speaking with a round Yorkshire accent, his tone unsteady and apprehensive. 'I can't take it all in, y'see.'

At that moment there came a cry from the deck. 'She's going! There she goes!'

The Englishman was transformed from that instant. He was no longer a hurt, shocked old man. He was as much a captain as the arrogant German who had shaken his hand, and with a grunt he pushed past von Steiger and climbed up on to the wing of the bridge.

'Why, the insolent pig!' Wildermuth stepped forward, his pistol half drawn from his holster, but von Steiger shook his head angrily, his eyes flashing. 'Leave him! This is his moment. It is all he has now!'

The little Yorkshireman glared down at the listless figures who lay on the raider's deck, their wet clothing making black shadows on the scrubbed planks. 'On yer feet, lads! Give the old girl a cheer!'

His men staggered to their feet, and stared first up at the small erect figure of their captain, and then at the great streaming hull which rose slowly from the water until its broken stern pointed straight up at the barren sky. For a moment she hung there motionless, as if unwilling at the last to leave. Then, with a final hissing roar, followed almost at once by the muffled thunder of her exploding boilers, she slid out of sight.

Von Steiger jerked his head. 'Clear the bridge. Leave the good captain alone for a while!'

Heuss tore his eyes from the great writhing whirlpool, its vortex seething with flotsam, and stared at the lonely old man in the corner of an alien ship. His lined face defied description, and the look in his eyes was similar to von Steiger's when he had joined the ship at Kiel.

Heuss shook his head and stepped into the wheelhouse. He felt that he should have learned something by all this, but he felt as if he had been deceived.

5

As THE wreck of the *Cardiff Maid* sank slowly into the bottomless depths of the Atlantic, to the deep unknown crevasses which lie undisturbed by current or tide and hidden by perpetual darkness, the German raider altered course due south, and even before the last pathetic remnant had been borne away on the remorseless waves, and the patches of coal-dust and oil had been scattered to the points of the compass, she had already started to alter her appearance and personality once more.

On either side of her hull hung a large sheet of steel painted red with a blue cross, and underneath, in clear white letters, 'NORGE'. The Norwegian flag flew from her gaff, and the name *Stella Polaris* decorated bows and stern alike. A large imitation pig-pen had been constructed of sewn canvas on the foredeck, to which some realistic washing had been fixed, so that to a keen-eyed observer the raider had all the appearance of a typical ocean-going tramp. Her decks littered with loose cargo, and the crew's washing flapping casually from every available space. The pig-pen altered her outline quite considerably, and hid the false deck-house which covered two of her guns. For although the remains of the crew of the *Cardiff Maid* were safely locked below, it was always possible that an enemy submarine might have spotted the raider through her periscope and reported both her appearance and nationality.

It had taken the hands most of the day to complete the change, and they had been driven mercilessly by their petty officers to get the work done before dusk. A series of brisk rain-squalls, each one heavier than the last, had not helped, and harried by the barked commands and cursing the keen edge of the wind, they had struggled with wet canvas which defied their efforts with brushes and paint, and hammered and

73

banged until few of them had been spared either a cut or a bruise for their pains.

With the night closing in around them, and the lookouts doubled at their posts, the seamen had at last been allowed to retreat to the safety of their messes. The *Vulkan*'s fo'c'sle was partitioned into small watertight compartments, each divided from the other by a steel bulkhead and one small door. Each compartment contained two messes, where the men, crowded together with hardly enough room to sit down, lived, slept, ate their badly cooked meals and gambled.

The yellow glow of the electric lamps cast a warm but feeble light over the men of Schiller's mess, as they sat packed together on the two long benches facing one another across the scrubbed deal table. The warmth of their bodies and the fierce heat which poured steadily from the steam-pipes, which ran throughout the ship's length, had made them drowsy, and they sat in vests and trousers, swaying comfortably to the heavy motion of the ship around them. In the background some men made belated efforts to wash their clothes in buckets of heated salt-water, and others squatted on the deck, sewing, polishing and darning, their faces tight with unaccustomed concentration.

Schiller struck a match and lighted the stub of a cigar. His eyes squinted to the sting of the smoke, but they did not waver from the cards held in the hands of his companions. He was wearing his blue trousers, supported by a wide leather belt. The belt was practically the only possession which he had retained throughout his service, and was decorated with badges and ships' crests, which he had carefully collected through the years. His other possession was his knife, which hung from the belt in a hand-sewn sheath. Otherwise he was naked, his thick-set body fearsome with tangled black hair, which he occasionally scratched with thoughtful enjoyment as he prepared to play his next card.

Schwartz stared stonily at his own cards and glanced quickly at the small pile of broken matches on the table. 'Pity we've not some real money to play with! I feel like a schoolkid playing at shopkeeping!'

Schiller grinned. 'We'll have plenty of everything before long. Just you wait till we get farther south. We will be able to stop and search ships at leisure!'

Blucher, another of the card-players, looked up, his wind-reddened face blank. 'What, looting d'you mean?'

Schiller laid down his cards and groaned. 'Looting! God Almighty! Commandeering—that's what they call it in wartime!' He winked at the others. 'Just think, a nice big merchantman with just us to look around! Deserted cabins, open holds!' He smacked his lips with relish. 'We'll be rich if we're careful!'

Hahn leaned on his elbows and watched. He wanted to pull out the gold watch and wave it at them. Stupid, ignorant fools! What did Schiller know about looting, anyway? He would probably break into the first cabin that he could find in an enemy ship and go straight for the whisky. It was well known that all the British officers carried good whisky with them. But Schiller would make a pig of himself, and probably get fighting drunk. Hahn grimaced. Then there would be another firing squad. Well, good riddance to all of them. They must be mad to cheer a sinking ship, or sing the praises of the Captain. One day they might learn that those sort of things got you nowhere. You had to look after yourself, and you could not do that by shouting and yelling like a lot of raw recruits. He could feel the smooth shape of the gold watch against his thigh as it hung heavily inside his pocket. Pure gold, and must have cost a small fortune.

Well, that was number one. A survivor from the *Cardiff Maid* had died almost immediately after being swung aboard the raider's deck. Hahn had been in charge of the purchase which had been hoisting him up the side, when the ship had rolled with sudden violence and the man —a British officer—had been dashed heavily against the hull. He had been badly wounded by shell-splinters, and his rough bandage had burst open on impact, so that as he was jerked urgently over the rail Hahn had felt the blood warm against his face. Lieutenant Dehler had snarled at him: 'Fix those bandages, you clumsy convict!' and Hahn had stooped over the dying officer, who regarded him with a fixed stare, his mouth opening and closing in silent protest.

Hahn had fumbled with the soaked bandages, his mind elsewhere. That swine Dehler was always riding him and calling him a convict in front of the others. Well, we shall see. He had almost stopped breathing when his searching fingers had found the officer's watch. It had been wrapped in a small waterproof wallet with some tattered letters, and Hahn had recognized its worth immediately. He waited, hardly daring to look up, even when the enemy ship sank, and everyone was dashing from one place to another. Then the wounded man had died, and Hahn had sighed with relief. The letters and wallet he had sent skimming over the rail, but the watch he had slipped into his pocket.

Lieutenant Dehler had stopped nearby and stared down at him. 'Dead, is he? Did you look after him all right? There might be some good even in you, then!'

Hahn smiled to himself. Dehler was like all the others really, for all his bluster. Too sentimental over things which really didn't matter. Ah well, it was their loss.

From a neighbouring mess through a watertight door came the plaintive sound of a mouth-organ, and he could hear voices, sad and emotional, as they harmonized the 'Lorelei' together. It was all so damned peaceful. They seemed to be doing just as they pleased on the seas. No British warships, and no real opposition anywhere. He leaned his back against the crude angle-iron support which had been built into the fo'c'sle to carry the weight of one of the five-point-nines. Opposite him Pieck sat in silence, his eyes tired and pensive.

Hahn regarded him carefully. A queer one was Willi Pieck. Flanked on one side by Schiller's hairy bulk, and on the other by that half-wit Alder, Pieck looked frail and smooth like a girl. Hahn licked his thin lips. I wish he was a girl. He frowned again. There was something else, too. Pieck was worried about the torpedo officer, Kohler. It was, he knew, the officer who had accused Pieck of stealing from his room at the barracks, and who had been the cause of the boy's imprisonment. That should have been enough, but Hahn knew it was not. He hoarded information carefully, knowing that such details could be useful, and he felt quite sure that Pieck knew more than he had told. Kohler was an effeminate-looking bastard. It might have been something like that. All the men in the ship pulled Pieck's leg about his girlish face and slim figure, and each time it occurred he looked as if he had been struck a blow.

He said casually, 'Seen any more of your friend Lieutenant Kohler, Willi?'

The boy started, his eyes suddenly alert. 'No. Not much. I try to keep out of his way!' He stared fixedly at Hahn's impassive face, a face betrayed as always by the restless eyes of a professional thief. 'Why do you ask?'

Hahn shrugged, his expression blank. 'Just wondered. I heard him mention your name on the bridge yesterday, that's all.' He watched the effect of the lie on Pieck's pale face. 'Thought maybe he was after you in some way.'

Slap-slap went the cards on the table, otherwise there was silence. Pieck felt mesmerized by the other man's cold eyes, and bunched his hands into tight fists in his lap. 'After me? How do you mean?' His voice was unsteady, and he knew that Hahn had guessed his secret.

'Well, Willi, you know what some of these wretched little aristocrats are like. Take this Kohler, for instance. Cool as they come, and as cruel as a cockerel. But I bet you he's never had a woman in his life!'

Pieck half rose, his mouth quivering. Hahn's eyes were mocking. He was enjoying himself.

Lukaschek, at the end of the table, threw down his cards and whined petulantly: 'My Christ, Schiller! You've won again! You've put a curse on my cards!'

Schiller scooped up some more of the matches and grinned lazily. His eyes, however, were on Hahn.

'Well, Willi?' Hahn's voice was sharper and more insistent. 'Has he been after *you*? Perhaps that was what got you in the detention barracks, eh?'

Schiller scratched his chest. 'What were *you* in for, Hahn? Stealing, was it not? Well, in the olden days, before the Fatherland was much more than a clod of mud, they used to cut the hands off thieves as a warning to others!'

Hahn turned on him, furious at this interruption. 'Well, what of it?'

'So shut your dirty little trap! That's what of it!' Schiller breathed noisily down his broken nose. 'I don't suppose you've had a woman either, come to that! She'd be afraid you were going through her pockets while you were proving your apology for manhood!' He relaxed slightly as the other men laughed.

Hahn slid from the bench, his face ugly. 'We shall see! Who was it reported that iceberg?' He gestured at Pieck. 'Him! Instead of going and telling poor Braun, he ran straight to the blasted bridge!' He clasped his hands like a girl and lisped: 'Oh, Captain, sir, there's a great big iceberg ahead! I saw it, sir! Not Braun, sir, he's left his post!'

Schiller's smile faded. 'You lying little bastard! You know damned well that if it had not been for Willi we might all be at the bottom of the Arctic!'

'I'm only saying——'

'I know what you're saying, you little snake! If you're so smart perhaps you know the name of the man who was supposed to have relieved Braun. Who was it, eh?'

Hahn checked himself. Time to break off. There was real danger in Schiller's hostile face. He shrugged. 'Well, it wasn't me. I don't let my mates down!'

Gottlieb, a fat ex-shoemaker from Landshut, laughed wheezily, his soft body jerking up and down like jelly. 'If we are away from land for a month or two, little Willi will be in demand by all of us, eh?'

Schiller scowled. 'You won't see land for months, maybe for ever! By that time the cooks will be looking at *you*, Gottlieb, but for other reasons! You'd be all right with some fresh cabbage and some baked potatoes!'

Alder, who had been sitting motionless beside Pieck, jumped as the laughter echoed loudly in the confined space. He peered sideways at his companions, and, realizing that nothing more was about to happen, resumed the complex task of unravelling his thoughts. The tension within his body was so great that it hurt him to breathe, and sometimes, when the mist across his mind cleared in a brief, confused picture, his thoughts became so frantic and jumbled that he wanted to scream and keep on screaming.

Below the edge of the table lay his hands. By leaning back very slightly he knew he would be able to see them. But he would not lean back. He would save it. Make the agony last a little longer. Then he could start again. Two hands . . . my name is Emil Alder. . . .

He frowned. Willi was leaning heavily against him, his body throbbing like a trapped animal's. Perhaps he too was lost. No, that was impossible. Willi was a good fellow. He tried to help, but did not understand. Perhaps one day . . . one day . . . He leaned back, his eyes wild. Two hands . . . my name is Emil Alder. . . .

Willi Pieck forced himself to sit quietly, his heart still pounding beneath his vest. Although Schiller had spoken up on his behalf, he knew it was only a matter of time before Hahn got him alone again. And the lie about the lookout, Braun. Even that had been used by Hahn to discredit him in front of the others. Why? He knew that although the men had laughed at Hahn, they would all remember his lies only as the truth under different circumstances.

He stared around desperately at his comrades. If only they knew how he wanted to be one of them. Tough, like Schiller; laconic and cool, like Schwartz; or even like Hahn. He at least seemed not to care what anyone thought of him.

Suppose I was to see Kohler, and explain that I did not intend to make any trouble. To tell him that all I wanted was to be a good seaman, and serve von Steiger.

Von Steiger. He remembered the Captain's keen stare. 'What is your name?' That had been a great moment for Pieck. Even Kohler's incredulous stare, as he had burst into the wheelhouse, had been unable to destroy it completely.

Perhaps he should just try to avoid Kohler and wait and see what he would do. Then, if he attempted something, he would report it to the Captain. He shook his head wretchedly. No, that was no good. If von Steiger could have a man shot for negligence it was unlikely that he would discredit one of his officers on the word of a common seaman. And on a cruise of such importance as this, Pieck's own life must seem of no value at all to the Captain, except as a mere cog in the great wheel of command and discipline.

If only there was someone he could approach. He bit his lip with concentration. Lieutenant Heuss was in charge of his watch. He seemed an unusual kind of man to Pieck, who was used to the more arrogant type of officer. He was popular with his men, and had taken a lot of trouble over their welfare and comfort, and might be the one to listen to him. He sighed. It was small enough comfort, but at least it was something.

A seaman named Erhard, one of the gunners, pulled a small bible from his trousers and began to thumb slowly through the worn pages. He was a sad-faced man who rarely showed any sign of humour.

Hellwege, the poop gunlayer, laughed noisily. 'Here we go again! How d'you do it, man?'

Erhard looked up suspiciously. 'Do what?'

'Well, this morning we sunk a damned British ship, and as a gunner you are not bad. We got off as many shells as the other guns, and you were quick with your training wheel!' He pointed at the small book. 'Yet now you read about saints, when all of you must be sinners in that book!'

'We are all equal in the eyes of the Lord, Hellwege!' He eyed him severely.

Schiller shouted from the end of the table: 'By God, that's true enough! So equal we're nothing!'

Erhard scowled. 'What do you know about the scriptures? All you think of is drink, women and any other evil which takes your fancy!'

Hellwege banged the table with his fist. 'Never mind *him*. What I want to know is, how can you reconcile all this with God? What can He think of our efforts to wipe out His creatures? Come on, man, answer me that!'

'He will forgive you!' Erhard stared back at him, unmoved and impassive.

'That's no answer! I want to meet one man who can explain it all to me! Here we are, the damned British, us and probably every other country that's in the war, all quite convinced that *his* cause is the just one! Each quite sure that God and Right are on his side! It make me sick, and I'll bet that God is a damned sight sicker of the whole lot of us!'

Erhard sighed and opened his book at the chapter he required. 'He has His ways,' he said calmly, and ignored the others from then on.

Schiller sighed contentedly and puffed at the cigar stub, while Schwartz re-dealt the cards. 'God is waiting to see who wins before He passes judgement!'

Schwartz cursed obscenely as a sudden lurch of the high bows made some enamel mugs clatter noisily along the deck. 'Keep still, you cow! How can I concentrate?' As he examined his cards, his heavy-lidded eyes sharpened with satisfaction. Aloud he added: 'Not that I am complaining as yet. We've had a nice smooth trip so far. Two ships sunk, and only two of our boys killed!'

Gottlieb put two matches tentatively in the little pile opposite Schiller and looked up quickly. 'You aren't including poor Braun as a casualty of war?'

'Certainly! It always follows like that. The officers get so keyed up with their own wind and importance that they have to kill off a few of the boys now and then just to let off steam!' He eyed Gottlieb with a cruel grin. 'If I were captain, I'd delight in polishing *you* off, you fat slob! You are a disgrace to the Fatherland!'

Schiller nodded gravely. 'That's what I think, too. All the poor people at home tempting their guts with nettle soup and watered beer, and this pig looks as if he had just attended an admiral's banquet!'

Gottlieb laughed nervously. 'I've always been fat. I don't seem to be able to help it!'

'Well, don't be so damned proud of it!' Hellwege nudged his companion. 'Otherwise you'll be the next one for the firing squad!' He pointed with a spatulate finger. 'Bang! Another pig for the pot!'

Schwartz yawned and shifted in his seat. 'All the same, we're lucky to be here as I see it. Some of the boys from the barracks in Wilhelmshaven were taken away and conscripted into the stinking infantry! What do you think of that?'

Gottlieb blinked. 'Really? What good would a seaman be in the firing line?'

Schwartz threw down his cards with relish. 'There! Me for the bank!' He gloated over the matches. 'Nobody's any good in the firing line, mate. You just fill up a space, and when some snotty little officer blows his whistle you just gallop over the top! They say that Flanders is chock full of corpses. Layer upon layer of them. And for what? A few yards of mud that nobody wants anyway!'

Schiller clicked his tongue with mock sadness. 'Nobody wants? What about the General Staff, heh? They must fight their little battles while the Navy is winning the war for them!'

'Do you think we will win?' Hellwege lowered his voice so that the men in the other mess could not hear. 'I mean that it's so difficult for us to know what's really happening.'

Schwartz smiled with his thin mouth. 'Perhaps we have won already and don't know!'

'Of course we shall win!' Gottlieb's pink face glowed with indignation. 'We have seen what we can do. The British are worn out by war, they have no stomach for it!'

'You at least are one up on them there!' Schiller grinned at the other man's hurt expression. 'Just because things have been easy so far, it doesn't follow that it'll always be so!'

Gottlieb half rose from the bench. 'You are defeatist! You forget you are a German. Your tongue will get you into trouble!'

'And who's going to tell what I say in my own mess?' His voice was deceptively calm. 'You? Because if so'—he paused and tapped his knife significantly—'you won't be around to collect your Iron Cross. A wooden one will be more suitable!'

Their laughter floated out of the screened door and on to the wind-swept deck outside.

Hahn twisted his head to listen as he leaned against the smooth barrel of a five-point-nine, his mouth sullen.

Fools. Laugh away and play at being brave sailors. You are gay enough now, but let us see how you behave in a little more time. He began to hum a sad little tune, and stood for a long while staring out at the creaming, restless waters.

·　　·　　·　　·　　·

Reeder, the Captain's servant, moved quietly and efficiently around the sea cabin, his long hands moving deftly as he endeavoured to maintain the appearance of both order and comfort in the small space behind the bridge. Occasionally his deep-set eyes settled on von Steiger, who sat behind the table, his face thoughtful as he studied the chart before him, his fingers tapping against the half-filled coffee-cup.

Reeder halted by the door, his smooth face worried and apprehensive. His fair hair was shaved so close to the skull that his appearance was deceptively aged, and even his shoulders had a premature stoop, as if he was endeavouring to ignore the Navy and its ways and concentrate on being the perfect family retainer. 'Will that be all, Captain?' He glanced meaningly at the bulkhead clock. 'May I suggest that the Captain tries to get a little rest now. It is well past midnight.'

Von Steiger looked up and stared at him. 'You are like an old maid, Reeder! Go to bed if you will, but I have work to do!' He was used to his pernickety ways, and secretly enjoyed the way the man was able to ignore his captain's rank and authority. 'We've been together a long time now. Five years, isn't it?'

'Five years and two months, sir. Very happy times we have had, too, if I may say so, sir. Until our recent unhappy loss, I think I might say that no one could have been happier than either you or, in my small way, myself, sir.' He shook his head sadly. 'Perhaps it is as well for you to have this task before you to drive away your memories.'

Von Steiger cleared his throat. 'Thank you, Reeder. Go to bed.

Bring me coffee at first light in the wheelhouse. We may sight something soon after that.'

The door closed silently, and only then did von Steiger begin to relax. His slight body seemed to ache in many places at once, and, as he poured another cup of coffee, he wondered if he was the only one aboard to be feeling the strain. Absently he leafed through the pages of his personal logbook, and wondered. They had been at sea for two weeks already, and yet about half of that time had been spent either in creeping up the Norwegian coast from Kiel or making that nightmare passage round Iceland.

He pulled out a cheroot and lit it with methodical care. Dehler thinks that I should not have made such a detour. He is a strange man. Full of violent impulses and as tense as a wild animal. One of these days he is going to lose control of himself if he is not careful.

He smiled wryly. If *I* am not careful, that means. There is such an unusual feeling throughout this ship, almost a type of gaiety, at present. I should be moved by their blind faith in my ability, but instead it frightens me. At any single second we might be surprised by an enemy warship, and what then? How will they react, I wonder? Right at this moment a light cruiser, or a patrolling destroyer, may be shadowing us; maybe the shells which will kill all of us are already lying in their breeches. He frowned. Ridiculous. I am tired and strained beyond my resources. For three weeks I have moved like a prisoner in this small world of my own choosing. The wheelhouse—where they watch my every move and speculate my every mood. Or in here— where the cabin walls already seem closer, and where loneliness and want make sleep an escape which is denied me. Yet all the time my officers wait and watch, and enjoy the comfort of their own alleged invulnerability. And the crew? They are better now than when we sailed. They have brushed with death and have emerged victorious. A man has been shot because of his ignorance, and the fact that an officer's word must be upheld above all else. Yet still they sing and argue, curse and hate, as sailors will the world over. Their protection is the basest of all: 'It cannot happen to me, only to others!'

I wonder how little Rudolf is getting on? Since we sailed I have tried so hard to rediscover my faith and hope in his memory. They say that a man can live on his own image after the loss of his wife. I want to believe it, but already it is difficult to picture him as being any different from any other small boy. Perhaps if I had had more time with him it might have been otherwise. Instead, when we did meet, during brief leaves, Rudolf was more interested in my exploits as a captain than as a father. He could see only the image created by separation, and the legend built up by others. I wonder if he will look up at the paintings in the gallery with pride and wonder, as I did? Or will he marvel at his forefathers' passion for duty and death?

The voice-pipe squeaked at his side and he lifted the cover almost before the sound had died.

'Captain speaking!'

'Masthead lookout reports a red glow on the horizon to the south-west, sir!' Heuss's voice sounded formal and guarded. 'He also reports that he has heard what he thinks was an explosion. A long way off, sir. About ten miles, perhaps more.'

He nodded to himself. 'Most likely a convoy, Lieutenant. Being attacked by our U-boats.'

There was a silence as the two officers listened without comment to the moan of the wind. Von Steiger frowned. How curious this was. Had he made such a remark to any of the others there would have been jubilation or excitement. But Heuss had merely accepted his captain's word without comment, as if he knew and understood von Steiger's detachment.

'Any orders, Captain?' The voice was weary.

'Yes. Bring her round two points to the south-east. Keep the alteration of course until that red glow has dropped away. We do not want to get mixed up with a convoy.' He paused. 'What is our position at present, Heuss? In relation to the Irish coast?'

'Six hundred and fifty miles west of Fastnet, sir.' The answer came without hesitation, and von Steiger smiled. 'Wind's freshened a bit, but the visibility is still hampered by the rain.'

'Very good. Call me at once if you need me.'

He forced himself to sit on his bunk, the tiredness within him making his eyes raw. It will do no good for me to go out there. There is nothing to add to that report, and I must not cause more excitement than necessary.

He stared across at the folded chart. It was strange how they had cut across the steamer routes without seeing anything but the *Cardiff Maid*. Once, during the afternoon, they had sighted a long pall of smoke hanging motionless along the western horizon. Another convoy. They had altered course away, as they were doing even now. A year earlier those same ships would have probably been sailing singly, or unescorted. It was all changed now. An empty sea. A desert in which a commerce raider could thirst in vain. It would be different in the South Atlantic, he knew. The ships would be unsuspecting at first, although they would be more scattered and harder to find perhaps.

He watched a cockroach scuttle down the varnished door and disappear into a crack. Two weeks at sea. One boarding steamer of little value, one hospital ship, and the *Cardiff Maid*. All those men, and all that waste. Would the world ever be able to recover from all this? The flower of its manhood dying and fading with each day that passed.

Had he been right to dispose of all the mines at once? he wondered. It was often argued that one large field across shipping lanes was better than small scattered ones. He shrugged with tired irritation and levered himself to his feet. He switched off the light and opened the deadlight which covered the scuttle. He leaned his forehead against the cool glass and felt the vibration of the distant engine pulsing through his head like life-blood. Every turn of the screw takes us farther south. Every turn of the screw means more coal. All the time, day or night, the stokers are flinging the precious stuff into their fires without thought or understanding. I must try to capture a good collier as soon as we strike south, and keep her in reserve. Whom shall I put in command of her? Heuss or Kohler? Or perhaps it would curb Dehler's ambitions to be given a ship for a while, and so learn his own limitations.

Some of the men are growing beards already. To save their ration of fresh water, or to copy me? They are a willing lot at the moment. So damned trusting.

He crossed to the voice-pipe as it squeaked once more.

'Lookout reports that the glow in the sky is fading, sir. Dropping astern now.'

'Very well. Bring her back on course, but tell the lookouts to watch for any signs of patrolling destroyers. They might be sweeping for stragglers. We do not want to be one of them!'

He returned to the bunk and gingerly lowered his shoulders on to the newly made-up sheets. He stared up at the damp deckhead and tried to rest his mind. There was so much to arrange and watch out for. Yet all the time he seemed to falter, as if to look over his shoulder.

Freda. I feel that you are so close to me, yet because you are unattainable, the pain is less bearable than ever. How much longer can I stand it?

Reeder moved silently into the cabin and stood blinking in the lamplight. With a petulant frown he covered the Captain with a loose blanket, and toyed with the idea of pulling off his seaboots. Von Steiger's eyes were still open as he switched off the light and moved silently into the passageway, but he knew that he had not even seen him.

He shuffled along the swaying corridor, his white jacket disembodied and unreal in the watchful darkness.

He ignored the collapsed bodies of the duty fire party and the Maxim gunners, who squatted like statues on their ammunition boxes. These men were nothing. Clay to be moulded by the Captain just as he pleased, and as such needed no consideration. He shut himself in his tiny pantry and climbed up into his solitary hammock. All the same, he decided, the Captain would have to watch himself. In the darkness his fingers groped for the bottle of plum brandy, and he sighed with contentment. This was the life. They can all have their duties and their ambitions for my part. I shall outlive them all.

· · · · · ·

The petty officers' quarters were built into the rear of the *Vulkan's* bridge superstructure, abaft and slightly below the small boatdeck. Originally they had been used as passenger cabins for company employees, and now made a snug and isolated haven, secure from the crowded life of the rest of the ship.

The main messroom was in darkness but for a tall oil-lamp, which swung easily in its gimbals over the green-baize-covered table, and which cast a circle of friendly yellow light over the two men who sat unmoving by a chessboard. Otto Lehr, the Coxswain, puffed thoughtfully at a large meerschaum and watched the concentration of his opponent's face. Petty Officer Weiss, the torpedo gunner, lifted his hand towards his bishop and sensed the big Coxswain stiffen. He immediately withdrew his hand and shook his head.

'No, Otto, not yet!'

A cloud of blue smoke floated free from the silver rim of the pipe, and Lehr chuckled. 'There is plenty of time, friend. Months if necessary.'

They kept their voices low, for the mahogany bunks which lined two of the bulkheads were occupied by silent, blanketed figures. It was almost midnight, and sheltered from wind and weather the small messroom was a peaceful place to be in.

There was a faded portrait of the Emperor hanging over the stove, and along one side of the messroom stood a gleaming rack of pistols and bayonets. By the rack sat two more figures, Petty Officers Brandt and Heiser.

Heiser was in charge of the signals section, and watched with mystified eyes as Brandt strapped a Luger to his hip and patted his uniform into position.

'Where are you going now? Why don't you just take the weight off your feet?'

Brandt bared his teeth in a grin. He was a hard, muscular man, who gave the impression of permanent watchfulness and energy. As if every ounce of surplus fat and useless weight had been stamped and sweated away on the barrack square.

'I have to muster my watch. I cannot trust my subordinate to do it correctly. Eucken is too soft with them. He is a fool, and wants to be popular with the men!' He glanced at himself in the mirror and put on his cap at the correct angle.

'I suppose you think that you alone are carrying the ship, heh?'

'Just remember this, Heiser.' He thrust his sallow face close to the other man's. 'We are the backbone of this ship, as in any other. Without us and our like the Navy is nothing! It is the same in the Army, too. Who keeps the men at their posts when the officers are scared of their own shadows? Answer me that! I will tell you. The N.C.O.s!'

'You worry too much. What do you hope to get, an Iron Cross?'

'All I want is the satisfaction of having done my duty!'

An unshaven red face rose above the edge of a nearby bunk, and Elmke, a man noted for his ability to sleep under most conditions, glared balefully down at them. 'Either shut up, Brandt, or get out! I was just dreaming of my little girl in Bremen, when I recognized your damned nonsense!'

Brandt sneered. 'I am going. When you are torturing your mind

with such childish dreams I shall be watching over you, so sleep well!'
He turned back to Heiser, his thin face triumphant. 'See what I mean?
Weak as gnats' water!' He clicked his heels at the Coxswain, the senior
member of the mess. 'Permission to leave the mess, Coxswain? I have
to muster my watch!'

Lehr took the huge pipe from his lips and nodded sadly. 'Carry on!'

Heiser pulled the black curtain across the door after the other man
and walked tiredly across to the table. 'What is the matter with
Brandt? He makes me nervous with all his spit and polish! You would
think we were all in the Admiral's flagship instead of this!'

Weiss moved his bishop and sat back hopefully. Lehr tamped the
embers of his tobacco and looked at the chessmen. 'Brandt is doing
his duty as he sees it.'

Weiss granted. 'I don't like the man, or any of his kind!' He was a
husky little man with a face that was all nose. A great curved beak,
which made his close-set eyes seem small and merely incidental.

Lehr didn't look up from the board, but he wagged his pipe-stem in
rebuke. 'You know you must not speak like that in front of me. It is
incorrect!'

'Sorry, Otto.' Weiss winked at Heiser over the Coxswain's massive
head. 'But I could be happy here but for him.'

Lehr sighed. 'I have been in the Imperial Navy for twenty years. I
have seen all kinds of men. Nothing can surprise me any more.'

.   .   .   .   .

Georg Niklas, the Chief Engineer, stood on his grating and rested
his gloved hands on the rail of the catwalk which ran across his
gleaming kingdom like a bridge. Here, in a world of thundering
machinery and harsh lights, the bowels of the ship had been cut away
to leave room for this maze of valves and gauges, of hissing steam and
great oiled pistons. Niklas was always impressed, and never got tired
of just standing on his perch above it all. Shadowy overalled figures
moved like spiders amongst the tangle of steel and brass, checking,
greasing and listening. The heart of the ship was never still, and could
never be left unwatched.

Anton Schuman, his subordinate, walked slowly along the vibrating
catwalk, his legs straddled against the uneasy roll of the ship around

him. He wiped his filthy hands carefully on his piece of waste, and greeted Niklas with a cheerful grin.

'Those damned stokers are getting quite good!'

He was shouting above the din, but Niklas was automatically watching his lips. Years in one engine-room after another had made speech almost unnecessary. 'Good. I am pleased they are settling down. The stokehold in this ship is not what they have been used to. We don't want any accidents if we can help it.'

Schuman glanced about him. 'How are things up top?'

'Not bad,' he answered vaguely. 'Still raining a good bit, and pretty cold. Typical Atlantic weather, but it could get rougher.'

He stared moodily at Schuman's youthful face. Just as I was once, he thought. Keen and full of hope. It is a weird life for a man to choose. It is not always enough to know that the whole ship is depending on you. His ear checked the even beat of the distant screw.

Typical of the High Command to choose a ship like this. Two propellers would have been better. Suppose anything happened to this single shaft? I wonder if Schuman realizes what we might be up against? He ticked off the little line of figures on the log-sheet. Coal consumption was favourable, although it was difficult to foresee the possible date of the next bunkering. Von Steiger no doubt had several alternatives in mind. He will tell me when he is ready.

He patted Schuman's arm and climbed heavily up the long, steep ladder. As he climbed, with the thick hot air swirling around him, he wondered if there would be time to get clear if they were torpedoed, or if a heavy shell plummeted into the boiler-room. A quick death? Who knew for sure? The hatch opened, and he sucked in his cheeks as the knife-edge of the wind slashed at his unprepared body. He paused momentarily by the lee rail and peered out at the angry whitecaps. I know why I chose the engine-room. It is because I hate the sea. I am afraid of it, and yet, like a woman, I am unable to leave it.

Part Two

'. . . . *war demands that sooner or later we must dirty our hands a little.*'

6

THE six-thousand-ton British freighter S.S. *Iolanthe*, outward bound from New York to Liverpool, gave another long-drawn-out shudder and seemed to settle even lower in the oily Atlantic swell. The fog which hid everything but a few feet of water around the hull was clammy and bitterly cold, and the ship's uneven outline was running with moisture and a frail covering of ice-rime.

With her engine stopped she lay beam-on to the sea, her decks set in a threatening list and her drooping stem barely two feet above the hungry water. Enclosed by the fog wall, the silence was all the more apparent, and when the seamen who were labouring below jamming great baulks of timber against the bulging forward bulkhead made some unexpected sound, those few who waited wretchedly by the lifeboats started, and stared at one another with fresh alarm.

The ship had been one of thirty in an England-bound convoy. For a week they had wallowed patiently across the Atlantic in some of the worst weather experienced for many years. The harassed captains had tried desperately to maintain their set course and speed, whilst all the time mountainous seas and screeching winds had battered down upon their overloaded ships and made station-keeping a nightmare. Dimly on either wing of the straggling convoy the hard-pressed destroyers had run this way and that, threatening, pleading and trying themselves to stay afloat. During one brief lull, when the labouring ships had been sorting themselves out, the shadowing U-boats had struck. Two ships had been blown apart before anyone realized what was happening.

Iolanthe had been in the middle of the port line of ships, and had received a torpedo in her bows, even as the Commodore signalled the convoy to scatter. Her captain had watched helplessly as the other

93

vessels surged past him, and one of the escorts had circled protectively nearby, her signal-lamp flashing through the rain.

'Abandon ship! I will pick up your crew and passengers!'

The captain read the signal slowly and bit his lip. Abandon ship? What was the fool saying? With a bit of luck the bulkhead would hold, and if they could get it shored up they would still make port. He thought of the thousands of frozen-meat carcasses in his holds and the urgent need for them at home. He thought, too, of his ship. Old, but well built. There must surely be some answer to the problem.

His mate, a young Scotsman, ran on to the bridge. 'We're shoring up, Captain! What shall I do next?'

'Signal yon destroyer that I'm staying put! The damage is not really so bad that I can't make a fight of it!'

He watched the light begin to blink. He was committed now. A ship, his crew and four passengers.

The destroyer circled warily round them, like a fox sniffing out possible danger. 'I regret that I cannot stay with you. Must reorganize convoy. Will return tomorrow and escort you in. Good luck!'

The old captain grunted and watched the mounting froth at the warship's stern. In less than five minutes she had vanished into the rain-squall after the other ships, and there was nothing but the swish of rain across his dead vessel.

He turned to the mate. 'Man the gun, Mister. We might have company soon. Have all the boats swung out and lowered to deck level. Tell the Second to check stores and fresh water, and see that the passengers don't wander off and get lost!' As the other man hurried from the bridge he added: 'I always said these convoys were no damn' good! Each man for himself, I say!'

Now, three hours later, the ship lay heavy and wallowing in the swell. It seemed to the four passengers who stood shivering by the second lifeboat that they had been there for ever.

The second mate, his oilskin glistening in the poor light, scrambled down from the boat and stood uncertainly, banging his red hands together. This was a fine business indeed. He looked at the four bunched figures in their cumbersome lifejackets and wondered what they were thinking.

Caryl Brett glanced across at her husband and shivered. She had been in her bunk when the torpedo had struck the ship, and for several seconds had lain quite motionless, as if paralysed. Now she pulled her fur coat tighter around her body and felt the bite of the air against her bare legs, which were protected only by the thickness of her nightdress. Her thick auburn hair hung damp and cold against her pale face, and she wondered what Arthur was thinking. It was so like him to be fully dressed and apparently in control of himself. He was wearing a thick camel-hair coat over his suit, and she saw that he was carrying his pigskin briefcase in one gloved hand. His handsome face, so often petulant or patronizing, as the mood took him, was filled with nervous irritation. She watched him numbly, and felt her teeth begin to chatter. Was it possible that at any moment they would be required to get into that scarred little lifeboat and be lowered down into the sea? She took a pace towards the rail and stopped as the damp air greedily explored her thighs. What were they waiting for? Why didn't somebody say something?

Arthur Brett turned to the young officer. 'Well? What the hell do we do now?'

'Wait and see if we can repair the damage, sir.' The mate stared past him at the lovely girl in the wet fur coat. If I had a wife like her I'd be thinking of *her* safety instead of a damned briefcase, he thought angrily. 'It might not be as bad as it looks. After all, the convoy lost two ships this morning, and I expect more'll go before they round up the stragglers! We might be safer on our own!'

There was a dull clang from aft. 'That's the gun, sir. They're keeping a lookout for U-boats.' He sounded doubtful.

Brett pushed a lock of fair hair from his forehead and groaned. 'God, Caryl! They've all gone off and left us to fend for ourselves! So much for the chivalry of the sea!'

Simon Gelb, a heavily built business man from the East End of London, clicked his tongue and sank his hands deeper into his pockets. 'Why did I have to take this ship, eh? Never get home at this rate!'

No one answered him.

Caryl Brett wondered if her husband had been drinking. He looked flushed in spite of the agonizing cold, and his eyes seemed a bit wild. It was ironic, really. He, of all people. The man who preached his love for his fellow humans, and had refused to fight for his country, was now marooned on a motionless hulk. Struck down by an invisible fellow human! She wondered when she had first started to despise him. Probably when he had taken the appointment in New York to lecture on Anglo-American Educational Co-operation. It seemed a curious way to fight a war, she had thought at the time. By refusing to put on a uniform he had been immediately accepted for a higher and better-paid post than he would have ever attained under normal circumstances. She stared at the young second mate and the shadowy shapes of the seamen who were waiting by the lifeboat falls. What did they get out of being brave and patriotic?

Mather, the fourth passenger, touched her arm lightly. 'Why don't you go to your cabin, Mrs. Brett? I am sure there is time for you to dress.'

He was a tiny, pale man who rarely spoke, but who had earned both her shame and admiration on his first appearance when he had said with emotion: 'I'm going back to join up. I can't stand working in my firm's American office when all the lads from my home town are dying in France.' It was not only his obvious sincerity that moved her. He was nearly fifty, and would be little use as a fighting soldier. Yet he was making his gesture.

'Perhaps I will. I am hardly dressed for this sort of thing.'

The second mate frowned. 'I'm afraid not, Mrs. Brett. But I'll go to your cabin and see what I can get for you.'

'Surely you don't expect me to change into my clothes up here in the open?' She smiled at his embarrassment. 'Thank you, that would be very good of you!'

Her husband stepped closer to her. 'Must you behave like a slut, Caryl? Sometimes I wonder if that's all you think about!'

She felt the sting of tears in her eyes. 'If you took a little interest in me sometimes . . .' she began.

But he shrugged impatiently. 'Oh, not again! Three years we've been married and that's all I've heard! For God's sake stop harping about it!'

She ran her fingers through her hair and twisted away from him. Her friends had warned her about him, and yet when she had been his secretary she had seen nothing but his firmness and strange aloof devotion to his work. He was so wrapped up in himself that he could barely find the time to speak to her. Yet, in spite of all that, he seemed to need her near him. Another possession, she thought bitterly.

'What do you think of the war now, Arthur? Is this how you imagined it?'

'Rather more stupid than I believed, that's all. I only hope to God some ship will pick us up soon. I have that important conference in London, and there's that series of lectures in Cambridge. I should have gone by a faster ship.'

She sighed. What was the use? If only he showed a small interest in her. Anything but this ridiculous pretence.

There was a rumble beneath them and the seaman nearest them looked up. 'Blimey! The old engine's goin' agin!'

Very slowly the ship began to move ahead once more, and on her bridge the captain let out his breath equally slowly. In the forehold the seamen toiled amongst the scattered cargo, to hammer wedges beneath the massive beams, and eyed the dripping bulkhead with mixed apprehension and pride.

It was at that moment that the fog began to move away. Slowly, lazily, it rolled clear of the ship, and allowed a frail, watery sun to cast its light across the pewter water. The captain stared with disbelief at the submarine which lay like a basking shark in the sun's path. Long, grey and completely evil, it looked as if it was waiting just for him and his ship.

'Hard a-port! Full ahead!' He swung his glasses up to his eyes and watched the submarine's deck. Already some tiny figures were running along the casing towards the long gun.

'But the bulkhead, Captain! It'll not hold against full speed!' The mate looked stricken.

'We must turn, Mister! We have to get our gun to bear. It's our only chance!'

He watched with narrowed eyes as his ship began to swing round. 'No sign of the convoy, but look yonder across the port beam! A bit of smoke, man! Send off a signal. S O S. Being attacked by U-boat on surface. Give position. Send it plain language! Jump to it, man!'

His voice was drowned by the crack of the U-boat's gun. The shell screamed overhead and hissed into the sea. In reply the freighter's gun barked back, and a tall waterspout rose significantly beyond her conning tower. 'By God, a good shot!' The captain banged the rail with impatience. 'Come on, girl! Give the bastard hell!'

The suddenness of the *Iolanthe*'s retaliation had taken the submarine by surprise, and the nearness of the first shot had obviously unnerved her captain. He reduced speed and began to drop astern. His shells still screamed overhead, and then one struck the bridge and exploded with a blinding flash. As the white-hot splinters sprayed across the wheel-house and set the varnished woodwork ablaze, the old captain and his mate were cut to ribbons, and the ship was momentarily out of control. To settle the ship's fate, the straining bulkhead collapsed, and the sea surged into the gaping hole.

On the boatdeck they felt the deck begin to cant, and with horrified eyes saw the boats swing free of their davits at a sickening angle.

The second mate staggered clumsily along the slippery planking, a suitcase in his hand. 'Lower away, lads! Abandon ship!'

He seized the girl by the arm and pushed her to the rail. He thrust his suddenly old face against hers. 'Listen. You'll have to jump for it! When you're in the water just keep swimming clear of the ship, or she'll pull you down.' He threw the case into the lifeboat and watched as it was lowered into the sea. Then with an axe he slashed at the falls. 'Come on, lads, over the side with you! Get that boat away from the side!'

The ship lurched and the angle became more acute. There was a crackling roar from the blazing bridge as all the distress rockets were ignited as one and added a final macabre touch to the ship's death-agony.

Caryl Brett folded her hands across the top of her lifejacket and stood terrified by the rail. The world had gone mad around her. Seamen were running wildly for the boats, and above the crash and whine of shell-fire the ship's siren wailed like an uncontrolled banshee.

She looked for Arthur and found that he was no longer in sight. Frantically she stared down at the bobbing heads and upturned boats, and then saw him swimming strongly towards one of the successfully lowered lifeboats. She was suddenly calm. She would wait on the ship and go down with it. There was no other way now. A hand gripped her arm and little Mr. Mather peered up at her. 'Come on, my dear. We will jump together!'

All at once she was up on the rail, the rough metal grating against her calves, and then she was falling. Falling . . . falling . . . and then choking under the tremendous pressure of salt and darkness. That was it. That was how it was meant to be. Arthur swimming to safety.

Leaving her . . . leaving her . . . leaving her. . . . She gave up the struggle and let herself go limp.

She was conscious of the great pain in her spine and the rough pressure of hands on her bruised body. A voice said: 'I think she's breathing. I've got most of the water from her guts!' She was staring down into the bottom of a boat, into a tangled mixture of feet and oars, of water and vomit. She had been saved. She tried to speak, but the hands kept kneading her, pushing her stomach down hard against the wooden thwart. Then Mather's dripping face floated down to her, and a hand began to push the hair from her mouth and eyes.

'Here, drink this!'

Hot, rasping taste on her tongue. Gin, whisky, brandy? She tried to concentrate. No use.

A voice said: 'Christ! She's gone! Poor old *Iolanthe*!'

Another said, 'The Captain bought it, too!'

A cracked voice interrupted: 'Blast 'im! I 'ope 'e rots in 'ell, the bastard! 'E let us in for this! The dirty, rotten bastard!'

'Shut up, you stupid sod! The Skipper was a good bloke! The best!'

Caryl Brett tried to think it out. A man was supporting her body from behind. That must be my vomit in the boat. Poor little Mather looks as if he is going to cry. I wish I could console him. A rough hand against her thigh. I must be naked from the waist down. Why am I not ashamed, as Arthur has made me feel in the past? What is that new sound? A harsh rattle. Distant. Then nearer. Like a lawnmower in the summer. This way and then that. Far, then near. What can it be?

Then she felt the hand on her body turn into frantic claws and something hot ran down upon her legs. She pressed her hands to her ears and tried to stifle the sounds of screams and curses that suddenly filled the boat. She tried to move, but a heavy body fell across her and pinned her to the seat. She should have recognized that sound. With relentless care the U-boat moved amongst the drifting lifeboats, her machine guns spraying them with cold efficiency, while their gunners looked for any sign of life in the scarlet-splashed carcasses which lay amongst the splintered planking.

The wisp of smoke on the horizon grew stronger, and soon a ship grew clear and hard in the watery haze. The U-boat turned reluctantly from its revenge, and dived. The convoy had to be caught and harried once more. The surface shivered under a sudden squall, so that the wreckage and shattered lifeboats bobbed like toys on the broken water.

Caryl Brett eventually pulled herself free from the dead seaman's body and dragged herself up to the bows. With wide, terrified eyes she stared along the boat's length. Men lay in horrible twisted attitudes of the dead and dying. One man lay across the gunwale, his empty eyes staring at the sky. The machine gun had cut him in two, so that his entrails lay across his lap in a grey, pulsating mass. The second mate sat by the tiller, his lifeless hand still pointing at the place where the enemy had dived.

A figure stirred amongst the carnage, and Simon Gelb rose up from the bottom of the boat like a great shaggy dog. Seeing the girl, her blood-spattered fur coat half up around her waist, he began to wade through the carnage, his face heavy with anxiety. 'Are you well? Are you hit? Hold on, my dear!'

A few feet from her he halted and peered down. A tear ran down his fat cheek. 'Poor bloke! He got his war in the end!' Mather lay curled up on a thwart, his tiny body broken by the force of the bullets as he had tried to protect the half-drowned girl.

Gelb reached her and pressed her to his chest in a great bear-hug. 'Don't cry, my child. See, another ship is coming! Soon we will be safe!'

She twisted her head and stared towards the other ship. It seemed huge from the small boat. It was heading straight for her, the sharp stem throwing up the white water with contemptuous ease. If only it would hurry. I cannot hold out much longer. . . . Safety. Away from this horror. She retched uncontrollably. The scarlet against the grey of the sea. The staring eyes and gaping wounds. This was what Arthur had sneered at. This was that other world she had only half understood. With shocked eyes she watched the great black ship slow down, and saw the boat being lowered down its tall side. Safety. Above her now she could see the towering riveted side and the proud Norwegian flag on the plates. And the name. *Stella Polaris*, bold and clear.

She forced herself to look again at the lifeboat and its crew of flayed men. Before she fainted she was conscious of a strange unwillingness to leave them.

Simon Gelb staggered against the hard gunwale of the lifeboat as the girl went limp in his arms. Her head hung back and he saw that her lips were blue with cold. This was terrible, a nightmare indeed. He could feel his heart pounding in his thick chest like a drum, and was reminded of his own state of shock. I am very out of condition too, he thought. Only forty-five, yet my arms are tearing from their sockets with the weight of this poor girl. He forced himself to look straight across the girl's head towards the fast-moving boat, which had been smartly dropped into the water by the newcomer. He watched it thoughtfully. He had spent most of his life travelling either to the Continent or to America for his firm, and, to ease the boredom of enforced inactivity which travel brought him, he had trained his eye to notice and observe all that went on around him, unrelated to the world of business. These sailors, for instance. They were not like what you would expect merchant seamen to be in a rowing boat. They pulled so smartly, and their officer seemed too well dressed for a mere deck officer. It was all so very odd. But then nothing had gone right from the moment they had left New York. Re-routed first to the north and then farther south, marking time while the convoy was checked and reassembled countless times. Then the terrible storm, and his own discomfort in a tiny cabin shared with Mather. He had inwardly sneered at Mather when he had told him of his reason for returning to England. To be blinded by some vague ideas of glory or saving the country seemed ridiculous to Gelb. He had always been brought up on the understanding that nothing was worth a thought unless it provided the substance for making money. Now he lay there just behind him. Ridiculous in death, as in life. His little legs drawn up to his chin, and his false teeth giving him an idiotic grin as they gleamed above the splintered remains of his mouth. Poor little man. What a way to die. Gelb wondered if he and the girl were the only survivors. What of her high-minded husband? Had he been killed too? The girl was very interesting, as well as being beautiful. It was quite unreasonable to expect her to stick with a pompous prude like Arthur Brett. He groaned as the sharp gunwale dug into his ample buttocks. What a life.

He realized that she had opened her eyes and was staring up at him without recognition. He rested her carefully against the side of the boat, but retained his hold on her. He would not allow her to suffer the horror of the boat's inhuman contents again. 'Keep still, my child. There is a boat almost here.'

There was a sharp, guttural order, and the oars stopped rising and falling. The smart white hull swung alongside, and a boathook struck down upon the waterlogged lifeboat.

Gelb swallowed hard, the words dying in his throat. It was too hard to understand. The uniforms, he knew them now. The seamen in their blue caps with the long trailing ribbons. And the name in gold on their cap-bands, S.M.S. *Vulkan*. What ship was she?

The young officer, his face grey beneath the smart peak of his cap, shouted across at him, 'Can you climb over to this boat?'

Gelb eyed him uneasily. 'Please, I have a girl here. She is near to collapse. Give me some assistance!'

Gelb was careful to speak in English, although he spoke better German than some of the seamen who were now within feet of him. They were a wild-looking bunch, who stared past him at the torn bodies, like hounds scenting blood for the first time.

The officer was rapping out orders. 'Gottlieb, get that girl aboard. Be careful with her! Schoningen, there's a man moving in the stern, see to him at once. His legs have gone, I think!'

Gelb saw the seaman detailed pull a short Mauser rifle from the boat and climb across to the bloody corpse in the stern. He blanched, and then pressed the muzzle against the man's skull. There was a muffled crack and the man moved slowly along the boat, his boots already smeared with blood. He came to the suitcase, and, without changing his set expression, threw it to Gelb. He indicated with his rifle. 'Boat! Get in! Understand?'

Gelb nodded and scrambled after the girl, who was being passed with something like awe from hand to hand until she lay beside the young officer.

Gelb spoke shakily, aware for the first time of the nausea within him. 'Why did you shoot that man? Who are you?'

'Orders. We have no doctor aboard. We could only prolong his agony.' He seemed to jump as a thin drawn-out cry, followed by more shots, sounded across the water. 'I am an officer of the Imperial German Navy. You are to go aboard the *Vulkan*, where you will be looked after.'

Gelb sat down shakily beside the girl. Five pairs of eyes regarded him as the oarsmen bent back to their pulling. The seaman called

Schoningen sat in the bows, his rifle at the ready. Twice more he fired into the water, and once Gelb saw a bloodied hand rise from the sea like a final denunciation of the human race.

A German ship. That was something he could not understand. She was probably a blockade-runner, and yet these were naval men. A raider, then? Yet he had heard that such things had been finished with a year earlier.

Caryl Brett pressed against him, her lifeless lips moving with difficulty. 'What are these men? They do not smile. Are they not pleased to find us?'

Her voice was very low, and Gelb said quietly: 'They are Germans. I am afraid we are prisoners of war!' He kept his voice level, yet the effect of the words was electrifying.

She jerked herself to her feet, her eyes blazing with green fire. 'Germans? Did you say Germans?' Her voice rose to a scream. 'Let me look at one of them!' She swayed towards the Sub-Lieutenant, who stared at her with alarm. 'Let me see what a hero looks like!'

'Please, fräulein! It was not our ship which did this thing!' He held up his hand to steady her, but she jumped clear.

'Don't touch me! You loathsome creature! How can you bear to be a German? Answer me!'

The officer looked awkwardly at Gelb. 'I make you responsible for her until we are aboard! Keep her under control, if you please!'

Caryl Brett slumped down again on the seat and began to sob uncontrollably, and the officer stripped off his greatcoat. He held it out to Gelb. 'Please put it on her.'

Gelb nodded, and slipped it over her shaking shoulders. His eyes gleamed. Perhaps there was hope after all. The important thing was to say little, and keep your head.

A harsh, metallic voice floated down from the sky. 'Get that boat alongside! Hurry, man!'

The officer stared up at the tiny megaphone on the high bridge. 'Very good, Captain!'

His voice sounded cracked with strain and emotion, and Gelb looked up at him with interest. Young and inexperienced. He asked carefully, 'Is your ship a raider?'

The officer regarded him warily. 'Yes. Now be silent. I have work to do!'

They approached the black hull and the swaying boat-falls. The seamen hooked on to the blocks, and within seconds they were moving jerkily aloft until the boat drew level with the ship's deck.

The deck space seemed jammed with uniformed figures, and many hands reached out to pull him across the yawning gap. Another boat was being hoisted on the other side, and Gelb saw Arthur Brett and three seamen from the *Iolanthe* being assisted aboard.

Another German officer jumped lightly from that boat and ran across towards Gelb. He was a slim, wild-eyed lieutenant, with the same sort of good looks as Arthur Brett. In German he said to the Sub-Lieutenant: 'Well, well, a woman, eh? How many more of the swine did you pick up?'

The ship trembled and began to move clear of the floating wreckage while the men were still securing the boats.

The young officer indicated Gelb. 'Just him. God, did you ever see such slaughter?'

'That is war!' He stared at him with a fanatical gleam in his eyes. 'There will be more of that before we are done!'

Caryl Brett hung on to Gelb's arm, staring at the ring of excited faces. She gasped as a seaman opened the sodden suitcase and pulled some of her clothing on to the deck. He held up a petticoat and grinned. Gelb stepped forward and then collapsed on the deck, his face contorted with pain. The Lieutenant had struck him a full blow in the stomach. 'Stand still! I'll teach you manners, you swine!'

The girl helped him to his feet, her face filled with anger and contempt. 'Why not hit *me*? Your bravery knows no limit, surely?'

There was a sudden hush on the wide deck and the men fell back uncertainly. She turned to watch as a slight figure in a salt-stained bridge-coat stepped between the sailors and moved towards her. His short beard did not hide the pain on his face, and he stood looking at her for several seconds. Then, in careful English, he said: 'I am sorry for what you must have suffered. I have given orders that you are to be well looked after.'

'Are you the Captain?'

He nodded. 'I am. Korvetten Kapitän von Steiger.'

'I shall remember that name, Captain. I shall be careful never to forget what you and your countrymen are capable of!'

For a second she saw the agony mask his remote, gold-flecked eyes, and then a shutter seemed to fall.

'Lieutenant Kohler, take the men to their quarters. Damrosch. Escort this girl to my cabin. I shall not be needing it. See that she has all that she needs.'

'Captain?' Arthur Brett stepped forward. 'She is my wife. Perhaps *I* could be permitted to look after her?'

Von Steiger regarded him coldly. 'You will kindly do as I say. Get below!'

Caryl Brett watched the others being led away and felt a hand on her arm. Damrosch looked past her towards his captain. 'Shall I put a guard with her?'

Von Steiger held the girl's eyes with his own. 'She has great courage. She also has intelligence, I think. She will not be any trouble.' He clicked his heels and turned back towards the bridge.

She allowed herself to be led into the sheltered warmth of the superstructure. The Captain's quarters were spacious, yet gave the impression of being unlived-in.

Damrosch shut the door behind them and indicated the door on the far side. 'Bathroom, fräulein. A hot bath will do you good. Your clothes have been taken to the boiler-room to dry. When you are ready the Captain's own steward will bring you food. You will please press that bell there.' He glanced around the cabin and swayed slightly. 'The steward does not understand English. Is there anything else you require?'

She stared at him in shocked amazement. The ship moved smoothly and steadily beneath her, and there was an air of order and security which had been lacking aboard the *Iolanthe*. This officer looked as if he was going to be sick. He, too, had been shocked by all that he had seen. She did not trust herself to speak, and shook her head. Damrosch nodded, and left the cabin in silence.

She walked dazedly around the cabin floor. There was a wide bunk and several comfortable chairs. A picture of the Kaiser glared down at her, and over the oak sideboard there was a smaller picture of a little boy waving a toy boat.

She swayed towards the bathroom and stood looking at herself in the tall mirror. Her hair was plastered to her face and flecked with salt. Her bare legs were caked with dried blood, and the fur coat was also deeply stained in several places. She switched on a tap and watched the steam rising. It was all a weird dream. She would awake in a minute. Or perhaps she had been drowned?

She slipped off the coat and tore away the last strips of her nightgown. For a long time she stood looking at her naked body in the mirror, shrouded in steam like a pagan goddess. If only Arthur and not Gelb had run to help her, had attacked the man who rifled her suitcase. But no. He had approached the German captain as if nothing had happened. Almost apologetic, even friendly.

She thought of the Captain, and tried to recall where she had heard of him. Von Steiger. Then she quivered. Von Steiger. She remembered now, the man the New York papers had described as the Sea Tiger. So this was the great raider.

With her mouth set in a sharp line to stop herself breaking down again, she lowered herself into the cleansing water. She paid great attention to her bath, knowing it was only that which was keeping her sane.

How simple life had become. Warmth, security and a hot bath. What had she expected? Rape, or sudden death, perhaps? She shied away from the thoughts which surged through her mind.

After carefully drying her bruised body she put on the long bathrobe which hung from the back of the door, and tied her hair back from her ears with a piece of cord.

In the cabin she found the white-coated steward, waiting as promised. He bowed and indicated a chair by the table. 'Eat,' he said shortly.

As he moved again through the door she caught a glimpse of a mounted machine gun, and shuddered. It would have been better to have died with the others, she told herself. That she could have understood. She felt unclean in spite of the hot bath, and empty in spite of the food.

Through the thick scuttle she could see the empty sea far below her and the creaming wake pushed back from the bows.

These Germans are like wild animals, she thought. They kill and apologize. They give freely, and then take what they want. She thought of von Steiger's cold eyes and began to shiver uncontrollably.

. . . . . .

Two decks below his wife, Arthur Brett was escorted with Gelb into a long rectangular compartment, which appeared to have been constructed from a section of cargo hold. It was filled with crudely carpentered bunks, each of which contained a straw-filled mattress and one blanket. Steampipes lined the compartment and filled it with a kind of sweating heat, which in turn mingled with the stench of oil and bilge-water.

As the two men entered, the sole occupant rose from a wooden stool and stared at them curiously.

Lieutenant Heuss, who accompanied Brett and Gelb, gestured towards the old man on the stool. In English he said: 'This is Captain Simpson, of the *Cardiff Maid*. He will be glad of your company no doubt. He will also tell you what is required aboard this ship in connection with security and your own comfort while you are here.'

Gelb looked around the bleak space. 'Does that mean that we might not be aboard very long?'

Heuss seated himself at the table. 'Perhaps. You are extra mouths to feed, and as civilians will be entitled to repatriation under my Captain's conditions, if and when we meet a suitable ship for your transfer.'

Brett felt the officer's eyes on his briefcase, which he had retained throughout the terror-filled moments in the lifeboat, 'These are papers in connection with education. You would not be interested.'

Heuss sighed wearily. 'We both know that I am going to see them, so put them on the table. Then turn out your pockets also.'

Heuss ignored the mingled anger and suspicion in their faces. He was thinking of the drifting lifeboats, and the smell of death which stayed with him. Had his people been changed so much by war? He could not forget the defiance and hatred in that girl's face, either. She had been right. What did it matter which officer had given the order? It had been carried out with fiendish relish. He had found Damrosch vomiting in the heads. He had waited until he had recovered sufficiently to talk and then pulled him quickly to his cabin. His own hand had shaken as he poured a full measure of schnapps. 'Here, Max. Drink this.'

Damrosch nodded dumbly and drank without protest. At length he stammered: 'It was horrible! I was so wrong about everything. I never dreamed such brutality was possible.'

Heuss turned the flask over in his hands. 'I, too, was ashamed to be a

German. But,' he stared at the other man, his eyes dark, 'what if *we* were ordered to fire on helpless survivors?' He watched the horror on Damrosch's pale features. 'I will tell you what I believe, Max. I think that we, too, would obey!'

Damrosch ran his fingers across his face. 'I looked into that lifeboat and saw the girl amongst all that broken flesh and blood! I nearly collapsed in front of the men!' He grasped the edge of the table. 'That was the weird thing, the men took it better than I!'

'Naturally. It was not their responsibility. It will always be ours alone!'

He stared at the neatly filed papers on the table before him. 'What is your work, exactly?'

'Education. I have important work with an Anglo–American commission which is studying all aspects of post-war planning.'

Heuss raised an eyebrow. 'But we have not finished the war yet.'

Brett shrugged. 'It will not be long.'

Gelb sat heavily on a bunk, his stomach rumbling for the food which he knew would follow the interrogation. It was lucky, he thought, that the other officer who had struck him was not here after all. Perhaps he was being held in reserve. He leaned forward. 'Mr. Brett is an authority on war. He does not believe in fighting. His conscience would not permit such foolhardiness!'

Heuss looked at the tall figure with new interest. 'So? That interests me. Yet you hold a good job? I would have thought that your work could have been given to a wounded veteran, perhaps.'

Brett's mouth curled. He was on familiar ground. So often he had crushed Caryl's arguments. 'Is that what happens in your country?'

Heuss leafed quickly through the papers. 'No. In my country we take the view that if it is worth living in, it is worth fighting for. Under similar circumstances in Germany you would be shot!' He smiled thinly. 'It is cheaper all round, you see!'

Gelb licked his thick lips. 'I have no such high notions, Lieutenant. I am a buyer of hides for leather. You might say that I am not a fighting man either. But by my efforts I have provided boots and equipment for half the soldiers in the British Army!'

'At a small recompense to yourself, no doubt?'

Brett snapped his fingers. 'Never mind all this! What will you do with those papers?'

'My Captain will no doubt wish to see them. He is well read. He will be interested to see if it is worth our prolonging the war when the Allies have such spectacular plans for after its completion!' To himself he added: We are all deluding ourselves. We can only think of that slaughter in the boats, yet none dares to betray his code.

'Where are the seamen you rescued?' Brett asked indifferently.

'In their own quarters. We have several prisoners already, but we separate officers from ratings, civilians from roughnecks!' He smiled wearily.

'And my wife?'

'She is well looked after. She has had a terrible experience.'

'Will she be molested?'

Heuss eyed him without expression. 'We are not all animals, Herr Brett!

'You will now be fed. I will question you again if necessary. You will be allowed on deck for certain periods, and you will at all times obey orders without hesitation.'

Brett yawned. 'Otherwise we will be shot, I suppose?'

Heuss signalled for the door to be opened. 'Yes, Herr Brett, I suppose so, too!'

.   .   .   .   .   .

Most of the wardroom air vents had been shut against the cold, and a thick blue cloud of tobacco smoke hung motionless across the white deckhead. The *Vulkan's* officers stood in a semicircle round the glowing stove, half watching the door, and speaking in unusually subdued tones. Outside, the night was quiet, and the thud of the engine could be heard, as well as the faint swish of water alongside the hull. The wind had not returned after the fog had departed, and only a thin drizzle and the bitter cold remained to plague those on watch around the ship.

Heuss rubbed his hands against his sides, his eyes dark and thoughtful. What had the Captain called a conference for? It was unlike him to leave the bridge merely to speak to his officers. He had already done it once today to greet the survivors from the torpedoed freighter. It was strange how affected von Steiger had been by the sight of the U-boat machine-gunning the lifeboats. Heuss had been on watch when the fog had lifted, and the drama had been played out before them.

Von Steiger had almost screamed down the engine-room voice-pipe: 'Full speed, damn you! Give me emergency full speed!' Then he had run to the wing of the bridge, his powerful glasses trained on the distant scene. Once, when Heuss had asked permission to signal the U-boat, the Captain had said bitterly: 'It's too late, Heuss! God damn that captain, I should have fired on *him*!'

Then the girl had been brought aboard. Von Steiger had left the bridge, even as the great screw began to turn once more. It was curious how like von Steiger's dead wife this girl was. Even covered in filth and in rags, he could see a certain similarity. He smiled ruefully. Or was his imagination working on him as well? It had been so long now since he had even seen anyone so defiant, yet so helpless, that his mind was probably playing tricks.

Kohler lit a cigarette exultantly. 'The sea is empty of the Royal Navy! It is better than I had dared to hope!'

Dehler, who had been brought off watch for the conference, scowled. 'What the hell are you talking about?'

'Well, it means that the war is in our favour at sea as well as on land! When our great offensive comes this spring we will finally break them in two!'

Dehler grunted with impatience. 'We shall still find a fight, sooner or later.' He was only half listening to the others. He was thinking about the raider's lack of targets. Apart from the *Cardiff Maid* they had done little so far. It was unlikely that the British had even guessed that a raider was abroad. He frowned. If I were to be captain, what course would I choose? If I carried on like this I might sink a few more ships and harm their supply lines. But if I made sure the enemy knew a raider was abroad, surely the forces they would have to deploy to hunt for it would be a greater handicap to them? They would probably cancel convoy sailings in some cases, too, until the seas had been cleared. Which course would be open to the Captain's own choice? he wondered. Probably the latter, and then dash back through the blockade before the squeeze got too dangerous.

Karl Ebert, the gunnery officer, smoked in silence. Eventually he said: 'I can't get used to having a woman on board. Right on the other side of that bulkhead she's probably combing her hair, or thinking about her husband.'

Wildermuth chuckled. 'I would not mind joining her, anyway!'

'She's too proud for the likes of you!' Ebert grinned with satisfaction. 'She's a little angel! An angel with a bite, I shouldn't wonder!'

Kohler eyed him with disgust. How could they talk like that about an enemy? He sighed and remembered his experience in the boat that morning. With his Luger he had leaned right over the gunwale to shoot one man clean between the eyes. He had not been badly wounded, but enough surely to warrant death by his hand. His men had been fascinated by him, he could tell from their glassy stares that they were amazed at his display of eagerness to kill. He had been unable to control it. He had felt almost a sexual urge compelling him to watch those frightened eyes before he squeezed the trigger. All this was like an anticlimax. In a moment I shall go to my cabin and play some Wagner on the gramophone. Then I will drink some schnapps in private and think about it all again. If only he could relieve his tensions on somebody, drive home his satisfaction and excitement. He thought of Pieck. It would be risky. But if he could win him back, things would be complete for him once more. He had been tried, and had proved himself true and unbeatable. He had killed for the Fatherland, and for himself. He knew now he could do it again. But Pieck might be difficult. He might make a complaint to the Captain about him. He shook his head. Unlikely. Von Steiger had already showed that he did not wish to interfere with his officers' methods. He licked his lips. Pieck was better than all the others. Simple and trusting. Yes, it must be tried. And if anything goes wrong the boy will have to be disposed of. He began to smile, and from the other side of the fire Heuss watched him apprehensively. Kohler looked slightly mad, he thought.

The door was flung open by a sentry and von Steiger entered the wardroom. He indicated that he wished the officers to relax, and then laid his cap on the polished table.

He opened his large coloured chart and laid it where they could all see it. They closed in around the table, their differences momentarily forgotten. The chart was marked with the raider's long rambling course, and pockmarked with tiny pencilled figures and notes.

Von Steiger gave them a few moments. 'Gentlemen, I have to tell you that I am dissatisfied with our efforts so far.' He pointed at the red trade-arteries which criss-crossed the North Atlantic and converged on the British Isles. 'The new convoy system has made our task here almost impossible, and to prolong our stay in this area will reduce us to the role of a scavenger!' He listened to the murmur which ran around the table. 'We are using up coal and food, and achieving little. And time is against us. Every ship which reaches England is crammed to the seams with war material, which within a week of being landed is on its way to the Western Front to await the spring offensive.' He slapped his hand hard on the chart. 'If we go farther south we have a better chance of causing confusion and disruption of those supplies nearer their source! Large enemy concentrations of warships will have to be deployed. It is a vast ocean, gentlemen, and will need a lot of warships! We will, in effect, be trailing our coats to the enemy. It is the only way!' He looked up, his eyes searching.

He glanced at Heuss's set face and waited. Of all the officers around him, Heuss was the only one who had the breadth of imagination required to understand what lay ahead. Yet he was blinded by his own conscience. It was as if he still tried to dissociate himself with everything which had passed, and which lay ahead.

It was Dehler who reacted first. 'But, Captain, what of the wireless message received today? Were you not ordered to remain in this area of operations for the present?' His face was blank, but his eyes seemed to throw a challenge.

Heuss watched them both. He, too, had seen the wireless message. Surely even von Steiger would not just ignore it.

Von Steiger folded the chart. 'The High Command are at Kiel. They are not only misinformed, but misguided!' That was all, but the bitterness in his voice told Heuss a great deal.

Von Steiger must have known that Naval Intelligence had been informed about the hospital ship's course under International Law. They must have known about it when he ordered the *Vulkan* to lay her minefield. It was as if they had wanted to brand von Steiger as a pirate, and so turn every enemy ship to search for him. Heuss's eyes followed von Steiger to the door, and for the first time he felt a rising admiration for the man, and began to understand the extent of his loneliness.

7

'SHIP bearing green two-oh!'

Lieutenant Heuss stared for a full three seconds at the telephone in his hand, as if unable to grasp what the excited masthead lookout had reported. He had known that another encounter was inevitable, and yet in his heart he had cherished a strange kind of hope.

'Call the Captain! Sound off Action Stations!' He still stood with the hand-set in his fist, his eyes staring unwinkingly at the silver-grey horizon, over which in a few minutes the stranger would take shape. Around him the ship awoke from its four days of uneasy waiting. Four days since they had found the lifeboats. For Heuss it had meant even more than that. He had been able to lose himself almost completely in the task of looking after the prisoners, or so he told himself, and he had been careful not to visit the girl any more than the other captives in the hold.

At first he had been saddened by the cold contempt which Caryl Brett had shown him, but the agony of shock and despair which he had seen behind her angry defence had acted as a challenge and given him a sense of purpose.

On the first morning after the sinking of the *Iolanthe* Reeder, the Captain's steward, had come running to his cabin, and in sharp, apprehensive sentences had reported that the girl was having hysterics, or something much worse. Grimly Heuss hurried after him to the Captain's quarters, wondering what von Steiger would do if the girl had gone mad. It was a strong possibility after what she had endured.

He shouldered his way through the group of idlers who waited curiously in the passageway, and pushed open the door. To Reeder he said shortly, 'Get rid of those men, and see that I'm not disturbed.' He regretted his words the moment that the door had closed behind him.

Apart from the throb of the engine there was a complete silence, almost as if the cabin was holding its breath. The large day cabin was empty, and through the gently swinging curtains, which partitioned off the sleeping quarters from the rest of the space, he could see that the disordered bunk was empty. He cleared his throat and took a pace forward. Perhaps that fool Reeder had imagined it all. He had said that the girl had been screaming, and writhing about in the bed like a madwoman.

He adjusted his mind to the careful English sentences. 'Fräulein? Where are you?' He could not address her as the wife of the prisoner, Brett. Her very isolation from him, and the strange way she had been brought from the sea, had already made her quite different in his eyes. There was a slight movement from the bathroom, and then silence. He licked his dry lips, and had a momentary vision of the girl trying to commit suicide behind the locked door. Something like panic and unreasoning alarm swept over him.

'Fräulein! Show yourself at once, please! It is I, Lieutenant Heuss!'

The small door opened, and she stood suddenly framed in the watery sunlight. She was wearing an oversize dressing-gown, which covered her like a shroud, and stood motionless but for one hand, which plucked slowly at the hair that hung down over each shoulder. Her pale face was quite composed, and but for her eyes, which looked rather wild, she seemed completely in control of herself. Heuss caught sight of himself in the mirror beyond her, and grimaced. Unshaven, his hair flattened over his forehead, and his greatcoat buttoned hastily over his pyjamas, he looked more in need of care than she did.

'What do you want, Lieutenant? Why have you come bursting in like this?' Her mouth moved slightly, as if she was having difficulty in breathing, and for a brief instant a spasm of nausea showed on her face.

'I was told that you were unwell, fräulein.' To himself he sounded ridiculously formal, like Kohler, he thought. 'I am glad to see you are recovered.' He tried to smile, but his features felt frozen. 'After all, I am responsible for you. My Captain would be angry if he thought I was not doing my duty!'

'I see.' The large green eyes moved slowly across his face, as if searching for something. 'I have just been sick,' she added simply.

'I am not surprised. You have been under a great strain.'

'You speak as if you are detached from all this, Lieutenant. That surprises me a little. You even sound a little concerned. That also is a surprise!'

Heuss saw the girl's face harden, and realized that the hatred which was again coming to the surface was giving her strength. He stood staring at her, undecided what to do.

'I awoke rather suddenly,' she continued in a flat voice, 'and all at once I was reliving that horror which I saw in the lifeboat. You are a man, a fighting man, so you could not possibly understand. In addition, being a German officer, I expect you would try to kill such sensitive feelings even if they arose. Just as your brave men killed those helpless sailors!'

The tone of her voice had become sharper, and through the folds of the dressing-gown he could see her breasts rising and falling in mounting agitation, as if she was only half in control of her emotions. He wanted to seize her, to pinion her arms and pull her against his body. To hide her lovely face with its steady, accusing eyes. To tell her that he did understand, and that it was she who was being without pity. Instead of these things he merely dropped his eyes and said evenly: 'I have seen such sights, fräulein. And believe me, I too know what fear and despair can do. So I realize well enough what you have suffered. I hope that you will try to have hope and understanding. We cannot alter life. We can endure it, or we go under.'

There was a nervous tap at the door, and Reeder's head appeared round its edge. 'Can I come in, Lieutenant? I have brought coffee.' His eyes moved across to the girl, and he added slowly: 'She is better I see! You are better than a doctor, Lieutenant!'

Heuss moved towards the door, feeling suddenly tired and dirty. For a moment longer he stood between the neat, white-jacketed steward and the tragic-faced girl in the far doorway, aware for the first time in many months that he was without bitterness. It was as if she had given him some purpose in life.

'Incidentally, Lieutenant,' her voice soft, yet cutting into his thoughts like a knife, 'I am *Mrs.* Brett. I shall assume that your familiarity is due to a lack of understanding of my language!'

She stepped back into the bathroom and slammed the door. Reeder shrugged and clicked his tongue sympathetically. He had not understood a word, but from the comical expression of anger and embarrassment on the officer's face he guessed a good deal. He laid the silver coffee-pot on the table and grinned.

'Never mind, Lieutenant! You saved the day, and the Captain's best coffee-pot will do the rest! It will be a good thing when the Captain gets rid of her and puts her aboard some neutral ship. I do not like women at times like these!'

'Oh, shut your blasted mouth!' As he had slammed the door behind him, Heuss had heard Reeder laughing. That, too, was strange, as he had never even seen the man smile before.

Now, as the alarm bells jangled throughout the ship, and the wooden decks vibrated beneath the thunder of running feet, Heuss tried to picture what Caryl Brett was doing. During any emergency she was to be put with the other prisoners under guard, and he wondered what her fatuous husband would have to say to her.

The door behind him clicked open, and he turned to salute as von Steiger came briskly into the wheelhouse. 'Ship on the starboard bow, sir! Closing us on an almost parallel course.'

Von Steiger nodded and glanced at the chart. 'Bring her round half a point. Have the starboard battery cleared away, and tell Lieutenant Ebert to shoot well when required. The afternoon light goes rather rapidly, and I don't want to start searching for a crippled ship in the dark.'

The ship moved easily over the short, wind-ruffled waves, and heeled slightly in response to the rudder. Lehr, the Coxswain, watched the swinging compass, and forced his shoulders to remain relaxed as the bridge lookouts reported that they had seen the ship through their powerful glasses.

Von Steiger waited in silence, his own glasses resting against the polished woodwork of the signal locker. Another ship at last. Probably making her way up from the south to rendezvous with a convoy. She might even be trying to make the journey on her own. For the last four days the *Vulkan* had steamed slowly southwards, and had now reached a point some two hundred miles north-north-east of the Azores. Beneath him the ship staggered slightly as a larger group of waves surged defiantly against the ship's side. He frowned. She was riding too lightly, he thought, and the empty hold forward was making quite an impression. It was amazing to think that it had once been jammed tightly with coal. Now, only a few piles of black dust remained. They had started on the second hold now, and after that the main bunkers would have to be tapped. A lot of coal for little result. In his mind's eye he pictured the pencilled lines of their course so far. Three weeks ago to a day they had sailed from Kiel. Up the Norwegian Coast, across the Arctic Circle and around Iceland, and then down into the Atlantic. Every minute of every one of those twenty-one days the giant screw had pounded at varying speeds but with steady and continuous demand, and the level of coal had rapidly fallen. He sighed and blinked briefly to clear his vision. He watched calmly as the strange ship hovered and then settled in the lenses of his binoculars. Another freighter. Almost certainly British. There was no mistaking that single black funnel, and the air of shabby efficiency which they all seemed to bear. Behind him he heard the signalmen preparing their lamps, and heard Heuss passing instructions through voice-pipes and telephones to the distant men who waited at their stations throughout the ship. Men who waited with hope or fear, and others who stared with patient indifference at their hidden weapons.

There was a sharp metallic clatter from the fo'c'sle, and he imagined the gunners slipping away the last catches which held the steel shutters across their charges. He eyed the other ship, and tried to see her as a mere target and not as a big, helpless fellow creature of the sea. About six thousand tons, and well laden. No armament visible, as far as he could see.

Near enough. 'Make a signal. Ask her name!'

The light began to chatter, and after what seemed an age of waiting a light began to flicker back across the white-capped waves.

'*Rockleaze*. Outward bound from Bridgetown.' Von Steiger nodded slowly. From Barbados. Mixed cargo, quite likely. The light still flashed in short, intermittent bursts. 'Have not seen another ship for days. Do you read me?'

Heuss gestured to the signals petty officer, but von Steiger shook his head. 'This one is talking too much. He might be playing for time. I don't like it.' He pressed the button at his elbow and added, 'Carry on, Heuss.'

The German ensign soared up to the gaff like a newly released bird of prey, and *Vulkan* made her own signal.

'German cruiser here. Stop your engines. Abandon ship.'

To sharpen the commands, one of the forward guns roared out, and a tall waterspout rose remorselessly less than a cable's length from the freighter's bows.

The light blinked again. 'I have stopped.' Already von Steiger could see the lifeboats being swung out.

Von Steiger heard Heuss sigh. Was it because another ship was to be destroyed? he wondered. Or perhaps he was just relieved because the other vessel was not putting up any resistance. Heuss was a strange person. Von Steiger wanted to like him, and yet he found himself constantly criticizing him and looking for faults and flaws in his cynical façade.

He watched the way fall off the other ship, and waited until Heuss had ordered a reduction of speed also. In silence the two ships drifted closer together, and von Steiger saw first one lifeboat and then another shove off from the deeply laden vessel and begin to pull towards the *Vulkan*.

'More guests for you, Heuss! About thirty by the look of it.' He kept his tone friendly, and wondered if Heuss was thinking about those other lifeboats, as he was.

'Yes, sir. They will eat us hollow at this rate.'

'I hope to get rid of them as soon as I can,' von Steiger continued thoughtfully. 'An opportunity may come along quite soon now.'

'All of them, sir?'

'Perhaps.' He had detected a sharpness in the other man's question, and eyed him gravely. 'I usually hold on to captains and chief engineers, but let the others free, or put them on a prize ship. As we have not caught a suitable prize yet'—he shrugged—'I do not have much alternative.'

The first lifeboat grated alongside, and vaguely they heard the First Lieutenant barking commands. Von Steiger sighed again. 'For them the war is over, Heuss. Perhaps we have done them a favour.'

'What about the woman, sir?'

So that was it. He studied Heuss's mask-like features, and for once the other man was unable to meet his eyes.

'The woman? She will have to go, I think. Unless you have any reason for her staying here?' He had seen the girl only once since she had been brought aboard. She had come on deck for one brief moment wrapped in her stained fur coat. Very slowly, and a little unsteadily, she had walked along the side of the boatdeck, her hair shining like deep chestnut in the morning sunlight. From his lofty position on the bridge he had followed her progress, and watched her shadow move below him on the salt-caked planking. Small, defenceless, yet so completely defiant. It was almost as if she had sensed his eyes upon her, for she had stopped and looked up at him. Separated by the length of the boatdeck and the height of the bridge, they had challenged each other, or so it had seemed to him. What a hell the war had made of both their lives, he thought. He had watched the line of her neck and the movement of her hair in the wind, and felt the knife turn in his chest once more. From that distance it might have been Freda standing there. Even as the thought had come to him, she turned deliberately away and disappeared below. Heuss must see a lot of her when he watched over the prisoners. He toyed with the idea of taking him off the duty completely, but instantly dismissed it. He could not be sure whether it was because of the feeling of unreasoning jealousy, or because of the taut anxiety on Heuss's face which made him change his mind. Keeping his voice level he said: 'I am not sure it will be a good thing to keep her in a ship such as this. In addition, I think she hates us too much for what has happened. She might make trouble in some way.'

'If you released her, sir,' Heuss was speaking faster than usual, his hands moving expressively, 'she might make more trouble.'

Von Steiger smiled wryly. 'You think we should keep her just to educate her? I thought that husband of hers was the educational expert!'

'I am quite serious, sir. I think that if we could show her what we are really doing, and how we do it, it might help us considerably.'

A voice-pipe squeaked and Heuss bent his head to listen.

'All lifeboats cleared and scuttled.' It was Dehler's voice. 'But the Captain is still aboard his ship!'

He sounded uneasy, and Heuss repeated the message to von Steiger. 'I don't see what he hopes to gain by staying over there, sir——' He looked up startled as the signals petty officer thrust his face round the door of the radio-room.

'She's sending an S O S, sir! Someone's still aboard!'

Von Steiger pushed past Heuss, his eyes blazing. The damned idiot! The poor, brave fool! He had seen that his crew were safe and had then stayed behind to show his defiance.

'Tell Ebert to open fire on her bridge!' He ignored the shouted orders and spoke sharply into the red voice-pipe at the rear of the bridge, 'Lieutenant Kohler! One torpedo, and be damned quick! Your life may depend on it!'

He snapped down the cover on the tube and walked slowly to the side of the bridge. He forced himself to stay still, a small hard core in a centre of anxious confusion. That shipmaster had played his last card well. He had known that the raider would relax after the departure of his crew in the boats.

There was a muffled thud beneath his feet, and through its protective canvas screen the lithe shape of the torpedo flashed over the rail and landed in the tossing water with hardly a ripple. There was a brief flutter of spray as its small propellers whirred into action,. and then it was streaking away towards the other ship, which stood tall and dark against the dying sun. Even in the frenzied whitecaps the watchers could see the straight hard line of the torpedo's course. A few seconds later it struck home. Through the water they felt a dull metallic clang, like the slamming of a great iron door, and then with a shattering detonation the side of the ship erupted in a great towering column of orange flame. Like a thunderclap the sound-wave rolled back across the water, and von Steiger felt the hot, foul breath of the explosion against his face.

The bow and the stern rose together, pivoting on the ship's broken keel, and as the water surged hungrily into the exploding boilers and tearing metal, another internal convulsion threw the complete bridge and funnel high into the air. He strained his eyes, as if half expecting to see that brave and fanatical captain appear on the dismembered superstructure before it crashed into the sea. A long wall of brown smoke rolled slowly across the space between them, and when the wind had cleared it away only a few pieces of flotsam remained.

'Secure the guns and get under way, Heuss. I shall be altering course shortly, so have the log ready.'

Heuss turned his back to the pall of smoke, and wiped his mouth with the back of his hand. 'By God, that was unexpected, sir!'

Von Steiger could hear the squeak of bogeys as Kohler's men reloaded the torpedo-tube.

'Do you think your lady prisoner would learn by that, Heuss? Or is our cause so weak that we must justify our every move, even to those who would hate us even if we were fighting *for* them?'

Heuss turned away. 'I will pass your orders to the engine-room, sir.' He looked tired and empty. 'Then when I am relieved I shall go and see to the new prisoners. I am sorry you do not agree with me, sir, but I merely thought it might help our cause.'

'Do not try to think too much, Heuss. You might build up something which, when it falls, will destroy you also.' He turned towards the chart-table and was momentarily aware of Heuss's expression of surprise.

He bent over the table and felt the deck begin to quiver once again. The men near him relaxed slightly, and on the wing of the bridge a man laughed noisily. He stared at the chart framed between his two hands and felt his heart thumping. I must be losing my grip. To allow the enemy to use a ruse like that. He kept his eyes on the chart, but his mind was busy with the S O S message. It was not possible to tell how much had been sent off, or if in fact any of it was received by another ship. *Rockleaze* had said in her signal to *Vulkan* that she had not seen any other ship, but that, too, may have been a lie. It would be well to have the prisoners searched and interrogated as soon as possible.

'Heuss, when you go below take Damrosch with you, and question every seaman and officer from that ship. I want you to search them thoroughly, too. Perhaps one of them might have a scrap of newspaper on him which might tell us something. The Barbados papers probably do not care quite so much about security, and we may learn something about ship movements, particularly warship movements.'

'Yes, sir.' Heuss kept his voice non-committal.

Lieutenant Dehler moved noisily into the wheelhouse. 'All secure, Captain. Prisoners below under guard and awaiting orders. A pretty quick kill, I thought, Captain.'

'Quite. What information did you get about cargo?'

Dehler laid his notebook on the table. 'It's all in there. She was carrying cotton, sugar and rum. Pity we couldn't get some of that liquor. It would be something to sweat out after a battle, eh?' He laughed harshly and glared at Heuss's impassive face. 'Are you still moping, then?'

'I was merely thinking.'

'Huh, I've had a bellyful of thinkers! You keep to your duties!'

Von Steiger watched the two men looking at each other with angry eyes, and grunted: 'Carry on below, Heuss. I will keep the remainder of your watch. Have a good look at those prisoners now.'

'The *male* ones!' Dehler called after him, and laughed again.

Von Steiger dropped his voice. 'Leave him alone, Dehler, he's more sensitive than you are!'

Dehler snorted. 'Why should *he* interrogate the prisoners? He's too soft! I could do it much better.'

'For one thing he speaks perfect English, which you do not, and another, he's not easily angered. You are a good seaman, Dehler, but inclined to be hasty in more personal matters. Do I make myself plain?'

Dehler breathed noisily, his cheeks flushing brick-red. 'There are a lot of things which I don't agree with, Captain! It's only fair that as second in command I should be allowed to have my say!'

Von Steiger looked up at him with interest. The man was obviously so jealous of Heuss that it shocked him to remember that *he*, too, had felt that same feeling. 'Don't be a fool, Dehler. I need you to run this ship efficiently. But if you question my orders again it will be the last time!'

. . . .

Simon Gelb sat uncomfortably on a bench, his body swaying to the motion of the ship, his large hairy hands resting flat on the scrubbed mess-table. He dragged his eyes from the sweating steel plates beyond the tiers of bunks, and tried not to think of the sea which surged persistently against them. When the raider's torpedo had exploded a few moments earlier he had imagined in one terrible second of agony that the *Vulkan* herself had been struck the mortal blow. The whole of the hold's dim interior had rocked and reverberated like the inside of an oil-drum, and the lights had flickered and slowly faded until the high, cheerless place was all but in darkness. They picked up again almost at once, and he found that he was staring now at the girl, who had jumped to her feet at the explosion, a silent scream on her parted lips.

The engine revolutions had increased again, and in the confined, stagnant air of the hold Gelb could hear the painful sound of his own breathing. 'Why should we worry? We are still alive, it seems!'

Arthur Brett ran his long fingers through his hair and peered upwards at the massive steel beams which supported the deck overhead.

His lip trembled, and he groped vaguely for a cigarette. 'Damn them! What wouldn't I give for a smoke now!'

'Did they take your cigarettes away from you?' Her voice was even again, but shy, like a child amongst strangers.

He turned towards her, his face bitter. 'I suppose *you've* had every comfort in your new quarters? Must be quite an experience for you!'

Her expression was pleading. 'Please, Arthur! Can't you stop attacking me? I don't think I can stand much more!' She waited, remembering his first greeting when she had been escorted into the hold.

'What the hell do you want now? It would have been more to the point if you could have persuaded the Captain to allow me to leave this filthy place! It shouldn't be too difficult for you!'

He looked changed already by his new circumstances. Unshaven, and his expensive clothes creased and rumpled. This should have been the moment to make amends for everything, to allow him to place the blame for all mistakes on their present predicament and to take her to him without recriminations on either side. It seemed incredible that even this disaster, and what they had seen happen to others, had failed to alter his self-dedication, and indifference to her, either as a person or as a wife. How much longer could she delude herself? she wondered. It had never really been any different. Even when he had proposed to her he had given the impression that it was he who was doing her a favour. She had seen that only in retrospect, and even then had imagined that the failure of their union was her fault. She tore her eyes from his empty face and looked from Gelb to the hunched figure of the old captain, who sat brooding on one of the bunks. He neither looked up when the torpedo exploded nor showed any interest in what the others were saying.

'God, what is the matter with us?' She turned back to Gelb, who peered at her calmly. 'We just sit here and argue!'

'You're doing all the talking, Caryl! What do you expect us to do?' Her husband began to pace back and forth, his salt-stained shoes clicking on the riveted plates.

'Do?' She held out her hands in despair. 'I don't know! It's just that I feel so small and helpless. It sickens me to be borne along in this ship while they do exactly what they like!' She crossed quickly to Brett's side and laid a hand on his arm. He paused in his pacing and stared

123

down at her in surprise. 'Please, Arthur. I need strength, don't you see that? Why must we fight each other now?'

'Why must you dramatize everything? It is bad enough to be here, without you trying to be heroic!'

Gelb shook his head, and watched the girl's hand fall from Brett's arm. Amazing, he thought again. Why was it that these impotent males always procured the most beautiful wives? A strange but surely undeniable fact. I would have thought that it would only make his lack of passion the harder to bear. Me, I am us ugly as sin and always have been. But if I thought it possible I would take her on a bunk here and now, even with him and that senile old captain for onlookers.

He cleared his throat and gestured with his head. 'Come and sit here for a while, my dear.' He watched with satisfaction as she slid on to the bench opposite him. See, he thought, she comes like a puppy. He has turned her away when she needs him, and she will come even to me. He studied her pale face and wide, listless eyes.

'I guess they have sunk another ship,' he said quietly. 'That will mean more prisoners for the gallant German. And that will mean less space here and less food in the storeroom, eh?' He reached out carefully and covered one of her hands with his huge paw. He was shocked to find it ice-cold, but she did not draw it away. 'So perhaps it will not be long before they let us go? That officer, Heuss, thinks we will not be aboard too long, and I have heard some of the seamen speaking of the difficulties of finding good coal for the ship. They say we might touch land somewhere. Who knows? You and I might be able to take some sort of revenge, that is if you are still interested, eh?'

'I hate them! I cannot tell you how I feel about them!' Her eyes lit up with a compelling brightness. 'They seem so terribly sure of themselves, so eager for destruction!' She looked him full in the face. 'You say you overheard the sailors talking? Do you understand German?'

He put a fat finger to his lips. 'Yes. But that is a secret between us. When the time comes, it may be useful. I already have the mere bones of a plan, but I cannot speak of it now.' He gave her hand a slight squeeze and felt the old feeling of power seeping through his bones. He had no plan at all, but the hint of mystery seemed somehow in keeping with their confidences. 'That officer I mentioned, do you see much of him?'

'Yes. He is always calling in to see if I am behaving myself!' She did not see the annoyance in Gelb's eyes, she was thinking about Heuss standing in the middle of the cabin, his greatcoat over his pyjamas. In spite of her cool answers to his questions, she had known even then that his arrival had saved her from a complete breakdown. All the frustrations had welled into her throat so that she felt like choking, and Heuss at that moment had been the personification of torment. Each time he called on her she tried to humiliate him and maintain her dislike, but his grave, even gentle, approach had made her regret her attitude the moment he had departed. She no longer saw him merely as a gaoler, a face behind a uniform, but as a man. And the fact that she trusted him frightened her more than her previous hatred. He would listen to her tirades and then talk about the sea and the places where he had been. He never mentioned the war, and always departed after a short while. A strange, lonely man. He had a keen wit, but his quick intermittent humour always seemed directed at himself, so that her anger seemed to lack purpose and weight.

Each time he visited her she noticed how he always made a point of reporting that her husband was well and was asking after her. She had wanted to believe him, but now she knew he had lied because he had seen the cause of her wretchedness, and she also knew that she would never turn again to Arthur for help.

The door banged open and two armed seamen stepped over the coaming. They gestured for her to accompany them, and one, a mere boy, blushed as she looked at his loaded Mauser. The other seaman, gaunt like a scarecrow, stared at her with eyes like stones. She shivered and pulled her coat closer. The man looked lost and slightly crazy.

She halted by the door, watching her husband. He smiled vaguely and thrust his hands into his pockets. 'I'll ask about cigarettes, Arthur. Perhaps I can get some sent to you.'

'See you next visitors' day, Caryl. You can bring me my briefcase next time. I've still got to polish up my report, you know!' A dismissal—amused, final.

She walked quickly down the long high passageway, conscious of the two seamen who followed her. A large rat scurried from behind a packing case almost at her feet, and involuntarily she jumped backwards into the arms of the scarecrow. Instead of releasing her he held her in a grip of steel, and she saw the look of alarm on the face of the younger seaman.

Alder peered closely into her eyes, his mouth loose and wet. He spoke excitedly, and as she struggled held her all the tighter, and raised his voice to drown her protests. He was trying to explain that he, too, knew what it was like to be in an open boat in the company of dead men. Perhaps she could help him.

Caryl Brett stared at the red-rimmed eyes and saw the spittle running from the man's frantic mouth. Her fur coat slipped from her shoulder, and she saw the other seaman stare with horrified eyes at the bare skin beneath.

Pieck seized Alder's arm, his voice frightened. 'Leave her alone, you fool! She doesn't understand you, she thinks you want to rape her! For God's sake leave her alone!'

The girl stopped struggling, and Alder drew slowly away, his eyes on the small door leading to the forward magazine. Lieutenant Kohler, a bundle of ammunition lists in his hand, was standing in the opening, his eyes blazing with insane rage.

'Stand to attention, you swine! Leave that woman alone!' In two strides he was in front of Alder, and in a savage thrust drove his fist into the man's mouth. Alder whimpered and closed his eyes as the officer struck him again. 'How dare you disgrace the Imperial Navy by degrading yourself in front of the enemy!' Kohler was almost beside himself with rage. He struck the half-dazed man first on one side of the face and then the other, so that his mouth and chin were streaming with blood. 'I have had my eye on you! Well, I shall see that we do not have to put up with your sort any longer!' He broke off, panting, as Pieck's terrified face appeared over Alder's shoulder.

'Permission to speak, Lieutenant! I can explain what happened!'

Kohler dropped his raised fist, gasping with the exertion of his blows. 'Shut your mouth! How dare you interrupt me!'

There was the sound of feet in the passageway, and Petty Officer Brandt with a sentry appeared in the already crowded space.

'Sir?' Brandt stood stiffly at attention, but kept his eyes on the girl. He drew in his breath sharply as he caught sight of her bared shoulder before she tugged the coat back into place. 'Is something wrong?'

'Wrong? I should damn' well think there is!' Kohler pointed accusingly at Alder, and looked again at Pieck, as if seeing him for the first time. For a moment he seemed confused, and then tossed his head angrily. 'Wait in the ammunition hoist with this man.' He indicated the wretched and bleeding man, who still stood rigidly at attention, a habit he had learned at the detention barracks when the guards had taunted him and jeered at his mental sickness. 'I wish to get a clear picture of what caused all this. Sentry! Take this woman to her quarters.' He was getting excited again. This really was a most fortunate happening. He had been congratulating himself on the success of his work with the torpedo when he had heard the commotion in the passage, but he had never dreamed that such an opportunity to regain his hold on Pieck would be so easy to come by. It was amazing. He had almost ordered Brandt to put that fool Alder in the cells. It might have been a case for a firing squad. That would have been interesting, but this new possibility was devastating in its simplicity.

The passageway was suddenly deserted and quiet, and he was conscious of the tension within him, and of the boy's sharp breathing. He frowned. 'Well, Pieck, this is very serious for Alder. What have you to add to the evidence?' He waited like a hawk, watching the torn emotions on his face and the wide, helpless expression he had known of old.

'Sir, it was an accident. Alder is a good man. He is a bit simple. He was only trying to sympathize with her, to tell her he, too, had been a survivor!'

'And when she refused to listen he tried to rape her, eh?' His pale eyes were brilliant with concentration. He was almost afraid to speak in case Pieck detected the excitement within him.

'No, sir! It was all a mistake!'

'And *he* made it! By God, I'll have him shot! If this sort of behaviour got around the ship we'd have a mutiny on our hands! Discipline! That's what these scum need!'

Pieck stared up at him miserably. He was a simple boy, but not too simple to see through Kohler's cat-and-mouse tactics. He thought, too, of Alder, and of their time together in the detention barracks, and of the man's mental self-destruction in the search for his memory. This way or that, what did it matter? Kohler would have won in the end. This way, at least, he might find some way out. Some small reprieve for all of them. He looked Kohler full in the face, his chin lifted. 'Please, sir, give him a chance. I'll do anything'—his voice shook— 'anything you ask of me.' He dropped his eyes and felt drained of life.

Kohler licked his lips. 'Splendid! I think you are coming to your senses!' He placed his hand under Pieck's chin and tilted his head towards him. 'After all, there's no need to bear old grudges, is there? Er, I must make you understand that. Things will be different from now on, eh?' He dropped his hand and called out sharply. 'All right, Brandt, you can release that idiot! Give him some extra work to keep him occupied, and watch him. But there will be no charge!'

The petty officer looked crestfallen. 'No charge, sir? But I thought you said——'

Kohler flushed. 'Damn and blast your stupid eyes, man! Do I have to do and say everything twice in this ship! Take that man aft and attend to your duty!'

'Sir!' The heels clashed together, and Brandt darted a look of hatred at Pieck, then, with Alder dragging his feet behind him, clattered up the steel ladder from the hold.

Kohler nodded. 'See? Nothing to it. So long as you behave yourself all will be well with your comrade. I think we understand each other, eh? Carry on to your duty then.' He waited until Pieck had reached the foot of the ladder. 'When you finish your watch you may visit me in my cabin. We can have a little talk.' He was still smiling as Pieck disappeared through the hatch. At last he was getting the luck and recognition he had earned. Humming cheerfully, Kohler began to check the ammunition lists.

∙　　　∙　　　∙　　　∙　　　∙

Heuss pushed open the wheelhouse door and then closed it behind him. He stared round the quiet orderly place with open dislike. It was always there waiting for him, it never slept. The nerve centre of a pirate. Every time that he was on watch and the telephone buzzed, or a lookout reported some vague object, his mouth went dry. He always felt sick and afraid to give the necessary orders which might commit the ship and himself to another cold, dispassionate engagement. It was all so inhuman, so unreal. He shook his head angrily and peered round the dimly lit wheelhouse. Damrosch stood at the rear of the helmsman, his hands deep in his pockets, his eyes quietly watchful. He tried to smile at Heuss, and then returned to his own thoughts and concentration. The helmsman leaned gently against the wheel, his face bright in the light from the compass bowl, impassive, like a carving on a cathedral. The telegraphsman, boatswain's mates, signalman and captain's messenger all stood like dim statues, without faces or personalities. On the far bridge-wing, dimly visible through the spray-dappled glass, he could see Dehler gesticulating and shouting at a lookout. A deaf-and-dumb show. All at once Heuss wanted to get away from the place and find sanctuary in his cabin. He might even make an excuse to visit the girl in her quarters. He strode to the dark door of the Captain's sea cabin. It was ringed with light, and he sighed deeply as he rapped lightly with his knuckles. Did the man never sleep? How could he go on without rest, without ever taking his hand from the helm?

Von Steiger was sitting at his table, writing in a small, leather-bound book. He looked up as Heuss entered, the electric light making his dark hair shine above his tanned face.

'Ah, Heuss. I have been expecting you. Have you found out anything?'

He laid his papers down on the table and shrugged. 'Not a lot, Captain. One real piece of news is that a British cruiser is, or was, lying at Bridgetown, H.M.S. *Waltham*, taking on coal and stores. She is not listed as one of the local squadron, so I suppose we might expect her to appear anywhere. To get back to the *Rockleaze*, she was two days late, it seems. We might have missed her otherwise.'

'What was the name of her captain?'

'Captain Louch. An old man apparently. His men speak very well of him. His first mate told me that the captain had an idea we were a raider. But he wouldn't say any more about it.'

Von Steiger lit a cheroot and watched the smoke sucked into a ventilator. 'Interesting, Heuss. A brave man, that master. But not foolish enough to make an empty gesture, I think. The wireless signals —I have been thinking about them. The signals department have informed me that as far as they can estimate the signals were short and repetitive. No mention of position at all.' He smiled gravely. 'That surprises you, I see. It may be, of course, that he was just trying to frighten us. Or,' he stabbed the air with the cheroot, 'it may be that he *knew* that there was another ship close by. A ship that would be able to estimate his position without further information by wireless. If that is the case, it is quite possible that the other ship will have passed on that information to the nearest British squadron.'

Heuss eyed him bleakly. 'That was more or less what you anticipated, sir.'

'More or less. Now, how are your other prisoners? Is the girl calmer now?'

'Yes, sir.' He was giving nothing away. 'She is getting used to us now.'

'You obviously have not heard that she was in a little incident this evening.' He watched the alarm in Heuss's eyes. 'Apparently she was frightened by one of the sentries. It is all settled now though. A little misunderstanding.'

Heuss stared at him. How did he do it? How did he know what went on everywhere in the ship without leaving the bridge?

Von Steiger laughed quietly. 'I hear a lot of things unofficially, Heuss. Don't look so surprised!'

'I'm only sorry I was not informed myself. I had better speak to the guard commander about it.'

'Let it go. The girl is affecting all our men, one way or another. They pause by her door and make an excuse to wait outside. They peer at her if she shows herself, and two seamen fought each other yesterday because one had made an insulting remark about her. She has become a symbol, Heuss.' His voice hardened. 'She could be a dangerous symbol. Still, we may be able to clear them all out soon.'

Heuss shifted uncomfortably, feeling the gold eyes direct on his face. 'I see, sir. It will be something for the British seamen to write home to their wives about, I suppose.'

Von Steiger regarded him distantly. 'It's coal I have to worry about. Things have changed so much in a year or two. No supply ships, nothing. I have one dump in mind where we can replenish, but I should like to catch a nice collier first. I think we will soon.' He tapped his forehead vaguely. 'I feel it. Strange, isn't it?' He waved the cheroot. 'You can go below, Heuss, I will not detain you any more.'

Heuss closed the door behind him and felt his anger drain away. I complain about my Middle Watch, he thought, and he is on watch *all* the time.

Von Steiger lifted a silver flask from his waste-paper basket and poured himself a stiff measure of schnapps. He grimaced. Filthy stuff. If we can catch a nice collier we might even find a few bottles of Scotch aboard. He tried to cheer himself up with the idea, but it did not seem to matter enough. He thought of Heuss and frowned. What was he up to? I must try to leave this bridge and have a look round. The girl, for instance. She had turned away from him, and yet nearly everyone else in the ship had been near enough to her to touch her. She and he were separated by something more than circumstances. Like the day when she looked up at him from the boatdeck. What other woman would dare to treat him like that? A prisoner, a woman already mourned as lost by the outside world, he could do anything he liked with her. He sighed. No wonder Heuss and some of the others were getting unrealistic about her presence.

A voice-pipe squeaked. 'Officer-of-the-watch speaking, sir. Permission to pipe for guns' crews to exercise action?' Dehler never missed an opportunity to keep the men on their toes.

Von Steiger gave his consent and snapped down the pipe-cover. It just was not possible on this trip to get away from routine and duty. He refilled the glass and continued to write in his log.

8

LIEUTENANT KOHLER stood on the weather wing of the bridge, forcing himself to breathe deeply in spite of the bitterly cold air. From his lofty perch he could see the seamen working about the raider's decks, putting finishing touches to her new disguise. She had been renamed *Jannsens* of Amsterdam, and a false funnel had been hoisted as a twin to the genuine one. In addition the poop had been lengthened by strips of painted canvas, to give the ship the appearance of a small Dutch cargo liner. A false deck-cargo completed the deception, and the raider now steamed slowly to the west, rolling heavily on her unwanted buoyancy, while from the maindeck came the clang of shovels as the stokers moved still more of the coal to replenish the hungry bunkers.

All around the slowly moving ship the sea was grey, cold and hostile, and for the one and a half days since the destruction of the *Rockleaze* nothing had been sighted. Nothing except one small sailing barque, hull down on the watery horizon, which had been allowed to go, unaware of its closeness to enemy guns.

Von Steiger had remarked to the bridge at large: 'After this war there will be few enough of those sailing ships left. I doubt if her cargo would cover the cost of one of our salvoes!'

Kohler frowned as he recalled the incident. Surely any ship was better than nothing. He watched the sunset move unhurriedly towards the horizon, until only a long silver line marked the edge of the sea and laid a metallic path for the ship to follow.

The ship felt sluggish beneath him, and for a moment his mouth curved petulantly. It seemed somehow out of keeping with the grandeur of his thoughts that the *Vulkan*, his God of Fire, should be wallowing along almost apologetically, and barely making steerageway. He had heard the Captain speaking earlier to that weird old engineer, Niklas. There had been a long and earnest conversation about consumption and the apparent shortage of fuel. Kohler thought the Captain to be far too tolerant with Niklas, who after all was only an engineer. He had stood beside the Captain, grubby, untidy and a bad example to the men on watch. He dismissed the question of coal from his mind. It was the Captain's problem, not his. He had done more than his share towards the ship's honours, and he was content to rest momentarily with his thoughts.

It had been the most tremendous experience he had ever imagined, and he still could not quite put his memories in order. Perhaps he had had too much to drink before Pieck had come to his cabin, or perhaps he had been so incensed with excitement that a clear recollection was no longer possible. It did not matter, there would be plenty of occasions to come when he could plan each move in advance as coolly as he had organized his mines and torpedoes. He bared his teeth in a savage grin as he thought of the boy's terrified face as he had locked the steel door behind him. It was incredible that it had all been so easy after all.

His pleasure faded as Sub-Lieutenant Wildermuth staggered clumsily from the wheelhouse. The bridge was swaying through such a wide arc that no movement could be made without holding on for support at each step.

'Well? What d'you want?' Kohler's voice was harsh. He wanted to get back to his thoughts.

'Masthead reports a ship, fine on the starboard bow!' Wildermuth watched Kohler's cold eyes worriedly.

'Well why didn't you say so before? Have you called the Captain?' He pushed through the wheelhouse to the other wing with Wildermuth padding behind him.

'I thought that the Captain would say it's too late to attack another ship now. The light will be gone completely in half an hour.'

'Leave thinking to me!' He picked up a pair of heavy glasses and scanned the horizon eagerly. Eventually he found a faint blob of smoke, like a stain in the grey sky. 'What does the masthead say?'

'He can't quite make it out. The light isn't very good.'

'Oh God, do I have to do everything?' He gestured angrily with his hand. 'Call the Captain, and ring down for full speed!' Stupid fool, he thought, wearing an officer's uniform, but more fit to clean out the heads.

Von Steiger was suddenly at his side. His eyes looked red-rimmed, and he waited until Kohler had made his report before going to the telephone.

'Captain speaking. What do you make of the ship?' A long pause while they all looked at von Steiger's face.

He felt their eyes on him but ignored them. He coaxed the distant voice of the lookout, he did not shout, nor did he make suggestions, he merely drew a picture of the other ship in his mind. He could feel the telephone hurting his fingers before he realized that he was gripping it too hard.

This was really fate coming back to mock him, he thought. He remembered his conversation with Niklas and inwardly cursed himself. If we go faster we use more coal; if we reduce speed we miss a target like this. He listened to the painfully slow voice of the man at the masthead. There could surely not be any doubt left. The ship he could see was almost definitely a collier. He felt like smashing the instrument into Wildermuth's blank face, or screaming at the others to get on with their watch. He peered through the glass windows at the darkening sky. Why bother to say anything? Just alter course to the south as you planned. This one at least has beaten you. But suppose you do not find coal there either? Suppose a cruiser starts to chase you when your bunkers are only filled with dust? He bit his lip until it hurt. They were all waiting for his decision.

Heuss stopped in the wheelhouse door on the way to the wireless room for his evening inspection. He, too, sensed something dramatic was happening and watched with the others.

Von Steiger waited. Outside his racing thoughts he heard Kohler say, 'I rang for full speed, sir!' In his mind's eye he saw the brass telegraph in the engine-room gleaming in the red glow from the gaping furnace doors, as Niklas's men shovelled the black diamonds into the ever-hungry fires.

He looked around the wheelhouse. They all avoided his eye, and yet he knew they were watching him like hawks. In a voice he hardly recognized he said: 'We will go after her. She is a collier. I cannot afford to turn my back on her now.' The pain in his chest seemed to ease a little, and he felt better. He smiled bitterly as they all moved their feet and readjusted themselves.

'Bring her round to starboard half a point, and sound Action Stations! Pass the word for the First Lieutenant, and tell the engine-room that this is an emergency.' He glared at them all, his eyes flashing with sudden fire. 'I want every ounce of steam they can manage!'

The ship, which had begun to settle down for the evening, came to life around and beneath them. Von Steiger rested his back against the open wheelhouse door and looked up at the ranks of darkening clouds. They moved overhead like a trapdoor which, when it met the thin hard line of the horizon, would blot out everything.

Dehler reached his side, his jacket undone, his collarless shirt open to reveal the reddish hair on his heavy chest. 'A collier, eh?' He stared at the Captain with cautious eyes. 'We will never catch her now. What's her bearing and course, anyway?'

Von Steiger flicked his pad across the chart-table. 'A converging course. We might get within gunshot before long if we keep this speed up.'

Dehler blinked around him as if aware for the first time of the terrible vibration which made every rivet and plate clatter and groan with noisy protest.

Von Steiger saw the sceptical look in his subordinate's face and despised him. He forced himself to remain calm, and walked to his tall wooden chair. In an even tone he continued, 'I am going to catch that collier if I have to blow up every boiler and burst every rivet in this ship!'

Dehler rubbed his chin with a rasping sound. 'I'll give the daylight twenty minutes,' he said doggedly. 'She'll get clean away.'

'The collier is probably making about eight knots. We are already doing over sixteen. In a quarter of an hour we shall therefore have drawn nearly seven miles closer.' The bridge lookouts were reporting the target in the background of other noises, and he smiled at Dehler's disbelieving face. 'We will do the whole drill this time, Dehler. I want a full boarding party ready to get across to her, fully armed and ready for anything. Heuss, you will be in charge of the boarding party, and will take Wildermuth as your second in command.' He picked up the speaking tube by his side and spoke to Lieutenant Ebert. 'This has got to be very good shooting, Ebert. I don't want her damaged at all if I

135

can help it. I shall signal her to heave to, and to wait for boarders. I shall tell her master that if he resists or tries to scuttle we will blow them all to hell!' He peered suddenly through the window. 'I will, too, if necessary. Put your best men on the machine guns, they may be more use when we close in.'

He turned calmly to the others. 'To your stations. Heuss, get the boats swung out now, and good luck to you.'

Damrosch wiped his eyes and lifted his glasses again. There she is, he breathed. What a queer-looking ship; no wonder the lookout was confused. Squat, low in the water, the ship seemed to crawl up over the horizon line like a giant beetle. She had a small, single funnel right aft, and her decks were lined with short, heavy-looking derricks.

Heuss passed him at the run, his face troubled. As he clattered below he said: 'See that she's gone below, Max. The girl, I mean!' Then he was gone. Damrosch strained his eyes to see the other ship, but considered Heuss's request. Strange, he's just about to be dropped into the sea with a boarding party and all he thinks about is his prisoners. He grinned in spite of the tension. Good old Emil, he can always be relied upon for an unexpected comment.

Von Steiger listened to the bark of orders and the clatter of running feet. This will drive away their cobwebs. They won't have time to groan about their misfortunes for a while. He realized that Dehler was still at his side.

'I think *I* should take charge of the boarders, Captain!' His voice sounded only half under control. 'I am the senior officer. It is my right.' He swallowed hard and lifted his chin in defiance.

Von Steiger barely gave him a glance. 'If I am killed you are in command here. You are no use to me on board that collier if anything happens here. If we were to be caught by a British warship at the moment when we had got our boats in the water I should have to steam away and leave them to fend for themselves. Would you rather be left in that predicament?' He watched the torn emotions on Dehler's face.

'No, sir. I did not know you would take such a course of action!'

He smiled without humour. To himself he thought: Of course you did not think that. That is why you will never command anything. Aloud he said: 'Try not to question my orders, Dehler. Until you can take an order properly you will never be in a position to give one!'

He waited until the angry, red-faced officer had left the bridge, and then he stood up and joined Damrosch in the open. He was aware of the returning tension within him and began to have doubts. A gesture was well enough, but it had to work. He would prove nothing by making a hopeless mistake now. It was when he had seen the resentment in Dehler's eyes that he had realized just how important this operation was, not only for the sake of the coal, but for his own sake as well. He was committed now, and nothing could save him but success.

In spite of the rapidly failing light the other vessel's outline was now more apparent, and from the bridge von Steiger could see her ugly derricks and lumpy superstructure without the aid of his glasses. He marvelled at the other ship's indifference to the raider's rapid approach. *Vulkan* was hurling herself through the water at nearly seventeen knots, a speed she had not bettered since her very first speed-trials as a banana-boat. The bridge supports were humming with the strain, and the wing upon which he was standing seemed to be jerking up and down like a diving board.

A messenger stood by the wireless-room door, ready to report the slightest sign of a signal from the other ship. The merest hint of Morse would bring a shattering salvo from the waiting guns. The collier, however, plodded on indifferently. She was, after all, clear of the U-boat hunting ground, and apparently took every other vessel for granted.

Von Steiger dared not leave it any longer. It would take some time to slow down and drop the boats in the water, and by then it could be difficult.

'Signal her now. Damrosch, go and press the alarm signal!'

He heard the steel shutters fall back from the guns, even as the light began to blink by his elbow.

'Stop immediately. German cruiser here. Do not use wireless or you will be sunk.'

In the dying light the sudden flash of a forward gun seemed all the more terrible, and although they could no longer spot the fall of the warning shell, the whining scream as it passed over the other ship was apparently enough.

An uneven light replied, 'I have stopped.' And then again, 'I have stopped.'

Von Steiger lowered his glasses. Speed was essential now. 'Stop engine. Lower the boats and slip them! Train the searchlight on her, but do not switch on unless I give you the order.' He heard the metallic chink of ammunition belts as the Maxim machine guns were swung to bear on the heavily laden collier.

Hoarse orders took up the signal from the bridge, and Dehler could be heard getting the boats away. 'Get a grip on those falls! Lower away!' Then, as the boats swung dizzily above the creaming water: 'Avast lowering! Slip!'

From his position on the wing, von Steiger saw the pale shape of the rakish whaleboat detach itself from the parent ship. There was a small delay, and then he saw the oars fan out from its sides and it began to move with maddening slowness towards the other ship. Around the *Vulkan's* stern the second whaleboat appeared, pulling strongly, its confined hull apparently crammed with dark figures.

He could hear Damrosch gasping with excitement, and smiled in spite of his own anxiety. He forced himself to take out a fresh cheroot and light it, and was surprised to find that he could still hold his hand steady.

Dehler came panting up the bridge ladder. 'Boats away, Captain!'

His features were indistinct, and von Steiger realized that in mere minutes they would be in complete darkness.

'Very well. Dehler, take over the watch, and keep her up-wind of that fellow. Watch her carefully, I don't want to drift down on to that great floating coal-mine, it would be like hitting a reef!'

Dehler hurried into the wheelhouse, and could be heard speaking to the Coxswain.

Damrosch banged his hand on the rail. 'The first boat is alongside, sir!'

They could just see its pale shape bobbing against the low black side of the collier, frail and ineffectual. The other boat tried to hook on also, but was carried clear by the surging water. The oars came out once more, and slowly and painfully the boat edged its way back towards the ponderous and seemingly immovable ship.

Von Steiger stared down at the dim black shadow and tried to estimate its rate of drift. She was so heavy in the water it was hard to tell, but one thing was certain: she was loaded to her deck-beams with coal. Too late to do anything now. Must keep together tonight and start loading at first light.

．　　　．　　　．　　　．　　　．

As his whaleboat was being lowered towards the plunging water, Heuss squeezed himself against the armed seamen who were jammed tightly in the tiny cockpit, and tried not to look up at the raider's gleaming plates as he plummeted downwards. The oarsmen sat hunched on their thwarts, already feeling for their oars, and making sure that they could slam them into the rowlocks without wasting a second. An overloaded boat, dropped carelessly into choppy water, could easily capsize unless way could be got on immediately.

Dehler's face peered down at them. The falls had stopped squeaking, and the boat hung suspended and helpless above the wave-tops. Heuss eyed the water grimly. The waves looked a damn' sight bigger than they did from the *Vulkan*'s high deck. He did not have time to consider his possible fate. 'Slip!' came the order, and the boat fell on to the remains of the raider's bow-wave with a sickening splash. Heuss felt the tiller bite into his hand, and he thrust his weight against it to bring the boat's head up into the cross sea. The small boat rose and fell with breathtaking swoops, and he had to grit his teeth together in order to control his sudden nausea.

'Out oars! Stand by!' The oarsmen leaned towards him, their eyes fixed on his face. 'Give way together!' Five pairs of arms heaved back, and the long blades sliced like scythes into the white-capped water which rose high above the gunwale.

All at once the momentary confusion had gone, and the tangled mass of arms, legs and weapons was moving in unison, and when Heuss looked over his shoulder he saw that the *Vulkan* had already dropped into an indistinct blur. He could see the other boat moving up rapidly astern of him, the oars rising and falling like wings, the high prow well clear of the water, so that it appeared to be planing across the wave-tops.

Wildermuth's boat was doing well, and if his own men did not watch out he would be alongside before them. He bared his teeth in an excited grin. 'Pull hard, lads! They're gaining on us! Put your blasted backs into it!'

The black bulk of the other ship grew out of the water ahead of him, until it seemed as if they would tear straight into her hull. Heuss tensed his body, straining his eyes into the gloom. Von Steiger had been right about sighting a collier. It was luck, of course, but uncanny all the same.

He poised himself ready, his hand upon the jerking tiller-bar. Nearer, nearer—God I must not misjudge it now! He could see the dripping black side and the tangled mass of rigging and spars overhead. Now! He slammed the tiller hard over. 'Way enough! Boat your oars!'

The seamen heaved the oars into the boat, so that, as it curtsied round in response to the rudder, their blades seemed to touch the collier's side. The waiting bowman flung his grapnel high over the ship's rail, and seconds later the boat swung obediently alongside.

Out of the corner of his eye Heuss saw Wildermuth's boat scrape against the hull and then stagger away again. There were muffled curses and the clatter of oars as the men fought to get back to grips with their quarry.

Heuss took a deep breath. 'Right, lads, follow me!' Gathering his strength he sprang for the rail. His clutching fingers scrabbled frantically, and then found a grip on the rust-covered bulwark, and then he was up and over. Immediately the collier's wide deck was about him, and the noise of the sea and the confusion of the tossing boat was lost behind him.

His men scrambled breathlessly over the rail, leaving only a skeleton crew to keep the boat from smashing itself against the iron hull, and stood peering around on what Heuss now realized was a deserted deck. He had expected the ship's crew to be waiting for him, or at least somebody to question his right of entry. There was no one.

He forced his mind to work. There was no von Steiger watching at his shoulder now, but he could well imagine the anxious eyes peering across the dark gap between the two wallowing vessels.

'Weiss, take four men and find your way below. You know what to do. Make sure they don't try to scuttle her!' He waited until they had padded away, and then he turned to the remaining four men. 'Can't wait for Wildermuth's party. There's something wrong here, and we must find out what it is. Follow me to the bridge.'

The collier's bridge was a small isolated island in the forward section of the hull, separated from the main superstructure by the long holds and loading derricks. As he ran towards it he felt a sense of unreality and alarm rising within him like a warning. He groped for the steel ladder and began to climb. The sound of the shot was so close that it sounded like a thunderclap, and he threw his body against the steel rungs as a bullet ricocheted off the plating and whined away over the sea.

'What the devil!' He groped for his pistol, his fingers fumbling with the holster-strap. They must be mad! There was another shot, and a man behind him gave a shriek and plummeted backwards on top of the others. His body bounced across the top of a winch and slithered across the deck. The man gave one more scream and then lay still.

For a moment Heuss stood stock-still, his first reaction one of complete terror. Then an unreasoning anger sent the blood rushing to his head and he bounded up the rest of the ladder. He saw a pale face through the glass window of the bridge door and he fired straight at it. The glass shivered to fragments, and the face vanished. From the darkness of the wheelhouse he saw the orange flash of another gun, and a heavy bullet thudded into the woodwork by his head. More shots came from aft, and he heard Wildermuth yelling for his men to take cover.

The whole bridge was suddenly laid bare in the unearthly blue glare of the *Vulkan's* big searchlight. Over his shoulder Heuss called to his hidden men. 'Use the lamp! Signal to the ship that we are being fired on!' He ducked behind the wooden bridge door as another shot whined past his face. He heard Wildermuth calling his name, and then heard him shout: 'We have rounded up most of the crew! What shall we do?' He broke off as a complete volley of rifle-fire sprayed down from the other side of the bridge and struck sparks from the metal decks below.

Heuss was thinking furiously. This was ridiculous, and yet it was more than just foolhardiness on the part of the collier's officers. They knew that the raider could not open fire with their own boarding party aboard, and they also knew that as soon as the boarding party retreated to give the raider a clear field of fire they could get under way again, and might easily slip away in the cover of the night. Why were they not using their wireless? He stiffened as he heard the sound of glass falling overhead. He strained his eyes upwards, and tried to see what could have made the sound. His back tingled, and he felt his heart thumping painfully in his chest. Someone might be trying to work round behind him and then shoot him like a sitting duck. He heard the rustle of clothing on the ladder, and saw Petty Officer Weiss's face appear over the rim of the bridgedeck. He sighed with relief and gestured with his Luger.

'Everything all right at your end, Weiss?'

The face moved cautiously nearer. 'Yes, sir. We've put the crew under guard, they're stupid Lascars for the most part. What the hell are we going to do, sir? I can't see a thing in this damned searchlight glare!' He broke off, his hand pointing upwards. 'By God, sir, look at that bastard!'

Heuss saw a figure leap from the top of the narrow wheelhouse and stand momentarily transfixed by the searchlight, and then, as Heuss's men fired wildly from the deck, he flung himself along a narrow catwalk and disappeared inside a small, isolated metal hutch.

A voice called from below: '*Vulkan*'s signalling, sir! Says that this ship must not be allowed to send signals!'

Heuss swallowed hard. These people were clever, he thought grimly, they were able to hold down all his own men quite easily, while one of their number had been allowed to make his way unchecked to that small cabin. Obviously, it was the wireless-room. He felt Weiss was watching him, and knew what was expected of him. If a wireless message went off now it would mean the end of everything. *Vulkan* would be chased away with her coal supply dwindling, and after that it would only be a matter of time. He thrust his pistol into his belt and stood up.

'Give me covering fire, Weiss, I'm going up.'

Without waiting for further events to change his mind, he wriggled round the side of the bridge, his fingers feeling upwards for the over-hanging lip of the wheelhouse deck. He felt quite cold, and as he moved along the metal wall, like a fly, he was aware of the menacing silence around him.

It is all my fault. I should have guessed that something like this might happen. The fact that the ship was deserted should have told me. He winced as another burst of shots tore the night apart, and the steel plates to his right shivered under the impact of the searching bullets. He had reached the catwalk now, and crouched like a runner waiting for the starter's signal. The catwalk was about ten feet long.

142

Then there was a small, verandah-like platform outside the closed wireless-room door. The moment he moved along the catwalk his back would be visible to the men behind him on the bridge. They could not miss. He bit his lip, his face set like a mask.

It was one of the collier's officers who gave him his chance. A rifle cracked from the front of the wheelhouse, and instantly the whole bridge was plunged into darkness. He had shot out the raider's searchlight, and in the sudden blackness which followed, Heuss hurled himself along the invisible catwalk. He threw his whole weight against the door, which gave unexpectedly beneath him, and with a cry he fell full length on top of the figure which crouched across the humming transmitter. The man rose easily beneath him, and in a trice had wrapped his arms around Heuss like a bear and butted his head hard under his chin. They staggered about the small space, grunting and struggling, while all the time the grip steadily tightened about the German's waist.

Heuss fought for breath, and bit back a scream as he felt his spine begin to crack under the strain. The eery light from the transmitter seemed to mock him across the other man's powerful shoulders and shining bald head. Heuss blinked away the mist of agony from his eyes, and in one final wrench tried to wriggle his arms free. In doing so they both lost their balance and fell heavily against the table. Heuss fell with the man's full weight on top of him. He kicked out blindly, and felt the pressure released and saw the giant stagger to his feet. He rolled on to his side as the man swung a kick at his ribs, and gasped as a million lights burst before his eyes. He groped blindly for his pistol, but it had gone, and the sudden fear which swept over him gave him new strength. He ducked away from the swinging boots and grasping hands, and fought his way into a corner. He seized a chair and tried to hold the man clear, but he brushed it from his hand like a toy and jeered wildly: 'Get up and fight, you bloody square-head! I'll fix you this time!'

He aimed a punch at Heuss's face, but in the semi-darkness misjudged the distance and hit him a shattering blow on the chest. Heuss jerked backwards, and felt glass raining down on his shoulders. He struck out wildly to save himself from falling once more, knowing that those great boots would finish him for good if he did. As he struck out his fingers encircled the wooden haft of a fire-axe, the glass case of which he had shattered with his head in falling.

He could not remember tearing it from its rack. He could see only the crazed angry face opposite him dissolve in sudden wild panic. The big man screamed as he ducked towards the open door, and, as the bald head glinted palely before him, Heuss struck out with the axe. It was the last of his strength, but it was more than enough. He felt the force of the blow paralyse his arm, and saw the convulsing figure plunge over the edge of the catwalk, the axe embedded in its skull.

From outside the wireless-room there came a sudden silence. Heuss stared at his hands on the cabin floor and realized that he was on his hands and knees. He heard a footstep on the catwalk behind him and waited for the impact of a bullet. Over his head the wireless still hummed with life. With a wild gasp he lurched to his feet and staggered towards it. Before he could reach it, two hands seized his arms and guided him firmly to a chair. Petty Officer Weiss was staring down at him, his face working with admiration and awe.

'Steady, sir! It's all over! The ship is ours!' Heuss looked at him with glazed eyes. 'Yes, sir, when that object came flying through the door just now, they lost their stomach for any more fighting!' He laughed shakily. 'To tell the truth, so did I!'

Heuss stood up and groped his way to the door. He dared not speak, for he could feel the vomit pressing upwards in his throat. He could see some of his men with rifles on the wing of the bridge, and another was signalling to the *Vulkan*, although he could not see her through the pink mist which swirled in front of his eyes. Some other figures were lined up on the deck below, their hands clasped on top of their heads. Five of them, yet enough to hold up the whole boarding party, and make him into a bloody murderer. He shook off Weiss's hand and staggered on to the catwalk. Below him he could see the broken figure of the wireless officer. It looked small and pathetic. Was it possible that a few moments earlier it had been a living, fighting giant?

Wildermuth appeared from the wheelhouse. 'By God, Emil, that was something!' His loose chins jerked with relief. 'I thought they had done for you!'

Heuss rubbed his knuckles into his eyes and tried to think. 'Signal von Steiger, and tell him we are ready to get under way.' His voice sounded cracked. 'Lock the crew below, and see that they are all made harmless.'

He walked towards the other prisoners, and halted in front of the one wearing a jacket with four faded gold stripes. He peered into the man's apprehensive face and then turned away.

Weiss said slowly, 'What about these, sir?'

'I expect our Captain would tell them how gallant and brave they were. I am afraid I have no stomach for that sort of hypocrisy! Just lock them up with the others for now. If you had asked me a few seconds ago, I would have ordered you to kill them!' To himself he added: But I remembered just in time what I told Max Damrosch. I said to him that we, too, might act like wild beasts under the right circumstances.

He climbed up to the bullet-scarred wheelhouse, and watched as Wildermuth took control of the telegraph. Far below, under the levelled rifles of their guards, the stokers began to toil at their fires, and very slowly the collier began to move through the dark water. Like a tamed beast she plodded behind her new master, unaware that he needed her as much as life itself.

On the compass platform Heuss reached for the collier's log, and then stopped, his eyes fixed on the vessel's name, which was printed across the cover.

It was called the *Nemesis*.

With his head on his arms he began to sob quietly, while the night closed in to hide his shame.

.   .   .   .   .

'Coffee, sir?'

Von Steiger eased his cramped body upright in the tall chair and passed his hands across his eyes. His breath hung in a damp cloud, and he was conscious of the cold which was eating into his tired bones.

He took the mug from Reeder and held the hot china gratefully in cupped hands. He glanced up at the wheelhouse clock, and frowned. Half past six, and still only a hint of grey light in the dark, hurrying clouds. From the deck below he could hear the subdued sounds of hatch-covers being removed, and in front of the bridge a seaman's body hung like a squirrel in the derrick rigging, an oil-can prodding at the swaying steel blocks. On the opposite side of the wheelhouse, huddled together as if for warmth, some of his officers stood as they had for most of the night, bleary-eyed, chilled and silent.

Von Steiger cleared his throat. 'Still see the collier?'

A figure moved to the rear of the wheelhouse and Damrosch answered swiftly: 'I can see her a bit better now, sir. She's keeping station very well.'

He grunted. 'Good. I wish the dawn light would come more quickly. This damned cloud is holding us up. We must break into the collier's cargo before the weather gets any worse. How is the glass, Kohler?'

'Falling, sir. But the wind is still steady.'

He sat back in the chair, and realized with irritation that the mug was empty. Reeder's white jacket floated out of the gloom, and he heard it being refilled. It had been a long night. He had not realized just how much the capture of the collier had taken out of his stored energy, and the strain of waiting for the dawn was beginning to make itself felt in other ways. It had been a near thing. Too near. When the firing had broken out aboard the other vessel he had nearly cracked. In the glare of the searchlight he had seen the running figures of the scattered boarding party, and had watched as Heuss had clambered up the side of the besieged bridge. The bullet which had shattered the searchlight had missed him by inches, and his cheek had been cut by flying glass. He had hardly flinched, so much had he been willing Heuss to succeed in his lone attempt to capture the ship. He wondered how Heuss was getting on now, in charge of the prize ship on his own. It might teach him that there was more to being a naval officer than wearing the uniform.

It was odd that the collier had not been able to transmit a signal of distress. Perhaps the set was an old one and took a long time to warm up. Careless fools, he thought with sudden anger. They had paid for their indifference.

He turned his aching mind back to his immediate problems. It would be tricky to get alongside the collier in this sea. The wind had mounted during the night, and the waves had increased in length and power, so that the whole ridges of white foam could be seen cruising relentlessly down towards the two ships, and the weight of their passing made the bridge heave with sickening violence, and thundered against the hull like the roll of drums.

Dehler was on deck with Sub-Lieutenant Seebohm, getting the ship prepared to take on coal. It was a job of pure seamanship, and he knew that they would both be in their element. Every man on board would be employed on some part of the work, and it would be damned hard work, he thought. The men would have to be shown their jobs individually beforehand, and a stupid display of impatience by a flustered officer could bring disaster on the whole venture. It was odd to think that most of his men had never been to sea before, and many of those who had had never been made to coal ship under these primitive conditions.

He was aware that the distant fo'c'sle head was clearer now, and he could even see the outline of the big winches beyond the foremast. Soon now.

'Make a signal to the *Nemesis*,' he said calmly. 'Tell them that I am about to drop astern of her.' He listened to the yeoman's pencil squeaking on his slate. 'Then tell them that I shall come alongside port side to. Estimated time of approach in fifteen minutes.'

Lieutenant Ebert watched the winking lamp and rubbed his chin with a frown. '*Nemesis?* That's an odd name, sir. What does it mean?'

Von Steiger smiled. Ebert was a good gunnery officer, and that was enough. 'Don't worry your head about it. It is when Nemesis catches up with you that you want to worry!'

The officers laughed dutifully, and von Steiger knew that they were getting more relaxed. That was good. It had been a long wait for all of them, and he knew that they had all been wrapped in their thoughts. When the collier's officers had put up a resistance in such a cunning and clever manner, von Steiger had again realized just how much the art of commerce-raiding had changed. With every merchant ship so far there had been complications, any one of which might have brought disaster and possible death to them all. Before, it had been quite different. A challenged merchantman would surrender at the first shot, or even a glimpse of the black German Eagle. Now, they turned and fought. The survivors had been more resentful than frightened. He frowned deeply. Try as he might, he could see only one explanation for this change of heart by defenceless seamen. They resented their fate now, at what they possibly imagined was the close of a war already won by their side. He chilled. They could take the threat of a U-boat's torpedo or sudden death on a lurking mine. That was part of the war at sea. It would go on until the last hour. But to be taken prisoner by him and to lose their ship in this way, that was too close, too personal, to be ignored. They would fight rather than give in like that.

He shook his head angrily. Why am I so surprised? I realized this fact long ago, but, like Heuss, I thought that I was too superior to share my knowledge.

'Collier's signalling, sir. "Forward holds open. Two derricks rigged, and manned by Lascars. Await your arrival. Good luck." '

Von Steiger smiled to himself. Good luck. It would seem that someone else had guessed his difficulties.

'Very well, Ebert, take her astern.'

The raider reduced speed and began to fall back. The bulk of the collier loomed large and black on the port quarter, and as she overtook them with ponderous dignity, they could see the bustle of figures on her low decks and the white faces on the narrow bridge.

Von Steiger watched her move ahead, and then slid from his chair. Slowly he walked on to the port wing and stood watchfully in the far corner, so that he could see the full length of his ship and down into the churning water below him.

Ebert stood by the helmsman, and Kohler waited by the wheelhouse door to relay his orders. Apart from a mere handful of men required as lookouts and sea-dutymen, every fit member of the ship's company was thronged on the foredeck by the already opened holds.

Von Steiger looked down at the gaping hatchways and remembered the great banks of glittering coal which had once filled them. He spoke loudly enough for the Coxswain to hear. 'I want you to steer fine, Lehr. Take her ahead until we are running exactly parallel with the collier. Don't worry about course or speed. The collier is steering south-west to take advantage of both wind and sea, so we shall just follow her.'

Lehr bowed his massive head. 'Yes, sir. I understand.'

'Ebert, watch the telegraph, and get ready for any emergency.' If only the ship had two screws. It was just like the Admiralty to select a ship with one screw. They thought of economy before the necessity of immediate manœuvrability.

'Very well, half speed ahead!'

The sudden jangle of the telegraph could be heard even down on the crowded foredeck, where the petty officers mustered their men into small, manageable parties. They felt the tremble of power through the hull, and saw the collier beginning to draw close once more.

Schiller stood swaying by the port rail, his thick fingers caressing the coils of his heaving-line and smoothing out any possible kink in its length. His two companions, Schoningen and Lukaschek, watched the other men moving warily round the gaping holds, and saw the first parties lowering themselves into the black depths with rakes and shovels.

Schiller snorted through his grotesque nose. 'Rather them than me! A man can get buried by the stuff when it first comes aboard!'

Lukaschek, shivering in his threadbare jacket, eyed the distant collier. 'Look at the waves breaking against that cow! She'll pound us to bits if the Captain makes a mess of it!'

'Make a mess of you, he will, if you don't stop whining!' Schiller grinned unpleasantly. 'God, how sick I am of lumping coal! All I ever seem to have done is coal ship!'

Schoningen shrugged. 'Well, if we stay here with the lines we might get out of it.'

'Huh! Pigs might lay eggs, too! You never get out of it! Dig and carry the stuff until your eyes are red and raw with grit and your nose feels like a wire brush! Then you have to hose the whole ship down and try to clean the muck out of your skin. Just in time to do it all again! God blast it! No wonder the old seamen went mad when they did away with sails!'

'Silence on deck!' Petty Officer Brandt glared at the sea of anonymous faces.

'Silence yourself!' Schiller spoke out of the side of his mouth. 'If I catch you near the edge of one of the holds, it will be just too bad for you!'

Sub-Lieutenant Seebohm watched some seamen lowering the large rope-fenders over the side at regular intervals, and wondered if they would be sufficient to withstand the shock. He stiffened as Dehler pushed his way through the ranks of men and peered angrily over the rail.

'Come on, you men! Move those fenders along! Put them ahead of the ship's frames, there is more support for them there.' He took a rope from a seaman's hand and snorted with impatience. 'Like this, you clumsy oaf!' He deftly tied the line around a cleat and stood up, breathing hard. 'You can recognize where the frames are by the lines of rivets down the hull!' He turned irritably to Seebohm. 'You could have shown him that! Don't just stand there like a priest at a whore's wedding!' He peered up at the bridge, his eyes fixed on von Steiger's distant silhouette. He was still smarting under the lash of the Captain's rebuke, and the man's apparent calmness did not help Dehler to forget. He glared towards the wheelhouse and tried to see the other officers. Half aloud he said, 'That's right, you all stay up there when there's a job of work to be done!'

The raider's stem moved past the collier's spindly funnel and remorselessly began to pass down the length of her side. They had all been so busy that the dawn had come unnoticed, and Dehler was surprised that he could see Heuss so clearly on top of the other vessel's bridge.

I should be up there. What could he do if anything went wrong now? After that skirmish last night, I expect von Steiger will fall on his neck and kiss him! The fool should never have allowed it to happen! Probably walked aboard in a stinking funk!

Seebohm muttered with alarm. The *Vulkan*'s bows had swung in very slightly, so that the gap between the two ships narrowed by several feet. They were steaming parallel now, and barely fifty feet apart. The *Vulkan* was a good ten feet higher than the collier, and already Dehler could see the ragged crew of Lascars cranking on their winches, and, even as he watched, the long booms of the loading derricks began to move jerkily towards the open holds. He watched with impatience mounting within him, then he bellowed across the water: 'Too low! You'll never make it!' He turned again to the bridge. 'We shall have to use our own derricks, sir! We're too high for hers!'

Von Steiger raised his hand. 'Very well. Get them ready.'

'Already done, sir!' Dehler glared triumphantly, and then turned towards a petty officer. 'Stand by with the heaving-lines!'

Closer and closer, so that the gap between them was darkened by their shadows. The water surged and thundered in trapped torment, and some of the men waved self-consciously to their friends on the opposite deck.

Schiller stood poised by the rail, his feet wide apart, his eyes narrowly gauging the distance from the collier's side. Behind him the first headrope was all ready to be passed across and secured once he had thrown his line.

Dehler jerked his thumb. 'Now!'

Schiller drew back his arm and threw the line in one unbroken heave. It soared cleanly across the collier's foredeck and was immediately seized by half a dozen hands. As the slack was gathered in, the eye of the big hawser began to ease its way through the forward fairleads and move jerkily across the gap.

Von Steiger watched the headrope being dragged aboard the *Nemesis*, and took a quick look aft. Another heaving-line had gone across, and already the sternrope was snaking into position. His practised eye sorted out the order from the chaos of running men, who surged across the decks between the long brown coils of ropes which still waited to be secured. Breastropes, springs, all were laid out, and filled every inch of the littered decks.

He could feel the great suction tugging against the side of his ship and sensed the tremendous strain which was exerting itself on the rudder. He signalled to the Coxswain through the wheelhouse window, and watched as the spokes were eased over to starboard. Just half a turn, yet the effect was immediate and final. He saw the headrope slacken, and held his breath as the *Vulkan*'s bows swung rapidly towards the other vessel.

The daylight vanished between the two ships, and then they struck. Even as the Coxswain applied opposite wheel, the first of the rope fenders took the impact, and then, with a scream of protesting metal, the two juggernauts thundered together. He felt the pressure of the bridge rail against his chest, and then held on as the ship rolled away for a second impact.

Dehler could be heard yelling orders, and, sensing the urgency, the seamen were passing the new lines across to the men on the lower deck of the collier. It was like lashing down two mad beasts which were trying to destroy each other. A six-inch breastrope parted with the sound of a pistol shot, but more seamen were there in an instant, a new rope already reeved through the fairleads. Von Steiger forced his hands into his pockets, and waited. The ship shuddered as it struck again, and two seamen were thrown from their feet. He watched the ropes tauten, and saw the seamen waiting to pounce like dogs. The headrope slackened as the ships nudged each other again, and instantly they had taken a couple more turns with it around the forward bollards. The ropes seemed to hum, but the strain was now evenly shared, and sullenly the two ships cruised forward together at reduced speed, the crushed fenders squeaking and writhing in protest.

Across the minute gap the first party of seamen poured with their petty officers. Dressed in old overalls, boiler suits or scraps of tattered uniform, they scrambled into the first pair of open holds in the collier's iron deck, to where the gleaming Welsh coal waited to be dug out by hand and loaded, shovel by shovel, into the waiting bags.

Already the two great booms on the raider's foremast were swinging across the collier's deck, while a score of hands steadied the dangling purchases and treacherous guy-ropes, which might pluck a man off his feet and send him spinning into the gaping holds.

Von Steiger relaxed slightly and groped for a cheroot. Already a thick black cloud of wet dust was rising over the two ships,. and the air was filled with the frantic ring and clash of shovels. He nodded with approval. Dehler had been right about the hoists. This was one advantage the *Vulkan* had over a warship. She could haul her own coal and not rely on the short-masted collier. In a battle-cruiser it would have taken ages to rig and operate the double whips, outhauls and complicated winch movements, which were difficult even with a well-trained crew in harbour. The *Vulkan*'s foremast derricks would be more than enough for this. He turned to the watching officers.

'Right, gentlemen. As you know, every available man turns to for coaling. That applies here, and to my officers. Carry on, and see that nobody even leans against a shovel until we are done. If they stop for a breath, they can never be restarted.' He watched the officers move from the bridge, their faces showing little enthusiasm. It would do them good, he thought, and in any case would show the men that their officers were quite capable of manual work.

Niklas appeared at his side, his eyes already rimmed in black. He waved his coaling plan towards the forward hold. 'It is much easier to load this way, but what a business it is to move it again into the bunkers!'

'Are we filling any bunkers now?'

'Two. I have the shoots already rigged, and my stokers can tend to them. If Heuss gets those Lascars moving we should really be able to pack it away!'

Von Steiger nodded in agreement. 'I shall be leaving a prize crew aboard, and will send the collier away independently as soon as we have taken on sufficient coal for a while. We can rendezvous with her later on at some prescribed places.' He called across to a messenger: 'Here, boy! Pass the word across for Lieutenant Heuss, and tell Sub-Lieutenant Wildermuth to report to the bridge with him.' To the engineer he added: 'Wildermuth can take her. See that your men pump across some fresh water and fill her tanks. I shall be putting some of our prisoners aboard. I think that we can get rid of all the unimportant ones.'

Niklas rubbed his chin. 'We shall be a bit short of water, sir. We may have to cut down the daily ration.'

'So be it then. I intend to milk some more off the next ship we meet. Until then, there will be no luxury uses for fresh water at all!'

Lieutenant Heuss climbed slowly on to the bridge. Von Steiger was immediately struck by his tired, empty face and the apparent heaviness in his limbs.

'You did well, Heuss. I shall want a full report later, but right now I want you to transfer all the prisoners to the collier. They can have the crew's quarters and any other cabin-space, and the Lascars will have to be content with an empty hold. The Lascars can help Wildermuth with the prize crew to work the ship, I think. They usually have little stomach for fighting.'

Heuss's eyes flickered with sudden concern. '*All* the prisoners, sir?'

'All the seamen, that is. Keep the senior officers, and any others that might be a security risk.'

'What about the girl? She can't very well go with that overloaded ship.'

'I realize that, Heuss. Although I suspect my reasons may be different from yours.'

'I don't understand, sir.'

'Pull yourself together, man! We have an urgent job to do here. Seconds are precious. You look like a man in a trance!'

Heuss stiffened, his face taut with suppressed anger. 'Last night was pretty hard on all of us, sir!'

'Quite so, Heuss. Well, carry on with your duty, and then go and keep an eye on the coaling party in our forward hold. We need eyes everywhere this morning.'

He turned to greet the perspiring Wildermuth. 'Ah, Wildermuth,

153

you have a command as from now. Come with me to the chart-table and I will write you your orders and give you a series of rendezvous for the next few weeks.'

As he passed Heuss he clapped him lightly on the shoulder. 'You have changed feelings now, perhaps? War is a little different when you can reach it at arm's length! It is not quite so humane and heroic as watching your enemy through a prismatic range-finder or a powerful telescope. That is the clean way to fight. Unfortunately, war demands that sooner or later we must dirty our hands a little!'

Heuss staggered down the ladder and cannoned into Ebert, who was supervising the rigging of another small derrick. He grinned, and wiped the coal-dust from his teeth. 'Ah, Emil! The hero returns! That was a nice bit of shooting you did!'

'Shooting?' His face hardened with pain. 'I killed a man with an axe!'

Ebert shrugged. 'Well, he didn't kill *you*, my friend, that is one thing. And I was saved from sending you to the grave too early!'

Heuss stared at him. 'What do you mean?'

Ebert grinned wider. 'When that fellow shot out our searchlight, von Steiger was not sure if you could stop that madman from getting to the wireless. So he ordered me to open fire on the collier's bridge with three machine guns!'

Heuss gripped his arm, his eyes wild. 'You're joking? You must be! Even von Steiger would not fire on his own men!'

Ebert sighed and turned back to his derrick. 'My friend, I like you very much. But if it meant saving this ship and the rest of the crew, I would have ordered my men to fire!' He laughed. 'But, you see, you surprised us all!'

.   .   .   .   .

The gaping hatch over the hold, which had first appeared like a grey rectangle above which the clouds moved in unbroken formation, was almost hidden in the swirling mists of dust, and in the shifting slopes of coal the men hacked and dug like victims in hell.

In the centre of the hold the sacks waited to be filled, but even as they were packed with the slippery, stubborn coal, and the men holding them cursed at their comrades for using their knife-edged shovels too freely, another hoist would swing hungrily through the filth and set them working more desperately than before. On deck, and even in the hold, it had been bitterly cold, but now, sweating and groaning with their efforts, the men were working stripped to the waist, their bodies grotesque and steaming with grime and filth. In their black faces their eyes glinted white and distorted, and their breath rasped painfully with each gulp for air.

'Get a move on down there! Work, you lazy pigs!' The harsh voice echoed and rebounded around their iron prison, but even Schiller was too weary to reply. His great barrel-chest heaved and panted with each vicious swing of his shovel, and his matted hair was streaked with black dust and sweat. He lurched drunkenly across to Pieck's small figure, which was crouched astride the sacks, his hands holding one open in readiness. Schiller hurled the load into the sack and paused, wheezing, on his shovel.

'All right, Willi?' He squinted through the blinding dust. 'God, why don't you take that damned jacket off? You'll never get it clean after this, and you'll need it for the next lot of work on deck!'

Pieck shook his head and held on grimly to the sack. 'No, it's all right,' he panted. 'I can manage!'

Petty Officer Brandt shouted again, 'Get moving, or I'll log the lot of you!'

Schiller swore and lashed out again at the shifting bank of coal. 'Bastard! I'll carve your face for you!'

Petty Officer Weiss, stripped like the others, reeled past them, his face contorted with pain. 'God damn this coal! I nearly crushed my foot!'

Schiller laughed. 'Good! I hope you choke yourself!'

The shovels rang, and the winches rattled and squeaked. Out of the black sky the empty hoists hovered and swung, always empty, always waiting to be filled with full bags.

Lieutenant Heuss shaded his sore eyes against the flying dust and watched the sullen column of prisoners being escorted aft along the collier's deck. Fifty less mouths for the *Vulkan* to feed. He pushed his way ahead to the shelter of the raider's fo'c'sle and stood looking down at the ant-like activity. It was still only an hour since the two ships had linked together, and yet the level of coal in the two forward holds had risen considerably and was even visible from his position in the bows. His ears were deadened by the din, and his mouth was thick with the dust, which, driven by the wind and laced with spray, had turned the *Vulkan*'s white bridge into a wall of streaked dirt. All that and more would have to be washed down before the men could rest.

He tried not to think about Ebert's remarks, but like a drill they worked into his aching brain. Von Steiger would have killed him if necessary. Would have swept the collier's bridge at a range of less than fifty yards with three machine guns. He closed his eyes and tried to think instead of the girl. He would see her as soon as he could. She at least would help him to forget the horror of the hand-to-hand struggle.

Von Steiger had been so matter-of-fact. He had been laughing at him. He had as good as said outright that Heuss now knew what it was like to control a ship for a few mere hours and have the decision of life and death to consider at first hand. He was not human. He was up there now on the wing of the bridge, watching them all. He had got his collier, and had held on to it. Yet even now he was issuing orders, making plans and still keeping his eye on both ships at once.

Heuss pulled his cap over his eyes, and walked to the edge of the hold and squinted down at the toiling men who hurled the empty bags aside and spread the new coal evenly around them with rakes and makeshift wooden trimmers. Like animals, he thought. Their skins shone like ebony, and their hands glinted with droplets of blood from broken blisters and the jagged cruelty of the black flood.

Wildermuth had the collier to worry about now, and good luck to him. With his two petty officers and twenty men he would be responsible for a ship over half full of coal and packed with prisoners. If he could keep clear of the shipping lanes as directed, and stay out of trouble, it might not be too bad for him. But if he lost control of that lot he could expect little mercy, either from the prisoners or from von Steiger when he found them again.

A whistle shrilled from the bridge, and the sound of shovels died away. The men were too beaten and winded to ask the reason for this unexpected rest, and merely leaned on their shovels or against the grimed bulwarks, their eyes closed and their chests heaving. The silence hung over the two ships once more, and left only the sea and the protesting groans of the two grinding hulls.

Dehler looked up, his face angry. 'They don't need a rest, Captain! There's much more to shift yet!'

156

Von Steiger had a megaphone in his hands and directed his voice to Wildermuth, who stood solidly on the collier's bridge. 'There is a ship on our starboard quarter. A big one. It might be an armed merchant cruiser! Range about eight miles, I think. Cast off immediately and proceed at full speed! Carry on, Lieutenant Dehler, stand by to let go, and clear our men off that collier!'

The whistle blasted again, and a different kind of activity commenced. Blackened, half-naked figures scrambled across the bulwarks, their bodies already shivering in their cold sweat, and dazed by this sudden change of events. Blistered hands fumbled with ropes and unhooked purchases, and all the time the officers shouted and cursed at them from every angle. It was as if the two ships were now reluctant to part, and every job took twice as long to complete. The half-blinded, gasping seamen had to be led to their stations and have their hands put on the necessary ropes ready for letting go.

Dehler peered anxiously along the confused deck and tried to estimate the degree of readiness. 'Let go breasts!' He was committed now. There was a sense of urgency in von Steiger's voice. Dehler raised his hand. 'Let go!' He swore at the delays. 'Let go springs!'

The men ran like puppets, heads down, heaving on the wet, gritty ropes. The headrope went next, but for another agonizing minute the two ships swayed and thundered together, and then a sliver of trapped spray rose over the rail and the collier began to idle clear. Her sides were streaked and scraped, and in several places, where the German ship had struck her really hard, her rusty plates were buckled and bare.

Telegraphs jangled, and at the collier's stern a mounting white froth beat the waves with urgent haste.

A whistle shrilled from the *Vulkan*'s poop, and Lieutenant Kohler gesticulated wildly at the bridge. 'The sternrope! It's jammed, sir! It's snared on the collier's deck!'

9

SIMON GELB stood beneath the overhanging boatdeck and studied the feverish preparations going on about him. He was cold and hungry, yet, because of the air of uncertainty which had disrupted his new existence, he was unwilling to return to the stifling shelter of the prisoners' quarters. The wind was whipping across the unprotected decks below him, and the coal-dust moved along the wet planking like black sand, making curious designs around the scurrying figures of the German seamen. He could not take his eyes off the other ship which lay lashed alongside, and now that a sudden order to cast off had been shouted from the *Vulkan*'s bridge and repeated by the harassed petty officers stationed across both vessels, a new sense of urgency made him apprehensive and uneasy.

He had seen the marching column of British merchant seamen escorted past, and had watched stores being carried rapidly across the heaving decks from hand to hand. He had expected to be taken across to the collier with the others, but nobody had shown the slightest interest in him or Arthur Brett, while the British officer prisoners had already been taken below again in addition to the newcomers from the collier.

He eyed the single seaman who had been left to guard him. A short, swarthy-faced man, with a heavy Mauser slung over his shoulder, he looked pleased with himself, no doubt because he was being spared the agony of coaling ship. Gelb had questioned him in English, but the man had merely shrugged, and then, when Gelb had persisted, had scowled threateningly and gestured at him to keep away from the maindeck.

Arthur Brett, who was being allowed to take his exercise with him, moved restlessly from one side of the boatdeck to the other. His hair was tousled by the wind and spray, and his pale cheeks were streaked with coal-dust. Gelb sighed. It was difficult to know what the man was thinking. He had gone completely to pieces in his new surroundings, and yet managed to stay aloof from him and the others. He did not even seem to be curious about how his wife was faring, and now that another ship had come from nowhere he could not, it seemed, think of anything but that. He paused by Gelb's bulky shape, his eyes desperate.

'What in heaven's name *is* going on? Why are they casting off from that ship, after taking such pains to get near to it?'

Gelb shrugged. 'It seems *another* ship has been sighted. Maybe they are going to attack it. Or perhaps they merely want to run away!'

Ropes were flying through the air, and wild-eyed seamen, their naked shoulders streaked with sweat and dirt, stumbled past them, unseeing and urgent.

Gelb swallowed hard. All at once it was quite clear to him what he should do. Brett was out of place here, and, once torn from his world of false values and meaningless platitudes, was not only useless, but a real danger to their safety. Keeping his voice level he said: 'I heard a sailor say that the prisoners have been taken to that ship so that they can be repatriated. Aboard here they will eat too much and hamper the crew. Soon they will be safe and sound in some neutral ship, or landed in a nice South American port.' He watched the last colour draining from the man's face. 'The Captain must think that we are too valuable to lose, eh? He will take us back to Germany with the captured officers!'

Brett grasped a steel rail and gripped it with all his strength. His eyes seemed to protrude right out of his head, and he stared down at the collier with disbelief. 'They wouldn't! It's unfair!' His voice cracked. 'Why should this happen to me?'

Gelb was shocked by the success of his lie. Unable to restrain himself, he said: 'Why not? The German Army shot nuns in Belgium, I hear, because they thought they were spies! Outrageous, of course, and I expect they apologized afterwards, but in a war like this the individual is a mere trifle!'

Brett took a pace towards the short ladder which led to the main-deck. His lips were slack, and he seemed to have difficulty in breathing.

With horrified eyes he saw the foremost line whipped aboard, and after a short pause the two ships began to stagger apart. Inches, then feet, and then he saw the tossing water surging up between the two fo'c'sles.

The sentry was watching the other ship with interest and did not look round until it was too late. Brett turned towards his companion, his taut face suddenly determined. 'I am going across to that ship! I must!' He pushed past Gelb, his mouth working quickly. 'Explain to my wife! She will understand!' Then he was running wildly along the slippery deck, his shoes skidding on the littered ropes and discarded shovels.

Gelb watched him go, his face frozen with excitement.

The sentry gaped down at the deck, his jaw dropping. 'Achtung! Halt!' He fumbled with his rifle sling, and then called again towards the seamen by the rail. They all had their backs to the running figure, and they were too weary to take their eyes from the collier as it moved clear.

A whistle shrilled from aft, and like a steel bar the sternrope jerked tightly against the poop fairleads, scattering the labouring men like skittles. The ship gave a great lurch, and seemed to hang suspended and helpless on the trapped rope.

Von Steiger leaned over the bridge rail and stared for a long moment at the stout rope. If he did not act at once, either the two ships would swing stern on together, or the rope would part and probably be sucked into the screw of one of them. He cursed silently and called over his shoulder: 'Hard a-starboard! Full ahead!'

The sudden clockwise turning of the great screw would tend to swing the bows to port and back alongside the collier. It would mean quite a collision, but only that way could his men on the poop clear the rope. It was a massive rope and it would take too long to cut it through, even if they had axes available.

The *Vulkan* gave a tremendous shudder, and the poop seemed to rise clear of the water in response to the sudden burst of power. From dead slow to full speed made every piece of the hull groan and kick in protest, but almost immediately he saw the action take effect.

Men were running with the lacerated fenders to take the unavoidable impact, while on the poop Kohler and his men waited to slacken off their end of the rope, so that the men on the collier could release it.

The rope acted like a giant hinge, on which the two vessels were inexorably drawn towards each other.

'Stop engine!' His attention was momentarily distracted by an armed sentry running crazily along the deck beneath him. What was the fool doing? He braced his body against the rail and waited for the shock of impact.

There was a tremendous crash, and he felt his fingers torn free from the rail. The momentum of the charging ship carried her cleanly along the collier's low fo'c'sle, smashing down a small derrick and tearing her starboard anchor completely from its hawsepipe.

As the *Vulkan*'s angry advance was momentarily slowed the stern-rope was released, and the dazed seamen on the poop plucked the dripping coils free from the sea and up on to the deck.

Von Steiger heard a chorus of shouts, and stared with disbelief at the figure silhouetted against the collier's white bridge. Arthur Brett stood swaying on the *Vulkan*'s bulwark, his arms reaching for support as the collier lurched and squeaked past him.

The breathless sentry had almost reached him, but, impeded by his rifle, was unable to climb fast enough to stop him.

Brett glanced once over his shoulder at the running men and clutch-ing fingers, and then jumped outwards and down towards the rusty deck of the collier. There was a single wire guardrail along the top of her bulwark, over which Heuss and his men had clambered the previous night. Brett's hands closed on it with relief, and his kicking feet groped vainly for a hold on the battered plates and scarred rivets beneath him.

As the sternrope was freed the Coxswain applied opposite wheel, and unwillingly the *Vulkan* began to sidle clear from the other ship. As she gathered way she seemed to brush almost gently against her for the last time, the full weight of her four and a half thousand tons nudging into Brett's body like a giant's hand upon a fly. When they were finally clear there was only a scarlet smudge down the collier's black paint to show where he had been, and that, too, was already fading beneath the spray and broken water.

Von Steiger stared back at the collier, his face filled with dismay.

All at once it started to pour with rain. It advanced across the tossing water towards the ship like a steel fence, and as it swept across the raider's decks and drenched the shivering seamen, and cascaded into the still-gaping holds, the collier vanished behind its protection, and soon there was nothing to be seen at all but the tumbling wave-tops quivering beneath the torrential downpour, and the mounting bow-wave as the *Vulkan*'s sharp stem gathered way once more.

.　　.　　.　　.　　.

The sentry in the narrow passageway crashed his heels together and held his rifle stiffly to his side. He did not relax a muscle until von Steiger had passed him and entered the lobby of his day cabin. Von Steiger paused with his hand resting on the handle, aware that he was more than just apprehensive about seeing Caryl Brett. He felt again at a disadvantage; it was curious how he always felt that way when he saw or spoke to her. She always put him on the defensive, whatever his own private convictions might have been, and this time it would be worse. He tried to tell himself that he was being stupid and over-wrought, and that it did not matter what she thought of him and his actions. He need not even see her. In fact, he had sent Heuss down from the bridge earlier to tell her of her husband's death, and even then had known that he was looking for a way out, an escape. He had sat brooding on the bridge as the ship gathered speed beneath him, and the decks bustled with frantic activity as the men were driven like exhausted animals to secure hatches and lash down booms and derricks, and all the time he had been thinking of Heuss and the woman below. The lookouts had been unable to see the other vessel, but the wireless room had picked up some faint signals, which appeared to be in code. He had forced his tired mind to concentrate, and had even endeavoured to placate himself with the thought that he had been able to get coal for his ship, in spite of doubts and disbelief and the incredulity of others.

His fingers closed over the door-handle, and without knocking he stepped quickly into the cabin. The three figures by the table froze at his unexpected entrance, and he studied them gravely without speaking. The cabin, warm and inviting, looked pleased with itself, he thought. The steel deadlights were clamped across the scuttles, and across them the velvet curtains had been pulled into place. Caryl Brett sat at the end of the table, facing him, her hands invisible in her lap. Heuss had risen to his feet, and von Steiger saw with sudden irritation that Simon Gelb was sitting on the woman's right.

162

He made a short half-bow and tucked his cap under his arm. He noticed that the girl had rearranged her hair, and was wearing a white, high-necked blouse. She looked quite different from the loose-haired girl he had expected, and it unnerved him. Although her eyes looked a little red, she seemed composed, even cool, and as he moved towards her he saw the small chin lift imperceptibly with defiance.

'I would have wished that I could have come earlier,' he said slowly, 'but I hope my officer explained what happened?' She did not answer, and he felt his gaze drawn to her eyes. Deep and green, they seemed to hold him mesmerized. It was as if they belonged to another being. Someone else who was peering at him through this calm, expressionless mask. He tried to dismiss the fantasy, and continued evenly: 'You must understand that there was nothing we could do to save him. He acted, I imagine, on a sudden impulse. It was all over very quickly.'

Gelb stirred for the first time. He had sat watching the Captain, his dark face almost entranced by his unheralded appearance. He stared up at the slight, almost youthful, figure, his deep eyes taking in the salt-stained jacket and faded medal-ribbons, and, above all, the black cross about his neck. He saw the neat brown hands twitch momentarily, and he marvelled that a man like von Steiger could betray any emotion. After a quick flicker of an eye towards the others, he decided that he alone had noticed it. The girl was too shocked, and the Lieutenant too overawed by the presence of his superior, to see anything. He said softly: 'He told me prior to his death that he was afraid. He would not tell me much, he was too proud, but he did say that someone aboard this ship had threatened him in some way.'

They all turned to look at him, their expressions as mixed as the thoughts which Gelb's lie had aroused.

Von Steiger eyed him coldly. 'Why did you not tell someone of this?'

'He told me to say nothing. I think he was afraid for his wife's safety.'

Heuss stared down at him with contempt. 'You are making this up! Who would want to threaten him? The poor fellow merely wanted to get aboard the collier for some other reason, not to escape!'

Gelb dropped his eyes to hide the triumph. 'As I said, Lieutenant, he told me but little. Of course, if somebody on board wanted him out of the way, perhaps so that he could try to interfere with this dear girl, then maybe that person might use threats against her husband, eh?'

'That's enough, please!' Caryl Brett spoke quietly. 'I don't want to hear any more suppositions from anybody! Arthur's dead. He can never be brought back by anything we say.' The eyes returned to von Steiger. 'Is that all you wished to say, Captain? That you are sorry? Always you seem to be apologizing. If your deeds are disgusting and treacherous, your manners at least are impeccable!'

Heuss caught his breath and darted a glance at von Steiger. She had gone too far this time. He stared at his captain in amazement. Instead of anger, there was something quite new on his quiet face. It was as if some door had been opened in his mind, and that some nagging worry had been part cleared.

Von Steiger answered, 'I hate to see civilians involved in the matter of war.' He paused, listening to the whine of the fans and the steady thunder of the engine. 'Everything has changed in this war. There is no longer security or isolation for anyone. The world is in flames about us.'

'I understand about war, Captain. But do you really call this a way to fight it? You slink about the sea like a pirate. You kill and maim without mercy!'

'You have had a severe shock, and I admire your self-control. For that reason I will ignore what you have already said.' Von Steiger stared across her head at the picture of his son on the far bulkhead. He tried to use it as an anchor, as something to hold down his self-control. He heard himself say: 'You British always talk so freely about the injustices of others! You never stop to think that *you* have everything! Yet you still want the world at your feet! I am a seaman, and a German officer, and although I loathe and detest this war and what it is doing to all of us, I will never turn my back on my duty!' He leaned forward, his eyes flashing with mounting anger. 'Do you imagine that my men enjoy being here? Do you think *they* find satisfaction in bad food and constant danger? Just because they wear uniform, it does not mean that they have no other life!' He waved his hand around the cabin, embracing the ship and the black water beyond. 'They have wives and children, too! And they are being made to fight for them. It is as simple as that!' He pointed suddenly at Heuss, yet remained staring down at the girl. 'Yesterday I would have killed this officer in order to save

164

my ship! Yes, I would have killed him, although I value him greatly. And I may have to sacrifice every last man aboard before I am through, but, in the name of God, do not imagine for one small moment that I am enjoying it!'

He stopped speaking and stood with his chest heaving uncontrollably. His eyes were low now, and he was aware that the others were staring at him, shocked by his outburst. All the pent-up anxieties had been too much for him. He knew that he had been waiting for this opportunity, or perhaps this audience, and he felt unsteady and yet elated.

He suddenly raised his head and looked once more at the girl. Her eyes, which had fixed him with that rebuking, contemptuous stare, were empty, yet there was something more. He studied her with new interest as the realization came to him. He cursed himself for not recognizing it earlier. She was afraid, desperately afraid. Perhaps not of him, but of the new meaning of complete loneliness which Brett's death had shown to her. He jerked his head. 'Take this man to his quarters, Lieutenant.' He waited, counting seconds, as Heuss moved unwillingly round the table.

He thought: God, this Gelb is cleverer than all of us with his cunning insinuations. Even if what he said was true, he would not have spoken as he did without some other reason, it is not in his make-up.

Gelb moved slowly towards the door. 'I shall see you again, my dear.' His voice was heavy with sadness. His sympathy seemed to throw a protective wall between her and the two officers. 'I shall be thinking of you all the time!'

The door closed, and he realized that he was alone with his prisoner. He forced himself to sit opposite her, and saw her eyes guardedly watching his hands as he groped for a cheroot. He lighted it carefully and dropped the match in a brass ashtray.

'Why have you stayed, Captain?' She sounded puzzled, like a child, yet with the constant wariness of a defenceless woman.

He smiled. 'I wanted to talk. You see, in spite of what you said about me, I know that you do not really believe it. I am merely the emblem for your hatred, a figurehead. With those who fight their war from behind a desk or through a bank account the emblem might be a flag, or a strange language. Unfortunately, the closer we get to war the more we discover that it is human, as well as inhuman.'

165

'Go on. I cannot ask you to leave your own quarters, anyway!' He saw her lip tremble slightly before she controlled it with an obvious effort.

'No, that is true. But you speak freely here, simply because you think you are safe with me. That is so, eh?' His mouth turned down with self-mockery. 'Because I am a man of honour?' He waved his hand wearily. 'You are right. I am safe enough. But you must not be too brutal in your accusations. Your husband is dead. I do not think he was a happy man, and I think he was twisted within himself.'

A glow of the old defiance showed itself in a small flush on her cheeks. 'How could you understand a man like him? He was above your world completely. He was a builder, not a destroyer!'

Von Steiger eyed her calmly. 'He was a fool, Frau Brett! I read right through his papers, and was amazed that he could delude others as well as himself, apparently, with such rubbish!' His eyes followed her as she rose from the table and moved quickly towards the sideboard. 'His theories were fine, but they were *only* theories. I felt that when he composed his opinions he was thinking more of his own advancement. Believe me, I would not say this to you so soon after his death, but for my anxiety for you!'

She turned towards him, and he was able to see that her eyes were filled with tears.

'What do you want, Captain? Was Gelb right, after all? Were you the man he spoke of?' Her voice trembled. 'Why do you try to tell me these things about my own husband? Surely I knew him better than you.' She passed the back of her hand across her forehead. 'I failed him in many ways I know, but I understood him, too!'

Von Steiger shrugged. 'I cannot think of you as failing *anyone* who needed you.'

She stared at him in surprise, the tears shining unheeded on her face. 'What a curious man you are!'

He stood up. 'I shall leave you now. If you need anything, let me know. And if anyone tries to molest you in any way, send a message with my steward.'

She watched him play uncertainly with the peak of his cap, and felt the loneliness close in towards her with each step he took towards the door. Yet she knew she must be on her own to recover her self-esteem. It had been inevitable that she should stand up against von Steiger, just as Arthur's death was unavoidable. She could not place her racing thoughts in order, nor could she bring herself to realize the finality of her position.

She heard him ask in that same level, polite voice, 'Are your parents waiting in England?'

She shook her head, and the completeness of her isolation had moved in one more pace. He stared at her from across the full length of the cabin. With each quiet question he seemed to strip her of her defences, and she felt she could no longer fight him. 'No, they are in India. They did not approve of Arthur, you see.'

He nodded gravely. 'Try to get some sleep. I shall put you aboard the first neutral ship I can find. I think you have seen enough of this war!'

She swallowed, and wanted to scream at him: What do you know about me? You are playing with me because you, too, are alone and need someone to impress, and to be near you when you are empty inside. You think I am afraid because I am your prisoner, but you are wrong. It is because we are so much alike that I am afraid. Not only of you, but of myself!

She watched the door close and sank wearily on to the settee. For a long while she stared at the pigskin briefcase containing Arthur's precious papers, her fingers moving restlessly over the gold initials. She wanted to cry, but the tears would not return. She searched her heart for grief, but was horrified to find that there was only guilt.

·　　·　　·　　·　　·　　·

Max Damrosch quietly closed the sliding door of his small cabin behind him and stood momentarily staring at his neat bunk, inviting beneath the intimate glow of his reading lamp. As the chill of the wind drained from his glowing cheeks, and the cabin's snug warmth enfolded him in what seemed like an embrace, he forced himself away from the door and began to peel off his clothes. A few minutes past midnight, and after four hours of strain and concentration on the First Watch this was the greatest pleasure of the day. The almost sensual feeling of luxury and well-being as he removed his oilskin and bridge-coat, and with difficulty tugged off his long leather boots. The heavy motion of the ship played with his tired legs, so that he swayed slowly across the tiny carpet, the effort of removing the rest of his uniform making him revolve in a grotesque dance. He sipped at the mug of coffee he had carefully carried down from the night galley, and peered at his dim reflection in the mirror. His cheeks looked hollow, he thought, and his hair seemed long and unkempt. He stripped off the rest of his clothes and stood naked before the mirror, his face critical yet pleased with his firm body. At first he had been worried about the stories he had heard of sea sores and salt-water boils, of scurvy and unaccountable swellings, which were said to be caused by tinned food and rancid vegetables. He grinned at himself and sat heavily on the prickly blanket of his bunk. He wondered what his mother would say if she could see her son now. His smile faded as he tried to remember how she had looked. He tried to recapture the peace and serenity of his home, but could not form a clear picture. He saw the dark wood of old furniture, and through the wide glass doors beyond his father's library the nodding beauty of the flowers and green lawn. He felt his eyelids droop, and lifted his bare knees to his chin.

I wonder if I am becoming a good officer. I did not turn away this morning when the Englishman, Brett, was smashed between the ships. Was it because it was so sudden and I did not have the agony of waiting, like that nightmare with the lifeboat? Or was it simply that I am getting matured by the hardness of my companions? As a young cadet he had formed many pictures of the war at sea and of life in the Imperial Navy. In the training ship and at the barracks he had been taught everything about tradition and naval history, of how to treat the men of the lower deck, and the finer points of discipline and obedience. In the spartan, almost sadistic, existence of those days he had learned a lot, but at no time was he ever told that any sort of personal life went on aboard any warship, let alone in the dangerous routine of a commerce raider. It was as if the ship and crew should have been as one, with only a godlike captain who could show opinion or understanding. Even a captain should be too dedicated, too perfect, to be swayed by either prejudice or personal beliefs. He drank the last of the lukewarm coffee, and listened to the pounding of the engine.

Inside this hull, he thought, there are men like myself. Not just a soulless crew without thoughts or fears, but men of all sorts. Right now, as I sit on my bunk, savouring the moment of sleep, they are all around me. Dreaming, or thinking worried thoughts. Arguing, maybe even discussing me, or playing cards. Others are stoking the boilers and just holding on to the picture of sleep and rest. It is strange I have never thought of them all as people before. Just officers and crew.

There was a sudden thud against the door, and as he looked up it scraped to one side to reveal Heuss, a bottle in either hand. Without speaking, he lurched into the cabin and kicked the door closed with his foot. He stood blinking at the light and peering uncomprehendingly at Damrosch's nakedness. He was quite drunk.

'I have come to share my drinks with you, Max!' He placed the bottles on the table with exaggerated caution and rummaged in the locker for glasses. Over his shoulder he added vaguely: 'Must drink with somebody. Go mad staring at the blasted cabin walls!'

Damrosch slithered hurriedly between the blankets, his astonished eyes fixed on the other man's stooped shoulders. It was incredible to see Heuss like this. He was muttering to himself and holding the glasses up to the light with unsteady concentration.

'Got to be clean, Max! Most important! Too damned good to waste!'

'Shouldn't you be on watch, Emil?' Damrosch was cautious. He could not imagine what had made Heuss act like this. 'You always have the Middle Watch. What's got into you?'

Heuss chuckled. 'Our Captain, overcome with remorse no doubt, said I could leave the watch to poor Karl Ebert and to him.' He belched, and stared down at Damrosch, as if seeing him for the first time. 'God, you sleep like a heathen! What it is to be young and fit!'

'Seriously, Emil, did the Captain really say he would stand your watch?'

'I would not lie to you!' He frowned with sudden severity. 'He thought I had done enough last night aboard the collier and needed a rest! And I imagine *he* has thoughts on his mind tonight, too!' He swore savagely as he lost his balance and sat heavily on the bunk. He was still wearing his bridge-coat, and his face looked lined with weariness. He poured a full measure into each glass and handed one to Damrosch. 'Here, try some of this, my friend.' He gave a conspiratorial wink. 'The real stuff!'

Damrosch sipped and then coughed violently, feeling the neat spirit burn his unprepared throat. He peered round Heuss's slumped shoulders. 'What was that?'

'White Horse whisky!' He gave an unsteady laugh. 'Got four more bottles off that Britisher, so drink up and let's console each other!' In another, strange, voice he added half to himself: 'Drink deep. Drink away the stain, the bloody stain!'

'I think you had better go to bed, Emil. You're worn out. You don't know what you're saying!' He tried to grin. 'I'm damn' tired, if you're not!'

Heuss turned his face towards him and Damrosch was shocked to see the deep maniacal gleam in the brown eyes.

'If you send me away, Max, I shall drink all the whisky myself! All of it, do you hear?'

'Here, calm down! The whole ship will hear you in a minute!' He smiled ruefully and held out his glass. 'All right, Emil. If I must get drunk for the first time, it might as well be in bed!'

Heuss studied him seriously and then laughed. 'Spoken like a true Prussian! Just think, all that whisky, and the war's been on for four years! The Tommies must be rolling in the stuff!'

He leaned back against the hump of Damrosch's knees and sighed. 'I have been drinking this blessed nectar for twenty-four hours. Last night I tried to get drunk, but couldn't. This morning I tried again, so that I could report to von Steiger that I was as sodden as a . . . as a . . .' He groped vaguely for a word. 'And tell him what I thought of him and the whole damn' ship!' He ruffled Damrosch's hair with affection. 'Except you, of course. You're too young and innocent to be so damned awkward yet!'

He slopped more whisky into the glasses, his face set with concentration. 'But I simply could not get drunk. Just vacant, like a damned country bumpkin! What do you make of it all, Max?' He did not wait for an answer. 'We're all changing, have you noticed?'

'In what way?'

'All changing,' he repeated, his voice growing thicker. 'At first I thought the Captain was trying to escape from the war and the misery of losing his wife. *We* were the heroes, the glory-seekers!' He laughed, as if seeing himself in his words. 'Look at us now! All plotting and scheming amongst ourselves because we don't like the war any more. People get hurt in war, and we don't like it! Christ, what's come over us!' His voice rose to a despairing shout.

'You are letting your imagination run away with you.'

'I wish I could!' He gripped his wrist. 'Max, last night I killed a man!'
Damrosch shifted beneath his powerful grip. 'I know, Emil. I heard about it.'

Heuss stared at him. 'So what did you hear? That I just killed an enemy?' He stood up and groped for the bottle. 'A big, bald-headed man. I smashed his head in with a fire-axe!' He shook with hysterical laughter, reliving the nightmare once more. 'Can you imagine that, eh? Me, the centre of every wardroom scandal, the life and soul of the Navy's genteel society, transformed in two seconds into a savage beast!'

'You had to do it. It might have been you!'

'By God, I wish it had!' He hung on to an overhead pipe with his two hands, his eyes glazed and no longer focusing. 'My life was bad enough before. It is double the hell now!' He groped for his glass and downed it with one swallow. 'Here's to the *Vulkan*! That was your toast, wasn't it? Well, here's to it!' His shadow danced across the cabin like a spectre. 'Vulkan, God of Fire!' He laughed, a short, bitter sound. 'It should have been God of Lust!'

Damrosch looked anxiously at the other full bottle. 'Please go to bed, Emil. If anything happened now, Action Stations or something like that, what would you do?'

'Do? I should go to sleep! Sleep, and tomorrow face von Steiger's firing squad with nothing but White Horse whisky on my mind!'

He sat down again, the strength gone from his legs. His voice was unexpectedly sober. 'I am in real trouble, Max, and that is God's truth!'

Damrosch stiffened. What the hell was he talking about? What had he done now?

'I have betrayed my trust, Max!' He stared at Damrosch's incredulous face. 'My oath of allegiance!' He rolled suddenly on to the floor, his head crashing against the table. Without changing his tone he continued: 'I have fallen for that damned English girl! I am so crazy about her that I cannot think straight!' He focused his eyes angrily towards the bunk above him. Damrosch had fallen back on his pillow, his face convulsed with laughter and relief.

'Oh, Emil! You had me worried then!' He gave another choking laugh. 'I thought you had done something really serious!'

Heuss ground his teeth. 'Damn your eyes, it *is* serious!'

'I am sorry I laughed. It was the whisky! But you really are imagining things. You have been away from intellectual companionship for so long that you are torturing yourself with fantasy!'

'It's not so. Don't you think she is lovely?' His angry red eyes were fixed with desperation on Damrosch's face.

'Of course. She is lovely. When I saw her in the lifeboat,' his face became quiet and grave, 'I thought even then that she was the most beautiful creature I had ever seen. Against all that filth and carnage, she was still beautiful enough to be noticed as a woman.' He swallowed with sudden embarrassment and tried to laugh. 'But you would be in love with *any* girl who came aboard, Emil! Even if she was a negress, or as ugly as sin!'

'No! This is real! I tell you I am going mad!' He tried to lever himself up but slithered back on the deck. 'Get me another drink, damn you!'

'You haven't told anyone else?'

'Of course not!' He was twisting his head to watch the bottle as Damrosch leaned out of the bunk to refill the glasses. 'Do you think I want *more* trouble?'

He grunted with frustrated anger as the spirit slopped over his chin. 'I think about her all the time. I try to be rational and to ignore my thoughts, but it only gets worse!'

'You might feel different tomorrow.'

'Tomorrow! I do not want any more shocks, Max. I have had my fill! Killing that man, and then finding out that von Steiger was about to slaughter me, that has been enough, I can tell you!' He lay back, his eyes closed, and Damrosch thought he had passed out. But his lips moved. 'Von Steiger is not human. I have never met anyone like him in my life, Max!'

'I agree with you there. I had heard so much about him. You know the sort of things we were told. The Sea Wolf, or the Tiger of the Seas, and all those other things that are said about him. But he's more than that.'

Heuss groaned. 'Enough! I cannot stand any more!'

'No, really! He is just a man, and yet, because of his strange, remote manner, he seems all the more unreal!'

'Unreal? You've hit it, my friend! He just stood there like a cadet in front of an instructor. Meek as you please. You should have seen him! She was defying him, goading him to destroy her like her husband, I think, and he just stood there and took it! He was almost humble for a moment.'

'Well, that's what I meant!' The whisky was having its effect, and both their voices were thicker and louder.

Heuss sounded despairing. 'I wish I could go to her cabin now! Tell her what I think about her, and see what she says about that!'

'Well, why don't you? Apart from the fact that you'd be arrested by the officer-of-the-watch for attempted rape!'

Heuss ignored him. 'But if she turned on me like she did on von Steiger, I know I could not accept it. It would finish me completely!'

There was a loud banging on the cabin partition, and Damrosch grinned sheepishly. Niklas, the Chief Engineer, had been awakened by their voices. He rolled on his side to remonstrate with Heuss, but saw with relief that he had fallen asleep. He lay on the frayed carpet as if crucified, his face already relaxed.

.　　　.　　　.　　　.　　　.

Simon Gelb sat in the darkness of the prisoners' quarters and watched the glow of a cigarette a few feet from his face. Captain Mason of the captured collier *Nemesis*, a lean, hard man, used to the authority needed to drive a native crew to any quarter of the globe in peace or war, grunted and propped himself on his elbows. He forced himself to listen to the tough, jaunty Londoner, who somehow seemed to have taken over command of the occupants in the locked hold. Around him the other prisoners tossed and groaned in their uneasy sleep, or lay like corpses in the tiered bunks.

Gelb was saying: 'Von Steiger must have made a series of rendezvous for the future, eh? Your old ship will be quite valuable, I expect?'

Mason stirred angrily, the pain of losing his collier returning with each of Gelb's words. 'I expect so,' he answered grudgingly.

Gelb's big hands glowed faintly in the light from a tiny blue lamp. 'If we could find out those meeting places, or get Mrs. Brett to find out something, we might get our own back on these ruddy square-heads.'

Mason still frowned. 'What the hell for?'

Gelb controlled his impatience with mounting irritation. Mason was like all professional seamen, he thought. No time for anybody who earned his bread on dry land.

'I have heard it said that the wounded and some of the prisoners, seamen and the like, will be landed, or maybe put in a neutral ship.' He felt Mason stir with interest, and sighed. 'If we get this information and pass it to one of those lucky men, it could be handed to the naval authorities or somebody like that, eh?'

Mason sat upright. 'By God, that's a damned good idea! I've had my fill of the bloody Jerries lately! I've been torpedoed and mined by them, and that's enough!' He rubbed his hands. 'So when von Steiger turns up to meet my old ship somewhere, he'll find instead a bloody great cruiser!' His voice showed his admiration. 'You are a dark horse, Gelb, and no mistake!'

Gelb smiled at the darkness. 'Can we trust your mate to join our little secret?'

'Jerry Cobb? Yes, he's a good bloke right enough. He'd be glad to get his own back!' He laughed quietly. 'Yes, Gelb, you *really* surprise me!'

Gelb moved towards his own bunk. 'Call me Simon, everyone else does,' he said affably.

. . . . .

Petty Officer Brandt ducked under the heavy canvas curtain which covered the entrance to the fo'c'sle and stood shaking the rain from his oilskin. He cursed as a small stream of water ran from his tilted cap and splashed across his unprotected neck. Middle Watch rounds were a waste of time, he thought savagely. The watch on deck were too scared to fall asleep at their posts, and too uncomfortable, in any case. And those below were all snoring their heads off by now. He eased the weight of his pistol on his hip, and listened to the wind howling across the deck outside. The ship was driving into a head sea, and the motion was not bad for the Atlantic in winter, he thought.

I would like to get my hands on whoever it was got me drafted to this ship. Must have been someone of influence whose poor little son I handled a bit roughly in the barracks. His lip curled contemptuously. They make me spew! Treat the Navy like dirt in peacetime, but come whining for victory as soon as things get bad. Seamen! These pampered civilian trash aren't ever likely to be that, but I'll make them see what a real man is like!

He stiffened, his alert ears detecting a small sound beneath his feet. He frowned, trying to trace the direction and substance of the sound. There it was again, like the movement of swilling water. He moved forward like a cat, his fingers feeling for the ladder which led to the deck below. Somebody was using the seamen's bath-space. They could not use fresh water, because it was turned off at the feed pump, but that was not the point. Nobody should be hanging about at this hour. He began to feel a bit better at the prospect of catching a man out, and he moved swiftly down the steel rungs and along the darkened passageway. A shaft of light shone from beneath the door at the far end, and he could hear the sound of a hose quite clearly now.

Brandt always found it easy to work himself into a rage. He could do it at any time and without effort, like giving a command, or shouting out a man's name. His face hardened as he flung open the door and glared with narrowed eyes at the single figure which stood transfixed on the tiled deck, a hose playing into a bucket containing a sodden piece of clothing.

Pieck stood quite still, his face ashen, as he stared at the petty officer. He could feel the water from the hose splashing against his foot, yet seemed powerless to move.

Brandt walked slowly round him without speaking. His quick eyes noted the coal scum in the water and the precious soap which the boy was using so freely to wash what appeared to be a seaman's working smock. He halted in front of him, his face without expression. Only his mouth moved, like the opening and closing of a tight trap.

'Well, Pieck? And what do you think you are doing here?' His voice was deceptively mild, almost caressing.

Pieck held his body rigid, his eyes trained at the top of Brandt's cap. 'Trying to clean this smock. I could not get the coal-dust out of it.'

'Don't you lie to me!' His voice was louder, and a small vein began to throb on his forehead. 'You were skulking away somewhere when the hands were cleaning ship and were too lazy to clean even yourself, isn't that it?' As Pieck began to reply, Brandt closed his eyes and screamed: 'Don't answer back! I have been watching you since you arrived from that detention barracks! I knew you for what you are, even if you *did* manage to deceive the officers! You are a useless, lazy, spoilt and lying little swine! Do you hear me?' Another thought came to him. 'And why were you wearing a smock when you were coaling ship? Afraid you might catch a cold in your precious little body? Answer me!' he roared.

'Yes, sir. I—I mean, no, sir!' He flinched as Brandt lifted his hand, but he was only readjusting his cap, and smiled sadistically to see Pieck's movement.

'It is time you stopped lying, Pieck! I have the rest of the Middle Watch, and longer, if necessary, to get at the truth.'

'I don't understand, sir!'

'You don't? Well, let me make myself clear. You are using the bath-space after lights-out, making a filthy mess, and you still persist in being insolent! Isn't that enough?'

Brandt was disappointed. Although the men were not expected to use this place after lights-out, as far as he knew there was no regulation in the ship's Standing Orders which made it a definite offence. But there was more to it. This shivering creature was hiding something more, he was sure of it. Shivering. . . . He smiled lazily.

'Take off your jacket, Pieck. Let me see if your body is still dirty as well! There *is* a regulation about personal cleanliness, you know. Or perhaps in your family they didn't wash at all!'

Pieck bit his lip until the skin broke and let the jacket fall from his bare shoulders. He tried to keep his back hidden from the petty officer, but had reckoned without the mirror behind him.

'Turn about! Quick, turn about!' Brandt stepped forward and stared incredulously at Pieck's pale skin. Across the shoulders and waist were six or more thin red weals. He could see the boy trembling now, and felt an excitement rising within him. Keeping his voice even he said: 'What are these? How did you get them?'

'I fell over, sir. I fell in the hold this morning.'

This time Brandt did hit him. With the edge of his glove he slashed him sharply across the most recent of the marks. 'Where did you get them?' He was shouting now. Already he knew or guessed that these marks were something to do with Lieutenant Kohler, and were indirectly connected with that incident when Alder had frightened the woman prisoner. He shouted again: 'This is the last time, Pieck! Who gave you those marks?'

There was a long silence, and Pieck stood swaying in the puddle of water, his jacket lying unheeded on the deck.

Brandt was breathing heavily. Suppose he took Pieck to the officer-of-the-watch? He rejected the idea immediately. It would finish Kohler, of course, but the Officer Corps would never forgive him. He would be a marked man for bringing discredit upon one of the Kaiser's élite. No, there was a better way, surely. If Kohler knew that he knew all about his affair with this boy, and was made to understand that he could, nevertheless, keep a secret, that would be much more beneficial. He smiled.

'Follow me, Pieck!' He marched out into the passageway and flashed his lamp until he found another small hatch leading to the deck below. He had to find out everything. But it might be a mistake to mark the boy unnecessarily. He listened to Pieck's dragging footsteps behind him and quickened his pace. The next prize ship that was taken would need a crew. Officers were short, but it was not unknown for a petty officer to be promoted at sea as prizemaster. That promotion, plus what he might find in the captured ship, would settle him on his course for good.

He halted in front of a huge wooden door, which ran with moisture and gleamed white in the glare of his lamp.

'Do you know what this is, Pieck?' He watched his eyes widen with fright.

'Cold-storage room, sir!' His voice was a mere quaver.

Brandt rested his hand on the door lever, his tone almost conversational. 'When they designed this ship for carrying fruit they certainly knew a thing or two. Refrigeration ships are scarce. We were lucky to get one of them.' He flung up the lever and pulled the great door open. The blue emergency light within gleamed on stored carcasses and wooden crates rimed with ice, and the cold air which blasted from the silent interior made Pieck's half-naked body quiver uncontrollably. 'Get inside! Now!' He reached out and pulled him against the edge of the door.

'Either you tell me everything, and I mean the whole truth, or you stay in there until you do!' With a jerk he thrust him skidding across the iced floor, and, as he cried out in terror, slammed the door in his face.

As he leaned his back against it he could feel the boy pummelling against the foot-thick timber and steel. He grinned, and groped for a cigarette. A few minutes of that would loosen his tongue, and it would also warn him against any treachery in the future. He was thankful for his oilskin and thick watch-coat. Even outside the door of the cold storage the temperature was low enough to be uncomfortable.

Above his head, his eyes shining like stones across the rim of the hatch, Alder watched him. He had followed them along the passage after hearing Brandt screaming Pieck's name. He was the only one in the mess to hear, because he never slept. Now, as he peered down, he could see only the grinning petty officer. He closed his eyes as if in prayer, and tried to assemble his jumbled thoughts.

10

It was another grey morning, and the rain followed the ship along its course in long heavy squalls which moved across the sodden decks with playful force, bringing discomfort to the party of seamen who laboured at the small derricks and shifted the coal from one of the holds to the gaping mouth of a bunker. The *Vulkan* still faced the rolling mass of a head sea, and as she met each lazily curling crest, the high fo'c'sle seemed to hang for long seconds before the ship could stagger up the face of the steep water and then plunge headlong into the following trough. On either side the ranks of whitecaps surged past, giving the impression that the ship was moving at a tremendous pace. Only the feeble froth beneath her high counter showed the lie, and told of the sea's immense resistance to the vessel's bulk.

Lieutenant Heuss felt his feet grate on the wet coal-dust by the open bunker, and blinked vaguely at the scudding clouds. He allowed the needles of rain to cleanse his face and play around his aching eyes. He shook his head like a terrier and tried to clear away the tiredness and the fog left by the whisky. He wished now that he had gone for some breakfast, or coffee at least, but von Steiger's summons to the bridge left him only time to clean himself and run the razor over his numbed cheeks.

He sighed, and began to climb the exposed ladder to the boatdeck. As he watched the pitching deck fall away beneath him, he tried to assemble his thoughts and prepare himself for whatever von Steiger wanted of him. Perhaps Kohler or one of the others had reported him for drinking to such an extent that it left him useless for duty. He had probably been worse than he could remember, although he could not be sure. He had awakened on the floor of Damrosch's cabin with the rain lashing against the scuttle and a bruise on his head which he could not account for. He licked his dry lips and grimly continued his climb.

The whisky had done one thing. Coupled with his complete exhaustion, it had given him the first real rest for days. Well, damn them all, he thought. Von Steiger took over my watch for that reason. If I choose to relax like that it's my own affair. He grinned at his fuddled reasoning, and, panting, reached the wing of the bridge. He stared hard at the crouching lookouts with their powerful glasses. Night and day, watching. Waiting for the sea to surrender its victims to the prowling wolf. He banged open the door of the wheelhouse and stopped, instantly on the alert. It seemed to be full of people, waiting in uncomfortable silence, and yet filled with expectancy.

Damrosch, red-eyed and weary, stood stiffly by the helmsman, and flashed a quick glance of recognition and what seemed like relief as Heuss entered, and then turned back to his duties as second officer of the Forenoon Watch. Dehler stood restlessly beside Lieutenant Ebert, and on the other side of the wide bridge some petty officers and a bosun's mate waited with obvious discomfort.

Von Steiger put down a china mug and nodded. 'Ah, Heuss. I am sorry to call you to the bridge, but I have just had something unpleasant reported to me.'

Heuss steeled himself. It was worse than he feared. After all, the whisky might have made some of the others envious enough to make a serious charge against him. He kept his face impassive and met von Steiger's cool eye.

'Sir?' He felt them all looking at him.

'Yes. During the Middle Watch, when I relieved you, a man was lost overboard! And although it was not then your concern, I feel you should be informed of all that we discover, so that you can keep an eye on your own men in future.'

'I see, sir.' He did not see at all. It was a great pity for a man to be lost at sea, but it hardly warranted such a gathering on the bridge of a naval vessel on active service. He waited for the rest.

'Right, I think we will start again, Dehler. Let us hear from the beginning what happened.'

Dehler, caught unaware, tore his small eyes from Heuss and cleared his throat. 'Er, Petty Officer Elmke was in charge of the Morning Watch, and should have taken over the rounds of the ship from Petty Officer Brandt. Brandt did not hand over to him, and upon investigation could not be found in the ship at all!'

Heuss listened fixedly, aware of the tension in von Steiger's gently tapping fingers as he watched Dehler ponderously making his report.

Elmke was speaking now. He was a portly, red-faced man, whose pouting lips gave him the appearance of an angry pig. 'I waited to see what was happening, sir. Brandt wasn't the sort to make a mistake, if you understand me, sir.' He swallowed hard, aware of the Captain's eyes. 'And when I couldn't find him I called the bridge. Then we searched the whole ship, sir, and found this!' He held out a blue cap, still sodden with the rain and spray, and somehow pathetic in his beefy hand.

Von Steiger nodded with sudden impatience. 'It was by the foremast, port side?'

'Yes, sir. Nothing else at all!' Elmke looked as if he could not imagine a man like Brandt being so unpunctual and careless.

Lieutenant Kohler appeared from behind the quartermaster, his face aggrieved. 'I had every man searching, Captain. When we found the cap I guessed what had happened and made a note in the log. I did not call you, sir, because there was nothing that you could do!'

He watched von Steiger anxiously, but von Steiger stared instead at Petty Officer Bener, who, in his soiled white overalls and smelling of cooking fat, looked more out of place on the bridge than anyone else. He gestured with his hand, cutting across Dehler's report. 'Let us get to the point! Bener, what did *you* discover?'

The *Vulkan's* senior cook frowned worriedly and wiped his hands in his apron. He was obviously regretting his discovery, but was committed to make the best of it. 'Well, sir, I went down to get a case of biscuits this morning. We're running a bit short, and I said to my assistant only yesterday that if we go on like this we shall run out of——'

'Get on with it, man!'

'Yes, sir. Well, I got the case, and when I was down in the lower store I noticed that the cold-storage room there was unlocked.'

Von Steiger waved him into silence. 'Right, that is enough. Any useful comments from anybody?'

Dehler groped for a suggestion. As senior officer he felt that the others were looking to him to clear up this matter. He could not understand what had got into the Captain. It was a pity about Brandt, but he was not indispensable. 'It seems to me that he was a bit careless, sir. And that's about the bones of the matter.'

Von Steiger spoke as if he had not heard. 'Now listen, we are all strained and tired. That cannot be helped. But the first hint of carelessness, and we could be done for.' He dropped his voice so that the helmsman and lookouts could not hear, although they were obviously straining their ears. 'Brandt is missing. Nobody saw him go, although he should have been visible from the bridge. Even if he was not, the deck is fairly sheltered there, and very little sea came aboard during the watch. I know, I was looking forward from the bridge the whole time.'

Heuss licked his lips. Thank God I was drunk, he thought. Had I been on watch this would have fallen on my shoulders. As it was, he could not follow the Captain's mind.

'Secondly,' the voice cut cleanly, like a surgeon's knife, 'the key of the cold-storage room is carried by the duty petty officer—at that particular time, Brandt! For some reason he unlocked that room in the middle of the night, then went on deck and fell overboard! No, Dehler, the bones of *this* affair are not even showing yet!'

Slowly the realization moved in on the small listening group, like an evil cloud of suspicion and fear.

Heuss was now fully awake. Brandt had been below, and had then been thrown overboard. Or he had been killed on deck, and his key taken so that the store could be robbed.

As if reading his mind, von Steiger added slowly: 'Nothing is missing from the store. I have been down there with Bener. There are a few faint marks on the floor, like footmarks, but I am not sure.' His eyes moved fleetingly along their faces. 'I will say what is uppermost on my mind. I think Brandt was killed. At the moment I know nothing. But by treating this matter as settled, we might yet find the culprit or culprits. In the meantime, every officer and petty officer in this ship must be absolutely vigilant and on his guard!' His eyes flashed with mounting anger. 'Let this be a lesson to all of you!'

They all drew themselves up to attention as von Steiger moved briskly towards the open door. They waited until he had reached his usual position by the weather rail and then dismissed themselves from the bridge.

Von Steiger called suddenly to Heuss. He did not look round, and seemed to be staring fixedly at the blue-grey line of the horizon.

'Heuss, I want you to give the woman, Mrs. Brett, something to keep her occupied. We have a few sick men, and she might like to help in that direction. Ask her, anyway, and give her any assistance in the matter.'

'I will, sir.'

'Yes, I think it might be good for her.' He was speaking half to himself, a slight frown between his eyes. 'She must get very uneasy, and she has much on her mind. Her husband's death, and other things.' His voice seemed to hang on the last words, but he did not explain what he meant by them.

Heuss waited, the rain bouncing on the shoulders of his coat. Von Steiger seemed to want to talk to him, and yet was unwilling to drop his guard.

'This other matter, sir. Petty Officer Brandt. It could have been an accident, I suppose?'

'Unlikely, Heuss. He was a bad petty officer, and a harsh man. He could have had many enemies in a ship like this.'

He was leaning on the low rail, heedless of the rain throbbing across his bridge-coat, and Heuss could look down on his face from an unusual angle. From the side it looked strangely sensitive and youthful, and Heuss had to force himself to compare this man with the hard, aloof captain he usually saw. He had called Brandt harsh, and yet it was very unlikely that he would show any mercy for the culprit, if and when he was discovered.

'You can never be sure, Heuss.' His tone was matter-of-fact. 'And to know that such passions are abroad in this ship is almost unnerving!'

'In war many things seem justified, Captain.'

'It is that sort of reasoning which can cause a mutiny, Heuss!' The other captain had returned, and Heuss saw the life ripple through von Steiger's shoulders as if he was reawakening. 'And, Heuss, never drink too much at one time! It does not help minimize one's worries. It merely distorts them!'

Heuss saluted gravely, and climbed wearily down the ladder once more. Pausing again by the bunker, he watched the labouring seamen with new eyes. Set, hard faces grimed with dirt and coal-dust. It might be one of them. He shivered, and tried to imagine Brandt falling into the ship's creaming wake, or being sucked down into the churning propeller. He walked slowly along the deck, his head sunk deeply into his collar. The ship would seem different after this, he thought.

.   .   .   .   .

Caryl Brett paused by the tall funnel and looked upwards at the thin streamer of smoke as it peeled away into the wind. She could feel the warmth from the casing, and sensed the great power which coursed up through the hungry engine-room fans. It was cold and wet, and she could feel the rain soaking through the headscarf which she had tied across her hair. Yet she was unwilling to go below until ordered, unready to face the quiet loneliness of the cabin.

She thought of her husband, and tried to remember exactly how he had looked when she had last seen him. Repeatedly she had endeavoured to see him as he had once been in England, confident, determined, yet a little defenceless. Instead, the picture of him swimming away to safety and the lifeboat, while she stood alone on the sinking ship, came foremost in her thoughts.

A shoe squeaked on the wet planks behind her, and Gelb moved to the rail at her side. She stiffened, waiting for his casual touch, the insistent kindness of his tone. A strange, deep man. He had saved her from cracking completely in that slaughter of the lifeboats, she knew, and yet she was unable to feel at ease in his presence.

Gelb stood in silence, as if searching for thoughts also. At length he said softly, 'I hear that they have asked you to work in the sick quarters?'

She turned towards him, her eyes wide. But his heavy profile looked quite unruffled at her surprise. 'How did you know? They only asked me an hour ago!'

He shrugged, almost apologetically. 'I hear a lot, my dear. It comes from being a good listener.'

'Yes, they did ask me. Their complete indifference to my own feelings amazes me!'

'I think you should accept their offer.' His voice was still casual, yet she could detect a slight edge to his words. 'After all, there are several British seamen to be looked after. You might be able to help them, eh?'

'I suppose so.' Her mind wandered off again to the officer, Heuss. He had tried to explain the idea to her almost as Gelb was doing. He had also suggested that it would pass the time until they could put her safely aboard another ship. So easy, so helpful. They all spoke as if nothing had happened. She turned back to Gelb. 'What else have you discovered?'

'A man was lost overboard last night. A petty officer.' He smiled at some inner secret. 'I believe there is more to it. You might be able to find something out, too!'

A bell chimed from the forward deck, and somewhere below a bosun's pipe twittered urgently.

Gelb moved closer, so that she could feel his coat brushing her leg. 'There is something else.' He dropped his voice so that she could hardly understand him. 'I should like you to make every effort to find out where we are meeting the collier again.'

She tried to pierce his impassive expression. 'Why? What does it matter any more?'

'I did not say this in front of the Germans, but I believe that there is a man aboard the collier that could help you. Your poor husband knew him, and I believe he alone knows who your husband was frightened of.' He let the words sink in. 'I have been talking to the collier's captain, and he thinks that the Germans will get rid of his ship after they next meet it. They will get all the coal they want, and then maybe scuttle the ship.'

'And the other prisoners on board the collier?'

'I expect they will put them ashore somewhere. We may not see them again after that.' He shook his head sadly. 'I feel that we would be doing something for your poor husband's memory if we made the effort to discover his persecutor. A small thing, but it would help. I am sure that we would never forgive ourselves if we allowed his death to pass unmourned and with no effort to find the cause of his unnecessary end.' He waited, hardly daring to breathe.

'What can *we* do? You have seen what these Germans are like. We are so helpless in their hands!'

'Not quite helpless! You try and discover the rendezvous, and I will try to contact that other prisoner, whoever he is. It will be something.' He hurried on, aware of the girl's quick breathing at his side. 'The captain of the collier will be able to recognize the rendezvous if you give him a clue. Any little thing might help, an island perhaps, or even some sheltered bay, who knows? But we must try!'

She nodded slowly. 'Very well. I shall tell the officer that I am willing to help with the sick. It is wrong, anyway, to keep thinking of myself when there are others worse off.'

His big hand closed across hers, and she felt something like relief. He has been wanting to do that since he came up here, she thought, I can almost feel the eagerness in his fingers. She removed her hand and brushed some hair from her eyes. She must try to like him. After all, he was doing his best to help her, whatever his motives.

A petty officer appeared at the top of the ladder and beckoned to Gelb impatiently.

'I must go below now. The dogs are barking again!' He walked slowly after his guard and left her alone once more with her thoughts.

She watched the surging water, and wondered where the ship had reached on its endless journey.

When I get back to England, what shall I do? Who will be interested in me now? Arthur would be missed by his friends, but his very life had excluded her in more than just the most important way, it had kept her quite apart from life itself. The completeness of her loneliness moved a step closer.

She was suddenly aware that someone was watching her, and she looked up towards the bridge. Von Steiger stared down at her, his features hidden by distance and by the heavy drizzle. She expected him to stay motionless, part of the ship, or to turn away, but instead he lifted his hand in a slow salute. She turned away and began to walk quickly along the boatdeck. She felt angry with herself, and yet strangely satisfied with the uncertain power she held over all these men. Gelb, who disguised his feelings for her with the sound of noble purpose. Heuss, who openly admired her, and even von Steiger seemed unsure of himself because of her. It was as if her presence disturbed the pattern of things, and had become a reminder and a link with another life, like a flaw in a piece of armour. She looked back briefly at the bridge, but he had gone. That is why he wants me to leave this ship. Because of himself, he is afraid of me.

She was almost running when she reached the cabin, and breathlessly she slammed the door behind her.

Her discovery had unnerved her, and she wanted time to think about it. It did not seem possible that such an impersonal, efficient machine as this ship of destruction could be weakened by human emotion, and yet, if it was, she knew that she would have to be doubly careful in future.

She spoke aloud to the cabin. 'I should like to bring him down from his perch. This arrogant, so-confident German!' It would be an achievement which might in part make up for all the suffering which she had seen and endured. But her words echoed back, unreal and meaningless.

.   .   .   .   .

The *Vulkan*'s sick-bay was situated below the boatdeck, and like the officers' wardroom ran the whole breadth of the ship, but, although spacious, gave the impression of overcrowding, with its neat ranks of white metal cots suspended from the deckhead and swinging easily in time with the ship's movement.

Caryl Brett paused momentarily in the entrance, her slim body silhouetted against the grey sky, and her cheeks glowing from the crisp morning air. Lieutenant Heuss closed the door behind her, and she was immediately aware of the complete isolation of this place from the ordered harshness of the rest of the ship. There was a mingled smell of disinfectant and soap, and the whole area gleamed with white paint, and neat racks of bottles and jars lined each bulkhead.

A tall, studious man in his middle thirties, dressed in a long white coat, stood alertly in the middle of the floor, his straight face and severe mouth betrayed by a pair of twinkling blue eyes. He waited respectfully as Heuss indicated the cots, six of which were occupied, and when at last Heuss beckoned him over he bobbed his head in a slight bow, and eyed the girl with approval.

'This is Steuer. He is our sick-bay attendant, but is more like a doctor than the real thing!' Heuss waved his hand around the large cabin. 'He is actually Swiss, and keeps this place as neat as a cuckoo clock!'

Eduard Steuer chuckled. 'Thank you, sir. You are very kind.' To the girl he said: 'It is very good of you to offer your help. Your presence here alone will do much for these poor fellows.'

'Huh! If we are not careful we shall have *all* the ship's company going sick now!' Heuss grimaced.

'Perhaps some of the officers, too?' The Swiss raised his eyebrows. 'But a good dose of my special tonic will clear them out again, in more senses than one!'

Heuss glanced at the bulkhead clock and frowned. 'I must go and attend to my work, Frau Brett.' The reluctance was obvious in his voice. 'But please do not hesitate to send for me if you need anything.'

When the officer had left Steuer seemed to relax, and led the girl to a small alcove at the far end of the sick-bay.

'There is a small cabin through there which you may use when I am doing the more unpleasant dressings, or at any other time. I have cleaned my patients up already, and they have been fed, so there is not much to do for the present.'

'You speak excellent English.'

'Most Swiss do.' He grinned. 'I would have made a good head waiter, eh?'

She coloured. 'I did not mean that. It is just that I have got used to the German sailors gesticulating or waving their hands when they want to tell me something.'

'That is true. The Germans are a bit like the English. They think that everyone should speak *their* language!'

She walked to the first cot, half afraid of what she might see. But the man was well hidden by his blanket, and from beneath a large head-bandage regarded her with dark, solemn eyes.

Steuer watched her across the cot. 'This is Brown. An excellent fellow. One of the seamen from the *Cardiff Maid*.'

Her heart quickened. 'How are you? Are you comfortable here?'

He watched her with fascinated eyes. Then his lips moved. 'Yes, thank you, miss. Just a bit stiff, like. I got a bit punctured by a couple of shell-splinters when the Jerries sunk the old ship.'

'Who removed them?' All the old anger was rising within her. The man looked so small and lost in the cot that she wanted to cry. 'Was it you?' She looked at Steuer, who shrugged.

'It was me. I am the only doctor here. I was a medical student and did all but qualify, so I manage quite well!'

'I think it's horrible! To let men suffer because they have not proper doctors! I know you are good at your job, but it's all so unfair!'

He stared at her bright, rebuking eyes and spread his hands. 'I know. But this war has taken every available doctor for more desperate things. On the battle fronts our men die like flies. They need all the help there.'

'You say *our* men? How can you speak of the Germans as your own people?'

'Serving with the Navy has made me look on them so, I suppose. I joined the German Navy because it was nearer than the British. I wanted to help the sick. I am little interested in national motives, and drum-beating!'

She smiled, feeling suddenly humble. 'I am sorry. I did not understand. My late husband felt much as you do.' Even as she said it she tried to imagine Arthur risking his life to help the sick and wounded. But the picture eluded her.

She moved to the next cots, where two more bandaged sailors painfully played draughts on a small board, balanced between the swinging mattresses. They were also from the freighter *Cardiff Maid*, and had obtained their wounds in much the same way as the first man.

One, a hard-bitten seaman from Bristol, reached up and took the girl's small hand in his large calloused one and grinned at her. 'You're a sight for sore eyes, miss! Wait till I tell the old woman about this! She'll never trust me away from 'ome again!'

'Garn, she'll be glad to see the back of yer!' The other man winked, and rattled the draught-board with his bandaged fist. Then in a quieter voice he said: ' 'Ere, say a good word to the bloke in the next bunk, will yer, miss? 'E's 'avin' a bad time.'

She moved softly to the still figure which occupied the cot the man had indicated, and stared down at the sunken white face which regarded her with fixed attention. It was young, yet already lined with suffering and experiences she could only guess at.

She smiled. 'And who are you? Are you from the *Cardiff Maid*, too?'

The grey lips moved painfully. '*Bitte? Ich—verstehe nicht, Fräulein.*'

She shrank back as if she had been bitten. 'He's a German!'

The British seamen watched her over the edges of their cots. ' 'Course 'e is! Poor old Fritz is in a bad way!'

Steuer leaned over and wiped the man's mouth with a piece of cloth. Without changing his expression he said: 'But you did not know that until he spoke? Please, if you cannot bring yourself to help me, I would rather be left alone!'

She moved closer to the cot again. The man's eyes were still fixed on her face; like a small, unwinking bird, she thought. At the sound of Steuer's words she had felt once again like a child at school. She was only just beginning to understand the meaning of what Steuer had said earlier. This was not just a matter of right versus wrong. This was something else she had to learn. She had not really been shocked by the surprise of finding the man to be a German. It had been the casual acceptance of him by the British seamen. The very men that this wounded German and his comrades had tried to kill. It was crazy, and yet it was happening. She forced herself to smile and said softly, 'What is wrong with him?'

Steuer's eyes were distant. 'Two bullet wounds. He may live. I am not sure.'

The wounded man watched her hand move down and adjust the blanket beneath his chin. A tiny tear moved from the corner of his eye. '*Danke, fräulein. Danke sehr!*'

The Bristol man called encouragingly: 'That's right, you bloody square-head! Start getting off with my girl friend, will you! You wait, mate!' They laughed.

The other two cots were occupied by Germans also. Steuer guided her quickly by them, and shrugged apologetically. 'Sores, I am afraid! Not very warlike, but just as painful. Too much salted meat and not enough fresh vegetables!'

'What is in that other cabin?' She pointed at a small door, half hidden by a curtain.

'Isolation. We have one patient there, admitted yesterday.' He frowned with sudden anger. 'It made me sick to see him! It is a disgrace that he should be allowed in the Navy at all, let alone at sea!' He saw her lips parted in a question and hurried on. 'He was apparently blown up by a mine earlier in the war. He was found in a waterlogged lifeboat with eight dead companions. He was frozen to the tiller, and I am afraid he became unhinged by his terrible experiences.' He became suddenly grave. 'I should like you to see him. He often mentions you, if not by name, and I think he wishes to tell *you* not to be worried by your own terrible experiences.'

Her eyes widened. 'But he does not know me. How does he understand?'

He shrugged. 'It is hard to say. He can remember little at all of his own life, and yet hearing about your ordeal from his comrades seems to have made quite an impression on him. Don't worry, he is harmless.

I shall keep him here for a day or two, and then ask that he be put on light duties, if that is possible.'

He opened the door, and the girl received her second shock. Alder, the man who sat dejectedly on the edge of the narrow bunk, was the man who had seized her. A flood of compassion swept over her. It was all clear to her now, and even without seeing the deadness in the man's eyes, she could understand his misery and his wish to save her from a similar fate.

Steuer spoke to the man quietly in German, his voice low yet compelling, and Alder nodded vaguely, muttering a reply in short staccato sentences.

'That is queer. He wishes to see another seaman. He wants to tell him something.'

They moved from the cell-like cabin and closed the door.

'Why is that strange?'

'Because he never speaks to anyone as a rule, and because the man he wishes to speak to is a mere boy, named Pieck.' He scratched his chin distantly. 'Very odd. Pieck was also in here yesterday. I thought he had got pneumonia or something like it, but there seemed nothing really wrong with him, after all. I put his condition down to being too long on watch in a cold wind. It is all rather strange. That was the night Petty Officer Brandt was lost overboard.' He saw her perplexed expression and smiled with mock despair. 'Forgive me! I am so long on my own that I think too much! Forget it, it is nothing!'

He watched her hair shine in the grey light from the scuttle, and pursed his lips with silent admiration. No wonder Lieutenant Heuss followed her around like a jealous suitor. She was beautiful indeed. Her very presence seemed to make the place brighter.

'Perhaps you would help me clean these bottles? It will pass the time for us both, and you can tell me all about England, and why the English come to Switzerland for their holidays.'

.   .   .   .   .

Von Steiger leaned against the side of his sea cabin and watched the tumbling water beneath his scuttle. Beyond the thick glass it was silent and unreal, and but for Dehler's voice it might have seemed like the world of the deaf.

'I have made enquiries, Captain, and as yet have discovered nothing fresh about Brandt's death.'

Von Steiger could hear the disbelief in the man's voice. He thinks I am mistaken, that I am merely wasting time. What a pity I have to have a man like him as First Lieutenant. If only he was someone I could confide in. Heuss would be more suited. With him I could be open, without fear of losing his obedience. Aloud he said: 'I see. Well keep on the lookout.' He waited, but Dehler still stood there, his heavy face uneasy yet determined. 'Well, is there something else?'

'Yes, sir.' He took a deep breath. 'I have done a lot of thinking lately. And I consider that we might not be making best use of ourselves and the ship!'

Von Steiger tensed. He had been watching and waiting for something like this. Dehler had been brooding over his thoughts, and now they were coming into the open. 'What is on your mind?'

Dehler looked away, and spoke quickly as if he were afraid of forgetting a carefully rehearsed speech. 'That wireless message you received, Captain. I have been doing a lot of thinking, and I believe that our orders were right! We should have stayed farther north, nearer the convoy routes!'

Von Steiger relaxed slightly. So that was it. Or was Dehler more afraid of the greater distance the raider was putting between herself and Germany?

'That sort of warfare is done for, Dehler,' he said simply. 'To wait in the hopes of finding a straggler from a convoy is no threat to the enemy, but it is to us. Do you want to die without a fight?'

Dehler blanched. 'I am not afraid to fight, Captain! But I am holding to my right as second in command to raise my objections, especially when your actions are in defiance of the High Command!'

'You have not understood a word I have said.' Von Steiger felt weary. 'You have said yourself that mine is the ultimate responsibility, and that is so. It is also true that upon me rests not only the weight of this command, but the successful completion of this cruise. Under the circumstances I think I am the better judge. The High Command may see us as a coloured counter on their chart. I have to see this ship as much more than that.' He turned away. 'As a symbol of honour, and as flesh and blood!'

Dehler drew himself upright. 'Nevertheless, Captain, I wish to register my protest!'

The door opened. Lieutenant Ebert watched the Captain, his face set and grim. 'Masthead reports a warship, sir! Fine on the port bow!' His words dropped like stones into a still pool.

Dehler blanched. 'What? Is he sure?' He opened and closed his big hands, and tried to realize what this could all mean.

'Alter course one point to starboard, Lieutenant!' Von Steiger reached for his cap, his mind clicking into orderly sections. For weeks he had considered this very encounter, toyed with it, imagined every conceivable angle. It had to happen, and he felt strangely calm. 'Keep that warship on our port bow at all costs, and reduce speed to dead slow!' He waited until Ebert had hurried away, his face etched with surprise at von Steiger's orders, and then turned again to Dehler, who had not moved. 'Sound Action Stations, and stand by to lower the starboard boat.'

'But—but, Captain! We can't fight this warship! We'll not stand a chance!'

Von Steiger regarded him with sudden hatred. 'We cannot run away, either! She could outdistance us, I expect, and if not could shadow us while she signalled every ship for miles to close in and finish the job!' He smiled with sudden amusement. 'You have your wish. We are no longer running away! Now, get that boat lowered and fill it with men!'

'Men, sir?' He sounded faint.

'Yes, I want it to look like a lifeboat!' An idea crossed his racing mind. 'And put the woman prisoner in it, too!'

Even as the alarm bells died away the ship rolled uneasily in the troughs as the engine was reduced still more. Perplexed seamen swung out the starboard whaleboat and lowered it until it was level with the guardrail.

Von Steiger watched the feverish activity impassively. Only his bunched fists betrayed the impatience within him.

There was a sound of hurrying feet on the ladder, and Lieutenant Heuss ran breathlessly on to the bridge. Without saluting he gasped: 'Sir! They are putting the woman in the boat! They said it was your order!'

Von Steiger lifted his megaphone as the girl was hustled into the swinging boat, her hair blowing in the wind. 'Lower away!' The falls squeaked and the boat dropped out of sight. 'Tell the Coxswain to pull clear as quick as he can and then stop where he is!'

Damrosch reported, 'Enemy warship bearing red one-five, sir!'

He nodded, and lifted his glasses. A mere patch, dark on the rim of the sea, betrayed by the rising white moustache of its high bow-wave. Destroyer, probably.

'Stop engine,' he said calmly.

Heuss said suddenly, 'Did you hear what I said, sir?'

'Get a grip on yourself, Heuss!' He tore his eyes from the small boat as it bobbed away from the *Vulkan*, the oars moving with difficulty amongst the crowded seamen. He could see the girl quite clearly, her frail body making a splash of colour against the sombre blue uniforms. 'Don't worry about her. If we are sunk she will be safe.'

Heuss stared at him with amazement. 'Is that why you did it, sir?'

'I am afraid not, Heuss. The warship will think that we are picking up survivors from a sunken ship, at least I hope she does! The sight of a woman in the boat might help.' Over his shoulder he rapped sharply: 'Signalman, make this signal at once. "Can you help? Am picking up survivors."' He watched the man bend over his biggest signal-lamp and waited until the shutter had begun to stammer out his message. He was aware that Heuss still stood staring at him. 'Well?'

Heuss shook his head. 'Nothing, sir!' He turned away to his position at the rear of the bridge, his eyes following the tiny tossing boat.

Petty Officer Heiser lifted his long telescope and steadied himself against the flag-locker. The tossing motion of the stationary vessel made his task difficult, and he tried not to contemplate the effect it would have upon the gunners. He examined the distant warship keenly through a practised eye. For many years he had stood on different bridges watching for the flashing lamp, the madly gyrating semaphore-arms, or the fluttering flags which were a meaningless jumble to anyone but a highly trained signalman. He had seen battle-cruisers and British Dreadnoughts, Japanese cruisers and French gunboats. He knew them all, and gauged their signalling proficiency accordingly.

'She's an American, Captain! One of their new destroyers!'

Von Steiger nodded shortly. He did not have to ask the man if he was sure. An American. He lifted his glasses and watched the newcomer without speaking. Fast, powerful and very well handled. There was an air of watchful preparedness about the ship, and an appearance of dash and recklessness which one always found with destroyers. Nevertheless, for all her power and the threat she offered to their very existence, there was one tiny consolation. She was American, and the United States were not yet hardened to the ways of war. It was little enough, but it was something.

'She's signalling, sir.' Heiser's lips moved slowly as he read the light without using the telescope. '"What ship?"'

The light blinked back, '*Janssens*, Amsterdam to Kingston, Jamaica.'

The white froth at the warship's raked stem died slightly and she began to sweep round in a wide semicircle, her narrow deck canting so that the Germans could see the torpedo-tubes and swivelled guns trained upon them. The stars and stripes streamed proudly from the gaff, and the ship's clean lines and well-painted hull gave the impression of untried newness.

'She's turning towards the whaleboat, sir!'

But her guns are following us—von Steiger bit his lip as he followed the warship's confident progress.

The lithe grey ship moved slowly across the raider's plunging bows, so that it appeared as if she were balanced on the stemhead.

Damrosch sounded strained. 'If she gets much nearer she'll see our empty davits! She'll guess what we're up to!'

Von Steiger lifted the small speaking-tube. 'Ebert, make sure of her wireless. She must not transmit! Stand by with the starboard battery!' He waited, counting seconds. It was now or never. He pressed the small button at his side. The steel shutters fell heavily against the hull and hung unheeded as the gunners swung their training wheels with such speed that their hands were mere white blurs against the dull grey guns. On the poop the long twenty-two pounder swept round in a tight circle, even as the men tore with savage frenzy at the canvas screens.

'Open fire!'

The ship rocked drunkenly as the two forward guns belched fire at the enemy and hurled their great shells at the fragile-looking destroyer. Damrosch ducked involuntarily as the twenty-two pounder fired at its most extreme angle from the poop and sent its shell screaming past the bridge, so that an acrid shock-wave tore through the wheelhouse door and stripped the chart from its table and flung it at von Steiger's feet.

'Full speed ahead! Hard a-port!' The waiting engineers were quick to respond, as if aware of the closeness of possible death, and the ship shook madly to the unchecked thunder of the screw.

'Missed!' said Heiser irritably. 'Too short by far.'

The guns cracked out again, but before they could see the fall of the shot the side of the destroyer rippled with orange flame.

The bridge shuddered, and von Steiger gripped the teak rail with both hands. They've hit us already. Good shooting. Too damned good.

From the maindeck he heard the rush of feet and a distant voice calling for the fire parties. Dehler would be busy enough for a bit, he thought bitterly.

Like a bursting star, bright and blinding above the sullen water, a shell exploded on the destroyer's maindeck. The foremast, black and slender, shuddered, and then with sad dignity plunged over the side, dragging a tangled web of wireless aerials, flags and rigging in its wake. Tiny, ant-like figures could be seen running with axes to cut away the wreckage.

Von Steiger drummed his fingers on the rail. Ebert had done his work. The enemy could sink them or be sunk. But she could not talk about it. He pulled in his stomach muscles as the ship leapt beneath him, and he felt the tearing crash of white-hot metal bursting and ricocheting around the boatdeck. Another hit. Thank God their guns were puny compared with the *Vulkan*'s. But the raider had tremendous vulnerability compared with the low-lying target presented by the destroyer, and was hopelessly outmanœuvred.

'She's turning!'

The American put his ship about like a toy yacht and flung her almost on her beam ends.

Von Steiger could feel his breathing growing faster. This captain was determined, and fighting mad. 'Hard a-starboard!' He pounded the rail, waiting for the heavy bows to swing after the elusive destroyer. He saw puffs of smoke from her spray-washed metal deck, and flinched as the torpedoes leapt from their tubes and bit into the racing water. Come on, old lady! He banged the rail with fierce persistence until his knuckles were numb. With all his power he willed the ship to swing end on to those racing, silver torpedoes.

'Torpedo running to port, sir!'

Another hoarse cry, 'Second torpedo running fine on the port bow!'

'Midships! Meet her!' The Coxswain blinked the sweat from his staring eyes and twirled the varnished spokes in response to the Captain's urgent voice.

Heuss looked across at Damrosch's white face. 'Missed, by God!'

The destroyer faltered, and seemed to shorten as she turned again to reduce the range. Ebert's gunners, their eyes sore from cordite and smoke, spun their wheels and stared wildly at the shape which danced with contemptuous ease across their sights. But for the few short seconds she had taken to loose off the torpedoes, she had laid bare her full length, open and exposed to their pitching guns, and there was a sudden crazed cheer as the enemy's quarterdeck erupted in a column of black smoke. Then she was round again and attacking like a terrier after a ponderous bullock.

·   ·   ·   ·   ·   ·

Lieutenant Dehler ducked his head beneath the iron bulwark and cursed aloud as a column of water rose alongside and sent a great mass of spray plummeting across the afterdeck. He skidded across the streaming planking and continued to run after the fire party. The black hoses snaked across the holds and ended by a huddled group beneath the poop ladder. The poop gun cracked overhead so that he thought his eardrums would burst, and he saw the men cower wretchedly as the shadow of the gun-muzzle moved across the deck like an accusing finger.

'Get under the poop, you stupid bastards! The blast will cut you down!'

He slithered to a halt behind the winch housing, pressing his wet hands over his ears, and waited until the gun had fired again. He felt the searing passage of the shell, and saw a dim figure wrench open the breech while a loader staggered forward with the next black shell, his face a mask dominated by a pair of terrified eyes.

He reached the shelter of the poop, and blinked at the long streamers of smoke which coursed rapidly through the heavy steel door which led to the main poop superstructure, from where they had laid the mines so long ago. He was breathing heavily, his brain numbed by the incessant roar of gunfire and the abandoned scream of shells overhead. The ship had been hit several times, and he had sent his damage-control parties running like madmen in search of the ragged holes.

Petty Officer Elmke, his face blackened by smoke, greeted him anxiously. 'Bad fire in that compartment, sir! Listen to it!'

Dehler listened. The fire sounded like pressurized steam, and was burning with such fierce intensity that the escaping smoke seemed to be ejected through the small cracks in the door as if by a pump.

A shell must have hit the hull low down, he thought, and exploded in one of the small storerooms below the poop. He licked his lips, aware of a sudden terrible urgency. Fanned by the draught and sucked through the poop with growing power, it might flash back to the small magazine which fed the gun overhead.

He gestured with his fist. 'Open the door! Every hose inside at once, and keep pouring it in!'

Elmke paled. 'But the draught will only fan the fire, sir!'

'And if it reaches the magazine we are all done for!' Dehler snarled. 'Now get moving!'

The seamen threw off the clips and pulled blindly at the heavy door. The flames had caused almost a vacuum inside so that they had to put all their weight on the handles. Then it was open, and the searing heat and hungry flames burst out on to the poop like savage beasts escaping from a cage. Two of the seamen screamed as the heat temporarily blinded them and a hose dropped unheeded on the deck. Another man whimpered and began to falter, whilst Elmke could only stare at the holocaust, which seemed to be burning away the very mounting which supported the gun above.

Dehler mopped his streaming eyes, and found that his Luger had somehow appeared in his hand.

'Get in there, you swine! I'll shoot the first man to fall back!'

They stared at his wild face and his teeth bared in a maniacal grin, and huddled together for support. Elmke seized a hose and turned it on the men around him. 'Here, I'll cover you! Get the other hoses up close!'

On the poopdeck the gun waited in sudden silence, its breech-block hanging open and the loader cursing with desperation at the delay.

Petty Officer Adolf Eucken, the gun-captain, banged the gun-layer on the shoulder. 'Carry on tracking the target! Something's gone wrong below!'

Hellwege blinked up at him, his red eyes uncomprehending. 'Maybe the ammunition party is wiped out! I think the whole damned poop is afire!'

But Eucken had already gone, and was lying full length over the small oval hatch with its hand-operated lift. His face practically collided with that of Pieck who stood half stooped in the narrow confines of the hatchway. His eyes looked incredibly large in his round face, and he seemed to be dazed by the fact that the ammunition lift was empty.

'What is the trouble, Pieck?'

Pieck blew down the voice-pipe at his side, but kept his eyes fixed on the petty officer. The cap and aggressive voice momentarily reminded him of Brandt, and he felt his senses reel.

Far below him, in the very bowels of the ship, a tinny voice called with sudden clarity: 'The fire's here, Willi! It's right outside the magazine door!' He swallowed hard, aware for the first time of the smoke which poured up over the gun in a dense brown curtain, of the shouted orders and the hiss of water against fire.

'The magazine's on fire!' He saw the petty officer's nostrils dilate like an animal scenting danger. 'He says there's a fire right outside the door!'

Eucken fell back. 'Christ! Here, let me use that tube!' He squeezed himself down the hatch, and Pieck could almost smell the fear mingled with his sweat.

'That you, Schmidt?' He tried to remember what the man looked like. 'How bad is it?'

The voice came to him, even above the scream of shells. It was thin and terrified, part of another world. 'Full of smoke! Great blisters coming up on the door!'

Eucken reached for the telephone which hung in its leather case, and cranked at the handle. This was very bad. The whole ship was coming apart.

'Gunnery officer!' Ebert's harsh voice sounded calm and normal.

Eucken shouted above the roar of flames, his eyes fixed on Pieck's white face. 'Magazine's in danger, sir! After flat well alight, and there could be a flashback!'

The smallest pause. 'Very well, flood it at once!'

'But, sir, I've three men down there! Can't I give them time?'

'I can see the fire from up here, Eucken! Do you want to die? Flood it!'

He felt the telephone fall dead in his hand. 'Come with me, Pieck.' He paused to look over the rim of the hatch. 'Send for the spare ammunition party and broach the secondary magazine, Hellwege!' He saw their expressionless faces. They knew what had to be done.

He reached the bottom of the ladder in one jump, and stared fascinated at the wide brass wheel, which almost filled the small space. He laid his hands on it and screamed, his cry filling the steel shaft with pain. He thrust his torn hands under his armpits, and called to Pieck through his clenched teeth. 'Turn the wheel, boy! Hold it with some rags, anything! But in God's name hurry!'

Pieck pulled off his jacket and laid it on the polished brass wheel. He stared as if mesmerized at the smoke which immediately rose from the folded cloth, and felt the searing heat through his hands. The wheel was stiff, and he was afraid his hands would blister before he could turn it. As it started to move he suddenly realized what he was doing. Eucken bit his lip with pain and nodded vigorously. 'Turn it! Don't think about it!' They held each other's eyes as the wheel squeaked round, and below their feet the sea-water surged in to flood the smouldering magazine and its three trapped inmates.

. . . . . .

The destroyer had turned right round so that she was steaming on a parallel course with the German. Occasionally, she zigzagged so as to move closer, and then dart away to leave only a great torn mountain of cascading water where the *Vulkan*'s last salvo had fallen.

Heuss crouched behind the steel shutters near the wireless compartment and strained his eyes through the smoke. The four-inch guns of the destroyer cracked like whips, and she had hit the *Vulkan* repeatedly. So far none of the shots had gone below the waterline, and the fire on the poop seemed to be under control. The American had received only three hits and seemed little the worse for them. It seemed incredible that such a frail ship could resist three heavy shells and survive. Around him the voice-pipes hummed and squeaked. Asking instructions, reporting damage and casualties. The bridge was misty with gun-smoke, and all of its occupants were specked with flaked paint brought down by the incessant vibration. Heuss felt ice-cold, and wanted to retch. He knew that if he allowed himself to think he was done for.

A messenger reported, 'After magazine flooded, sir!'

Von Steiger wiped the lenses of his glasses with a handkerchief, and cocked his head as the poop gun reopened fire. He saw Heuss watching him and smiled crookedly. 'It's hot work, Heuss!'

There was a bright flash behind the bridge, and the dummy funnel vanished in a single tongue of flame, leaving the wire stays dancing and humming like live things. There was a great shout from the deck below, and von Steiger lifted his glasses. Two of the destroyer's four slender funnels had vanished, and in their place was a wide black crater from which came a sullen orange glow with surprisingly little smoke. He felt his heart tighten in his chest, and he knew that the worst was over.

'She's making a smoke-screen, Captain! She's falling away!'

A strangled cheer rippled along the torn decks and was carried even to the men in the inferno of the boiler-rooms below.

Damrosch had to tear his eyes from the foremast to take in what the cheering meant. He had seen the long scarlet line running unchecked down the full length of the tall mast, to form a shining pool at the bottom, after a shell-splinter had passed through one side of the crow's-nest and out the other. His glance fell on von Steiger, who had placed both his hands palms down on the ledge by the voice-pipes and was staring intently at nothing. His gold-flecked eyes were without expression and empty, and for an instant Damrosch thought he too was watching the blood on the mast.

Heuss rapped out fresh orders to the fire party below the bridge, and ran back into the wheelhouse. They were drawing away from the warship. Von Steiger was breaking off the action. Now there was one urgent task to be done. They must find that whaleboat. He collided with Damrosch and glared at his colourless lips.

'What's the matter, Max?'

Damrosch had difficulty in speaking, and his voice sounded brittle. 'The Captain! He has been hit!'

II

As the wind freshened the sides of the wave-troughs grew steeper and more menacing, so as each new roller appeared the small wooden whaleboat yawed dangerously and then slithered down the crumbling wall of water, heavy and unresponsive to the sweating oarsmen who had pulled almost ceaselessly since the boat had been lowered. At first the terrifying spectacle of the destroyer and the *Vulkan* engaging each other in the near distance had left them little time for thought of their own plight, but as the two ships slowly drew away and were finally lost beyond the jagged horizon of tossing waves, and the thunder of guns mingled with the crash of exploding shells faded and finally merged with the roar of the sea, they felt the smallness of their own craft and the immensity of the water which towered around them.

Apart from the five oarsmen and the coxswain, six other seamen were crammed into the sternsheets, their uniforms already grey with salt and their bodies stiff with cold and wet.

Caryl Brett had made herself as small as possible beside the coxswain, a thin, sick-looking man, who gripped the tiller with a hand like a claw, and peered over the heads of the oarsmen and watched for the next creaming wave-top.

When the destroyer had first appeared round the bows of the *Vulkan* she had felt a lump rising in her throat and could sense the despair in the boat around her. The German seamen had watched dully, their hands limp on the oars, as the lithe grey hull had curtsied across the water, the white wave-crests reflected in her sleek raked bows. By comparison, the German raider had looked old-fashioned and clumsy, an amateur beside the professional. The warship looked so proud, so reassuring, that the helplessness of her own position and her inability to help had made her leap to her feet and wave her spray-drenched headscarf. A man had cursed her, and someone had pulled her backwards to the stern, just as the raider's starboard battery swung into view and the German ensign soared up to the gaff. She had been terrified yet thrilled by the speed and viciousness of the action, and had watched the two ships firing at each other without a moment's respite, and apparently heedless of the damage being done to both of them.

The *Vulkan* appeared to be on fire in two places, and her tall black side was ripped open in three or four savage gashes, the red lead beneath the paint looking like blood in the grey light. Now that they had gone she felt sick and dazed by the suddenness of events. The very feel of the boat brought back the searing memory of the lifeboat and its cargo of slaughtered men. She was aware, too, of the bitter cold and the feel of the spray lashing against her unprotected body. Someone had handed her an oilskin as she was bundled into the boat, but she no longer had it. It had probably been whipped away by the wind as she had stared, transfixed, at the battle.

She tried not to look at the seamen, but she could sense their eyes on her—bitter, resentful and hungry. They looked tired and dirty, their faces reddened by the wind and their movements lacking purpose or meaning. One of the men scrambled forward with what looked like a large canvas bucket on a long line. He paid it out over the bow so that it streamed away, the line taut and black against the dark-green water. The sea-anchor helped to steady the boat and keep its bow heading into the crushing water, and gave the oarsmen time to rest. As they lay panting on the looms the oars stuck out each side of the boat and looked like the bones of a gutted fish.

She jumped as the coxswain said: 'Good, eh? That will hold her for a bit!' He grinned down at her, his thin, pointed face creased like a mask.

She pulled the sodden scarf about her shoulders and tried to stop her teeth from chattering. 'You speak English? What do you think will happen now?'

He watched her lips carefully. 'Maybe they come back for us. Either the Captain or the American. Who knows which?'

Her stomach seemed to crumble as the boat dropped sickeningly into a deep trough, but she forced herself to keep talking. It was as if she was afraid the coxswain would revert to his own tongue and once more alienate her from the hard resentment of the others. 'Where did you learn English?'

'I was steward in Hamburg-Amerika Line before war, you understand? Plenty of opportunity there!'

She looked at him more closely. He was too old for this, she realized. Nearly fifty, with his flesh stretched across his skull and his eyes aged by the harshness of this unnatural life. She thought of that gleaming warship and the soldiers she had seen in America. Clean, fresh and somehow invincible. To see this worn creature in his ill-fitting jacket and clumsy boots should have filled her with contempt, but she recognized the pity which came instead to her mind.

'Where are we now? Will we be found out here?'

He shrugged. 'I dunno. I just do as I am told. We could be in China for all I can guess!'

One of the seamen shouted from the bows and some of them laughed. The coxswain scowled and said to her: 'Take no notice. They are afraid and do not know what they are saying.'

She opened her mouth to reply, but saw the man nearest to her staring at her body, his eyes unblinking and unmasked. She knew that her clothing was plastered to her by the spray, that her blouse was moulded to her like another skin, and as she watched the hunger on his face she felt naked and defenceless. These men had been away from their homes for how long she could only guess. They had been sent to sea, bullied, half starved and threatened on every side by punishment or death. She had not thought of them as individuals before. They had been an anonymous background for men like von Steiger or Heuss. But now, as she felt the scrape of rough serge clothing against her body, she could sense the yearning and the primitive emotions of these very men.

Hauptmann, the man who had called from the bow, glared at Schaffer, the coxswain, with sudden fury. 'What's the risk, you fool? Maybe we have been left to die, eh? What do you think of that?' He turned to the others, made bold by the apprehension on the coxswain's face. 'What have we to lose, comrades? If we die, we die! But if the *Vulkan* finds us, we will say that the girl fell overboard! Come on, let us use her while we can! God, I have not had a woman for months!'

Some of the men looked uneasy, but others murmured their assent.

Hauptmann, a short, muscular ex-docker, showed his uneven teeth. 'Agreed? One at a time, and we will find out what an officer's woman is like!'

Schaffer moved closer to the shivering girl. 'I will kill the first man to come near!' He unshipped the heavy tiller-bar. 'I swear I will!'

'You old fool, we can finish you as well!'

In English Schaffer muttered: 'Keep close by me! That one is like a madman!'

She watched Hauptmann move down the middle of the boat towards them. He stepped carefully over the banked oars and the watching seamen, the motion of the pitching boat making his walk like a swagger. He was grinning broadly, but his eyes were like slits as he watched the tiller-bar in the coxswain's hand. He stood swaying on the last thwart, his thumbs in his belt.

She could sense the animal power in the man, and saw the contemptuous ease with which he maintained his balance in the madly tossing boat. She felt her nails biting into the palms of her hand. This was what she had expected would happen from the first. Von Steiger's courtesy and Heuss's eagerness were only a veneer to this.

The man at the second oar suddenly laughed, a great hoarse bellow of sound, so that Hauptmann paused, uncertain and off his guard.

Schiller leaned his elbows on his oar and laughed again. He saw the gratitude in Schaffer's apprehensive eyes and the terror on the face of the girl. He had almost allowed Hauptmann to carry out his threat. It would be something to add to his list of memories. He had never seen a girl taken in a drifting boat before, but somehow Hauptmann was not the man. A useless ex-docker, who was more of a boaster than a seaman. He spat on the loom of his oar.

'Sit down, bonehead!'

Hauptmann faltered, aware of the others watching him. 'What's the matter? If he is scared we can manage him, too!'

'That's right, mates!' Schiller grinned. 'All you have to do is beat me and you can have the girl!' He tapped the haft of his knife. 'Who's first?'

A man shouted shakily, 'Smoke! Look, lads! Smoke!'

They were all on their feet in the madly swaying boat, trying to see the cause of the smoke-trail which occasionally showed itself above the wave-tops.

Schaffer gestured with the tiller-bar. 'Man your oars!' He was in control again. To him it did not matter what the other ship was; there would be officers, discipline and safety.

The oars creaked and bent under their concerted efforts, and as they moved painfully towards the smoke the *Vulkan*'s tall funnel and raked masts swept forward to greet them.

All at once they were beneath the lee of her hull, and the men were snatching at the dangling falls to hook on their boat. They could see the scarred plates in her side, and smell the tang of cordite and burned timber. As the boat was hauled skywards towards the davits the raider began to move forward once more, and the men who laboured at the torn decks and doused the last piece of smouldering wreckage hardly gave a glance to the eager, whooping seamen who clambered down from the rescued boat.

Caryl Brett turned to find the men who had been with her in the boat, but already they had been swallowed up by the rest of the crew. Only the coxswain stood patiently supervising the securing of his boat. She started to thank him, but he stared past her, already part of that other world she could not share.

As she made her way along the littered boatdeck she could hardly realize that this was the same ship she had left that morning. The white paint was blackened and blistered by fire, and several parts of the bridge were riddled with small, savage holes, which had burned away the steel plates and left the edges of the punctures smooth and bright like molten metal.

An officer barred her way, and she gave a start as she realized that this tall, blackened figure was the normally spruce and youthful Damrosch.

'Would you please go to the sick quarters! We have had many casualties, and Steuer cannot manage without your help.' He stared at her soaked skirt and disordered hair. 'But first you must get some dry clothing! I must apologize for not thinking of that!'

'I do not have to help with your wounded.' She lifted her chin and momentarily forgot the misery of her wet body and the experience she had just suffered. 'I was forced to go as a decoy in your boat, I cannot be forced to help with any more of your chivalrous ideas!'

She had expected him to strike her or to shout at her, but instead his face seemed to crumble, and his shoulders sagged with sudden despair. 'You must do as you wish,' he said. 'I cannot blame you for your anger.'

She stared at him, aware for the first time of the shock and misery in his eyes and the vague, disjointed movements of his hands as he spoke.

At that moment Lieutenant Heuss appeared round the side of the bridge ladder, his eyes unnaturally bright and searching, his air almost jaunty as he hurried towards her. There was neither caution nor pretence in his tone, as brushing past the other officer he seized her cold hands in his and peered down into her face, his teeth white against the powder smoke which seemed to cover him from head to foot.

'Thank God you are safe! I thought we should never find you!' He ran his eyes over her soaked clothing, and the hair disordered across her forehead. 'I cannot tell you how pleased I am. It has been hell enough here without worrying about you!'

She wanted to protest, to pull away her hands from his, but something in his voice and in his manner prevented her and seemed to bring an ache to her mind, like an old memory.

Heuss glanced at Damrosch, who still stared blankly at the confusion of scurrying seamen. 'You get forward, Max,' he said gently, 'and keep an eye on the men up there.' And then, in a slightly sharper note, 'Hold on, comrade, it could have been worse.' As Damrosch walked slowly away he turned back to the girl. 'It could have been *much* worse!'

She heard herself say, 'They need me in the sick quarters?'

He shook his head. 'I think it better if you stay away from there. It is not a pleasant sight at the moment. No, it would be as well for you to keep away.'

A thin cry floated along the deck, and she felt his grip tighten. 'Poor devils,' he said quietly, 'they are not used to this.'

She thought of all the things she had intended to say. About how it was paying them back for what they had done to others and for what they and their kind were doing in Europe. It all seemed too trite, too hollow, now. Instead she said, 'I am glad you were safe, too.'

He seemed to forget the ship and the battle, and his face was suddenly very intense. 'Do you really mean that?'

She stammered: 'Yes, I do. You have been very kind to me. I do not think you really had to be.'

'I should like to talk to you again. I should like that very much. But I have been told to escort you to the bridge. The Captain wishes to speak to you.' He squeezed her hands tighter as he saw the fires light up in her eyes. 'Please do not get angry. Von Steiger has asked for you to go. I think your going away in the boat has been on his conscience.'

'Has he got a conscience? I think he is a law unto himself!'

'Perhaps, but he is also responsible for all of *us*.' He dropped his voice. 'He has been wounded. Yet he just sits there directing all of us, driving us until we hate him. Nothing can stop him.' He grinned sheepishly. 'He behaves like the devil, but does not have the decency to look like him!'

A seaman came at the double, a thick bridge-coat in his hands.

'Ah, here it is.' Heuss helped her into it and lifted the high collar around her throat. 'Are you ready?'

She followed him up the ladder, shutting her eyes to the dark stains splashed across the planking and a still shape covered by a piece of canvas.

The bridge lookouts stared at her with amazement as she stepped on to the sacred deck, forbidden to all but those with authority there.

Inside the wheelhouse a man was already fixing a new plate of glass in a window, and another was sweeping up the mess of wood splinters and torn paintwork. Heuss paused outside the varnished door at the rear of the bridge, his eyes bright in the half-light. 'Ready?' She nodded, and he knocked on the door.

The small cabin was seemingly crowded with people. Niklas, the Chief Engineer, was squatting on the edge of the table, a pencil dashing across a notebook, and Sub-Lieutenant Seebohm, his arm in a sling, was stolidly reporting progress with repairs on the upper deck. Three petty officers waited by the bulkhead, either writing in their notebooks or merely awaiting instructions, and somehow, through this throng, Reeder, the steward, threaded his way, his expression rather disapproving as he refilled the cups from a large coffee-pot.

Von Steiger sat on the edge of his bunk, his jacket thrown over his bare shoulders, beneath which showed a wide bandage, which crossed his body like a white sash. The girl saw him grimace slightly as he rose to his feet, brushing away the hands which reached out to steady him.

He studied her face carefully, and glanced briefly at Heuss, who stood close at her side.

'I want to offer my apologies for what happened, Frau Brett. Under the circumstances, you were safer in the boat, although I must confess I was thinking mainly of my plan of action when I ordered your removal.' He winced, and sat down heavily. 'Excuse my sitting down in your presence, but I find that I am not so invulnerable as I would have people believe!' He snapped his fingers at Reeder. 'A fresh cup of coffee for our guest.' He looked across the littered table, his face suddenly relaxed. 'And a guest is what you have become, whether you like it or not. I am sure there are some who will be indeed sorry to see you leave this ship, although I am equally sure you will be relieved.' He smiled, but seemed uneasy, as if he depended greatly upon what answer she might give.

What is happening to me? The words pounded in her brain. I hate this man and all that he stands for. He is more than a German, he has become a personal enemy. Of course, he wanted her to submit to his new mood of humility, if only that she should be silenced. If she told him of the men in the boat and what might have happened to her, he would speak differently. Those men would be punished, she had no doubt of that, and the resentment in some of the crew, that Gelb had told her about, would be fanned into a more dangerous flame.

Niklas, the engineer, looked up from his list and watched the emotions chasing one another across her face. He waited until she had sat on the proffered chair and had the large coffee-cup cradled in her small hands. Hands which were still dainty and fascinating, in spite of the cold and misery of an open boat. He said gruffly: 'Only Lieutenant Heuss and I can understand what is being said by you and the Captain. The others are content with their own language, as you are, so you can answer freely. But, my dear, before you speak your thoughts, and I can guess what they are, let me tell you something.' He turned his back deliberately on von Steiger as he leaned forward to protest. Usually Niklas's dishevelled appearance made him stand out against the other deck officers, but now his white boiler-suit looked almost smart beside the battle-weary men who were standing around him.

'We had quite a fight with the American. It was a near thing, whatever some of us might say now that it is over. We have broken off the action, so that we can put many miles between him and us, so that by the time he is found by his friends we shall be well clear to the south. We are steaming at full speed now'—he smiled wryly—'I should know, eh? But in spite of the risk and the danger, the Captain insisted on turning back to find you.' He watched her soberly. 'That was quite a deed. He would not receive medical attention, although he had a shell-splinter in his chest as big as this pencil, until his men were cared for and until he was sure his ship was prepared to fight again if need be. Think of these things before you judge. I am an old man— I could be your father, almost a grandfather in fact—and I have nothing left to hide, but although we are enemies, because we are ordered so to be, I think you will remember this deed with pride, if not with gladness.'

Von Steiger groaned. 'For God's sake hold your tongue!' He laughed, a short, nervous sound. 'He is not only old, he is senile!'

She placed the cup on the table and watched it vibrate to the thunder of the engine. 'Thank you for coming back for me, Captain,' she said quietly. 'I shall not forget that.' Immediately she sensed the relief on von Steiger's face, like the passing of a cloud.

She stood up. 'And now, in spite of what I have been told, I should like to go and help Steuer with the wounded. Are there many?' Her voice was level and calm, yet she could feel the trembling in her limbs. I am mad, she thought. What am I doing?

Von Steiger kneaded his forehead with his knuckles. 'Eight dead at present, and another fourteen wounded. Some more slightly injured men are resting in their quarters, and I hope will not concern you.' He lowered his head. 'Thank you for your help. As I think you have already discovered, wounded and sick men have no nationality at all.'

Heuss touched her arm and she stepped through the door. As it started to close she heard von Steiger's voice again, crisp and impatient. 'Now, Niklas, I want you to get all available men from the engine-room working to repair the plates we have lost. I have ordered Dehler to get the whole ship repainted above decks before the next forty-eight hours!'

The door closed, and Heuss shrugged at her in mock despair. 'You see? What can you do with such a man?'

. . . . .

A whistle shrilled, and the seamen threw themselves wearily down on the deck or wherever they had been working for a few moments' respite. The light was beginning to fade, but the sky had cleared and the air was keen and dry. Soon the first pale stars would be seen in the sky, but even the rarity of such a sight made little impression on the men, who crouched or lay, breathing heavily and staring with hatred at the tools and shovels which were scattered around them, at the fresh planks which the carpenter and his mates had prepared for the torn gaps in the decks, and at the great pots of boiling pitch with which they had yet to pay the open seams. All afternoon the air had been filled with their clamour, the screech of saws on metal and wood, the bang of hammers or the never-ending commotion caused by the work of shifting coal to the ever hungry bunkers.

Schiller lay back against a sweet-smelling baulk of timber and closed his eyes. Half a cheroot protruded from his lips, and his cap was tilted jauntily over his forehead. He half listened to the grumbling and whining of some of the men near him, and smiled to himself. It had been a very near thing in the boat that morning. Still, he could have been killed by a shell, or be screaming like that wretch under the knife in the sick quarters. As they had worked he had heard the dreadful cries, even above the din on deck. And to think that girl was in there helping, after what that fool Hauptmann had tried to do in the boat. He shook his head, amazed at the stupidity of his fellow creatures. She could be living like a queen in the Captain's quarters now, her feet on a silk cushion and a bottle of schnapps at her elbow. Instead, she was amongst all that blood and pus up there. He opened one eye as somebody slumped down beside him. It was Pieck, pale and grim-looking.

Schiller sighed. More trouble. Poor Willi had been a bit queer lately. Something new on his mind. Still, the detention barracks were enough for anybody, let alone a boy like him.

'Hello, Willi! Where have you been? We've been slogging out our guts up here!'

The boy drew his knees up to his chin, his eyes on the other men. 'I've been to the sick quarters. I tried to see Alder.'

'Oh? What for? Leave him be, boy! He's a damn' sight better off than we are!'

Pieck turned towards him, his eyes desperate. 'You don't know what happened the other night!' His mouth trembled. 'You've got to help, Gustav! I don't know who else to turn to!'

Schiller drew in on the cheroot. 'Spit it out, Willi! But keep your voice down a bit.'

'Petty Officer Brandt is dead.'

'Christ! Is that all? I knew all about that!'

Pieck's voice sounded as if it would break. 'Alder killed him!'

'What?' Schiller sat upright, his eyes suddenly alive. 'Say that again!'

He nodded. 'Yes, he killed him. Brandt locked me in the ice-room, and I nearly died. I could not move.'

'Locked you in?' Schiller stared at him incredulously, as if he had gone mad.

Pieck closed his eyes, reliving the terror when the great door had banged behind him. At first he had pounded the door with his fists, and had then decided to make one last effort to keep control of himself. He had marched back and forth across the iced floor, his naked shoulders gleaming blue beneath the emergency light. He had lost sense of time, and when he began to stumble and cannon into packing-cases and frozen carcasses, a warning flashed in his tortured brain. He was beginning to lose control of his limbs. The intense, almost searing, cold had killed his resistance, and he knew that he was almost finished. It had been then that he had flung himself again at the door, his feet, hands, even his head crashing against the unmoving, ice-sheeted plates. He vaguely remembered falling and the light flooding in through the door.

His feet banged against the rungs of the ladder as he was dragged slowly upwards through the hatch and along the silent passageways. Then he fainted away once more, only to recover, spluttering and choking, as the burning schnapps flooded his throat and spilled down his chin. He was wrapped in blankets, and painfully aware of the feeling returning to his body.

He suddenly realized that he was telling all this to Schiller in a flat, toneless voice.

'It was Alder,' he said at length. 'He saw Brandt lock me in and came to help me.' He shuddered, imagining the feeble Alder, alone with his terrible mission. 'He made a noise, and Brandt saw him. He was going to come for you, but Brandt saw him and ran after him before he could get away. I think he chased him along the starboard passageway to where that inspection door opens into Number Two hold. He got the door open just as Brandt reached him, and then . . . and then . . .' His voice died.

'Well, go on!' Schiller's face was like stone.

'Alder jumped into the hold on top of the coal. When Brandt looked over the coaming he smashed his head in with a piece of coal!'

Schiller sat back, his brain working fast. 'So that bastard's carcass is still on board, eh? Well, who planted his cap on deck to make it look as if he had gone over the side?'

'Alder. He must have had one of his saner moments. What will we do? If they find the body they're bound to suspect one of us. They've been hounding Alder and me since we came aboard!'

Schiller grunted. 'Number Two hold, eh?' They both looked at the hold cover nearby. 'Lucky it wasn't Number One. They're moving coal from there right now!' He creased his face into a frown. 'We'll get rid of him tonight.'

'You'll help, then?' He stared at him with relief and gratitude.

'Suppose so. Us gaolbirds must hang together!'

The whistle shrilled once more, and Schiller reached for his hammer. 'I'll work something out, Willi.' As he put his cheroot carefully in his cap he asked, 'By the way, Willi, what did Brandt want to know?'

Pieck went even paler and shook his head. 'I—I am not sure!'

'He'd found out about you and Lieutenant Kohler, eh?'

Pieck dropped his hammer on the deck, his lips ashen. 'You *know*?'

'Of course! What did you expect?' As the men began to move to their jobs, he grabbed the boy by the shoulder. 'Do you want to go on with it? Do you really like what that swine does to you?'

'No, no! I've been so afraid, I didn't know what to do! He threatened to tell my parents, he——'

Schiller had seen a petty officer drawing near. 'Listen, don't go any more! Keep away, see?'

'But if he makes more trouble?' He hung his head. 'I couldn't bear any more detention and punishment, and what it would do to my family!'

'If he tries any more he'll follow Brandt!'

'You *wouldn't*! Not an officer!'

'Wouldn't I? Look at my face, Willi, and tell me what *you* think!'

.   .   .   .   .

Eduard Steuer pulled the blanket across the man's face and stood up, his eyes dark with fatigue. His white smock was daubed with dark-brown stains, and his bare arms were also disfigured with patches of dried blood.

'Another one,' he said quietly, and two seamen, who had been sitting in a corner of the sick quarters playing cards, reached for a folded stretcher and began to roll the lifeless body out of the cot.

Steuer did not look round as the men shambled out with their burden, but as the heavy curtain was pulled back and the door opened on to the moonlit deck he felt the cool air on his cheek, and some of the pain and misery seemed to fade before that small contact with the outside world.

He crossed to the small table at the far end, and stood looking down at the girl. She, too, was wearing a white smock, and her hair was tied back from her small ears with a piece of bandage. He noticed the tiny droplets of perspiration on her forehead and on her upper lip, but also he saw her composure and strange serenity.

Her voice was low and husky. 'What time is it?'

There was a clock above her head, but he answered: 'After midnight. I think you should turn in, as the British would say.'

She did not appear to hear. 'It is quiet now. I did not notice it happening. It just came, like the darkness.'

He nodded. As he looked along the ranks of shaded cots, swinging gently in the ship's easy motion, he wondered how they had managed to restore order and peace to what had been a scene out of hell. He had worked steadily throughout the action, deaf to the shattering explosions which rocked the ship, and the awful cries which echoed around the hull like souls in torment. The first case had almost unnerved him. A man with no feet, kicking and screaming, fighting his two comrades who had carried him from the boatdeck above. His bloodied legs opened and closed like scissors, and before he could even get him on the table he was dead. He had stood for several seconds, just staring at the man's contorted face and broken legs, with the bones protruding from the blackened flesh like splintered wood. He had made himself look, and had told himself, This is where you decide whether you can go on playing the doctor, or run away from it. After that he had cleared his mind of all else but his work, had treated each new case with the efficiency of a mechanic, and not as a mere human.

The floor space had gradually filled with soiled dressings, broken splints and bloody rags. His unwilling working party emptied the enamel pails repeatedly, sometimes retching at their contents, and sometimes thanking God that they at least were spared.

It had seemed hopeless, and then the girl had come in, as she had that first morning. Frightened, fragile but so grimly determined to help, that she swung the scales in his favour. Now the place was quiet. Nine men had died so far, and another thirteen lay in the cots. Some were as still as death, rescued from horror by hurriedly applied anaesthetics. Others lay apparently asleep, but with their eyes open and unblinking, no doubt thinking of their wounds, and dreading the dawn.

She handed him his cigarette case, and he smiled. 'Thank you. I think I need one now.'

'What was it like on board during the battle?'

He shrugged, and watched the smoke pass into the fan. 'It was outside, it did not seem part of all this. I felt like a man who runs into a church during a terrible storm. It is hard to explain.'

'What about the Captain?'

He darted a quick glance at a cot, as one of the men moaned violently and then fell silent. 'That was the only time I left here. It was after the action; in fact, I did not know he had been wounded. He was sitting in his chair on the bridge, and opposite him there was a small hole in the glass. A stray splinter had hit him without anyone seeing.' He shook his head, still unwilling to accept it. 'It was uncanny! He was soaked in blood, and yet would not let me do more than stick a shell-dressing under his shirt.'

Her wide eyes were watching him gravely. 'He must have been in great pain?'

'Terrible. It must have been half spent when it struck him, probably a ricochet, otherwise it would have gone right through him!'

'You admire him, don't you?'

He drew in on the cigarette before answering. 'I don't know. All I know is that today he would not give up until your boat was sighted.' He smiled sadly. 'He ordered Heuss to stay at his side in case he fainted. I think he is always afraid that Dehler will jump at the chance to overthrow him and take command! After today I think he has little to fear in that way!'

215

'Why is that?'

'Dehler has had a stomach full of fighting.'

She shook her head. 'If I try to reason it all out I become dazed by all that has happened. It makes me verge on hysteria.'

'I am not surprised. You have suffered more than all of us. Yet you are in so many ways stronger than the rest, even than von Steiger.'

She forced a smile. 'You are teasing me!'

'I am quite serious. For all that you may hear or see, I still believe he is a sentimentalist. He laughs at others who preach idealism or boast of their private beliefs, but he is affected by other forces as well.'

'What drives him? What makes him so completely dedicated?'

'I think it is despair. He is no ordinary commander. He is a thinker. He is like that old British captain from the *Cardiff Maid*. He has only his ship now, and I think he is just beginning to realize it.'

She stood up and stretched, aware of the great tiredness which enfolded her and chilled her body. She felt dirty, and ached in every bone. All at once she wanted to get out of this place, with its smell of living death, and find the peace and privacy of her cabin. She suddenly remembered that the fresh water was turned off, and the bewitching picture of a hot bath faded like a distorted mirror.

As if reading her thoughts, the Swiss smiled. 'A salt-water shower is as good as anything for freshening you up.' He held out a small packet. 'Have one of these, and I guarantee you a good sleep. It is what you need now more than anything.'

She paused, her hand on the curtain, the fatigue making her sway. 'Where are we going, Eduard? What will happen?'

'I do not know. South, to a better climate. I have heard a rumour that von Steiger intends to touch the South Americas somewhere to get rid of the wounded and the "unwilling passengers"!' He seized her hand inpulsively and held it to his lips. 'I shall always thank the fates for permitting me to meet and work with a real lady! It has all been worth that!'

She stepped out on to the deck, the bridge-coat heavy across her shoulders. The ship was quiet and still, and she realized that the engine had stopped. She crossed to the rail and stood silently in the shadow of the boatdeck. The afterdeck was dappled in bright moonlight, criss-crossed with black bars, made by the shadows of the rigging and spars overhead. Beyond the rail the dark water gleamed silver, and the horizon below the pale moon looked like a long, scattered necklace.

She saw the small huddle of figures by the rail, the bared heads, and the rank of still shapes on the scarred planking. She saw, too, von Steiger, his coat still hanging like a cape across his shoulders, reading the burial service by the light of a shaded lantern. Her heart jumped each time one of the pathetic bundles splashed over the side, and she found herself counting. Nine men. Some of them might have spoken to her, or leered at her passing. And some of them she would never have noticed. Now they were on their last journey. The night was so beautiful that she wanted to cry. Someone should cry, she thought, before hatred took even tears away.

When she looked again the deck was clear, and the small party of mourners had vanished. She shook herself, and found that she was almost running along the boatdeck. The sentry at the end of the passageway did not move as she passed him, his chin was on his chest, and he slept on his feet.

She closed the door behind her, and without even switching on the light sat down on the wide bunk. The packet of pills rolled across the polished floor, and she, too, was asleep.

Outside, the mast spiralled gently around the distant stars, and the engine began its symphony once more.

.　　　.　　　.　　　.　　　.

Niklas slid his buttocks forward to the edge of the chair and thrust his thin legs beneath the table. His chin, stiff with stubble, was resting on his interwoven fingers, so that he appeared to be squinting at his captain like a knowing sparrow.

The sea cabin was heavy with smoke from cheroots and the old cracked pipe which Niklas usually favoured, and the table was still littered with books, charts and scraps of paper of all sorts. Von Steiger lay on his bunk, his body bare to the waist and one hand gingerly exploring the bandage across his chest. He looked spent, but his voice still sounded controlled and even.

'Well, I have buried nine good men, Niklas. I am only sorry that their passing will hardly be noticed by those other than ourselves!'

'You did well to bury them at night. The crew are doleful enough after their little battle, without being reminded of their closeness to the grave!'

Von Steiger frowned. 'I am afraid they have a lot to learn! It was all fine while we were doing as we pleased, but a bloody nose is not the same when *you* have to wear it!'

Niklas looked at the clock and groaned. 'Look at the time! It will be dawn in a few hours! Why do I encourage you in your campaign against sleep?'

Von Steiger tried to laugh, but the soreness in his chest made him quiver and a rash of sweat break out on his forehead. 'Go away, you old fraud! Go and find peace with your engine!'

Niklas noticed the freckles across von Steiger's shoulders, and envied him his ability to hold on to youth. 'I am going. Why not do what everyone else but the watchkeepers are doing? Go to sleep yourself!'

As he moved stiffly from the sea cabin, the Captain swung his legs over the edge of the bunk and stared with distaste at the disordered cabin. It would all be waiting for him when he awoke. The chart with its new course—a near-straight line, desperate in haste, running to the south and to the sun. He tried to remember what a clear hot sky looked like, and what it was like to feel clean.

He remembered the beauty of the sea as he had buried his dead seamen, and its apparent emptiness. It was just another illusion. Even now, as he sat here, they were being hunted. The air would be alive with signals, and weary captains would probably be called from their beds to weigh anchor, or to leave a convoy and search for the German raider.

He shook his head. Not much of a raider. Not much to show for his efforts. It was strange how he was changing. He had wanted only peace in which to hide his misery. His officers had desired otherwise. They thirsted after honours and glories, which he knew were not to be had; they wanted to destroy the enemy, when he could have told them that their own destruction was the more likely. Now it was all changed. One action with a destroyer and their eagerness had collapsed into fear and resentment.

He scrambled to his feet and began to pace. Aloud he said: 'Now I am the one who has had the legacy of their ideals passed to me for solution. Against my will, and in spite of what I know must be inevitable, I must now drive them along a course which I despise! I can no longer find comfort in knowing them to be wrong, because their realization has come too late for all of us!'

He halted, breathing painfully. Why did not that splinter do its work? When it had struck him, the agony had rendered him incapable of thought or even the ability to cry out. As the seconds passed he had waited to die, expecting the peace which he had always imagined would follow the one final wound. He had tried to think of Freda, but even through the mists of pain he was unable to recall her face. This shock alone had jolted him back to life. He had returned with the knowledge that in some strange way he had been cheated.

When he had inspected the damage to his ship he had realized, perhaps for the first time, just what she had come to mean to him. As he had limped painfully from deck to deck, the men had stood back, respectful, yet hostile. He represented their safety, but at the same time he was the one man who could destroy them.

He had peered into the open door of the sick quarters and watched the girl helping Steuer. He had wanted her to see him, so that he could tell if she had changed since her return from the sea and her appearance on the bridge. She had thanked him for taking the ship back for her. She would never guess just how important that had been to him. Returning from the dead, he had driven the ship like a madman. A cheated madman, who could not remember the face of his wife. Because she had been part of another life and another world which had rejected him, and which he had rejected. Only here in this ship was there reality. But the girl in the white smock had not seen him. Her eyes had passed over him like a blind girl's, and her face had been empty of everything but determination.

He looked at his bunk, and reached instead for his black leather coat. The fur collar felt warm about his ears, and the lining soothing against his skin and chafing bandage.

He clapped on his cap and strode purposefully through the wheelhouse. The dark figures stiffened into watchfulness as he passed. Ebert by the chart-table, no doubt dreaming of how well his guns had behaved. Heuss on the far side of the bridge, his shoulders hunched against the chill air.

He passed them without speaking, behind the lookouts and down the exposed ladder to the forward deck. All around him his ship was asleep and resting. As his boot stubbed against a torn plank he smiled gently and felt his own wound. It was right that he had suffered with his ship. He passed close to a hidden gun, and laid his hand on the long barrel as if still expecting to feel the heat of its fury. It was like ice, and he hurried on to the ladder which led up to the high fo'c'sle. He stepped between the unused anchor-cables, feeling the rust scraping his foot, and walked right forward to the eyes of the ship. He turned his back on the stem with its angry turbulence of white foam, and stared back along the full length of his ship. Nothing moved but the shadows caused by the low moon and the occasional lift of spray over the rail. In the moonlight it looked like a phantom ship, driving on, committed to an endless journey alone with its captain.

The glass of the bridge windows glinted like black eyes and seemed to be watching him, and he could see the dim shape of the crow's-nest spiralling high above the deck.

I wonder how the lookout feels up there now? Knowing that a dead man had earlier shared his post. It was strange that he had stressed its importance so early in the voyage, and how much tragedy it had brought, either for the enemy or the men who had kept a lonely vigil there.

He walked slowly back towards the bridge, his chin on his chest. The walk had weakened him again and his feet were heavy. He passed two seamen and sensed their animal surprise, but did not look up as they passed. He turned the end of the boatdeck and saw the shape of the sentry in the unlighted passageway.

She was in his cabin, asleep. He had taken her from the sea to make her humble and grateful. Instead, he was the one who had been humbled. He dragged himself back to his tiny cabin on the bridge and lowered himself on to his bunk.

There was so much to think about. Coal, repairs, even disguising the ship would have to be tackled in the morning.

In the mirror he saw a bright-red spot in the centre of his bandage and cursed weakly.

A bell chimed in the distance, and he heard the Morning Watch assembling on the lower deck.

He lay down and tried to place the different sounds, which were like the heartbeats of his ship, and think about the nine men he had buried.

Von Steiger fell into an uneasy sleep as his ship carried him to the south. Behind the ship, and beyond her wake, lay confusion and the rallying calls of pursuit and vengeance.

As the Morning Watch moved listlessly to their posts, Schiller and Pieck sat in their messdeck, looking at each other.

Pieck said: 'The Captain did not see us! He walked right past!'

Schiller grunted, and clambered into his bunk. 'Von Steiger would understand! After all, he has buried nine of us, we only buried one petty officer!'

Part Three

At thirteen-fifteen the enemy opened fire.'

12

EXTRACT from von Steiger's report:

January 31st, 1918.

It is now thirty-five days since we sailed from Kiel, and in that time we have covered over six thousand miles. At noon today our approximate position was one thousand miles north-east of the Brazilian coast, and eight hundred miles west of the African Continent. At this moment we are crossing the Fifteenth Parallel, and also what was once the busiest trade route between the South Americas and Europe.

It is nine days since our skirmish with the destroyer, and yet we have sighted nothing but a small ship in the far distance, which altered course away from us before its size and class could be identified. The sea is empty, and yet I feel that we are being hunted for every mile that we steam.

Another of the wounded men has died, bringing the total to ten, and of the wounded, two of the seamen are in real danger, having succumbed to gangrene poisoning.

Food is a problem, there being no vegetables of any kind left in the stores, and personal fresh water is rationed to a pint a day for each man aboard. Morale is as good as can be expected, but the majority of the ship's company are still unused to the demanding ways of the sea, and are finding the hardships of bad food and lack of personal cleanliness difficult to surmount.

It is eleven days since we replenished the bunkers from the collier Nemesis, and I shall endeavour to make contact with her at the first opportunity, as coal is getting dangerously low once more.

Against this, however, I am pleased to see the change in the weather as we move still closer to the Equator. The skies remain clear, and the sun helps to make up for much of the harshness of life on board for my men.

There is still no fresh information about the loss of Petty Officer Brandt, but I feel an undercurrent which I cannot explain in connection with this matter.

The prisoners are in good condition, and the woman has been a great help to the sick, and quite unselfish in her voluntary help with these unfortunate fellows. I shall, however, try to put them aboard a neutral ship, or perhaps land them at an early opportunity.

I am desperate for information of the outside world, of the conduct of the war and of the deployment of enemy naval forces. I am like a blind man, and must feel my way at every step.

My officers are doing their duties well, but are showing signs of strain.

Yesterday we passed the area where our very first commerce raider, Kaiser Wilhelm der Grosse, was sunk by the British within a month of the declaration of war. We would all wish to avenge her and her successors, but so far this cruise has been disappointing in its lack of prizes.

My own wound is giving me a little trouble, but the sun is helping to give me strength, and patience. . . .

. . . .

It was at two bells of the Afternoon Watch that the ship was sighted. She was so low in the water that against the glimmering sheen of the sea her upperworks appeared as a mere smudge against the hazy horizon line. The *Vulkan*, still under Dutch colours, but shining dully in her new paint and renamed *Van Diemen*, altered course immediately to intercept, the men running unwillingly from the midday meal, squinting with nervous apprehension first towards the bridge and then at the smiling sea, which shone warmly, like pale-green milk.

Von Steiger closed the leather-bound book in which he had been writing his daily report, and listened to the alarm bells and the sudden urgent clamour of noises within the ship.

The pale, fresh sunlight faded as Reeder slammed down the steel deadlight across the scuttle and swept the remains of the Captain's meal on to a tray. He scurried away to his station with a first-aid party, his unhealthy face set and miserable.

Von Steiger forgot his steward and his report as he stepped on to the bridge, his eyes taking in the orderly preparedness which, in control of everyone present, hid the worries and anxious thoughts he knew were plaguing his men as they prepared for action. Was it another warship? Why not just run away? They were the mad fleeting questions they would be asking themselves as they tore away the gun-muzzle covers and slammed the shells into the gaping breeches.

'Ship closed up at Action Stations, Captain!' Heuss saluted formally, his face impassive. 'Masthead reports target fine on the port bow. She is just breaking out of the haze.'

A voice-pipe crackled irritably as Ebert reported that the range-finder had found and was tracking the other ship.

Von Steiger pursed his lips as a twinge of pain moved in the scar beneath his jacket. He decided to ignore it, and strode impatiently to the side of the bridge and felt the power of the sun magnified by the plate-glass windows, so that it enfolded his body in comfortable warmth.

It was amazing the difference finer weather had made, and had they been better stocked and equipped, as his other raider had been, this cruise could be almost enjoyable. The bridge superstructure shone in its new buff paint, and the tall, yellow funnel, bearing a black star, gave the ship almost a holiday atmosphere. Not so the crew, he thought. Their faces looked drawn and grey with stubble, and their shoddy uniforms added to their dishevelled and wild appearance.

It was as if they had given their own strength and vitality to the ship itself, and had been left with only their empty husks. For over a week they had been driven without mercy and reprieve, and only at close quarters could the repaired shot-holes be recognized and the new planks on the scarred decks be visible for what they were.

Von Steiger frowned. Tomorrow he would get the ship's company changed into white uniforms. That alteration of routine and sur-roundings, plus the warm air, would help to shake them out of their doldrums. The extra washing which that would entail would keep them too busy to grumble, and salt-water would have to suffice for the moment.

The bridge lookouts had picked up the other ship and were passing their information to the wheelhouse. Von Steiger remained silent and aloof, like a spectator. He could now trust his officers to cope with the preliminaries. He did not want to tire himself too early in the operation and make the one small slip in judgement which might kill them all.

Damrosch manipulated the power of his binoculars, his lips pouting with concentration. He rarely smiled any more and his tone was always sharp, but more confident than before the action with the American warship.

'She is not making any smoke, sir! I think she is stopped!'

Von Steiger looked at the newcomer with immediate caution. She was still well away from the raider and not closing the range as she should have been. She must be stopped, he thought. He squinted painfully as an orange shaft of sunlight lanced up from the unbroken water. The sea was so inviting, he thought, yet gave the impression of immeasurable depth and patient cruelty.

As they drew nearer he knew the reason for the stranger's indifference. Her bow was barely a few feet above the gently lapping water, and her screw glinted brightly where her rounded stern jutted dangerously clear of the sea.

Von Steiger could feel the taut silence within the bridge, but concentrated on that small circular world within the lenses of his glasses. The smokeless stack, the empty boat-falls dangling loose and swaying down the rusty sides, the buckled guardrails and splintered foremast, with its attendant mass of torn and tangled rigging. All these things were familiar to him. Torpedoed and abandoned, probably hundreds of miles to the east of the African coast, by one of the new ocean-going submarines, and carried dismally across the Atlantic by the Equatorial current. A ghost ship, a relic already forgotten by its crew and its country.

He cleared his throat and saw Damrosch jump nervously. 'Clear away port battery! Fire one round across her bows!'

He waited as the orders were passed and the big five-point-nines showed themselves to the sun for the first time. Another agonizing pause, and then a shot. Even the shot seemed reluctant to trouble the lonely wanderer, and in the warm, moist air they heard the shell thunder away across the strip of glittering water with the sound of tearing silk.

Far away, the tall waterspout rose and vanished. Leaving only the sound of the *Vulkan*'s engine and the smudge of brown smoke around her fo'c'sle.

'Stop engine!'

They glided slowly towards the other ship, the gun-muzzles still following her, like uncertain dogs around a dead rabbit.

Von Steiger made up his mind. 'Pass the word for Lieutenant

Kohler! My compliments to Lieutenant Dehler, and tell him I wish to have both whaleboats ready for lowering.' The messengers scurried from the bridge, and he turned to Heuss, who was watching him from the shadowed chart-space. 'We shall board her and find out if she has any coal in her bunkers.'

'Is that wise, sir? She looks very low in the water and has a bad list.'

'It is necessary. That ship has managed to get this far, so I imagine she might stay afloat a little longer.' He frowned. Why should I try to justify myself to him? Is it because I feel guilty in some way? He thrust the idea from his mind as Kohler appeared at his side.

'You sent for me, Captain?' His handsome face was tense.

'Take two boats and a boarding party. Twelve seamen and three stokers. In addition, I want the Second Engineer to go with you and two petty officers. Search that ship from end to end! First, I want any coal that you may find, and then food, if there is any.'

Kohler looked across at the rusty ship, his eyes doubtful.

'Furthermore, you yourself can try to find any information which might be of use. Newspapers, old logbooks, anything—understand?'

Kohler saluted. 'At once, Captain! I shall attend to it immediately!'

Von Steiger walked on to the open wing of the bridge, conscious of the sun's warmth reflected from the sea. It was a poor wreck to scavenge from, but it was better than nothing. Now that they were closer together, he could see the blackened stains on her bridge where she had also been damaged by shellfire. In spite of himself he cursed his fellow Germans of the submarine service. They had probably torpedoed this ship and then fired on her as the crew tried to abandon her. He sighed. It was a race of self-destruction.

Lieutenant Kohler sat stiffly in the sternsheets of the whaleboat as it was lowered briskly into the water, aware of von Steiger's eyes and the important duty he had to perform.

As the boat was unhooked from the falls and started to move away from the *Vulkan*'s tall side, Kohler looked quickly at his companion and wrinkled his fine nostrils with distaste. Anton Schuman, the Second Engineer, seemed to stink of his trade, and his young face, shaded by the peak of a greasy cap, was pasty-looking, as if starved of fresh air and sunlight. The pores of his skin were starkly ingrained with coal and oil, so that it looked like a mass of blackheads. In spite of his appearance, however, he was cheerful enough and peered with interest at the listing ship ahead.

'By God, she has taken a pasting, Paul! There will not be too much left to salvage!'

Kohler flinched at the free use of his Christian name by this inferior creature. But they were too close to the men for comment. He would put him in his place later. He contented himself with a non-committal grunt.

They scraped alongside, and in the deep rhythmic swell the whaleboat bowed and dipped easily near the dangling falls and a worn rope ladder. Kohler noticed that the ladder and falls were slime-covered near the water, and wondered just how long the ship had sailed alone. He dismissed these thoughts and clambered over the gunwale of the boat and seized the ladder. He climbed carefully, aware that the other whaleboat was also hooking on below him, and conscious, too, of the *Vulkan* as it rode comfortably on the green water.

The decks were a shambles. Blasted planking, pieces of unidentifiable metal plating and pathetic bundles of clothing and personal belongings which the crew had dropped in their mad scramble for the boats.

The boarding party jostled into line on the broken deck, their tired faces curious and hopeful, while the two whaleboats shoved off, as ordered, and idled nearby awaiting fresh instructions.

'Do you know what you have to do?' Kohler looked at his companion. Why did they allow these fellows to be called officers? he wondered.

'Yes. I shall take my petty officer and the three stokers and see what can be done about coal. It will not take long, I think.'

Kohler waited until they had vanished through a twisted hatchway, their lamps switched on in readiness, then turned to Petty Officer Elmke. He was gasping painfully after the climb up the ladder, and his piggy face was streaming with sweat.

'Split your men into pairs. Three pairs to cover the accommodation aft and three pairs below. Watch all of them, and don't let them wander off and get lost. If I get an order to abandon this ship, I shall not wait.'

Schiller found himself with Hahn, and together they climbed up the rust-flaked ladder behind the bridge and into the small group of cabins. The ship had been a small freighter, and all the accommodation was huddled together behind the main superstructure, and below the thin funnel which leaned so drunkenly against its broken stays.

Schiller kicked open the first door and sniffed dubiously at the mildewed air.

Hahn passed him quickly, his eyes darting round the wrecked cabin. He jerked open drawers, searching their contents with deft, practised hands, and scowled when he found only damp clothing or sodden bundles of old letters. He glared at Schiller, who was watching him with amusement. 'Christ, there *must* be something? It's a British ship, so they must have some loot aboard?'

Schiller kicked a broken chair across the cabin with sudden anger. 'I wonder if there's any drink about?'

Hahn's ferret face eased. Of course, that would be the answer. If this fool had a drink under his belt he would be content. It would leave him in safety to find more valuable things. Already, without the big seaman being aware of it, Hahn had pocketed a small clock in a leather case and a pair of cuff-links which looked quite good.

'I will find you some, Gustav!' He strutted to the next cabin, marked 'Chief Officer', and rummaged about in a large chest of drawers which had been torn from its lashings by the torpedo's explosion. Hidden beneath a pile of shirts he found two bottles. One of whisky and one of gin. He showed them to Schiller, who smacked his lips.

'Ah! Now that is more like it!' He took them in his big hands and looked from one to the other. 'God reward the fine fellows who design our torpedoes! They can destroy a ship but preserve the drink!' He forgot Hahn and sat comfortably on the edge of the bunk.

Hahn watched him carefully and waited until he had drawn a cork with his teeth, and then he began to search in earnest.

Gottlieb and Erhard reached the small boatdeck and made their way along the slime-covered catwalk which connected it to the bridge. They stared down at a yawning crater where the torpedo's blast had blown away the upper deck and left the broken deck-beams protruding like black teeth. Far below them they could see the glint of trapped, uneasy water.

'Christ, that's a big one!' Gottlieb stood and mopped his face.

Erhard sighed wearily. 'Don't blaspheme! You'll pay for it if you do!'

'Sorry!' He chuckled and rattled the big sack in his hands. 'Two tins of beef and a bottle of vinegar! Not much of a haul so far, eh?'

Erhard frowned. 'To think we should do this sort of thing! Like scavenging dogs in a back alley! Still, let's go and look at the bridge.'

They moved cautiously into the wide bridge, their feet scraping noisily on the slanting deck. Gottlieb gave a little squeak and gripped his companion by the sleeve. 'Look at that!'

An officer stood propped against the engine-room telegraph, his hands gripping the brass handle as if making a final effort to obtain more speed. His alien uniform was covered with patches of pale-blue mildew, and his hands were more like claws as the bare bones burst through the parchment-like skin to grip the handle better. But his face. Without eyes, and with little skin, it was terrifying enough, but the large yellow teeth bared in a huge grin made Erhard cross himself and mutter beneath his breath.

Gottlieb laughed shakily. 'Nice welcome to get! Scared the daylight out of me!'

He walked slowly round the officer and then stooped to pick up a cap from the deck. He dusted it against his fat leg and placed it carefully on the corpse's head. 'That's more like it!' Regaining his nerve, he saluted. 'An officer should *always* be an example to his men!'

Lieutenant Kohler had found the captain's quarters below the wheelhouse and was leafing through some papers in the old varnished desk. As he searched, his ear listened to the noises made by his men as they groped through the ship or piled their prizes on the upper deck. The whaleboats were passing back and forth to the *Vulkan* with their scanty finds, and even the big dory had been lowered to assist with the work. Tinned food, two barrels of rum and a case of rancid butter had already gone over. In addition, some twenty sacks of small coal had been found in the ship's galley and had been speedily lowered into a waiting boat. Enough for an hour's steaming? He wondered how long they could go on like this. Surely a better plan should have been envisaged by the High Command?

He sat back in the swivel chair and glared at the useless mass of papers. He tried to concentrate on his duties, but all the time he kept seeing Pieck's face and feeling the pain of loss and frustration. He had approached him twice in two days, but the boy had said nothing, just shaken his head as if something greater was frightening him. Perhaps someone else had got hold of him? He dismissed the idea instantly. It must be something else which was making him more afraid than he was of him.

The ship gave a lurch and Kohler jumped to his feet with alarm, but it stopped just as quickly, and he walked nervously into the narrow passageway which led to the other cabins.

Another small sound reached his ear. The chink of metal. He was instantly alert, and creeping on his toes he moved carefully towards a cabin which was partly hidden by a tattered curtain. He halted outside, his ear close against the flaked door. A drawer opened and shut, and he heard a man curse quietly.

As the door crashed open under Kohler's foot, Hahn fell back on his haunches, his startled face wide with surprise and then terror.

'Stand up!' All Kohler's gnawing anxiety of the past few days swept through him like a sheet of flame. 'Drop those things on the deck!'

Hahn opened his nerveless fingers and allowed a bright silver tankard and a cigarette case to fall on the carpet.

Kohler sighed. This would help him to ease his taut nerves. He slipped his hand slowly into his long holster, enjoying the agony in the seaman's eyes as he followed the movement. In the dim light of the cabin the Luger gleamed every bit as brightly as the silver tankard.

He spoke softly. 'You swine! It was wrong to bring your sort aboard. Germany has need of strong, dedicated men, not the sweepings of a gaol! You took your own way, as a filthy pig like you would!' The safety-catch clicked with the sound of a giant gong in Hahn's ears. 'So now you must pay for your greed!'

In spite of the discipline which had held him rigid watching the gun and the mad light in Kohler's eyes, Hahn's legs buckled and he fell on his knees. 'Please, Lieutenant! Don't shoot me! Oh God, have mercy on me! Please give me a chance!'

'You have half a minute!' He gestured with the pistol towards the laughing sunlight which played across the deckhead. 'Prayers, perhaps? What does a swine like you do when death is near?' His thin lips quivered in a smile.

Hahn heard himself babbling and sobbing, his vision distorted by the tears of fear which poured from his eyes. He knew that Kohler would shoot, and would enjoy it. A sudden idea came to him. It would give him time. That was all he wanted.

'Lieutenant Kohler! Just listen, please! I can help you! Seaman Pieck, sir!'

Kohler stiffened, his finger hard against the trigger. 'What about him?'

'I know what he has done, sir! He was there when Petty Officer Brandt was killed, sir!'

Kohler took a pace forward. He was lying. He must be. And yet why should he, on the point of death? 'How do you know?'

'I heard him talking about it, Lieutenant! Brandt had found out about you and him, sir, so they killed him!'

'They? Who was the other man?'

'Alder, sir. But he is mad. He won't tell!' Some of the old craftiness came back to his eyes. 'They thought I was asleep, sir. But I heard them.'

'You are lying!' The pistol lifted a little. 'Why should I believe you?' As he half listened to Hahn's whimpering reply his brain was working at full speed. Of course, that was it. Brandt had been suspicious of him and Pieck, and resented it, too. So Alder had killed him and somehow they had got rid of the body. His throat went dry as he thought of Pieck carrying such terrifying knowledge with him. And this dirty little thief knew all about him! About those visits Pieck had made to his cabin during the night watches.

He breathed in deeply, and Hahn saw the gun waver. He got slowly to his feet, conscious of a great weight being lifted from his shoulders. He had been wise to save that piece of information. Ever since he had learned of Brandt's death and Pieck's ordeal in the ice-room he had wondered how best to use it. He had never dreamed it would save his life.

Kohler nodded gravely. 'I believe you. I am glad you told me.' He gestured with the gun. 'Pull up your jumper.'

Mystified, Hahn dragged out the bottom of his serge jumper, conscious of the damp air cool across his stomach. He controlled the elation which had followed his terror, and felt the mad desire to laugh in the Lieutenant's face. Perhaps he fancies me?

Kohler looked with distaste at the man's scrawny stomach-muscles and grubby skin. Gently he placed the muzzle of the Luger against his navel and squeezed the trigger.

·   ·   ·   ·   ·

Anton Schuman waited impatiently as the seaman at his side signalled with his semaphore flags to the *Vulkan*. Behind him most of the boarding party had drawn up in a small squad, their faces grim and resentful. Petty Officer Elmke was shouting at them to get ready to leave, and already one of the boats was hooking on to the loose falls.

Schuman jumped as his own petty officer, a gaunt engine-room man called Heinemann, touched his sleeve. 'Have they replied yet, sir?'

He shook his head. 'I've told them about the coal in the bunkers. That torpedo made such a great gash in the hull that only one bunker is clear of water. If we remove the coal, the weight of water in the other side will pull her over. I don't know what's holding her up now!'

They both watched the man with flags, his lips moving soundlessly as he spelled out his signal.

Heinemann said quietly, 'Is it true that a man has been shot?'

'Yes. Lieutenant Kohler found him looting and the man went for him. The Lieutenant shot him in self-defence!' Their eyes met, and Heinemann saw the raw disbelief in his officer's face.

'The men are a bit on edge, sir.'

As he spoke there was a great bellow of laughter from the boatdeck, and Schiller loomed unsteadily into view. His face was flushed, and he seemed to have difficulty in walking.

Petty Officer Elmke scowled and moved towards him, his mouth twisted into a mask of anger. 'Come here, that man! By God, I can see what you have been doing!'

Schiller threw back his head and sang, 'I knew a girl in Singapore, she was the fairest of them all!' His unmelodious voice echoed along the broken deck and rang around the silent wreck of a ship.

Schuman crossed quickly in front of Elmke and stood looking up at the great seaman. 'Right, Schiller, that will do! Fall in with the others, will you?'

Schiller beamed at him. 'Say please!'

Elmke sucked in his cheeks and looked to see if Kohler was coming. But Schuman, although young, was used to drunken stokers, and had learned that brutality was not the only way to control a man.

'If I say please, will you let me have a drop of whatever you've found when we get aboard the *Vulkan*?'

Schiller nodded gravely. 'You are a good officer! For you I will fall

235

in!' He glared at Elmke and the other men. 'But only for you! Not for that other pigdog!'

Schuman turned quickly to the pop-eyed Elmke. 'Not a word about this man. There will be trouble enough as it is, without adding to it!'

The signalman said suddenly: 'The Captain says to get what coal we can. He is coming alongside.' He sounded apprehensive.

'What was that?' Kohler walked briskly to the rail, his eyes darting from face to face. 'Coming alongside? Right—prepare the fenders and any spare ropes you can find. Heinemann, open up the port bunker and rig that small derrick!' His nostrils dilated like an agitated horse. 'Well, what are you staring at? Are you all deaf?'

The men broke up and shuffled away, their voices low but protesting. Kohler yelled at them to halt. As they stood in a little ragged group he walked right up to them, his thumbs in his belt.

'Just a moment! There seems to be a little misunderstanding amongst you! Some officers might overlook your unwillingness to obey my instructions, but I will not!' He stood directly in front of Schiller and stared straight at him. 'You are worrying yourselves about Seaman Hahn, is that it?'

The men glanced at Schiller and then at the pale-faced officer but did not speak.

'Well, let me tell you this. I killed him because he was a dangerous, lying pig of a man who regarded life as a right! It is not a right, it is a privilege while you serve in a ship of war! You talk and threaten amongst yourselves, but understand this! I will shoot dead the first man who dares to question *my* orders! Is that clear?'

Schuman found that he was biting his lip until he could taste the blood. The man was a maniac. He was goading the men to complain or start trouble. He actually *wanted* them to!

Elmke said huskily, '*Vulkan's* making for us, sir.' But his eyes were fixed on the figure of the Lieutenant.

Before Kohler's piercing stare the men fell back, cowed and beaten, their eyes on the officer's slender fingers as they played a little tattoo on his holster.

Gottlieb hissed between his teeth: 'It's not fair! They kill us like pigs!'

Schiller grunted and then belched. 'Never mind, mate! It will make *his* death all the more pleasant when it comes!'

Kohler turned to Schuman and frowned with sudden severity. 'And for God's sake don't imagine that they respect kindness. To them it is weakness!' He continued briskly: 'Stand by to hoist coal. It will have to be quick!' He slapped Schuman's arm with sudden gaiety. 'You know, Schuman, I feel better already!'

. . . . .

Unlike the first time the raider had coaled at sea, the impact this time as the two ships came together was hardly more than a shudder, and the water lapped and gurgled playfully between them until the fenders took the strain. Ropes were thrown, and in minutes there was a line of men passing bags of wet and dripping coal across the slanting deck of the shattered freighter to the waiting hands aboard the *Vulkan*.

Caryl Brett stood quietly on the boatdeck, her cheeks warm in the sunlight, watching the activity below. There was no coal-dust this time, and she could see that each sack of coal was sodden with the water which had slowly penetrated every part of that sad hull.

There was a movement at her side, and she was aware that Simon Gelb had joined her. She saw his thick fingers interlaced and strong, as he leaned heavily on the teak rail.

'They seem to be scraping the bottom of the barrel,' he said softly. 'How are things in the sick-bay?'

She shrugged, feeling guilty that she had hardly thought of him since before the battle with the warship. 'They are pretty ill.'

'Good. I hope they die!' He moved his shoulders restlessly. 'They locked us below when that battle was going on. We might have gone down with the ship.'

She could smell the dried sweat on his large body, and again felt guilty. He must surely be aware of her own fragrant smell. Heuss had given her a large bar of scented soap which he had found aboard the *Nemesis*. It was odd that she had been delighted with the gift. She should have thrown it down, denounced it, but against the backcloth of suffering which she had witnessed already it seemed a small thing, but a strangely welcome one.

Gelb said, 'Have you found out yet about the rendezvous?'

She shook her head. 'I do not know if I can.' She found that her heart was pounding uncomfortably. 'It is very difficult.'

His fingers gripped her bare wrist. 'Nevertheless, you must find out! People might get the wrong idea about you, otherwise!'

She turned on him, her eyes flashing. 'How dare you!'

'Not me, of course!' He held up his hand placatingly. 'But you are out of touch with England. Back there they might think you were too friendly with the Germans.'

Her eyes filled with angry tears. 'That is cruel and unfair! I am mixed up, all this has got me completely confused!' It sounded weak, but she still stared at him defiantly. 'We are out of place here. We cannot try to understand what is happening!'

'Maybe. But I am only saying how it might seem to others!'

He stared down at the listing hulk, choosing his words carefully. He must not spoil it now. But it was as he had suspected, she was only a woman after all. He had heard about her ordeal in the small boat and how near she had been to being raped by the seamen there. He had heard a guard saying to his companion that it was only to be expected when men were forced to keep apart from their women. He watched the girl from the corner of his eye. *How long is it, I wonder, since she knew the real meaning of being loved?* He cursed his own weakness and felt the pain in his groin. Nevertheless, she must be made to understand what would happen to her if she started that sort of thing with these filthy Germans. He added evenly: 'Do your best. It is very hard for us down below to know what is to become of us.'

She relented, and felt ashamed at the hurt tone of his voice. 'I believe von Steiger is to drop the wounded if he can somewhere in South America. That is what I have heard. Maybe we shall go, too.'

'Do you want to leave this ship?'

'What a stupid question! Really, you are quite impossible!' But somehow the conviction was lacking in her answer. She could feel the heat mounting her neck, and wanted to hide her face from him and his careful questions.

Gelb nodded towards the other vessel. 'It brings back sad memories, I expect. Of your poor husband?'

He smiled to himself as he saw his shot go home. She was staring at nothing, but he knew she was remembering how Arthur Brett had died. He watched her breasts moving painfully beneath the thin blouse. She was so lovely that it hurt him to watch her. He said, with sudden anger, 'God, why doesn't the Navy catch up with these arrogant animals!'

She saw Steuer go aboard the listing ship, his white jacket out of place amongst the debris. She could see him talking to Lieutenant Kohler, who was grinning broadly and waving his arms about. Steuer did not smile at the officer but followed him below. Another man hurt, she thought. Another dazed and frightened face for a cot in the sickbay. The very thought made her remember the stench of gangrene and the pitiful cries of the two dying men. The smell seemed to pervade the whole ship. She could tell that the other sick men were willing their companions to die, and die quickly.

Sub-Lieutenant Damrosch crossed the boatdeck, his face clearing as he saw the girl. 'Ah, Frau Brett. Could you come to the bridge? The Captain is ill and requires a change of bandage. Everyone else is occupied, and I thought your knowledge of these matters . . .'

His voice trailed away as Gelb said loudly: 'How dare you! Are you aware that under International Law no prisoner can be compelled to do such things? Especially a woman! Go and tell your captain to attend to his own misfortunes! We have enough of our own!' He waited, watching not the young officer but the girl at his side.

She shook a loose strand of hair from her eyes. It was almost as if she had been expecting this to happen, but she tried to tell herself that it was just the right opportunity to get the information Gelb required.

'I will come at once.'

'Thank you. Please follow me.' Damrosch eyed Gelb with hostile dislike.

'I hope you will not forget your loyalties,' Gelb called after her.

* * * * * *

Lieutenant Heuss lowered his megaphone and wiped his forehead with the back of his hand. The men who crossed and re-crossed the deck beneath him seemed to move with the slowness and caution of beetles, and the supply of coal from the ship alongside had slowed to a mere trickle. As each group of men returned from the *Vulkan*'s bunkers they would pause, reluctant to board the listing hulk for fear that they might be the ones trapped below when she rolled over.

Heuss looked at his hands and saw that they were still shaking badly.

He was the only officer on the wing of the bridge and was conscious of the mingled responsibilities of watching the slow process of coaling ship and the task of gauging the seaworthiness of the other vessel. As each lazy swell rolled beneath her counter she would rise wearily and grate against the *Vulkan*. He watched the mooring lines tauten, his hand gripping his whistle in readiness to sound the alarm. Then the lines would slacken slightly and the old freighter would appear to nestle closer to the raider, as if for protection.

He dashed the sweat from his eyes and stared at the stooping corpse in the freighter's wheelhouse. It was horrible, and yet it fascinated him. The wide grin and the black, sightless eyes added the right macabre touch to this whole affair, he thought.

Dehler looked up at him from the maindeck, his face red and angry. He is wondering how the Captain is getting on. If von Steiger is put out of action *he* will have to assume command, and I think that no longer appeals to him.

He tensed again as another bank of green glass lifted against the two ships and broke with a noisy gurgle across the exposed propeller of the freighter.

Heuss glared at his opposite number on the fire-blackened bridge. 'Yes, my friend, you can well afford to smile! Your watch is over for good!'

As the freighter nudged the ragged fenders a tremble seemed to move through every rivet in the *Vulkan*'s hull. The stokers paused as they waited by the coal shoots, and grimaced at one another and wondered if such a risk was worth while. The tiny trickle of wet coal which occasionally appeared in the shoots hardly seemed to justify the chance of being locked against a sinking ship.

Caryl Brett rolled up her sleeves and glanced quickly at the bandages which had been brought from the sick-quarters.

Damrosch cleared his throat and held open the door of the sea cabin. 'Would you go in, please?' He watched her pass him, his eyes creased with worry.

The sunlight beamed through the open scuttle in a long, solid ray. In the golden glare she saw the spartan fittings, the well-worn uniforms swaying on their rack and the mass of charts and logbooks which had been pushed to one end of the table to make room for her case of dressings. Von Steiger was lying on his bunk, his shoulders propped up on three pillows and a rolled jacket. His tanned face was paler than she had ever seen it, and his breathing was quick and sharp. He appeared to be listening, straining his ears as if willing every shipboard sound to come in through the open scuttle.

Reeder waited at his side, his eyes on the girl.

She stood looking down at him, seeing, too, the sodden red bandage across his heaving chest.

He did not flinch as she tore away the old bandages and mopped carefully at the raw, star-shaped wound. His gold-flecked eyes were quiet as he watched the tilt of her head and the loose strand of chestnut hair, which defied her repeatedly as she bent over him.

She could sense him watching her, and at first tried to appear unconcerned, even indifferent. But she could feel the heat rising in her cheeks, and immediately felt angry with herself.

There was a tremendous crash from outside the bridge, and von Steiger was halfway from his bunk before she could stop him.

Emboldened by the English girl's indifference to his captain's rank and status, Reeder ran to her aid, and together they forced him back on the bunk. She stared down at his agonized face and, for a second, thought his wound was worse than she realized. But he struggled weakly in their grip, his eyes desperate.

'What are those fools doing? For God's sake find out for me!'

He barked an order at Reeder, who scurried from the cabin like a frightened dog.

'I never thought I should ever give in to anyone like this!' He ran his fingers through his hair, his eyes almost dazed. 'The ship might be breaking in two, and here I am, as useless as a broken boat-hook!'

She carefully laid the new dressing on the wound, and held it firm with the palm of her hand. She could feel the steady beat of his heart, and was suddenly conscious of the closeness of his body. Coldly she said: 'And I never thought a grown man could behave so badly! Now lean forward while I put on a new bandage.'

Without a murmur, von Steiger leaned towards her, and she passed the bandage round his body like a bandolier.

She looked over his shoulder, seeing the freckles and the smooth, clean line of his back. A strong, youthful back, seemingly wrong for the captain of a ship of war.

'Right,' she said at length, 'I have finished for the present.' But von

241

Steiger still stayed upright, his bent head resting against her shoulder. She could feel his warmth and his vitality, and was suddenly afraid to move lest the moment was broken.

Quietly she said, 'Are you feeling more comfortable, Captain?'

He lay back with a great sigh. When he looked at her again she could no longer meet his eyes, for fear of what he might see in her face. Her voice sounded shaky as she added, 'I must go now.'

Reeder entered the cabin and spoke to von Steiger, who said calmly, 'He says that the ship alongside is about to capsize.' He groaned. 'For your sake I shall refuse to lose my temper. In fact, I doubt if I shall ever be the same in your presence again!'

Reeder helped him from the bunk, and he slowly straightened his body, his hand resting on the white bandage. He joked with the anxious Reeder, but all the time he remained looking at the girl, his eyes trying to convey another message.

She stood back to let him pass towards the bridge, his arm resting on Reeder's shoulder. He paused at the door into the bridge, where his men waited for their orders. He seemed to be trying to say to her: 'Do not take any notice of this pretence! Remember me as I really am!'

She leaned back against the warm bulkhead, her body pinioned by the sun's shaft. She ignored the harsh orders and the jangle of telegraphs, and no longer wanted to see what was happening outside. Her eye fell on the chart which lay across von Steiger's bridge-coat. It held all the secrets which Gelb wished to know, and she was horrified to find that she no longer cared. She could not trust herself to move or speak, and her body trembled uncontrollably. I should feel ashamed, her brain said, but for the moment I feel only a terrible longing.

·   ·   ·   ·   ·

Von Steiger brushed past the watching men on the bridge and stepped out on to the sun-warmed wing, his jacket hanging like a cape across his shoulders. He was immediately aware of the closeness of the battered freighter's funnel, as it hung drunkenly across the slanting deck and cast a dark shadow against the *Vulkan*'s fresh paint.

Heuss watched him searchingly, his eyes troubled. 'I think we should cast off, Captain! She is going over, and one good swell under her stern might throw her right into our hull!'

Von Steiger frowned. 'Keep them at it. I want every bit of coal they can find!'

Some of the men on deck were peering up at the bridge as if listening to their distant conversation, and Heuss gestured briefly to Niklas, who stood watching the slow intake of coal by the bunkers. The men still stood uncertainly, their faces now turned towards the listing ship alongside.

'The men will not like it, sir!' Heuss sounded angry.

'They will do as they are told!' Von Steiger watched the petty officers pushing their men over the rail and saw their unwilling and dragging footsteps. I would not like to go down there either, he thought. But there will be worse to come and there is no longer room for sentiment.

The metal of the two hulls ground together with heavy, uneven thuds, and to his probing ears each concussion seemed heavier than the last, and every strain on the mooring lines appeared to be final.

He could hear Heuss breathing hard behind him, and could feel his eyes on his back. What is the matter with him? Has he so little reserve of nerve that waiting for disaster has become more real than disaster itself?

He thought suddenly of the girl and her cool hands on his shoulders. A warm flush seemed to creep over him, so that he felt uncertain and off guard. I must be mad to behave as I did. And yet why did she not laugh, or challenge me as she did when she first came from the sea?

Heuss said suddenly: 'Shall I send more men across? There is another delay!'

The men in the freighter's bunkers were working with the speed of fear, and had produced more coal than the working party of seamen could cope with, so that it lay in a shining black heap on the ship's torn deck. Some was in bags, and the rest just lay in a great disordered pile into which the men drove their shovels with frantic haste.

'No. It is nearly time.' Another long shudder moved along the bridge, and he saw that the weight of the other ship had torn away some of the fenders so that the rusty bulwark was beginning to gouge the raider's hull.

A man slipped and fell on the deck's extreme angle and the others stopped work to watch him. A petty officer shouted an order but the man stood his ground, his face frightened but stubborn.

243

Von Steiger cupped his hands and called down to Dehler: 'Get those men working! There is still some coal to bring across!'

Dehler turned away from Niklas and squinted up into the sun. 'She'll go at any second, sir! The men are afraid!' He sounded defiant, even pleased.

'Heuss, stay here. I am going across!'

Cutting short the protests which came from several directions at once, von Steiger began to descend the long ladder from the bridge. Every step was agony, and he could feel the new bandage plucking at the edges of his wound. His jacket fell from his shoulders and floated down to the deck below, but he ignored it and continued to lower himself to the maindeck. He knew that his anger was getting a hold of him and that reason had been replaced by the driving force of despair. His boots thudded on the warm planking, and he stood swaying in the sunlight and blinking up at the great towering mass of burned metal which had once been the freighter's bridge.

Reeder ran after him and again placed the jacket across his shoulders. Von Steiger moved briskly between the grimed figures of his men, his eyes fixed on that pile of coal. Grimly he picked up a shovel and clambered across the guardrail to the other ship's tilting deck.

It was even steeper than it had appeared from his bridge, but gritting his teeth he climbed up to where some transfixed seamen stood with their bags, and without a glance in their direction thrust the shovel into the black, moulded mass of coal. His jacket fell once more, but he waved Reeder aside and grinned up at him, his teeth white against his beard. 'Drop it, man, and get a shovel yourself!'

He worked savagely, the sweat coursing down his hard body, his eyes filled only with the coal and the gaping sack held by his terrified steward. Lieutenant Kohler appeared at his side, his pale eyes incredulous. He swallowed hard, and then, with all the dignity he could muster, called to one of the seamen, 'Fetch *me* a shovel!'

All at once there was a great bellowing laugh, and Schiller's black face showed itself over the rim of the bunker. He was drunk, but fighting drunk, and wielded his shovel like a battle-axe. 'By God, dig, you bastards!'

And then, around the slight, doubled shape of the Captain's half-naked body, everyone was working like a maniac. Shovels clanged and rang, and the air was filled with flying grit and the wild curses of the labouring men.

There was a loud crack like a pistol shot from the bows, and instantly the deck seemed to fall from under them as a five-inch rope parted like a thread. Von Steiger felt his men freeze and knew that any panic could kill more than half of them. From the corner of his eye he could see the axes already slashing at the remaining ropes as Dehler freed the *Vulkan* from her terrible burden.

'Right, you men!' His voice was harsh and halted the men, even as they began to move. 'Take your shovels with you, we shall need them again! Now clear the ship in an orderly manner!' He watched them scamper for the rails, their hands like hooks as they grabbed at the waiting ropes and dangling ladders. He turned to Kohler, who still stood dazed and panting, his face streaked like a clown's. 'Have all your men got clear?'

Kohler pulled himself together with a visible effort. 'All but one, sir! I had to shoot him in self-defence. He was looting; I——'

Von Steiger cut him short, aware that Reeder still waited with the two officers, his face ashen. 'Make a report later, Kohler; in the meantime, get back on board!'

He was aware of the great bank of faces which lined the *Vulkan*'s side above him, and conscious, too, of the muffled gurgling roar beneath his feet as the impatient sea began to thunder into the ship's gaping wounds. His limbs were shaking and he could no longer see anything clearly. The coal shimmered in a haze and seemed to mock him, but something still forced him to stand on the trembling deck. He looked at Reeder and smiled. It was a savage, victorious smile. 'A cheroot, if you please!'

The gaping, fascinated crew of the raider watched their captain and his steward, as the latter searched frantically through von Steiger's jacket until he had found the leather case. Another horrifying pause while a match was lit and held for von Steiger's use, and he bent his head with apparent concentration.

The freighter lurched again, and the corpse on her bridge plummeted from his place by the telegraph and crashed against the bridge screen, his frightful face hanging through the shattered window as if to see the cause of the delay.

Dehler watched von Steiger, his hands balled into tight, painful fists. The Captain seemed to be looking at him across his steward's shaking hand, mocking him, humbling him to his true world of jealousy and pettiness. He felt the sweat pouring down his forehead, and did not see the sad concern on the face of Niklas the engineer.

The girl saw it too, her hand pressed to her breast, as von Steiger clambered up the ladder, his body filthy and streaked with sweat, yet the jutting cheroot and bright eyes giving him the appearance of an impish schoolboy who was playing at being a man.

The raider idled clear as the other ship rolled over on to her beam ends, her remaining mast shivering to fragments against the German's bridge and showering the watching crew with splinters.

Caryl Brett saw the tension break like the mast, and watched the bedlam suddenly break around von Steiger as his dirty, resentful men became a mass of cheering, laughing pirates, their haggard faces shouting and yelling as they reached out to pat his bare shoulders as he pushed through them.

He paused at the foot of the bridge ladder and turned to watch the freighter's last moments. A weed-encrusted bilge-keel wallowed like a submarine in a turmoil of giant air-bubbles, and then she was gone.

Von Steiger began to climb, his senses reeling, yet feeling the grin on his face like a mask. The cheers rang in his ears, and his shoulders ached from the blows they had received. They were cheering with all the power they could muster. Shame, pride and relief bonded together in a great wave of noise. He reached the safety of the bridge, and forced himself to look at the whirlpool and its attendant flotsam as the wreck plunged towards the sea-bed. Tomorrow they might be cursing him once again, but at the moment they were happy.

He smiled grimly as he heard Reeder being sick behind the bridge.

The telephone buzzed like a wasp, and Heuss jerked himself from his trance. 'Masthead reports a ship on the port quarter, sir! A merchantman!'

He drew on his cheroot. 'Stand by to engage! Alter course to intercept, and sound Action Stations!' He watched the consternation on the Lieutenant's face. 'With the crew as they are at the moment, Heuss, I would not hesitate even to fight with the Grand Fleet!'

13

A few tiny clouds, their fleecy underbellies pink in the evening sunlight, drifted across the peaceful sky towards the fine gold line of the horizon. The unbroken green water moved with rhythmic slowness, like deep breathing, and showed clearly the reflections of the two ships as they lay beam-on to each other, watchful and tense. Under the raider's trained guns the other vessel seemed vulnerable and helpless, her towering size and deep-laden hull adding vividly to this impression.

She had been surprised by the raider's swift approach, and quite unprepared for the harsh suddenness of events which changed her from a proud, independent ship to a cowed, motionless prize.

Von Steiger watched the boarding party in the two whaleboats drawing nearer and nearer to the big freighter, the oars rising and falling in perfect unison, and seemingly incongruous with the wild, coal-spattered men who manned them. He moved his glasses slowly along the full length of the waiting ship. Between eight and nine thousand tons, she had reported herself as the Italian freighter *Romolo*, outward bound for Rio de Janeiro and on passage for France. It had been a copy-book attack, and the Italians could not have responded better. One warning shot, the sight of the German ensign, and they had been running for the lifeboats, only to be halted by another signal from von Steiger to stand fast and await the boarding party.

He breathed deeply as he saw the first whaleboat ride alongside and glimpsed the flash of sunlight on a rifle-barrel as the first of his men shinned up the proffered ladder. Then the second boat, and more scrambling figures. It was so maddening to have to stand and wonder, he thought. He felt the gnawing uncertainty growing as he watched the tiny figures of his men fan out across the *Romolo*'s deck and move

247

towards her lofty bridge. Such a fine-looking ship, even her drab grey paint could not disguise the proud flare of her bows and the neat rake of her tapering masts and streamlined funnel. The next few moments would decide her fate.

Lap, lap, lap, went the clear water against the hull, and he could feel the warm air like a tonic, replacing the strength which he had lost when wielding a shovel. As he thought of it, he smiled with something like embarrassment. What had prompted him to make such an exhibition? he pondered. He lowered his glasses and ran his coal-blackened hand across his chest. It had been just one more moment of decision. No other officer could have done what he had done. It would have lacked impact and purpose. He grinned in spite of his uncertainty. Suppose the men had still stood back and had left him alone shovelling coal? Dehler at least would have been delighted. And yet why should that be? Dehler had as much to lose as anyone. Was his hatred so pointless that he no longer cared about himself?

'Lieutenant Heuss is signalling, Captain!' Petty Officer Heiser levelled his big telescope, puffing out his cheeks as he always did when reading the stabbing light. 'Cargo as follows. Six hundred tons of gunpowder. Five hundred tons of meat carcasses. Two hundred tons of salt meat. Three hundred tons of steel tubing. Latter for use as rifle-barrels.'

There was a pause, and von Steiger could sense the excited air on the bridge.

'In addition,' Heiser continued, in his flat voice, 'twelve hundred horses for the French Army.'

He sighed deeply. In his mind's eye he could see the poor, terrified animals, penned in the half darkness, on their way to slaughter. Either the French would ride them to ribbons, or they would be used as food. No doubt some fat business man was making a nice profit from their agonizing journey. He shook his head angrily.

'Make this signal.' He plucked his beard, his eyes brooding. 'Send across fresh meat in three lifeboats and salt meat in two others.' He eyed the placid ship with sudden dislike. 'Next, same boats to carry fresh water to maximum capacity.' He waited, tapping his foot, as Heiser wrote the signal on his slate, his pencil squeaking noisily. He imagined Heuss and his men waiting for the signal, and remembered how the Lieutenant had looked when he had come on to the bridge and seen his wound dressed by the girl. He bit his lip. So *that* was it. Of course, it would explain Heuss's taut features and barely controlled anger.

By God, am I to be watched and judged every single minute! He snapped with unnecessary sharpness at the waiting Heiser: 'And tell them to get a move on! I want to sink this ship in one hour!' He felt a childish satisfaction as he watched Heiser's thick fingers manipulating the light shutter.

He turned to Ebert. 'Lower our dory and get all hands to work! Double the lookouts, but fall out the guns' crews! Now see that they get moving! I do not want another exhibition of temperament!' Ebert saluted and hurried away.

'Well, Damrosch? What do you think of the prize?' Von Steiger watched the tired eyes become alert, as if looking for a trap in his words.

'It seems a terrible waste, Captain.' He sounded cautious. 'All that to be destroyed.' He faltered. 'I am not squeamish any more, sir, but there is more to destroying a ship than just blowing it up!'

'How right you are.' Von Steiger spoke half to himself. 'Nothing can be destroyed that has ever been created. This type of fighting is not as you expected?'

He shook his head. 'No, sir. It is almost as bad as unrestricted submarine warfare!'

'My God, I hope you are wrong!' The gold eyes gleamed dangerously.

Damrosch fumbled for words. 'At least the U-boats make no pretence, sir! They are the butchers, and they are content with their label!'

Von Steiger's voice was cold. 'Then what have you left to fight for?'

His eyes looked tortured. 'That's just it, sir, I don't know any more! I love my country, and will die for it if necessary!' He moved his hands helplessly. 'But how can I remember *these* things with pride and honour!'

My God, thought von Steiger with sudden despair, he wishes me to console him and to bring back his confidence. Me, of all people.

Gently he answered: 'When all this is over, it will only be important to many people who won and who lost. The method is often overshadowed by the result.'

Damrosch searched his captain's face intently. 'You are trying to be kind, sir!'

Von Steiger smiled dryly. 'I am merely being practical.'

A messenger saluted and handed von Steiger a folded sheet of paper. He flicked it open, noting Kohler's spidery signature at the bottom and the official wording of the report. Short, official, unfeeling. It summed up the death of a seaman caught looting. It also summed up Lieutenant Kohler.

'So it was Seaman Hahn who was shot?' He nodded briefly and thrust the report beneath a paperweight on the chart-table.

'That's the sort of thing I mean, sir!' Damrosch seemed unable to stop himself. 'Even amongst ourselves we loot, fight, even murder.'

'Murder? Do you mean Petty Officer Brandt, or Seaman Hahn?'

He flushed, aware that he had gone too far. 'I am sorry, sir. My tongue ran away with me!'

'Quite so. Let me give you a word of advice. Try to be a good officer. That has to be enough, even for an idealist. If you want to find something else in all this, let me tell you, you are wasting your time and energy!' His face hardened. 'There is *nothing* else, do you hear? Nothing!'

He walked away from Damrosch and past Heiser, who was studiously examining his lamp. Damn them, he thought viciously. What do they want of me? He slumped against the screen and stared down at the gently rolling decks below him. Yet, in spite of everything, I cannot turn my back on any of them. Even that man Hahn, thief that he was, did not deserve such a death as that. Alone, in an alien ship, on the bottom of the Atlantic. Braun, the masthead lookout I had shot for cowardice, or the men who died in battle. Even that pompous fool Arthur Brett did not deserve to die in such a fashion. He shied away from that thought immediately, knowing that in reality Brett had deserved to die, if only for not loving his wife.

He passed his hand across his face. I am so tired I am incapable of reasoning and dead to reason. He watched the white lifeboats pulling towards him, their oarsmen hidden by the piled meat and crates of vegetables. Fresh food for my men. Like that drunken brute Schiller, whose blind hatred of any sort of discipline had saved the situation aboard the hulk. And Heiser, who listened to his officers around him on the bridge, yet never repeated a word of anything he heard. Yes, they were a good crew, in spite of their shortcomings, and in spite of their helplessness. Like those poor horses in the Italian ship, they had no choice any more. Decisions were made in spite of them, not for them.

.   .   .   .   .   .

Lieutenant Heuss moved restlessly across the freighter's wide bridge and peered down at the nearest lifeboat as it shoved off from the side and started another journey to the *Vulkan*. The ship's forward deck was littered with broken packing-cases and bundles of meat carcasses, whilst beneath the watchful eyes of the Germans the freighter's seamen ran to and fro from the broached holds, their faces strained and averted from the levelled rifles.

Nearby, his round face filled with misery, the Italian master stood motionless and limp. As each new order was shouted, or another boat moved away from the side, he glanced at the clock, as if wondering how much time there was left. From aft came the muffled stamp of hoofs and the frightened cries of the horses, unnerved still more by the silence of the ship's engines.

Heuss gritted his teeth until his jaw ached, and tried to stop his ears to the sounds. Across the peaceful green water the *Vulkan* rolled lazily in the slight swell, her masts spiralling against the purpling sky.

'Please, *tenente*, tell me what is to happen?' The captain spoke English like a schoolboy, and no German at all. 'What will become of my ship?'

Heuss turned on him, hating the hurt in his voice, and stared at the man's gentle, liquid-brown eyes. 'How do I know?' The man looked at his feet and shifted uncomfortably. Heuss compared him and the other Italian sailors with his own ragged men. Even taking their coal-streaked faces and stubbled chins into consideration, the comparison was plain to see. The Italians were without exception well fed and sleek, their uniforms pressed and neat. They looked like innocent bystanders caught up in a war not of their own choosing.

Petty Officer Weiss clattered on to the quiet bridge, his tiny eyes gleaming. 'Here you are, Lieutenant! Are these what you were looking for?' He held out a bundle of well-thumbed newspapers which he had collected from the messdecks.

Heuss nodded, and spread them hungrily on the chart-table. Newspapers in unfamiliar languages, yet with stories plain enough in any tongue. He gestured impatiently to the captain. 'Here, read this one. I do not read Italian.'

The captain did not look at the proffered paper, but stared instead at the distant *Vulkan*. 'It says, *tenente*, that a German raider is at large in the Atlantic.' He paused as Heuss scanned the stark headlines, picking out familiar words and fitting the captain's own into the gaps.

'It says how you have murdered innocent men, and have sunk ships without warning.' The captain's sad voice seemed to gather strength. 'It also reports that you are pirates, and outcasts from human society.' He stopped, as if waiting for Heuss to strike him.

'And this?' He gestured to a faded photograph which showed a jubilant French *poilu* planting a tattered pennant on a broken gun-carriage. 'What do they say here?'

'The Allies have defeated a German offensive in France! Your army has lost ten thousand men!' The Italian spoke calmly now, without malice and without interest. 'You are being destroyed, *tenente*!'

Heuss folded the papers into a bundle and handed them to Weiss. 'Send them to the Captain. He will want to see them!'

He walked into the cool evening air, his brain burning with jumbled thoughts. What are we doing here? Why do we not go home and fight there, if we must?

The Italian's voice intruded yet again. 'Are you going to kill us?'

He whirled round, his face white with fury. 'Kill you? What do you think we are? Savages? Are you the only damned people with right on your side? For Christ's sake stop looking so damned pious and righteous!'

The Italian looked confused. 'Please, *tenente*, you are speaking too fast!'

But Heuss hurried on, his ears deaf. 'God in heaven, how sick, sorry and tired I am of all this humbug! If only I could find one man honest enough to say that he was fighting because he is afraid of the alternative! Why must the cause be justice?'

Heuss started as Lieutenant Dehler climbed the ladder of the bridge and stood blinking in the half-light of the wheelhouse. He looked tired, and suddenly old.

'Everything all right, Emil?' He sounded apprehensive and nervous, and Heuss stared at him in disbelief. He had called him by his Christian name for the first time.

Guardedly he answered: 'Nearly finished. The water is going across now. Every available drum of the stuff!'

'Yes, I saw it as I came over.' Dehler spoke vaguely, as if trying to make up his mind. 'Why are we hanging about? It's asking for trouble!'

'Well, *you* should know! You are the senior officer!' Heuss's voice was cutting, but there was no response. Instead, Dehler's fat shoulders seemed to sag.

'I know I treated you badly, Emil. A man can have his reasons.'

'I suppose so,' he answered coldly. 'You made it obvious enough!'

'Look, do you want me to grovel? I've got a bit of pride, whatever you people think!' With a trace of his old bitterness he continued: 'Oh, why should you understand? You've always had everything!' He lifted a red fist to silence the other man. 'You don't know what it's like to drag yourself from the stinking gutter, always having to be grateful, and servile! I've never owned anything.' He laughed, a short, barking sound, which made the Italians draw together even closer. 'No, not a damned thing! I've tried all my life to get on, to make good, and all the way there has always been a clever, stuck-up bastard with position and "breeding" behind him who has beaten me to the plum job!' He glared across at the *Vulkan*, his eyes misty. 'She should have been mine by rights, but look who has got her! Another damned aristocrat, who doesn't even begin to care for the likes of me!'

Heuss could hardly credit what he was hearing. Dehler, the hard, competent, self-made man was cracking open before his eyes. He tried to grin, but his own uncertainty choked his words of comfort. 'Perhaps you will have the last laugh after all.'

'How so?' He eyed him cautiously, for fear of Heuss's sharp tongue.

'Well, you'll have to know soon enough. There has been another push on the Western Front. Ten thousand more have been buried, it seems. *We* are in the news, too. We are murderers and swine of the first class!' He laughed bitterly. 'I also found out from an officer's diary that two British cruisers are on the South American coast hunting for us! They mean to get us, just as we really knew they would!'

Dehler buried his massive head in his hands. 'My God, I don't want to die out here! I want to go home, I shall be ready enough for anything there!'

Petty Officer Weiss returned to the bridge and saluted. 'Signal from the Captain, sir! You are to order all the Italians into the boats immediately, and then send a signal on their wireless. Give your position, and say that you are being attacked by a German raider.' He trained his big nose towards the Italians. 'They are to be left in the boats, sir. We are not to take them aboard the *Vulkan!*'

'What?' Dehler seemed to come to life, and seized Weiss by his jacket. 'What did you say?'

Weiss repeated his message, and Heuss shrugged wearily. 'That'll be right enough. Von Steiger will leave them behind, and when we wireless our position some ship will come and pick them up. Simple, eh?'

'My God!' Dehler banged his fists together. 'He is raving mad! He will have those cruisers and everyone else on our backs before we can move!'

'Maybe he has another plan. I just don't begin to understand him!'

Weiss waited and then said, 'Any reply to the signal, sir?'

Heuss looked at his superior. 'We will carry out the order, I take it?'

Dehler shook himself and pushed past the gaping petty officer. 'Do what you like! I must go and think!'

Heuss shrugged. 'No reply. Order will be executed. Pass the word to abandon ship, and send the ship's wireless officer up here!'

Weiss saluted and moved away.

'And, Weiss, you did not hear anything!'

'No, sir. Not a thing!'

As the S O S flooded from the powerful transmitter, Heuss stood smoking his pipe and watching the Italian operator's busy finger on the key. 'Any reply?'

After a while the man nodded with relief. 'Yes, two ships!'

'Right, that's enough! Follow me!'

Together they ran out into the fading light and scrambled down the ladder into their waiting boats.

Feeling the anxiety rising within him, Heuss said sharply: 'Pull harder, men! Time is running out!'

As the Italian lifeboats pulled one way and the raider's whaleboat the other, a crisp white line parted the clear water between them.

Heuss felt his mouth go dry as the torpedo sped like an arrow towards the abandoned freighter.

The double, shattering roar as the torpedo exploded and ignited the stored gunpowder rent the sky in two, and the shock wave made the little boats dance like white leaves on a disturbed pool.

They pulled in silence back to the raider, their faces grey, and no longer able to understand the magnitude of events about them.

.   .   .   .   .   .

The stars, which seemed to fill the sky from horizon to horizon, were large and bright, and the night air, although cool, was sweet and refreshing to the men of the Middle Watch.

Lieutenant Ebert sat at the side of the wheelhouse, checking the deck-log, his face yellow in the small shaded lamp, and his neat hands moving in time with his eyes as he read and re-read the lines of pencilled figures.

All the wheelhouse windows were lowered, and in the bright moonlight the forward deck appeared white, as if covered with snow.

Seaman Pieck moved quietly around the bridge, picking up the empty coffee-cups and placing them on a tin tray. He paused by the chart, his eyes fixed upon the wavering line of the *Vulkan*'s course and the countless alterations, inserted times, compass variations and bearings which told his untrained mind only some of the concentrated effort which had brought the ship thus far.

After sinking the Italian freighter they had steamed away purposefully to the east, towards the distant African coast, and under the full observation of the men left behind in the lifeboats. Then, under cover of darkness, they had altered course to the south-west, and were now steaming at full speed back towards the South Americas. He had heard some of his messmates discussing von Steiger's tactics with admiration and surprise. At first it had seemed madness to send off a wireless signal advertising their position, but he could now see what the other men were so jubilant about. When the rescuing or avenging ships arrived to pick up the Italians, the latter would waste no time reporting the raider's last known course and position. By the time they all discovered their mistake the *Vulkan* would be many miles to the south-west. He leaned over the chart, his round face set in a concentrated frown. The new course, roughly marked in by the Captain, seemed to lead directly in to the Brazilian coast. He stooped lower, squinting in the feeble light. That part of the coastline seemed empty of names but for one small town, or perhaps village, Corata.

Against it, in small neat writing, von Steiger had inserted: *See Chart 707, E.T.A.? 4th February.*

He could feel his heart pounding against his ribs, and glanced with sudden guilt at the helmsman's stalwart back and the hunched shape of Lieutenant Ebert. He licked his lips and peered again at the chart. That meant they would reach this place within four days. He tried to gauge the size of the tiny anchorage, and draw a mental picture from the wavering lines and mysterious figures which he knew represented the depth of water. It appeared to shoal away to nothing, except around a jumbled mass of minute islets, which looked as if they had been tossed carelessly down from the mainland by some giant hand.

A lookout coughed in the darkness, and he picked up his tray of cups, his mind working at a furious pace.

Before, it had only been a wild dream, either to torment him further with its improbability, or in rare moments of peace to afford him a strange comfort. But now the idea had suddenly grown into a real possibility. Somehow he would leave the ship. Would desert. He no longer had any option. He had to get away before they could guess what he was up to. He thought of Lieutenant Kohler, and shivered. He had almost collided with him in the small space below the bridge where the torpedoes were housed in their hidden tubes. Remembering what Schiller had told him, he had saluted the officer, his face ice-cold, and stepped aside to let him pass.

Kohler no longer pleaded or threatened. Instead, to Pieck's horror, he smiled amicably, his coal-streaked face adding to the sense of unreality. 'I *know*, Willi!' He spoke quietly, almost matter-of-fact. 'Do you understand? I *know*!'

He stood back to watch the impression his words had had on the boy. He was not to be disappointed, for Pieck looked as if he had received a blow in the stomach and could no longer draw breath.

'Know, sir?' When he at last answered his voice was faint.

Kohler grinned wider, like a wolf. He said one word, 'Brandt!'

Pieck swayed and would have fallen, but Kohler seized him by the front of his tunic and held him against the cool steel. 'Listen, you little fool! You need *me* now! If you start to get stupid ideas I will have you arrested, and Alder too! He will soon confess with a little persuasion, and then you know what will happen to both of you, eh?' His smile faded abruptly. 'But such things are not necessary, as you well know!' His tone became suddenly smooth, almost caressing. 'I need you, Willi! Why must we be enemies?' Then as a party of seamen hurried towards them he concluded sharply, 'There is no escape, Willi, believe me!'

Pieck moved across the wheelhouse, his cups rattling on the tray. He could see Lieutenant Heuss on the port wing of the bridge, his binoculars moving restlessly across the dark water. Pieck faltered. Should he tell this officer? he wondered. He dismissed the idea as soon as it was born. All his young life he had asked and depended on others. The result, as it had been for poor Alder, produced nothing but misery and shame.

He moved down the ladder, along the maindeck and down the oval hatch which led to the prisoners' quarters. Outside the barred door the sentries stiffened into alertness, and then one of them laughed.

'It's only Willi! We thought it was the duty petty officer!'

The other man, Schwartz, his dour face concentrating fiercely as he rolled a crude cigarette, grunted: 'Well, what's happening up top, Willi? Any more fat prizes yet?'

Pieck felt the pain prickling behind his eyes. He had wanted so much to be one of these men. To belong. But it was too late now. He looked around for their dirty cups, and answered, 'We are going to Brazil.'

The two sentries gaped at him.

'Brazil, did you say?' Schwartz sounded doubtful. 'Are you sure? Hell, Willi, Brazil is at war with us!'

'Saw it on the chart. Three days from now!' Pieck answered stubbornly.

Blucher, the other man, belched and massaged his stomach thoughtfully. 'Could be, at that. Brazil, just think! To put your feet on solid earth once more, eh?'

'Forget it!' Schwartz laughed. 'Von Steiger will drop the wounded, grab a bit of coal and then disappear on the high seas again! He cannot find the time for the fleshpots, like you!'

Blucher refused to be distracted. 'What part, Willi? Did you see that?'

'A place called Corata.'

'Never heard of it!' Schwartz sounded triumphant. 'Sounds more like a disease!'

But when Simon Gelb, who had been pressing his ear to the other side of the door, roused Captain Mason from his uneasy sleep and told him the raider's destination, he sat up immediately.

'Corata? Of course I know it! Miserable little place right on the north-east corner of Brazil. Nothing but flies, sand and a few stupid fishermen.' His hand rasped across his chin. 'Corata. Well, that's something we've found out! Von Steiger is taking a hell of a chance to touch an enemy coastline, lonely or not!'

'*I've* found out.' Gelb smiled in the darkness. 'All we have to do now is get ashore. Maybe von Steiger will get rid of us there.'

'I think not. Too dangerous for him. Just the wounded, I expect. Lucky swine!' he added bitterly.

Gelb sat on the edge of the bunk, thinking of Caryl Brett. 'We must find out some more, my friend. Things are beginning to get interesting!'

.   .   .   .   .

The sun was still low on the horizon, and the decks fresh from their morning scrub and wash down, when the bosun's mates ran the length of the ship, the pipes twittering in the crisp air, their voices hoarse and self-important.

'Clear lower deck! All hands lay aft!'

Looking strangely different in their creased and little-used white duck uniforms, the *Vulkan's* crew flowed along the gently pitching decks to congregate in a great murmuring crowd in the narrow confines of the afterdeck. The petty officers came next, checking that no one but those on watch remained idling below, and finally in a small group came the officers, all but Kohler, self-conscious in their white tunics.

Dehler stood swaying on the top of a hold and glared round at the circle of upturned faces. Some men stood on the bulwarks and some clung to the mainmast stays to get a better view of the proceedings, and anyone more imaginative than Dehler would have marvelled that so many men could live, sleep and fight in such a small ship. But he frowned, and stuck out his lower lip.

258

Lehr, the big Coxswain, saluted formally. 'Lower deck cleared, Lieutenant!'

Von Steiger stepped from the poop screen door and mounted the hold-cover. He returned his first lieutenant's salute and waited until the big man had shuffled away to join the officers. Then he placed his hands on his hips and slowly looked around at the silent men, who in turn were waiting for him to speak.

He noticed that some of the expectant faces were already getting tanned and losing their barracks pallor, and some of them looked different in their new beards, and hair worn longer than regulations ashore would have permitted.

'Now listen to me! We have come a long way from Kiel, and I have not had much opportunity to speak to you before!' He forced a wry smile. 'We have, as you may have noticed, been too busy of late!' That brought a rumble of laughter, as he knew it would, and he hurried on. 'But I think you should all know more of what is happening outside this ship, and not be made the victims of rumour!' He had their full attention now. 'I am steering for the Brazilian coast, as I am sure you knew before I did'—another, even louder, laugh—'and I shall put ashore some of our less fortunate comrades, who have done their duty well but are too ill for the sort of life we are leading here. In addition, I want more fuel and information about the enemy. We are alone at sea for so long that we sometimes tend to get careless, even over-confident. But be assured, the enemy is there.' He waved his arm across the milky green water, and several heads turned to look. 'He is there in strength, and looking for us! We have had some success, and we must try our hardest to hit the enemy, and hit him again and again where it hurts, in his supply line!'

His voice dropped, and the white-clad figures pressed closer. 'Our comrades in the field are having a hard fight, and, right at this moment, when some of you may feel that you have a grievance about food or lack of sleep, our soldiers are fighting for their very lives!' His eyes flashed as he turned towards the rising sun, so that he did, to some of the watching men, indeed look like a tiger. 'Our enemies are hunting for us, and will leave no piece of water unsearched until they can bring us to battle! The Americans are flooding to the Western Front, and the Fatherland can expect no rest, no weakening of pressure, at any time.' He scanned their faces once more. 'I want to believe that, whatever happens, *we* will never tarnish the name of the Imperial Navy, and will be remembered with pride and not shame by our countrymen, and, later, even by our enemies!'

There was a great silence, and he could see the impression of his own words making themselves plain on the faces around and above him. He wondered how his officers were reacting to his speech, and wished that he could turn and confront them.

I should like to say: 'Do *you* understand? Do you realize your own responsibility? You, Dehler, with your ever present fears and petty hatreds. And you, Heuss, too idealistic to see the truth in front of your eyes! By God, I will drive this ship with or without you, be assured of that!'

He realized that they were all still waiting for him to continue.

Did these men realize what they were up against? he wondered. How would they thank him, when the trap was finally sprung? A sudden flame seemed to sear his breast, like a reopening of his wound, and he shouted up at the masthead, as if to tell the ship herself: 'But let you all be witness of my words! So long as I have strength, and as long as the ensign flies, by God, I will never surrender!'

He felt his shoulders fall limp, the tunic damp against his skin. Another display, another exhibition—for whose benefit?

He started as Petty Officer Weiss jumped up in front of him, his ugly face beaming.

'Come, comrades, three cheers for the Captain! Three cheers for the Tiger of the Seas!'

Damrosch found himself pressing forward with the others, his cap waving above his head. The mad, uncontrollable impulse to cheer and scream, to yell and reach out to pat the Captain's shoulder, gripped him like the most junior seaman aboard.

Dehler watched in silence as the stamping men seized the slight figure of their captain and hoisted him up on to their shoulders, shouting his name, laughing, and, in more than one case, weeping at the same time.

His eyes met von Steiger's across the waving arms and thrown caps, and he felt his body cringe. There was a sad smile on von Steiger's mouth, but his eyes were defiant, like those of a conqueror.

.   .   .   .   .

Heuss stood in the entrance to the sea cabin, the sun from the open scuttle hot across his impassive face. 'You sent for me, Captain?'

Von Steiger glanced up briefly from the chart and nodded towards the chair. 'Yes. Sit down a moment.'

Heuss sat, his body tense and unrelaxed as he saw the Captain's brown hands manipulating the brass dividers deftly across the worn chart. His tunic was undone, and Heuss could see the bandage across his chest and the hardness of his stomach muscles as he bent forward across the table. He realized that von Steiger had tossed the dividers aside and was staring emptily towards the bright-blue circle of the scuttle.

'You heard what I told the ship's company this forenoon? Well, it may not be quite so simple as I painted it for them.' He smiled pensively and rested his chin on his cupped hands, his eyes on the Brazilian coastline outlined on the chart. 'We shall anchor, if possible, under cover of darkness, and then I shall want you to go ashore and contact our agent in Corata.'

Heuss leaned forward, his mind being drawn unwillingly to concentrate on the Captain's calm voice.

'His name is, or was, Renato Fleiuss. A coffee planter by trade, but in the past he has been the chief organizer in these parts for getting fuel and information for our commerce raiders. A year or so ago he would have arranged for a train of colliers to rendezvous with our ships at prearranged places, a whole supply chain right across the South Atlantic. Quite a feat of organization, as you can imagine!' He shrugged. 'Of course, with Brazil now in the war that is no longer possible, but I am hoping that he still has a few cards to play.'

Heuss cleared his throat and shifted in his seat. 'Is he reliable, sir?'

The gold-flecked eyes settled on his face. 'Is anyone? He is, I think, an odious man, but not without a sort of patriotism.'

'He is German, then?'

'He was *born* a German. But for necessity is a Brazilian, and by choice a rich man!' He laughed, as if at some secret joke. 'We must handle him with care!'

He stood up and began to pace, his hands behind his back. Heuss watched him carefully, his dark eyes following von Steiger's shadow across the small cabin.

'We shall be there in three days, all being well. There is a lot to do.

Boats to be made ready, anchor cables to be well greased and above all, Heuss, a good leadsman for the chains. We shall have to feel our way in there, and I have no wish to leave our keel on the reef!'

Heuss leaned over the chart and stared at the tiny cluster of broken rocks. It would be difficult to get the *Vulkan* in there by day. In the darkness it would be a test indeed. His voice guarded, he asked quietly: 'Should not the First Lieutenant be here, sir? It would be of more interest to him, surely?' He thought of Dehler's frantic, miserable face and wondered how much von Steiger knew.

'You are the next senior officer, Heuss. You will be the one who has to go ashore.' His voice suddenly became harsh. 'And if I am killed or seriously disabled, *you* will have to take command!'

Heuss stared at him as if he had been struck. 'But, sir! That is hardly fair to Lieutenant Dehler!'

He crossed to Heuss's side and stood looking down at him. 'Forget your little textbook of etiquette, Heuss! I am no fool, and I know who can and cannot be trusted. I want a possible successor, not just somebody to take over command! Think, man! Try to see the difference!' He resumed his pacing, his face bleak. 'We have been sent to do a job. It shall be done. When things were easy, everyone wanted my position of command and the honour it implied. But now that our task grows more complex, I am alone! Dehler is a good seaman, a reliable navigator, and that is all. But if he were to be left in command, and the choice was his, what would he do? Stand and fight, or run for a neutral port and be interned?'

Heuss stood up, his face hot. 'How can you say that about a brother officer? He should be allowed to answer that slur!'

Von Steiger laughed softly. 'Well, well, Heuss! How you have changed! A month or so ago you would have been the one to sneer at such old-fashioned codes of honour and tradition! I thought you were above such sentiment!'

Heuss writhed in the neat trap. 'I agree with Dehler, sir! We are facing great danger, and the odds mount day by day. But, like him, I would fight if required!'

'You have not understood a word! Fighting is not enough! It is as empty as committing suicide and as craven as collecting duelling scars to impress young women!'

'I think I have proved my reliability in battle, sir, I——'

Von Steiger waved his hand. 'Sit down, Heuss! I want no heroics! I know that you dislike me, but that is also unimportant. I am the commanding officer of this ship, and you will listen to me!'

Heuss glowered at him, his mouth a tight line.

'You are intelligent and not easily diverted by others. You think for yourself, and that, God knows, is rare enough with some officers! For those reasons, if none other, I trust you. Personal differences are unimportant. If we were back in peaceful times, Heuss, I would come halfway to you, and listen to your ideas.' He smiled with sudden sadness. 'You might have found me more of an idealist than yourself! But those days are over, gone perhaps for a lifetime. Even if I believed in your way of thought I could not say so. And I do not believe! Things will not be right because we want them to be. Men will not love one another because we think it is nicer that way! Men must be driven and battles must be won if they are to be any use at all!'

'Even if the end is unchanged?'

'Even so! The British have a saying that they lose every battle but the last one. But, Heuss, that last one is not the only battle which counts in the end. The record and behaviour of every man is just as important for the loser as for the victor. It is a foundation on which to build anew!'

'And what of Dehler, sir?' Heuss felt unsure of himself.

He shrugged. 'I have spoken to him. He is too old for this sort of war, Heuss. Like the poor *Vulkan*, he should be carrying bananas!'

Heuss stood up, his features controlled. 'Is that *all*, sir?'

'See that the wounded men are got ready to leave. The agent can arrange for immediate medical care and proper surgical treatment. The poor devils have earned it.'

'And the prisoners?'

The eyes rested on his face searchingly. 'They must stay. The officers are good hostages, and the man Gelb is quite a valuable prize in his way. Or so he seems to think!'

Heuss still faltered, and von Steiger's hand moved to the bandage on his chest. 'And the woman? Was that what you wanted to know?' He stared unseeingly through the scuttle. 'I shall see. If it is safe I shall put her ashore. I may leave it to her to decide.'

'Is that fair, sir?'

'No. Perhaps you had better ask her what she wishes.'

263

'I shall be sorry to see her go, Captain.' Heuss could have bitten off his own tongue because of the smile which hovered around von Steiger's mouth.

'You have made that rather obvious, Lieutenant!'

.   .   .   .   .

She watched Heuss's face change from apprehension to puzzled anger as he moved restlessly round the wide cabin, his fingers unconsciously touching the furniture and fittings.

'What are you trying to say, Lieutenant?' Her voice was soft and husky, and yet Heuss stared at her with surprise. It was as if she, too, was mocking him. As if she shared some secret that he could not understand.

'The Captain wishes to know if you desire to be landed at this port. If you say that you want to leave, then he will arrange it, and you can contact the British Consul at the nearest town.'

'Is there an alternative?'

Heuss felt the sweat prickle at the neck of his tunic as he watched her parted lips and the firm, rounded curves of her body. 'You could wait aboard until you can be put in a neutral ship.'

'We have not met one yet. From what I have heard, it seems more likely that we shall meet a British cruiser!'

He spun round, his face bitter. 'Then you would be pleased! But who can blame you, after all this!'

He sat heavily on a chair and stared down at his hands. 'But perhaps when we are blown to hell you will no longer think so harshly of us. We are individuals now, not just a foreign flag!' As his face was lowered, he did not see the brief spasm of pain in her wide eyes.

He tried to laugh. 'Perhaps my conscience is troubling me, eh?'

'Is that so bad?'

'They say that conscience can make cowards of us all. It is hardly appropriate!'

She moved nearer to him, so that he could feel the warmth of her body.

'You have been kind to me. I shall not forget,' she said simply. 'It has made things bearable for me, and all the other survivors, too.'

On a sudden impulse he seized her hand and held it tightly against his cheek. 'My God, that it should end like this! What a damned waste it has all been! To come all this way and be cheated of something worth while!'

Gently but firmly she withdrew her hand. 'Have you no faith in your commander? Surely the danger of defeat is worse for him?'

Heuss felt the sting of her words like a taunt, and he staggered to his feet, his face flushed. 'What do you care for von Steiger? How can you pretend to understand a man like him?'

Her cheeks seemed to lose their colour, but her eyes flashed back at him scathingly. 'Why do you ask? Because I am only a woman, a prisoner? Or because I am not good enough for a high-bred German?'

He fell back before her anger. 'So I was wrong! You are like all the rest, and set your cap at the highest available!'

Her mouth trembled. 'At least your Captain is a man! I cannot see him whimpering just because he cannot have his own way!'

She cried out as Heuss's palm struck her cheek, but did not falter. Only her eyes were misty, and her fingers were clasped into the folds of her skirt so that the knuckles gleamed white.

Heuss stood dazedly staring at his hand. 'Forgive me, I do not understand what I have done!'

Her voice sounded different, controlled and flat. 'Will you leave, Lieutenant? Or shall I call the sentry?'

As the door closed her hand flew to her cheek, feeling the force of Heuss's anger and despair. I should hate him, she thought. But at least he made me say what was uppermost in my thoughts. No, I *wanted* him to hit me!

She stared at her face in the mirror and was frightened by the look in her eyes.

14

WITH the engine at dead slow the *Vulkan* slid smoothly through the black water, the gentle thrust of her sharp stem hardly making a ripple to disturb the reflections of a million bright stars. The night air was heavy and humid, and on the bridge every man felt the quickening of his heart as the scent of invisible land moved inquisitively around the wheelhouse.

Von Steiger's shadow moved from the port door until his small beard shone wickedly in the binnacle light. 'Steer south-west by south!'

Lehr, the Coxswain, repeated the order, and the silence was broken by the discreet creaks of the wheel's spokes being eased over.

From the forward deck the silvery chimes of two bells rang out with unexpected suddenness, and von Steiger cursed in the darkness. 'For God's sake send a man down there! Do you want every damned Brazilian to hear us coming!'

He tried to relax and concentrate on the impenetrable black curtain ahead of the ship. He could almost feel the great mass of land beyond the bows, but instinct and training made him stand quite still and control his anxiety. There was no moon, and although this helped their stealthy approach, it made the actual navigation a nightmare.

Behind him by the chart he could hear Dehler's heavy breathing as he bent over the small pool of light, his thick fingers working with parallel rule and dividers. Poor Dehler, he thought absently. Second in command in name only. He had taken the news of von Steiger's choice with surprising calm, his heavy face devoid of expression. Von Steiger had looked for relief, anger or even open disagreement, but the man's eyes had been blank.

He heard the scrape of metal as the machine-gun crews on either wing of the bridge swivelled their oiled weapons and clipped the long belts into place. Every other gun was still covered, and as she moved so quietly towards the land the *Vulkan* was more like her true self than she had been since leaving Germany. All the false deckhouses had been either removed or completely modified, and a hastily applied layer of white paint had once more transformed her upperworks. She wore neither flag nor name, and was ready for instant action should she be challenged.

Von Steiger watched the pale blobs of white on the distant fo'c'sle head where Sub-Lieutenant Seebohm and his anchor party waited to let go. He could see the triangular shape of Seebohm's arm-sling as he gesticulated to the rating with the hammer who would, with luck, knock away the slip and let the great anchor go plummeting to the bottom, for the first time since leaving Kiel.

'Start sounding!' He could sense the excitement in Damrosch's voice as he repeated the order. Every man aboard was keyed up to the limit. It only needed them to be pinned down by a Brazilian searchlight or challenged by a gunboat, and all hell would be let loose.

Far out on his small platform on the ship's side the burly figure of the leadsman ran the long line through his hands and tested the fourteen pounds of lead on its end. When he heard the order he lowered the lead slowly over the edge of his platform and allowed the slender chain rail to take the weight of his body. Slowly, rhythmically, he began to swing the line back and forth, the heavy lead almost touching the gurgling bow-wave on each downward stroke. Then, as the arc lengthened, he jerked the line towards him, so that in a few seconds he had the lead swinging in a complete circle. Then, with one final mighty heave, he cast it from him, feeling the line with its telltale markings snaking away through his fingers. Forward and down into the clear water, its passage making a gay commotion of green phosphorescence. He waited, felt it strike the bottom and called, over his shoulder, 'By the mark ten!'

Von Steiger grunted. They were right in the narrow approach to Corata. A cable or so either way could be the finish of the *Vulkan*. It hardly seemed worth the risk. He shook his head angrily. He was committed now, and, in any case, the risk was more than justified. It had to be.

267

Heuss moved silently to his side. 'All watertight doors closed, Captain! Wounded on deck, and boats swung out as ordered!'

'Good. I am not expecting trouble, but one cannot be sure.'

'You have been here before, sir?' Heuss spoke coolly, but von Steiger could sense the tension in his tone.

'Yes. Nearly two years back. When Brazil was still neutral. It was one of the places shown in the Intelligence Log supplied to all commerce raiders. Reliable then, but a lot of water has flowed in that time.'

'And blood, sir.'

Von Steiger smiled grimly. How like Heuss to find double meanings in everything he said.

'This man Fleiuss, his attitude may have changed, too.'

'*I* shall tell him his attitude, Heuss! Make no mistake about that!'

'By the mark ten!' The leadsman's chant floated eerily up from the darkened deck.

'Good. It will not be long now.' In a sharper tone he added: 'In a few moments we shall be sighting the first of the islets. Fine on the starboard bow it should be. Coxswain, when we have found it I want you to bring her head up to the eastern tip and steer as close as you can! The channel is no more than half a cable wide at that point!'

'I understand, Captain!' Lehr hunched his massive shoulders and sniffed at the air through the open window in front of him.

Von Steiger fretted with concealed impatience. They all accept my word without question, although we might be right off course. A bead of sweat formed beneath the rim of his cap at the thought of *Vulkan*'s twenty-two feet of draught moving towards what might in reality be one of the outlying reefs.

'By the deep eight!'

'Damn!' He swore softly. 'Bring her head up half a point!'

A few agonizing moments, then, 'By the deep nine!'

That's more like it, he breathed.

'Well, Heuss, you know exactly where you have to go? If there is anything else you wish to know, let me have it from you now. There will be no time at all in a moment!'

Heuss seemed to relax slightly. 'Take both boats and make for the beach. The beach is at the south-western end of the anchorage and is at the bottom of a giant cleft in the rock cliffs.'

Von Steiger interrupted: 'The beach is nothing at all really, so watch for those two pinnacles of rock on either side of the cleft. Just think of two great book-ends, and there you are!'

Heuss nodded. 'Up the path from the beach, and right at the top of the gully. Through the coffee plantation, and straight on to the house. It is the only one there?'

He grunted. 'Intelligence reports so!'

'See this man Fleiuss, and bring him to the ship.'

'That is about all there is to it,' said von Steiger wryly. 'But do not forget to deploy your men right round the cove and up on the rocks above. When dawn breaks they will be able to see miles out to sea, so I shall be relying on them to a great extent. The ship will be invisible from a seaward approach, but then, too, will any intruder be invisible to me!'

'I have arranged all that, Captain.' Heuss refused to respond to the Captain's humour. 'They are all picked men, and Lieutenant Kohler is in charge of the beach party.'

'By the mark seven!' The chant was like a dirge.

Damrosch's voice broke in on his thoughts. 'There it is, Captain! At green four-five! Look, sir, land!'

Heuss lowered his glasses, and stared at the Captain. A quick glance had verified Damrosch's report. There was no mistaking the faint white line of breaking waves and the imperceptible darkening beyond. Land, after all this time. The last glimpse for him had been a nightmare vision of snow-capped mountains and screaming winds in the Denmark Strait. He felt himself sweating slightly and trembling with furious admiration. How did he do it? He had willed the ship here, that was the only explanation he could find. Nothing else fitted. No wonder that girl admired him. He felt the pain reawake in his breast. Two people like Caryl Brett and Felix von Steiger, a nation—a war —apart, and neither a stranger to pain and hatred, yet both so similar it was uncanny.

He wondered if she had reported him to the Captain for his behaviour. He felt the shame burning his cheeks as he recalled her face and the crimson mark where he had struck her.

'Bring her round, Coxswain!' Von Steiger's voice was terse. 'She won't bite you!'

Heuss followed his captain's ghost-like figure on to the starboard wing and stared past him at the black mass of land. No cheerful buoys, no lighted houses, not even a nodding fishing boat to guide them in. Just the calm sea, broken at the far edge by a writhing line of pure white breakers.

The engine was so muffled that they could not hear its pounding rhythm. Only the persistent vibration and rattle of glass and instruments showed that it was still alive.

Von Steiger placed his hands on the teak rail and breathed deeply. 'That smells good! Peace must smell like that!'

'By the mark five!'

'Christ!' said von Steiger calmly. 'That coxswain is so nervous of losing his pension he is still holding her head round! I imagine that new depth will change his mind for him!'

Heuss heard the wheel spin round, and saw the black wedge of the bows sidle nearer to the whitecaps on the shore.

'I shall get below, Captain. The landing party must be ready to get away as soon as you give the order!' He saluted, and moved to the top of the ladder. He faltered, the nagging question bursting from him. 'What if he will not come to the ship, sir?'

'Persuade him, Heuss. You should be good at that!' His white-clad body turned at the rail, his face hidden in the darkness. 'If anything goes wrong, and it is the fault of this agent, shoot him!' He added, half to himself, 'He has got fat enough at our expense!'

'By the deep eight!'

The land seemed to swoop up and over them, and all at once the ship was no longer the only thing to share the sea and the stars. A great ragged dome of black rock towered high above the mastheads and shut out the stars like a curtain. At its foot the waves leapt and curtsied in a mad dance of worship, and, as the silent ship glided past, a few nodding gulls rose screaming from their nests, disturbed and querulous.

'Hard a-port!' His voice rapped across the polished machine gun and galvanized the helmsman into action. Von Steiger watched a gap-toothed rock sidle past and vanish astern. He remembered that rock from before. He remembered, too, the ship he had then commanded, and the wave of cheerfulness and optimism with which they had greeted the shore. It had been a tremendous cruise and had taken him as far as the Indian Ocean. He had cut the British blockade twice. Once to break into the Atlantic and start a raid on the enemy's commerce, which had been unbeaten and stupendous in its results, and again when he had returned victorious to Kiel. He could remember the cheering crowds, the brass bands and the house-flags streaming like yachts' pennants from every halyard and yard, each flag taken from a victim or captured prize. Freda had been there to greet him, too. He recalled her face briefly, like a portrait revealed in a flash of lightning, as she had stood by his side before the Emperor. The greatest decoration pinned to his tunic, more crowds and screaming applause and the quiet dusty road to Plön. The nodding horses with their heads together over the polished shafts, and Reeder sitting proudly on his piled baggage.

'Second islet on the port bow, Captain!'

He lifted his glasses, the small dream dispersed as if by a wind. 'Take her straight for that next reef, Coxswain. I will tell you when to swing her round!'

Trust me! You big, obstinate ox, he thought angrily. I have no wish to sink my ship either!

Dehler loomed behind him. 'We shall be coming into the tide-race soon, Captain!'

'Very well. Increase speed. Half speed as we come up to the reef, and then full ahead! Tell the Coxswain that if he wishes to draw his pension he will have to move very sharply. Wheel hard over when I give the signal!'

'I have been telling him what to do for the last twenty-four hours, sir.'

'Even so, Dehler, watch everything!'

'By the mark five!'

Von Steiger winced. Only a few feet beneath the raider's barnacled hull now. He watched the angry surf, his eyes slitted as if gauging the strength of a human enemy.

He lifted his hand, and the telegraph jangled urgently. The great screw sprang to life, churning the water into a mad white maelstrom and making every plate shudder in protest. Another brief signal, and the bows, which were rushing straight for the barrier of rock, pivoted round like a bull warded off by a matador's cape.

Von Steiger held his breath until he thought he would burst. Ten seconds, twenty seconds, while the maze of islets swung past the bows in a madly pivoting panorama.

'Full speed astern! Wheel amidships!' A great hand seemed to seize the ship by the stern and pulled her slowly back from her headlong flight.

'Stop engine! Slow ahead!' He peered over the rail, his glasses looking for those two pinnacles of rock. He grunted; there they were. Like the steeples of a shelled and deserted cathedral, black against the stars.

'Stop engine! Stand by to let go!' He heard the orders being repeated and passed forward to the cable party. Another painful ten seconds, while he waited, in spite of his outward calm, for the keel to slice into the rocky spines beneath it.

Then, 'Slow astern!' With a muffled roar the greased cable thundered through the hawse-pipe, the great rust-marked anchor breaking the quiet of the enclosed water and making a mad dance of phosphorescence. Slowly the ship moved astern, paying out the cable ahead of it. The telegraph jangled again, and the engine fell into silence.

Von Steiger felt the vibration die in the teak rail under his hands, and was aware of the great peace which fell over his ship like a cloak. Only the slap and ripple of wavelets alongside and the muffled sigh of the deep water beyond the shelter of the islets and reefs disturbed the humid air. He could imagine Niklas and his engine-room staff leaning on their silent wheels and scarred shovels, and staring at the great, demanding dial of the telegraph, which, for the first time, read, 'Finished with engine!'

.   .   .   .   .

Renato Fleiuss, the German agent in Corata, shifted uncomfortably in his chair and watched von Steiger across Reeder's stooped shoulders as the steward poured two large measures of Scotch whisky. In his expensive drill suit his bloated body looked gross, and the oily skin of his face was covered by a sheen of sweat as his dark, gimlet eyes studied the neat Captain with a mixture of apprehension and fury.

Reeder left the cabin, and Fleiuss's anger burst like a flood. 'And now, Captain, perhaps you will tell me the meaning of all this? You must be a maniac to come here after all that has happened!'

Von Steiger raised his eyebrows, and lit one of his cheroots. He did not reply, but watched the other man with interest.

'When my men reported the presence of your ship I could hardly believe my ears! Here, in Brazil, a hostile country, you dare to show your face!'

'It is too dark for anyone to see!' Von Steiger pointed to the whisky. 'Drink some, Fleiuss, it will calm your nerves!'

'What are you thinking of, Captain? There is nothing for you here! Things have changed since you last came in the *Isar*. Then Germany was great and feared. A chain of resources and supplies stretched around the world. Neutrals turned a blind eye to your comings and goings, provided that our money was good. But now even Brazil is against you! Because the stupid U-boat commanders repeatedly sank her shipping.' He wagged a fat finger, so that the ruby rings glinted like droplets of blood. 'After fair warnings, too, and again after other provocations, Brazil declared war. Every door is shut to you. It is over!' He mopped his face with a silk handkerchief. 'Please go away! You are endangering us all here!'

'Have you finished?' The voice was still calm. 'Surely you realize better than most that I want stores and fuel? I can see that you have feathered your nest here, but for me the war still goes on.' His voice hardened. 'Already my men are going ashore. Before dawn I want every sort of supply you can provide. My officers will give you lists. Fresh fruit, vegetables, water and, above all, fuel!' He watched the mounting indignation on the man's face. 'I believe your coffee steamers still call here once a month?'

'What of it?'

'Then you will have retained a good supply of coal for them, and the lighters to ferry it from the shore.' He smiled faintly. 'I want all that coal, Fleiuss!'

'It is not fair! I was warned by the courier that you might come! But still I could not believe you would be so foolish! And now you are trying to ruin me!' He waved his hands. 'I have won the confidence of people here, and they trust me! I have become one of them!'

'Enough! For years you have waxed fat at the expense of Germany! Without too much risk you have settled here and made yourself more than just comfortable! You are rich, and powerful in your own way!' He waved down the man's protests, the gesture brief and scornful. 'I want to hear no more! I am landing my wounded men also. You will see that they are cared for and taken to the nearest town. Maybe they will be repatriated, but in any case they will be well cared for. You will do all these things, Fleiuss, whatever your scheming brain is plotting right at this moment. You may think that you can destroy me by informing your powerful Brazilian friends, either now or later, when I am once more at sea. Forget such things, and face what you have to do!'

'Betray you! I am a German, Captain!' The shifty eyes blinked with discomfort.

'I am glad you remember! But I am not merely relying on your own interpretation of patriotism!' His lip curled with contempt. 'If you try to betray me you will never live to enjoy your revenge. After the war, if Germany wins you would soon be hounded down for your cowardice, and should we lose the Brazilians would be quick to dispose of you also, provided they were given certain information about your activities!'

Fleiuss's mouth hung open. 'You would not inform on me?'

'For my ship I would do much more than that!' He turned away as the sounds of oars and boats drifted through the open scuttle.

The wounded were on their way. Von Steiger had been on deck to see them, while he had awaited Heuss's return with the agent. The men had been brave, but frightened. Like most sailors they were unwilling to leave their ship and the illusion of security it offered. His eyes had stung as he had moved about the darkened decks. A handshake here, a fumbled embrace there, and teeth which gleamed in smiles at his quick, well-used jokes.

Fleiuss sighed, recognizing his own defeat in those brooding eyes. 'I will get the stores, Captain. Before dawn if you wish it so.' He fumbled in his pocket and handed across some folded papers. 'The courier brought these for you. I was to give them to you if you called.' A small spark of pleasure showed in his heavy face. 'It would appear from what the courier told me that you are not too popular with the High Command? You are still headstrong perhaps, and resent the interference of your superiors?'

Von Steiger leafed through the brief reports. Local shipping, warship movements, etc., there were still a few conscientious agents about, he thought. He opened the last envelope, and felt his heart chill.

Fleiuss downed his whisky and looked up with interest. 'Bad news, Captain?'

Von Steiger walked to the scuttle and lifted a corner of the black curtain. So Heinz was dead. Killed, as he had prophesied, leading his men into the wire and the machine guns.

'My brother-in-law is dead,' he answered sharply, excluding the other man who sat like a fat spider, his face working with fresh ideas.

'But, Captain, surely you can see that it is all hopeless now?' He spread his hands, his voice wheedling but insistent. 'The war is lost for Germany! If you carry on as you are doing, what difference can it make? The big days are gone for ever. The eagle is reduced to picking up crumbs!'

Von Steiger turned on him with sudden fury, his eyes blazing. 'What do you know of war? You, or your stinking kind? Better men than you are shot for cowardice, or fall weeping in the mud of Flanders! What do *you* want me to do? Surrender and scuttle my ship I suppose? Or perhaps sell her to your friends? Do not endanger your skin even by suggesting it!'

'I am sorry, Captain. I was only trying to help.'

'And so you will! Attend to my orders, and at once! You will be guarded at all times while I am here, just in case your memory should lapse, and my pickets will surround your estate. You are far from any other town or village, and I think you are intelligent enough to understand what I mean. I will leave when I have replenished my stores, and you will be in peace. But see that my wounded are cared for. Your own life will be measured against their security!' He looked suddenly tired. 'Now go away! I want to think.'

He stared at the picture of his son until Fleiuss had left the cabin, and then poured another glass of spirit. Poor Heinz. He tried to picture him as he had last seen him. Instead he saw a one-armed man, old before his time, leading his ragged soldiers into nothingness.

With a jarring crash the door flew open, and he swung round to confront a wide-eyed petty officer.

'Captain! I am sorry to burst in!' The man swallowed, and waved his hands hopelessly. 'Something terrible has happened!'

'Speak, man! Don't gabble at me!'

'Some of the prisoners have escaped in the dory! They overpowered a guard and got away in the darkness!' The man stared at his captain, appalled by his own words.

'Who were they?' Von Steiger thought he already knew that answer, but forced himself to wait.

'The Captain of the collier, Mason, and his mate Cobb. Also the man Gelb!' He had turned white, and von Steiger knew there was worse to come. 'They took a rifle, and then overpowered Lieutenant Heuss. They knocked him unconscious and took him as a hostage. They also took the woman, Captain!'

Von Steiger crossed the cabin in two strides and shook the petty officer by his jacket. 'What? Are you certain of all this?'

'Yes, Captain! The sentry who was tied up saw the whole thing! She screamed and fought them! But they dragged her away!'

'Call the Quarter Guard! Summon all the officers at once, and alert the pickets! They cannot get very far tonight!'

He paced across the cabin, listening to the sounds of shouted orders and the clatter of the guard boat alongside.

It would have to happen now. Hardly a man still aboard, and that swine Gelb must have waited for just this moment. His senses and thoughts reeled and surged in disordered confusion, but through it all he seemed to feel one strange steadying message. Caryl Brett had fought them. She was a hostage, as much as Heuss. She was no party to Gelb's plan. He walked to the bunk in the sleeping quarters. He imagined he could sense the feel of her presence or still hold on to the comfort of her belonging in this place.

Dehler and Kohler arrived together, their faces apprehensive as they saw the cold anger in von Steiger's eyes.

Von Steiger did not waste words. 'You have heard what has happened? This is what I intend to do. At dawn I want every available man on the beach. Split them into platoons and cover the whole area. Kohler, you can take your men and start from the far end of the gully, and I will move towards you from the beach. Ebert can take his men along the west side of the cove and beat out every cave and cranny in the rocks there. We must find those men! If we sail without them they will have a hornets' nest around our heads before we have gone a hundred miles, or much less. If we cannot find them soon we will be pinned down here, and maybe discovered by a police patrol or casual ship. Gelb is in a strong position if he can remain hidden, and he knows it. He is not a fool, I think, but dangerous man!'

Kohler blinked his pale eyes. 'We will shoot them like dogs!'

'We must make contact first, Kohler! I can deal with them then. They have two hostages, and will want to bargain. I do not want them hurt!'

'Two, Captain?' Dehler frowned. 'Surely the woman is as dangerous as they?'

'She is a hostage also. No harm must come to her!'

Dehler licked his lips. 'But, Captain, she is not worth the risk! She is only a prisoner!'

Von Steiger smiled straight at him, and ignored Kohler, who was already peering at the map of the cove.

'Dehler, I can read you like a book! Do not imagine I cannot see how your thoughts are going! Attend to my orders at once, and do not try to be clever at Heuss's and Frau Brett's expense!'

He turned away, dismissing them. 'Now we must get that coal! Tomorrow there will be much for all of us to do.'

As he walked on to the darkened deck he felt the pang of loss even stronger. The sick-bay door was open, and the place was deserted. She had not wanted to leave. Whatever she had wished to do later, she had not wanted to leave him like this.

He watched the first coal-lighter being rowed alongside, and rested his hands on the guardrail. Somewhere out there, inside his ring of pickets, the three escaped prisoners and their hostages were waiting and hiding. The land was unbroken and wild, and too dangerous for movement by night. Von Steiger lit his cheroot and wondered if they could see the glare of the match from the shore. Perhaps the girl could see it and would feel hope. If Gelb saw it he might even recognize it as a warning. Von Steiger glanced at the watchful shape of a machine gunner and threw the cheroot over the rail.

Heuss may already be dead, but if they have harmed that girl it will be my own doing!

If Gelb could have seen his face, he might well have known the meaning of fear.

15

HEUSS half lay against the sharp-edged rock, feeling its warmth through the back of his crumpled tunic. His head ached fiercely, and when he moved his face muscles he winced and felt the clotted blood hard against his cheek. His hands were pulled tightly behind his back, and he knew it was useless to try to free them. The British mate, Cobb, had tied the line efficiently and with relish, so that his hands were numb and his shoulders felt raw in their sockets. He moved his head slightly and stared up at the fine blue sky and the tiny white gulls which circled above the hiding place, and tried to estimate their position. He could hear Gelb's thick voice as he talked with Mason, the collier's captain, and he could see Cobb's left foot sticking round the side of a diamond-shaped boulder as he watched the gully below him. He wondered what the girl was doing, and what Gelb intended to attempt next.

It had all happened so suddenly that he still could not quite realize that he was away from the ship and a prisoner. He had gone to the sick-bay to apologize to Caryl Brett for his behaviour. She had greeted him warmly, yet with a reservation he had recognized as their new relationship. He had wanted to tell her so much, to make her understand his longing, but it was not to be. Gelb and his two companions had burst into the sick-bay, and again Heuss's world had changed. This was a new Gelb, a man who felt the strength of his new power. He had told the girl that she was going with them. When she refused Gelb had twisted her arm behind her, and pushed her to the door. Heuss had seen too late the swinging rifle-butt and the look of hatred on the British mate's face. There had been sharp pain and then oblivion. A chance of escape never came twice, he had once been told. Gelb must have been plotting and planning for just this one chance. He never seemed to do things on impulse. Perhaps that was the way of business men, he thought, a type of commercial training which service men lacked. He bit his lip, realizing that his mind was wandering; he even felt light-headed from the effects of the crushing blow he had received. He wondered what von Steiger would do now. It would be just like him to open fire on the whole cove with the ship's main armament, he thought. Blast the whole hillside to fragments, and him with it. He dismissed the idea with irritation, and tried to estimate the seriousness of the threat Gelb offered to the raider.

On the other side of the rock Gelb rolled over on to his stomach, and peered down at the tiny white figures which moved with painful slowness along the floor of the gully. The sea was invisible, and the air was alive with bird-song and the scream of enraged gulls. But for the distant, jerky figures, Gelb might have imagined that they were already safe and clear of danger.

He turned to listen to Mason. It was so typical of his kind, he thought, to want to assume command again now that they had got this far.

'We can lie low here,' Mason spoke slowly, his slitted eyes on the nearest of the search party, 'and wait to be taken. Or we can try to get further inland. If we get found up here we can hold off an army if necessary. But what's the point in that? We're free, that's all that matters!'

Gelb glared at him with sudden anger. 'What about your ship? I thought you wanted to get back to it?'

'Oh, for Christ's sake! I'm alive and free! That's good enough for me! The bloody Navy'll take care of the Jerry when they get round to it!'

'Ah, but suppose von Steiger manages to get clear, eh? Maybe gets back to Germany. Have you thought of that?'

Mason shifted uncomfortably beneath Gelb's concentrated gaze. 'We can't be expected to stop him on our own!'

'He will get back to Germany, and the effect on his country will be tremendous! With their backs to the wall, the Americans in the war against them and their army dying like flies! But one splash of bravado like this, and who knows what might happen? Try to put yourself in von Steiger's position!'

'How the hell can I?' He sounded uneasy. 'I don't see what we can do!'

Gelb smiled complacently. 'You should always try to put yourself in your enemy's skin, my friend. In business or war. It makes no difference.'

Cobb called from beyond his rock barrier. 'That lot of square-heads are moving clear! Look at 'em! Like dogs on the wrong scent!'

Gelb hummed softly, enjoying Mason's discomfort. 'What did I tell you, eh! They will never look for us here! They will expect us to make for the other end of the cove, or maybe that plantation!'

The white figures moved away and vanished into the green fringe at the edge of the plantation.

Gelb smiled. 'Don't you see, man? We shall be able to get back to England, all being well. I have friends here in Brazil who will be happy to pull strings with the government. We will not be delayed, I think. We shall go home with more glory than von Steiger has ever had! A captured German officer, the destruction of the raider due to our information, what more could you ask!'

'*You'll* be all right!' Mason stared sourly at the wheeling gulls. 'But I'll be sent back to sea again! That's all the thanks I'll get!' His leathery face split into a tired smile. 'Still, you didn't do so well with the girl, did you? I saw your eyes on her! But it looks as if she's already been sampled by the Jerries, eh!' He laughed at Gelb's face, which was transformed into an expression of hatred and anger. 'Don't take it so hard, chum! She's only a woman! A damned pretty one, but a woman for all that. There's no accounting for any of 'em. I've been married twice, so I should know!'

Gelb muttered under his breath, and moved, stooping, along the natural parapet of the hiding place, away from Mason and his harsh laugh.

Caryl Brett sat beneath the overhanging wall of rock, like Heuss, her arms tied behind her back, although not so cruelly. Her skirt was torn and covered with wet sand, and her blouse was stretched tightly across her full breasts by the pressure of her arms. She stared up at him, her eyes startled but unafraid.

My God, you are beautiful, you little bitch! He sank on to his knees and ran his eyes hungrily over her body. She thinks she is too good for me, like all her class. I saw it in her eyes when we first met. Just a common jumped-up Cockney, she was thinking. Not to be trusted, but we must be nice to him because he is a fellow passenger. But no warmth, no open friendship. When the lifeboats were attacked by the U-boat, where was her damned, stuck-up husband? There was only me to help her!

In his brooding rage he involuntarily reached out and laid his hand on her thigh. He saw the alarm give way to revulsion in her eyes, and felt her leg go taut beneath the torn skirt.

'It need not be like this, my dear!' He had to control his voice with real effort. He could feel the mounting pain in his groin, and her helplessness and sudden fear filled him with mad desire. 'Stop acting like this and I might be able to help you!'

She lifted her head and stared at him, as if seeing his face for the first time. 'This is *your* moment! You have engineered all this, so do not spoil it by pretending to be a hero, too!'

He leaned closer, so that she could see the furrows of dirt on his unshaven chin and the beads of sweat forming and re-forming on his thick neck. The pressure on her thigh remained, and she could almost see the indecision in his mind.

This is all my fault, she thought, all my doing just as much as his. Suddenly she wanted to hurt him as she was being hurt herself, to break that bursting pride which had transformed Gelb into a bully and a sadist.

'I wish you could see yourself!' She felt her mouth go dry as Gelb's face darkened. 'Why, you dirty, cowardly beast! Why don't you stop deluding yourself? You think because I don't fall at your feet that I am a traitor to my country. That because you were the only man available to me I should give myself without reserve or question. You're mad! The very nearness of you disgusts me!'

'Shut your mouth!' Gelb lifted his hand threateningly. 'Don't try to talk down to me now! Those days are past for you, unless I choose otherwise!'

'Talk *down*! Before I married Arthur I was a typist, not a lady in waiting, or a countess! Stop deluding yourself! You only think I am talking down to you because you know full well that you are nothing, in spite of your money, your connections and your damned, know-it-all conceit!'

Her head jerked back as he struck her across the cheek. She closed her eyes, waiting for the other blow. She almost wanted to be beaten, as if to drive away uncertainty and fear.

Instead of striking her again, he moved his hot hand along the line of her neck and around the soft curve of her shoulder. She could feel his hand shaking as he ran it down to her waist to join the other one on her thigh. He seized her arm with sudden fury and shook her so that her wrists ground against the rock.

'You little bitch! I could take you now if I wanted! Right here! But I have other things in store for you, my pet! When I tell them what a slut you are, you will be sorry for the rest of your life!'

She tried to meet his anger, but as she looked at him he hit her again across the face, and again, and again, until she thought he was trying to kill her.

Mason's harsh voice interrupted him. 'Come back here, man! There's some more of 'em coming!'

Gelb tore his eyes from the limp figure at his feet and ran his fingers through his thin hair. She lay panting on her side, her face in the dust, her hair tangled across her shoulders. Through the torn blouse he could see her smooth skin and the painful movement of her breasts. He was suddenly thankful for Mason's interruption. He realized that in another minute he would have killed her.

He blinked away the sweat from his eyes and peered over the rocks to where a long straggling line of weary seamen had toiled up the side of the slope from the gully, and now waited listlessly, staring up at the high rocks or at the sky beyond.

A figure detached itself from the rest and began to move up the slope. It was an officer, and from his quick steps Gelb could recognize him as Lieutenant Kohler. He halted in a natural rocky basin, his uniform bright against the slate-coloured floor, and stared blindly upwards at the overhanging rocks and silent cliffs.

'Listen to me!' His sharp voice rang out and was echoed and re-echoed around the towering walls of stone. 'Listen to me, wherever you are! We know you are somewhere up there, and will give you a chance to surrender!' His clipped accent gave menace to the words, and Gelb glanced quickly at Mason's dark face. The voice continued: 'You have five minutes to decide! After that we shall take reprisals!' He started to walk back towards his men, his shoulders braced as if expecting a shot.

'Reprisals? What the hell does he mean?' Cobb leaned round the rock, his face uneasy.

'Bluff!' Gelb sneered at him. 'He does not know for sure where we are, he . . .' His voice trailed away as Mason pointed at another tiny group of men behind the first line of seamen. Even at that distance there was no mistaking the dark-blue uniforms and tarnished gold braid.

'Christ, they've got the rest of the prisoners!' Mason half rose, his face pale with anger and fear.

'Get down! They won't do anything!'

Kohler's distorted voice echoed around and above them. 'Your time is up! We will shoot one of your men for every additional minute you wait!'

Even as Mason staggered to his feet, his face contorted in anguish and his arms outstretched, there was a single crack, and one of the figures fell on its face beneath a faint hovering cloud of smoke.

Mason called out: 'Stop! Don't shoot any more of them! They had nothing to do with it!'

All the pale blobs of faces were upturned towards the hiding place, and here and there a rifle moved restlessly and a man gestured towards them.

Gelb grabbed at Mason's leg. 'Get down, man! We have hostages, too!'

'Don't be a fool, Gelb! They'll kill every last one of those blokes! And if we shoot this Jerry officer, what then? What will happen to us?' He stared at Gelb with open hatred. 'Just too clever by half! We should have got away when I said!' He jerked to his feet again as another shot rang out, then he was running crazily down the slope, his arms waving like semaphore arms.

Cobb threw down the rifle and stood up, his face determined. 'Me too! I'll not see anyone else butchered!'

Gelb watched him go, his mind reeling with shock.

The seamen started up the slope, their rifles levelled, their eyes searching and alert.

Below, Mason and his mate walked together through the advancing line of men. The rank parted to let them through, and the British captain walked straight towards the familiar figure with the short beard and small black cheroot, who stood at the far side of the gully, a pistol hanging in his hand. Mason was a hard man and expected no mercy, but his own anger swept away caution and prudence. He stopped before the levelled rifles of two seamen and glanced down at the sprawled figures in the dust.

Von Steiger nodded coldly. 'I thought that you would have the decency to come down, Captain!' From the corner of his eye he saw Gelb being hustled over the rim of the boulders. He saw two other figures being assisted down by his men, and felt the claws of anguish relax from his inside. He even smiled as he gestured to the two still figures at his feet. 'All right, Reeder, Schaffer! You can get up now!'

The two dead men rose from the ground and grinned self-consciously in their borrowed uniforms. Von Steiger turned away from the two Englishmen, unable to watch their discomfort. 'Take them back on board! But see that there are no reprisals!'

Mason stared at his mate and shrugged. 'Well, can you beat that!' He clapped the younger man on the shoulder, and together they walked down the gully towards the sea. 'Still,' Mason said cheerfully, 'we gave the bastards a run for their money!'

    .   .   .   .   .

Lieutenant Ebert, closely followed by Petty Officer Weiss, came running breathlessly across the sun-baked sand, momentarily distracting von Steiger's attention.

Ebert saluted, his face pouring with sweat. 'Captain, I have to report that two men have deserted their posts on the picket line!'

Lieutenant Kohler stamped his foot. 'Who were the swine?'

Ebert still watched von Steiger's set face. 'The men were Pieck and Alder, Captain!'

Von Steiger frowned. 'Why should they desert now? That Pieck was a good boy, I thought.' He did not see the look of surprise and shock on Kohler's face, and continued: 'We cannot worry about them now. We must get the rest of the men aboard and see that they are rewarded for their double efforts. Tell the cooks to prepare them a real feast!'

Ebert looked at him with surprise. The Captain had not flown into a rage as he expected. Now he was talking of rewards, and a feast! It was as if he were celebrating something personal, and wanted to share it with his crew. He heard von Steiger add: 'Beef and haricot beans, and a double ration of sausage and bread! Give them some of Fleiuss's wine and tobacco, too! They have earned it, and the chance may not come again!' Von Steiger turned away from their surprised faces and walked to meet Heuss and the girl.

'I am glad you are well, Heuss! It might have been worse!'

Heuss tried to find the words to answer, but when he turned he saw that von Steiger was talking to the girl. He seemed oblivious to the stares of his officers and the grins of his tired men. For a long moment von Steiger and the girl appeared to be isolated from everything and everyone around them.

.   .   .   .   .

The ship was quiet, but for the faint hum of a generator and the perpetual whirr of fans. The upperworks were too hot to touch, and the pitch in the deck seams was wet and bubbling beneath the sun's probing glare.

The wardroom had every door and scuttle opened wide, and the interior was deep in shadows, which gave the impression of peace and coolness. The white deckhead shimmered in dancing lights and reflections from the water below the scuttles, while from the closed pantry came the peaceful clink of crockery as the stewards prepared the evening meal.

Heuss stretched out his legs and felt the sweat trickle across his thigh. In spite of the schnapps, or perhaps because of it, his headache was worse, and he kept his eyes tightly closed in a tired frown. He could feel the chair-back sticking to his shoulders, and thought back to that morning and the painful wait on the top of the ridge. He could still feel the sharp pain of the cod-line which had bound his wrists, just as he could clearly remember the shock at seeing the girl lying on her face in the dust with the rescuing seamen bending over her. And now I have to be even more humble and grateful to the Captain, he thought bitterly. He had made the prisoners' efforts to escape seem pitiful and slightly ridiculous. He could still hear the laughter of the seamen who had come blundering up the hill, and the way they had chuckled at von Steiger's ruse. He frowned again, the pain in his head making him gasp aloud. It was as if I was included in their derision. As if they saw through my inadequacy, as I have done.

He opened his eyes and stared gingerly at the shimmering deckhead.

He suddenly felt that he hated the sea and all that it offered for the future. He realized that Ebert was watching him from another chair, a look of concern on his round face.

'Feeling rough, eh, Emil?'

Heuss smiled thinly. 'That describes it!'

Ebert put down his tattered book and yawned. 'It doesn't seem real, does it? Sunshine, good food and nothing to do! I shall be glad to get to sea again in a way!'

'Sadist! I suppose you want more fighting?'

Ebert was unmoved by the sarcasm. 'I have been listening to the things the Captain was saying about the war and the serious situation at home. We must do our best, Emil. We *have* to!'

Heuss groaned. 'A forgotten ship! I was mad to volunteer for her!'

'You make me sick!' Ebert clenched his fists angrily. 'You have all the luck, and yet you still grumble!' He waved down Heuss's protests. 'No! Hear me out! The Captain has fallen over backwards to give you every chance, he has even made it pretty clear that you would take command should he be killed or badly wounded. He knows you don't like him, yet he acts like that to show he is a big enough man to ignore personal tittle-tattle! If he was like some of the captains I have served, you'd have been court-martialled ages ago!'

Dehler entered the wardroom and peered questioningly at the two officers.

Heuss avoided his stare, but Ebert asked, 'Any fresh orders?'

'Yes. We shall sail at dawn tomorrow. The Captain thinks it too difficult to manage in the dark. There are no leading-marks on the outward passage!'

Ebert said, 'Good-bye to the smell of earth and the sound of birds.'

Dehler did not seem to hear. 'A whaleboat will lead us out, taking soundings all the way. Before the day gets going we should be well clear of the coast and in the open sea again.' His voice lacked enthusiasm, and he walked over to Heuss's chair. 'God, I'm tired! I've aged about ten years in the last month or so. Just let me get home, and I'll never set foot on a ship again!'

'How is the woman?' Ebert sounded uneasy, and wanted to turn the subject away from Dehler's despondency.

He shrugged. 'Laughing at all of us, I should think! By God, she is getting a first-hand look at us, and no mistake!'

Heuss staggered to his feet. 'Well, I hope she likes what she sees! I am afraid that *I* do not!'

. . . . .

To the north-west of Corata the rocky coastline was sliced at even intervals into deep crevasses, as if a giant axe had hacked at the inhospitable coastline to get at the lush green interior.

The sun blazed relentlessly down on the two small figures as they moved slowly along the edge of a tall cliff, pressing them on to the baked rock and making the surrounding landscape shimmer in a madly dancing haze.

Pieck paused and peered dizzily down into the nearest crevasse. Something told him he should follow the coastline, and yet these crevasses kept appearing across his route, so that he had to retrace his weary steps inland and then back to the sea, to stare down once more at its mocking glare. He leaned on his rifle and waited for Alder's shadow to join his own. If only he would say something, question his intentions, anything. But Alder seemed content to shamble along in his world of silence, his eyes in-looking and dead.

Pieck wiped his lips with the back of his hand and tasted the salt from the sea. He blinked away the moisture from his eyes and watched the smooth interwoven patterns of the deep blue water, which glittered towards the faint horizon, or changed to a warm green hue at the foot of the cliff, where it shone like a giant magnifying-glass above the pale sand.

He uncorked the water bottle and lifted it to his lips. Alder gave a great sigh and sat down on a stone, as if some invisible string had broken. 'Here, have a drink!' Pieck held out the bottle. He watched as Alder sipped unwillingly at the half-empty bottle, and felt the tears of frustration and despair pricking behind his eyes.

'We *had* to leave!' he said again. 'They would have shot you otherwise!' He tried to smile at Alder's blank face. 'Never mind. We will manage somehow!'

He pulled Alder to his feet, and they started off once more. He tried to estimate how far they had come since they had left the guard-post on the hill and moved away from the sea and the darkened ship. When the dawn had found them, they had already moved several miles up the coast, but the heat and the exhaustion in their starved bodies had made careful preparations impossible, and Pieck had to grit his teeth until his jaw ached to keep himself moving at all. His stomach rumbled painfully, but he could not face the dry biscuits and half-sausage which he carried in his bag. Perhaps when it was dark and cooler they could rest, and then he could try to think out what he was going to do.

Alder fixed his eyes on the boy's narrow shoulders and the patch of sweat on the ragged uniform, and felt the hard ground jarring through his thin boots with each painful step. He played a little game as he walked. He tried to keep out of step with his companion, and put his feet down carefully, concentrating on Pieck's jogging limbs in case he should catch him out. Left right, left right. He grinned quietly as he changed step with sudden alarm and then continued his silent counting. He wondered where they were going and when they would meet the others. It was quiet without Schiller and Hahn. He tried to fathom what was happening, but gave it up with a wild grin of resignation. After all, if Willi wanted to show him something, he must try to follow. Left right, left right.

Alder stopped dead in his tracks, his face suddenly filled with fresh apprehension. He was standing on the top of yet another crevasse, and as he stepped forward, his boots gingerly releasing a stream of loose pebbles, he saw the water far below him, breaking with tiny, silent cat's-paws across a line of black rocks. He shifted uncomfortably and peered from side to side. He was quite alone. Of Willi there was no sign, and after several long minutes a frown of petulant annoyance crossed his vacant features.

Then he heard it. . . . A voice crying out in pain, and he thought that perhaps he had been hearing it all the time. But the outside world was so often disconnected with his jumbled thoughts that this no longer worried him.

Biting his tongue with concentration, he took another pace forward. Then he stopped and peered incredulously downwards over the edge. Splayed across a small ledge of outflung rock, some twenty feet beneath him, he could see Willi's white uniform and terrified eyes.

Pieck tried again to move, but the pain in his ribs made him whimper. He began to sob uncontrollably as he lay staring blindly at the sun and Alder's distorted figure on top of the cliff. With the sun on his neck and his limbs moving automatically, he had literally walked over the edge of the cliff. He had struck the ledge with a sickening crash, so that, as his ribs cracked like twigs on the sharp rock, he had seen a thousand stars explode before his eyes, and had waited to die.

Instead there was silence again, and as he felt the sand spray across his face he realized that Alder was lowering himself carefully down the cliff towards him. He realized, too, that he no longer cared. He had failed once more, and now he was as helpless as Alder.

The latter moved with surprising agility and total disregard for the height of the ledge above the water. Muttering to himself, he tied Pieck's wrists together and pulled him up across his stooped shoulders. Then, carrying the boy like a sack, he began to feel his way up the treacherous wall of rock. Each step brought a moan of pain from his burden, but Alder did not alter his expression of concentrated effort.

As their heads rose above the edge, Pieck saw Alder's pack which contained the telescope and some more biscuits neatly placed on a flat stone, with his cap balanced on the top. His pain-racked body shook in a paroxysm of inane laughs at the sight, but Alder pursed his lips severely and lowered him to the ground.

He ripped open the boy's jacket and ran his hands across the heaving body, his eyes staring blankly at the raw skin and angry-coloured bruises. Beneath his probing fingers he felt the uneven ridges of bone, and sensed Pieck holding his breath against the agony of his discovery.

He grinned down at him and walked to the pack. Pieck craned his head to watch, as the tattered scarecrow figure pulled out the long telescope and began to peer seawards and along the glittering coastline.

Alder hummed to himself as he swung the big brass tube and watched the distant cliffs and beaches spring to life in sudden close proximity. But they were, of course, empty. In spite of the heat and their haphazard course they had covered a lot of ground, and Alder frowned with vague disappointment. Not even a small fishing boat moved to break the glassy brightness of the sea, and no birds swooped over the inviting water. Alder felt himself tremble with unaccountable anger.

Pieck let his head fall on the hard ground, and waited for Alder to stop acting as he was. He began to think of his parents and wondered how they would receive the news.

All at once he heard Alder muttering with excitement, and as he turned his face towards him he saw him pointing with the telescope towards the horizon. His heart sank. He must have seen the *Vulkan*. Perhaps she had sailed, and was already standing well out to sea.

With sudden determination he gritted his teeth. 'Here! Let me see her!'

Alder supported his head and obediently held the telescope. For a long while Pieck searched the empty sea, and began to think that Alder's mind had given out yet again. He had to see the *Vulkan* just once more. He had to. He grunted with agony and leaned his frail body against Alder. Then he saw what Alder had seen. At first he thought it was a part of the haze on the horizon, and then he realized that the hard outline was unchanging, unmoving.

At the training ship he had seen pictures of such ships before. There was no mistaking the outline of that squat tripod mast and the clean grey funnels.

He dropped the telescope and stared into Alder's deep, expressionless eyes. 'A British cruiser!' And Alder nodded.

·   ·   ·   ·   ·

Lieutenant Kohler marched purposefully along the deserted beach, his patrol boots squeaking noisily in the darkness, his arms swinging energetically with an almost parade-ground precision. Behind him, his pig-like body making hard going of the uneven ground and treacherous pieces of rock, Petty Officer Elmke kept a respectful distance, his chest heaving with exertion.

Kohler halted suddenly and glared round the black shadows of the darkened cove. As officer-of-the-guard he was taking his duties extra seriously, and had already awarded punishment to two sentries who had been nodding at their posts. His hand played a little tattoo on his holster as he listened distastefully to Elmke's heavy breathing. Great fat oaf, he thought angrily. Fancy anyone, even a ranker, letting himself get so gross and ugly.

He turned right, up the side of the gully, and began to climb up the narrow goat-track which led to the top of one of the tall rock pinnacles. He increased his stride, finding amusement from Elmke's painful grunting.

'Halt! Who goes there?' The sentry's voice was sharp in the still air.

Elmke managed to reply, 'Officer-of-the-guard!' and Kohler marched up to the two white figures with levelled rifles.

They saluted, and the taller reported:. 'Seaman Schoningen, Lieutenant! All correct!' They stood quite rigid as the officer prowled around their post, which spanned the goat-track and covered the approach to the beach and another overgrown path from the cliffs beyond the cove. He sniffed, but could detect no cigarette smoke. A pity, he thought viciously. It was bad enough having Pieck, and that other ungrateful idiot Alder, desert, without letting the sentries get slack and take advantage of the Captain's leniency.

Schoningen smiled to himself as he watched the officer's petulant behaviour. He and his companion had heard Kohler long before he had reached the bottom of the path, and had had ample time to douse their cigarettes. When darkness had fallen Schoningen had run down the path and had strewn it with dry branches from a dead tree. The blundering feet of the two men across the tinder-dry twigs had given him plenty of warning. Officers! Think they're so damned clever! Look at him now, trying to find fault with Blucher's rifle. I'd like to poke this bayonet right into his guts.

Kohler handed the rifle back. 'Filthy!' he roared. 'Report to me in full marching order at the end of your duty!' He smiled in the darkness. That would teach him. It would take him hours to find and assemble the complicated mass of belts, ammunition pouches, helmet and entrenching tool which the German High Command in all their wisdom thought fit to issue to sea-going sailors. He turned to Schoningen. 'Your rifle, man!' He felt a little pulse begin to pound in his head as the man stared past him. 'Did you hear?'

Schoningen said quietly: 'I heard something, Lieutenant! Along that path from the cliffs!'

Kohler glared at the man's shadowy face. 'If you are merely saying this to distract me . . .' Then he turned and listened also. Probably one of Fleiuss's estate workers, he thought. 'Has anyone come along here while you have been on watch?'

'No one, sir!'

Kohler smiled as he heard the sound again. A seaman from the ship, most likely. Slipped through the guards earlier to steal something from the estate. These two guards were probably accomplices. It would be worth something to see their faces when the other man arrived.

They could all hear the dragging footsteps now. It sounded as if the man, whoever he was, was dragging a considerable load with him.

Schoningen lifted his rifle, his thumb on the safety-catch. Through the dried brush and tangled trees which had overgrown the twisting path he had already seen a faint white shape. It seemed to be swaying, and his heart sank. Some fool must have broken ship and gone off on his own to get drunk.

Resignedly he yelled: 'Halt! Who goes there?'

The shuffling footsteps stopped, and they could hear the man's wheezing breath.

Schoningen shifted the rifle unsteadily. 'Advance! You are covered!' Must be a drunk, he decided.

They gave a combined gasp of surprise as Alder's bent shape staggered up the last few yards, his eyes like two black holes as he peered short-sightedly at the tense group in front of him.

Kohler stepped forward, aware of the limp shape which the seaman carried across his back. Pieck. It could be no one else.

Alder laid the boy on the sand and then fell on his knees beside him, his narrow chest shaking with strain and exhaustion.

'Get up! You mutinous swine!' Kohler lashed out with his foot and kicked the man on the arm so that he toppled on to his side.

Pieck's voice, weak but desperate, called out: 'Please, sir! Do not touch him! He has carried me for miles! He would not leave me. I told him to, but he would not put me down!'

Kohler clenched his fists, a white-hot rage sweeping over him. 'Get up, I said!' He kicked Alder again, but the man lay limp and indifferent to the cruel blows.

Pieck moved his head jerkily, as if to clear away the mist of pain which closed in on him. 'Sir! We came back to report that we have seen a ship! A British ship!'

Kohler laughed, an ugly sound. 'A likely story! Where did you see it, in the hills? You'll have to plead better than that before I have you shot!'

'Surely you don't think I'm lying, sir?' There was despair in the boy's voice.

'Yes, you damned hound, I *do* think so! And I think you fell and

292

injured yourself, so you came crawling back for mercy!' He stooped over the spread-eagled figure and groped savagely for the bare skin. 'Where does it hurt you? Here?' He pushed down hard, and the boy's thin scream shattered the stillness.

Kohler laughed delightedly. The touch of that smooth skin under his hand reminded him again of this boy's treachery and the frustration it had caused him. He could feel the broken ribs move beneath the pressure of his hand, and trembled with excitement. 'Admit it! You deserted your ship, and came back because you were hurt!' He pushed again, and quivered to the shrill scream.

Elmke stood staring at the torture with glazed eyes, his mouth dry with fright. Schoningen felt the sweat cold on his face, and gripped his rifle with such force that his knuckles cracked with pain.

There was a metallic click from the path behind them, and Schiller's unmistakable voice said quietly: 'Stand up, Lieutenant! And don't do anything foolish!'

Kohler leapt to his feet, his head swinging towards the faintly gleaming rifle with its fixed bayonet. In Schiller's hands it looked like a child's toy. 'What are you saying?' It was Kohler who was screaming now. 'Are you mad? This will mean death for you, for all of you!'

Elmke stepped forward. 'Please, sir, it's not my fault!' He blinked from Kohler's pale shape to the steady bayonet. 'I did not know he had left his post!'

'Shut up, you fat pig!' Schiller's voice was a dangerous snarl. 'Schoningen, Blucher, carry Willi down to the Quarter Guard on the beach, and call for the boat. Elmke! Help Alder down to the boat as well!'

Kohler shook his fists in the air. 'Don't move, any of you! This is mutiny! I'll have you all hanged! I'll have——'

'You will have this bayonet in your belly, Lieutenant, if you don't do as I tell you!' Schiller lowered the rifle an inch so that the saw-edged blade was level with the officer's stomach. 'We are going back to the ship to see the Captain. I heard what Pieck told you, and I believe him. But then I know him better than you do!'

'You'll pay for this! You'll wish you'd never been born!'

Schiller gestured towards the edge of the path. 'Be careful, Lieutenant! A man could fall here in the darkness, and might never be found!' In a louder voice he bellowed: 'Hold on, Willi! We'll look after you!'

Schiller followed the silent party down the narrow path, his chin hard on his deep chest. Well, you've done it this time. You've stuck your stupid neck out once too often.

But he thought of Pieck's terrible screams, and was glad he had done as he had.

. . . . .

The sentry outside von Steiger's quarters stamped his feet together and banged the butt of his Mauser sharply on the polished deck as Lieutenant Heuss pushed open the door and entered the wide cabin. Heuss glanced from Dehler's grim face to Damrosch's apprehensive stare, and then at the Captain, who sat behind the polished walnut table, the low light shining on his neat dark head.

Von Steiger looked up and nodded. With a steady hand he poured a large measure of brandy into a vacant glass and pushed it across the table. 'Sit down, Heuss, and drink this. I am sorry to call you to my quarters like this, for I know you must be feeling quite shaky still.'

Heuss picked up the glass and watched von Steiger over the rim. He tried to detect sarcasm in the level voice, but could find none. Von Steiger looked calm, even composed, but Heuss had learned enough to know this was only a façade.

'I understand there has been some more trouble ashore, Captain.'

'Trouble? I should think so!' Dehler's thick voice broke in. 'A mutiny more like it!'

Von Steiger's eyebrows twitched slightly with irritation. 'There *has* been some trouble. Ebert is up forward questioning two sentries and the petty officer of the Guard, and I have had the man Schiller placed under arrest. For the moment, I am letting Lieutenant Kohler quieten down in his cabin, but I shall question him again myself in due course.'

Dehler stuck out his lower lip. 'And the deserters, sir?'

'Both in the sick-bay. I shall go and see the boy Pieck in a minute, but first I want to ask you what you know about all this. Why is it left to a crisis to show me what is happening in my ship?' His voice was still level, but his eyes were cold and bitter.

Heuss placed the glass slowly on the table. 'Perhaps we all thought you were too aware of what was happening, sir. We have all seen the power you hold over the crew.'

Von Steiger's eyes flickered. 'Do not be frivolous, Heuss! Let me put it plainer to you. I can have all these men shot. The sentries for not coming to an officer's aid; Schiller for mutiny, and the other two for desertion! Are you prepared to carry out those sentences, Heuss?'

Heuss shifted in his chair. 'I don't see that it's any part of my duty——' he began, but von Steiger leapt to his feet and killed the words in his throat.

'Don't be so damned smug! Men's lives *are* your duty! You exist because of them! I do not expect to have to lecture any of you, but you have made it obvious once more that you are still only half aware of your duties!' He swept the three of them with a scathing glance. 'Are all these men to be sacrificed just to uphold the prestige of one of my officers? Well, can't you answer me? Prestige is like respect, it is something to be earned, it is not issued with the uniform!' He was shouting now, and Heuss felt the words like a whip across his cheeks. 'I have had a man shot already for that purpose, but, by God, if I had only known then what I know now . . .' He left the threat unfinished, and sat down wearily in his chair.

In a calmer tone he continued: 'The boy Pieck has reported seeing an enemy warship off the coast. If he is right I shall have to change my plans. It could be serious!'

Heuss said slowly, 'Shall I speak to him, sir?'

'No, I will. There are a lot of things I wish to know in good time. What happened to Petty Officer Brandt? Why was Seaman Hahn's body left in that sinking ship? And what would make two men desert and then come back to the ship because it was in danger of destruction? Does that sound like the act of a coward or a traitor?' He picked up his cap and stood up, the black cross glinting in the lamplight. 'No, gentlemen, as officers you have had your opportunity to prevent these irritations. By failing to do so, it falls to me to solve them!'

Damrosch knew in his heart that von Steiger's bitterness was directed at the other two officers, and yet he felt his cheeks sting with humiliation. There was no answer to his words, no defence against his lashing tongue. Damrosch stood back to allow the Captain to pass and then followed the others along the narrow passageway. They walked in single file, and he was reminded of the same feeling he had known when following his first headmaster to his study to be questioned over some minor prank. Except that this was in deadly earnest, he thought. As they crossed the boatdeck, he could sense the watchfulness of the ship, and saw several groups of silent figures standing in corners or waiting on the darkened deck.

The sick-bay smelt clean and unused, and beneath the glaring light above the operating table Steuer's face looked drawn and angry. He stood back as the Captain approached, but Damrosch could sense his unwillingness, as if he no longer trusted the behaviour of his fellow men.

Pieck looked very small on the table, and beneath the probing light his face seemed almost transparent. Von Steiger's eyes lifted briefly to Steuer's, an unasked question in his grave face.

Steuer said quietly: 'I have nearly finished with the dressings, Captain. I cannot yet say the extent of his injuries, but his lungs are not pierced, and that must surely be a miracle.'

Von Steiger leaned across the table, his eyes taking note of the savage bruises which showed above the temporary dressings and the painful, uneven breathing.

'Well, Pieck, you came back,' he said at length. 'Can you understand what I am saying?'

The boy licked his lips and rolled his eyes to stare first at the closeness of his captain and then at the grim-faced officers behind him. He swallowed and tried to speak, but the agonizing pain flooded through him again like fire.

Von Steiger said quietly, 'I have a book of pictures here for you to see.' He lifted a well-worn album of photographs into the boy's line of vision and raised the cover. He saw Pieck's frightened eyes move uncomprehendingly to the first photograph, which showed a British light cruiser making full speed through a blurred and choppy sea. 'If you recognize the ship you saw today with your telescope, let me know.' He began to turn the stiff cardboard pages, his eyes fixed on the boy's face. He saw the fear replaced by something else. Urgency, desperation or eagerness. But neither cunning nor deception showed on his undernourished features. He could hear Heuss moving closer, and guessed that he, too, was aware of this important fact.

The minutes dragged on, and once they had to pause while Pieck lowered his head with exhaustion.

Steuer said sharply: 'Captain, sir. He is in great pain! Could not this wait for a while longer? I know it is important for him, but he has suffered a great deal!'

Von Steiger took Pieck's cold hand and held it. 'It is important for all of us, in more ways than you imagine, Steuer!' In a quieter tone he continued, 'Just move your hand if you see the ship!'

Damrosch could feel himself sweating as the stiff pages rasped over the sleeve of the Captain's jacket. If he cannot find that ship, what will von Steiger do to him? He winced as he remembered the angry, mutinous faces of the seamen when the Quarter Guard had brought Schiller and the others to the ship. He thought, too, of Kohler's stricken face. Not a shadow of guilt, or sorrow for the boy he had tried to cripple, but only shock to find such humiliation at the hands of his own men.

The page began to turn, and then von Steiger felt the unsure movement in his hand. Hardly daring to breathe, he held the book steady and watched the pale eyes moving jerkily back and forth across the clearly etched photograph.

'That is the one, sir!' The voice was weak, but filled with conviction. 'I can recognize her by that forward funnel. It seems to be built into the tripod mast!'

Von Steiger squeezed his shaking hand and nodded. 'So it does, boy! So it does!' He had seen the small caption under the picture: H.M.S. *Waltham*, 1915. One of the cruisers which Fleiuss had reported as being in these waters. He felt as if a great weight had been lifted from him. For a brief moment he forgot the menace of that sleek cruiser and what would have happened if the *Vulkan* had waited until dawn before she sailed. The two ships would probably have met, even as the raider left the coastal waters. He forgot, too, his fear that Kohler had been right and this boy had come back to save himself and not the ship. He forgot all these things for a short while and stared almost humbly at the boy's searching eyes.

'You have done very well, Pieck. Very well indeed. Once before, your eyes averted what might have been a disaster. This time I cannot even begin to guess what might have happened!'

He felt Steuer relax, and saw the tears of gratitude well up in the boy's eyes.

'Is there anything I can do for you, Pieck?'

He felt the grip tighten on his hand. 'Please don't put me ashore with the other wounded! I shall be all right after this, sir! I swear it!'

Von Steiger tried to smile. 'I would not part with you now if you had no arms or legs at all! Is there anything else I can do?' He knew that he should not be here. There was a great deal to do, and at once. But for nothing on earth would he have broken the spell.

'Perhaps, sir, you would find the time to write to my parents? It would mean a great deal to them, for all the trouble I have caused them.' His voice trailed away, as if he feared that he had gone too far.

Von Steiger stood up. 'I shall do so at once. I shall see that it goes ashore with my despatches tonight.' He moved to the door, aware of the ring of watching faces. 'I shall also be happy to tell them that I am recommending their son for the Iron Cross!' He pushed past the startled Dehler and reached the rail in three strides. He drank in the cool, crisp air as if he had been starved.

All my life I have lived with ships and the naval tradition, he thought with quiet amazement, and I have been able to regard it all with detachment, as if it was incidental, like a backcloth. It has taken the faith and uncompromising loyalty of that poor village boy to show me that my life was a delusion, and everything outside this ship has become false and unimportant.

16

In the humming engine-room the telegraph jangled and the brass pointer swung suddenly to 'Stand By'. Niklas pushed the greasy cap to the back of his head, settled his buttocks comfortably against the rail of his catwalk and ran his eye over his gleaming kingdom. He could faintly hear the scrape of shovels and the sound of coal cascading down from the bunkers, while through the rising curtain of steam he could see his artificers making their last checks. He sighed and returned his gaze to the implacable dial, and wondered why he had not found the time to stretch his legs ashore.

Two decks above, and right forward in the eyes of the ship, Dehler leaned right out over the narrow guardrail, his shaded torch pointing down into the gently swirling water. Behind him he could hear the steam hissing on the capstan and the sharp regular clicks as the pawls dropped into place with each turn. The dripping cable moved reluctantly upwards through the hawse-pipe, where it was quickly hosed and scrubbed with long brooms before it finally vanished into the deep cable-lockers below the fo'c'sle.

Clank, clank, clank, each link of the slime-streaked cable drew the ship slowly forward towards the straining anchor, and to Dehler it seemed as if they were being drawn bodily to something even worse than before. His men whistled and chattered quietly to one another, indifferent to him, and seemingly oblivious to danger. They had changed, he thought, as if relieved of some great threat. He thought also of von Steiger and the boy on the operating table. How would *I* have handled that situation? He tried to believe he would have acted like the Captain, but his uncertainty only increased with the realization that he would probably have shut his ears and relied on Kohler's explanation as the easiest way out.

He craned his thick neck as the taut cable suddenly jerked downwards to point straight at the sea-bed. 'Up and down!' he yelled, and heard the report being passed to the bridge. The ship trembled, and he felt the distant screw begin to turn. A few more clanks from the capstan and the cable shook convulsively and began to swing gently like a giant pendulum. 'Anchor's aweigh!' They were free of the land once more.

Von Steiger listened to the hoarse voice shouting from the shadowed deck and dug his impatient hands into his pockets.

'Half speed ahead! Port twenty!' He walked briskly on to the open wing and stared at the two dancing blue lights on the oily water. The whaleboats bobbed obediently on the gentle swell, the oars waiting to send them scudding ahead of their mother ship to guide her through the treacherous channel.

'Midships! Steer north-east, Cox'n! When we are in the middle of the channel keep her head between the two lights!' He watched the wedge of the bows settle and steady around. 'Slow ahead!' The vibrations died and quieted to a low, confident rumble.

He imagined the sweating oarsmen in the boats and the two leads-men who would be leading their crews like blind men with their sticks. He had put two good petty officers in the boats, and had made sure they understood their importance.

He watched the uneven black shadows sidle past, and once caught a glimpse of a match flaring halfway up the hillside of one small islet. Probably a peasant out searching for his goats, he decided. Very soon the land will fall clear and we shall be away again. The land. So important, and yet so unknown. It might have been anywhere, any country. We touched it, and then left as quietly as we arrived. And yet we have all learned a lot by our brief visit. He thought of the relief on Fleiuss's fat face when he had handed him the secret despatches for Berlin. The carefully worded report which he doubted if anyone would trouble to study. And Pieck's recommendation with the letter to two lonely old folk in far-off Schleswig-Holstein. To us all these things are so vital, he thought, but who else will care?

The last islet fell clear, and he could feel the heavier thrust of the unbridled water beyond the reef. 'Stop engine!' To his messenger he said curtly: 'Signal the boats alongside. Quickly, man!'

A shadow joined him by the screen, and Heuss said formally, 'Anchor secured for sea, Captain.'

300

'Very well. Clear lower deck and hoist in both boats at the rush!' He listened to the twittering of the bosun's pipes and heard the rush of feet along the boatdeck. Although an anonymous voice rapped harshly for silence, he heard a man laugh equally loudly. A free laugh, free of the land perhaps. The blocks squeaked noisily, and the two streaming boats jerked rapidly up the tall sides.

He did not wait to see them rise above the deck level. 'Half ahead! Steer north eighty east.'

The helmsman repeated the order, and he heard the Coxswain's rumbling instructions as he handed over the wheel.

He leaned his chin on his hands and stared unblinkingly at the black curtain with its sprinkling of stars. Faintly against the velvet he could see the thin, sharp line of the foremast, and the watchful pod at its top. Well, H.M.S. *Waltham*, where are you now? Sleeping, perhaps, and resting until the dawn, or still prowling as close as you dare to the hidden coastline?

Heuss left the wheelhouse once again. 'Ship secured for sea, Captain. Boats hoisted!' He still waited after von Steiger's non-committal grunt.

'That was a fine thing you did for that seaman, sir. And I have left Alder in the sick-bay too, as you instructed.'

'That man should never have been sent to sea, Heuss. He has suffered enough in this war. His reason is smashed. He cannot even remember if he is missed by those he has left behind, or indeed if there is anyone to miss him.'

'And Schiller, sir?'

'I have released him. A first-class seaman, Heuss. Not at all diplomatic, but not afraid of responsibility. I would make him a petty officer, but I see from his record that he has held the rank three times already, and never for more than a week! I think he will be more use as he is.'

Heuss tried to see the Captain's expression, and continued slowly: 'I am sorry to hear of your new loss, sir. Your brother-in-law. I have heard that he was a fine soldier!'

'A fine soldier.' Von Steiger repeated the words half to himself. 'Yes, he would have liked that.' He tried to picture the tall, one-armed officer as he had last seen him on Kiel railway station. The haunted eyes, the lost youth. He had looked at the *Vulkan*'s replacements and had said that his own men were like them. Untrained, pathetic in their helplessness. I hope they followed you as my men followed me, he thought bleakly. I am leading them to their death, yet they follow like sheep. They are happy because I have not turned my back on injustice, yet they are all here because of an even greater injustice. Aloud he said, 'When I think of men like him, and what they are enduring even at this moment, I thank God that my father put me in the Navy!'

Heuss asked guardedly, 'And will you put your son to sea, sir?'

'Rudolf? If I am spared, I should like to see that. When all else has been smashed, there is always the sea.'

He craned his head to see the wheelhouse clock. 'I am going to work on my charts, Heuss. Double the lookouts, and alter course *away* from any other vessel. *Anything!* Do you understand?'

As he moved into the wheelhouse, Heuss swallowed his pride and said quietly: 'And I apologize, sir! I ask your pardon.' He waited, half expecting von Steiger to prolong his agony.

But he laughed sadly instead. 'You have come a long way, Heuss. Make the most of it!'

.   .   .   .   .

'Captain, sir?' The gentle but insistant grip on his shoulder brought him instantly awake, although his brain still hung reluctantly to the uneasy refuge of sleep. His joints seemed to creak as he levered himself upright in his tall chair, and his body felt chilled and bruised. Rubbing his eyes with his knuckles he glanced quickly at the bridge clock and then at Reeder's puffy face and the steaming mug of coffee.

Heuss looked lined and grey in the faint dawn light, and his drill tunic was creased and grubby from the long, searching vigilance. 'Dawn coming up now, Captain,' he reported, as von Steiger glanced towards him.

There was a long silvery light, an endless stroke of brushwork along the eastern horizon, which grew even as they waited. Brazil and the unimportant anchorage of Corata had already been swallowed up in the distance, washed away in the creaming straight line of the *Vulkan's* wake. The ship vibrated from stem to stern, and the bridge seemed to be alive with loose fittings and protesting rivets as the thrashing screw pushed the raider along at her maximum speed. Once clear of the hostile coast, the straining engine-room staff had gradually worked up the revolutions until the sharp stem threw back the bow-wave in two great unbroken wings of crested water. The light hardened and strengthened, and a dozen telescopes and binoculars scanned the deep-hued sea and the darkness which the night was still unwilling to vacate.

Von Steiger sipped the scalding coffee and waited. His eyes strayed occasionally to the brass telephone nearby, and he tried to imagine the masthead lookout peering with sick apprehension from his lonely eyrie.

There was no warmth in the air as yet, and the decks and rigging gleamed dully with dew, while from forward the guns' crews could be heard removing the canvas covers from the long muzzles.

He reached for his leather case, and then dropped his hand on his lap. His mouth felt bitter and sour, and he knew that a cheroot would bring him no comfort.

As the grey-and-silver light spread slowly down from the horizon, they saw, too, the golden tinge in the colourless sky, and imagined the warmth which would soon follow.

On the forward deck a small party of men were connecting up the salt-water hoses, and a petty officer unlocked the cabinet which contained the scrubbers and buckets for the first task of the day. There was a smell of coffee and bacon coming from the spindly galley funnel, and only the extra tension on the crowded bridge marked this dawn as different from any other.

He slid from the chair and massaged his forearms, conscious of the tingling irritation in his wound. The dressing could come off today, he decided, the air and sun would do more good than that.

He moved towards the door, and froze in his tracks as the telephone buzzed with jarring insistence. He forced himself to keep still as Heuss snatched it from its hook. They had been expecting it to call, and yet the shock now seemed all the greater.

'Ship, Captain! On the port quarter!'

He moved quickly to the wet and glistening port wing and swung his powerful Zeiss glasses astern towards the glittering sea. There was a thick haze already, but the man at the masthead would have better vision from his height above the deck. He rested the glasses against the canvas shield which draped across the searchlight and began a systematic search of the open sea. He was peering directly into the path which the sun would follow, and the glare rebounded harshly into his eyes. He held his breath. He waited a moment longer, being well used to the tricks which dawn at sea could play with a man's eyes. It was no illusion. A tall, unmoving cloud of smoke, fine and clean against the brightening sky. No ship as yet, just that white cloud. He lowered his glasses and wiped the lenses with great care, his mind busy and excluding the sharp lookout reports behind him and the sudden clatter of feet on the bridge ladder.

He glared towards the masthead lookout, and resisted the temptation to call for another report. The man was probably in great difficulties without putting him into a panic. He would be peering almost dead astern, and, with no wind to clear the heavy vapour from the *Vulkan's* tall funnel, he had trouble enough. He made up his mind, and, slinging the glasses round his neck, he began to climb the narrow ladder to the top of the wheelhouse.

Lieutenant Ebert sat behind his camouflaged range-finder, a pair of headphones clamped across his ears. His three ratings were already crouched by their hand-sets and voice-pipes and were conversing in low tones to the hidden gunners.

There was an additional compass on its tall wooden stand at the rear of the tiny deck, and von Steiger climbed up on to the scrubbed steps from which the officer-of-the-watch could take bearings and fixes under happier circumstances. Apart from the masthead man, he was now higher than any other person aboard. He was slightly below the lip of the funnel, and found that when he raised his glasses his vision was clear and unimpeded.

The white cloud was still there, motionless.

The sea had already changed colour and had allowed the early sunlight to flow down into the deep troughs and glittering gullies. It was a fine, unspoiled blue, broken only occasionally by a brief whitecap and the aimless crowd of gulls which still spiralled hopefully above the ship's taffrail.

He stood for several long minutes, his eyes sore from strain, yet unwilling to shut out the picture of that pale cloud.

He was about to step down from his uncomfortable perch, even if only to wipe his eyes, when the *Vulkan* ploughed into yet another of the long swelling rollers which moved easily across the empty sea in quiet, dignified columns. By a chance freak a similar roller, probably one which had long before lifted the raider's keel, passed beneath the other vessel. Imperceptibly, the horizon's sharp edge was broken by a faint but definite black triangle. Then it was gone again, and only the mocking smoke remained to stain the bright sky.

He stepped slowly from the compass platform, his mind making rapid calculations. That had been a tripod mast, it was useless to think otherwise. No other superstructure was visible as yet, which indicated that the warship was pointing straight towards him. He stared through Ebert's questioning face and past the swinging tube of the range-finder. Allowing for the haze and the height of the other vessel, we must be about eighteen miles apart. He frowned as the pounding vibration of the engine intruded on his thoughts. She was already going at full speed, and he doubted if they could give him even another knot, no matter what the emergency. He climbed rapidly down the ladder, his thoughts dropping into place as he moved.

'It's the cruiser, no doubt about it!' He saw the hope fade in their eyes. 'Allowing a mile, more or less, she is about eighteen miles clear, but we will check with the range-finder as soon as the haze breaks.' He smiled as if at some secret joke, and continued: 'H.M.S. *Waltham* is a fairly new ship. She has twelve six-inch guns and the same number of smaller weapons.' He walked to the vibrating chart-table, aware that so far none of his officers had voiced a reply. 'The *Waltham*'s speed is the problem. It is listed at twenty-one knots, but I imagine she will go much faster if the hounds pick up the scent!'

He pushed the brass ruler across the chart and steadied the pencil against the quivering paper. 'Alter course, Heuss. Steer south seventy-five east.' He walked to his chair and stared at it with dislike. 'Dehler, pipe all hands aft. I want the whole ship's company, gunners as well, under the poop. Their extra weight will lift the bows a little and add to our speed.' He saw the man's face blanch as the telephone buzzed once again.

'Masthead reports the warship, sir. Dead astern now. Range about seventeen miles.'

Von Steiger smiled. 'He's guessing!' He saw Heuss's taut features relax into a grin, and added, 'If it had not been for Pieck, I fear we would already be hard-pressed!'

Heuss peered astern at the unmoving white cloud. It was so sinister,

305

so permanent, that he found himself standing on tiptoe as if to see the invisible ship. The cruiser's guns, he knew, had an effective range of about eight miles. But a fluke shot at an even greater range could be just as disastrous. He remembered the great screaming salvoes of shells which had plummeted down from the sky at Jutland. But there at least they had had armoured decks. The *Vulkan*, apart from a few extra sheets of hardened steel about her superstructure and sandbags jammed around the sheltered gun-mountings to protect the gunners from flying splinters, was much the same as the day she was launched. He bit his lip. The guns, too, were mainly mounted in the forepart of the ship. It had been assumed that she would be chasing, not being chased. The twenty-two pounder on the poop was as much use against an armoured cruiser as a hatpin against a charging elephant.

He listened to von Steiger rapping out his orders in that sharp, clear voice which had become the centre of their little world.

'Pass the word to the galley to take the men's breakfast aft to the poop. And tell Petty Officer Weiss to get his concertina. I have heard him play quite well, and it will take their minds off our new companion if they can sing a few of their bawdy songs!'

Damrosch said uncertainly: 'What will the enemy do, sir? Have they seen us yet?'

'It is better to assume that they have seen us. They might be following us by accident, but I doubt it. I expect they are checking all craft in this area and want to have a talk with us. When they discover that they are not overhauling us, they will begin to get suspicious.'

'Perhaps they have guessed already.' Damrosch tried not to look astern.

Von Steiger shook his head. 'It is too quiet. No frantic wireless messages, nothing. If I know the Royal Navy, the *Waltham*'s captain will have sent his men to breakfast first. "The strange ship can wait until after that!" It is a good rule, too. A man can always fight better on a full belly!'

He shaded his eyes against the shimmering glare on the water. To himself he added: A full day of empty water and clear sky. If I can keep clear of those guns until dusk I have a chance. If not . . . He shut his mind to the other choice, and called to Reeder, 'My breakfast, if you please!' He walked towards the sea cabin, keeping his movements slow, even casual. 'I shall have my own food now, Heuss. As the British respect their own appetites, they can at least do the same for me!' He saw Heuss relax and Damrosch's stiff face break into a shaky smile.

But when the door was closed behind him and Reeder had gone, he could not even bear to look at the breakfast on the silver tray. He was so conscious of the threat which followed his ship, and, once alone, he could think of nothing else. He felt, too, a sense of failure and a helplessness which his victims must already have known and understood.

He rested both hands on the edge of the table and closed his eyes so tightly that little lights jumped within the darkness. The strain of always having to be right is killing me as surely as any shell. Every command I give must leave no room for uncertainty, and any decision could be final. He opened his eyes and stared emptily at the trembling table. Final indeed, he thought.

    .   .   .   .   .

For two nerve-stretching hours the *Vulkan* continued along her set course, the hull and superstructure shaking so violently that several plates began to work and strain in the lower part of the vessel, and above the thunder of the engine could be heard the monotonous clank of the power-operated bilge-pumps as the engineers dragged themselves from one warning leak to another.

Von Steiger had resumed his place on the port wing of the bridge, his glasses resting on his forearms as he steadied them on the screen. Dehler joined him in the hot sunlight, his face haunted. 'We must slow her down, sir! She's shaking herself to pieces!'

Von Steiger watched the telltale smudge of smoke on the horizon. 'Alter course and steer due east, Dehler. If the cruiser hauls off I shall order a reduction of speed. If not,' he shrugged wearily, 'the slow destruction of this ship will have to continue.' His voice suddenly heated, he added, 'Damn all those fools who sit in their offices and make such decisions and issue the orders which will send a ship like this to war!'

Dehler did not answer, but he heard him pass the order and felt the firm but gentle pressure of the screen against his chest as the charging ship responded to the alteration of course.

Minutes dragged by, and every glass was trained on the faraway wisp of vapour. The angle of sight increased with agonizing slowness, until the smoke-trail seemed to merge with the shimmering edge of the horizon itself. An hour passed, and the miles grew between the two vessels, and it took great skill to find the warship's position, once you had lowered your glass for a second.

Von Steiger stared doubtfully at the empty sea. It was small comfort to lose the cruiser, but it would have to suffice. The least sign or suspicion could bring her dashing back at a speed which could overwhelm the *Vulkan*'s with ten knots to spare.

Ebert left his range-finder and joined the others on the bridge. In a voice clearly audible to the lonely figure on the port wing he exclaimed: 'He's done it again! Lost that cruiser when the Tommies could have had us by the tails!'

Damrosch said: 'What was the matter with the British? Why did they let us get away?'

'Who knows? They probably sighted another ship and wanted to investigate. After all, there is nothing more harmless than a ship apparently steaming from a "safe" country!' They were still laughing when the telephone buzzed and cut the humour dead in the air.

Heuss said: 'Masthead reports two ships, fine on the starboard bow, Captain! Two freighters, well down in the water and on a converging course!'

Von Steiger frowned. 'Why did he not report them earlier? If we had ten masthead lookouts I suppose they would all be gazing after that cruiser!'

Ebert said ruefully: 'What rotten luck! Two fat freighters and we can't touch them! That beats everything!'

Von Steiger perched himself on his chair and wound down the big window in front of him. 'Clear for action, Lieutenant Ebert! We will engage both ships together!'

The words dropped like boulders in a quiet valley. Dehler could not check his disbelief. 'You can't mean that, sir?' His eyes were popping from his head. 'You have not forgotten there is an armoured cruiser just beyond the horizon?'

Heuss said nothing, but watched the Captain's set face, seeing the fleeting shadow of surrender in his gold eyes.

Von Steiger twisted suddenly in his chair. 'Do you imagine that I shall let them escape? If we are sunk immediately after these ships, at least we shall have done something to justify our existence! Now, do as I say!'

Dehler sweated visibly but stood his ground. His heavy face was fearful but determined. 'But what about the men, sir? If they knew what you were doing they would turn on you!'

Von Steiger sighed and stared past Dehler's head towards the twin columns of greasy black smoke which lifted lazily over the skyline.

'At any other time such consideration for the crew's welfare would be highly commendable, Dehler. But what you are saying now is akin to mutiny. Do you understand that?'

Heuss stepped forward. 'I agree with the Captain!' He met Dehler's glowering face calmly. 'We have been deluding ourselves, I can see that now. We have to sink these ships, Dehler. If we start running away we are done for.'

They jumped as von Steiger dragged a match noisily across a box and lighted a cheroot. He had apparently dismissed them all and was patiently waiting for results.

Dehler turned towards the bridge ladder, his eyes downcast, even ashamed. 'I hope I know the meaning of duty, Captain! I think I have done my share!' Then he was gone.

Heuss wiped his brow with a soiled handkerchief and spread his hands to Ebert. 'These chaps are so jumpy! I don't like to say it, but anyone who comes from the lower deck, no matter which service, will never make a good officer.'

Ebert pulled down the peak of his cap and placed a foot on the bottom rung of his ladder. He stared intently at Heuss. 'I hope you are wrong, Max. *I* came from the lower deck, and, as a matter of fact, I am rather proud of it!'

Heuss walked to the centre of the wheelhouse, his face resigned. He stared at von Steiger's firm shoulders, and in spite of his feeling of humiliation, grinned at himself. I shall never learn, he thought. I have been so wrapped up in myself that I have never considered making a decision which might put me in one category as against another. Now I have offended Karl, the one man who has tolerated my moods and bad temper for so long. He sighed, and lifted his glasses towards the approaching black shapes.

Von Steiger said calmly: 'You acted wisely then, Heuss. Another second and Dehler might have said something stupid, which I could not have overlooked. Perhaps you should have been a politician?'

Heuss watched him carefully. How does he do it? He looks so controlled and unimpressed, and yet I know he is wound as tightly as a gun-spring. I hate him for his arrogance, his godlike superiority and his utter ruthlessness. Yet I would do anything for him because of his humanity and complete integrity.

'Would you have ordered an attack on these ships, Heuss?' The sudden question startled him, and he tried to gauge the Captain's real motives for asking.

'I think it is important, sir,' he answered slowly, his eyes fixed now on the black smoke and small dark shapes on the glittering water. 'A combined effort is important in this war, but I think perhaps that the individual acts are the more telling in the end. We are like a branch of a great tree, or even like one of its twigs. Small but important to the whole. And all over the world ships and individuals, even men like Fleiuss, are doing what they think best for their country.'

Von Steiger turned and smiled at Heuss's serious face. 'Very well put. Unfortunately, if someone cuts down your tree at its roots, the twigs are not much use!'

A voice distorted by a mouthpiece said, 'Range ten thousand yards!' And another, 'Both ships appear to be British!'

Von Steiger's smile faded. 'It will have to be quick! In fifteen minutes signal them to heave to and abandon ship! Give them another three minutes, and then open fire!'

. . . . . .

The two travel-stained freighters steamed in line ahead about half a mile apart. Both were well down in the placid water, and as the *Vulkan* bore down on them the watching officers could see the clean white crates stacked on their crowded decks and the tattered British ensigns which hung limp and unmoving from their gaffs.

A cluster of signal flags soared upwards to the raider's yards, and simultaneously the big, crisp German ensign flapped out over the bared guns. 'Stop immediately! Abandon ship! This is a German cruiser!' Signal-lamps clattered on either side of the bridge to finalize the fate of the two unprepared merchantmen.

Von Steiger watched the bow-waves die away on the two freighters, and saw the decks suddenly blossom with scurrying figures. A lifeboat moved jerkily in its davits and began to slither down the nearest ship's rusty side. Then another, and on the other ship he could see the crew following suit. He reached for his megaphone and strode out on to the sun-bathed starboard wing as the raider moved in a cautious semicircle round the bobbing lifeboats. The two freighters already looked abandoned and wretched in their stillness.

The *Vulkan* stopped her engine and glided towards the nearest boats, her great black shadow falling across the upturned faces and motionless oars. 'Where is your captain?' His voice was metallic and eerily distorted on the gently heaving water.

A man in a white shirt stood up in the nearest boat, shading his eyes with his hand. He did not answer, but merely stared at the high bridge and the officer with the megaphone.

'I am taking you aboard, Captain! I will give you your position, and the boats can make for the Brazilian coast! It is safe enough for them!' The man still stood silently swaying in the boat, and von Steiger called sharply, 'What is your ship?'

The voice was husky but strong enough to show its anger. 'S.S. *Pitcairn*, outward bound from Pernambuco!'

A rope ladder was thrown down the raider's side, and the boat idled nearer. Heuss, standing close by von Steiger's side, saw the upturned, sun-reddened faces, the hastily seized possessions and the mixed expressions of hatred and anxiety. One man in the bow of the boat held a small black-and-white cat cradled in his brawny arms. The English captain seized the swaying ladder and stepped from the boat. He turned and smiled at his silent men, and one of them gave him a thumbs-up sign.

The *Vulkan* moved slowly forward towards the other group of boats. The second ship was the seven-thousand-ton *Dover Light*, also from Pernambuco and bound for England. Her captain shook his fist at von Steiger and seemed about to refuse to leave his boat. A seaman poked a rifle over the raider's rail and gestured with nervous impatience.

The master, an elderly, grey-haired man in an old tweed coat, glared at the rifle and the line of heads along the rail. His voice cracked as he yelled hoarsely at the watching ship: 'Don't shoot! Let my men go, you bloody murderer! I thought women and children were more in your line!'

He grasped the ladder and began to climb. Heuss threw down a small canvas bag containing the course and position for the stranded seamen, and turned to watch von Steiger's chilled face.

'Did you hear that, Heuss? Do you hear what they are calling me?'

The two captains were brought to the bridge and stood in silence as von Steiger finished rapping out a string of orders.

He turned and faced them, his eyes hard. 'I have to sink your ships! It is war. I do not like to destroy any ship, but it is my duty!'

The captain of the *Dover Light* moved as if to step forward, but a levelled bayonet dropped across his chest. The man stared at von Steiger's outstretched hand and sucked in his breath in astonishment.

'I'll not shake your hand, Captain!' His chest was heaving in a mixture of fury and misery. 'I would feel unclean for the rest of my life! I've heard about you! I've read of your sort of duty! Wounded men in a hospital ship, unprotected merchantmen and the rest! Why not shoot us too, you bloody butcher!'

Heuss tore his eyes from von Steiger's stony face. 'Silence! You are speaking lies! The Captain has never——'

'That will do, Heuss!' The voice was tired. 'Take them below!'

Heuss's outburst was finished and overthrown by the sudden shattering roar of the forward guns opening fire. The first shells exploded on the waterlines of the wallowing ships, and the second salvo settled their fate. Together on passage, the two ships slowly sank in company, their deck cargoes breaking free and crashing across the listing decks and smoking superstructure.

Heuss turned angrily to the two English captains. 'Take these men below!' How different, he thought, from the sad dignity of the first prisoner, the old captain from the *Cardiff Maid*. He swallowed hard and turned back to von Steiger. 'All lies, sir! How can the people who write such things believe them?'

Von Steiger watched the two ships canting on to their sides and imagined that he could hear the roar of inrushing water. Already the lifeboats had drawn together and were hoisting small triangles of buff sails. 'They don't believe them, Heuss. But the people who read such things will swallow every word. Just as they do at home in Germany!'

The screw lashed at the blue water, and with mounting revolutions

312

the raider increased speed away from the widening path of flotsam and gently exploding air-bubbles.

Damrosch crossed the bridge. 'No sign of the cruiser, Captain!'

'Good.' He sounded disinterested. 'Fall out Action Stations and secure the guns. But keep all lookouts on their toes. I have a feeling there is more trouble yet.'

Heuss waited until von Steiger had moved clear. 'My God, Max, I have never seen him so shaken! That Englishman really cut him with his words!'

'I suppose that is how the enemy sees us.' Damrosch looked back at the tiny, shimmering lifeboats.

Heuss snorted. 'We could have left them like that U-boat did! But we did not, we treated them fairly and humanely! It sickens me to hear such rubbish! If we ruled the seas, as the British have done for centuries, would *they* stay quietly in Portsmouth or Scapa Flow?' He laughed bitterly. 'By God, they would be worse than we are!' He stared at Damrosch's brooding face. 'The Captain has more control of himself than I have. I could have beaten that man into the deck for what he said.'

Damrosch shook his head. 'I just can't get used to all this. Two ships sailing quietly, and then nothing!' He peered at Heuss's angry face as if to find an explanation. 'Nothing at all, Emil. It's so final!'

Heuss shrugged. 'That's it, Max. We are against the whole damn' world!' He laughed suddenly and freely, so that a lookout momentarily lowered his glasses and listened.

'They used to tell us at the beginning of the war that we would conquer the world. What a laugh, eh? Now, we've got the whole world to conquer!'

.   .   .   .   .

The sun was high above the mainmast and its power defied the puny efforts of the fans to stir the lifeless air between decks. Speed had at last been reduced, but the ship still thrust forward at a steady thirteen knots, the vibration adding to the discomfort of the men off watch, who lolled half naked about the decks and avoided the searing heat of the metal plates and the vicinity of the funnel casing, which seemed to glow from the straining efforts of the engine-room beneath.

313

Dehler and Heuss sat in the two chairs in von Steiger's sea cabin, watching their captain as he moved restlessly back and forth near the open scuttle.

Heuss could feel his eyelids drooping with strain and weariness, and tried to concentrate on what von Steiger was saying. It seemed incredible that it was only a few hours since they had despatched the two freighters, and only twenty-four hours since his rescue from Gelb and the two British seamen. He wondered how Caryl Brett was faring in the isolation of Von Steiger's quarters, and whether her seemingly inexhaustible resistance against her hardship and shock had at last given out. He had wanted to go and see her, but the night escape from Corata, the nerve-racking race with the cruiser and the short, ruthless destruction of the two ships had left him no time at all. He could not remember when he had last been able to sleep, and now von Steiger had summoned him to another conference.

He looked at the Captain and wondered. He was still brisk and apparently fresh, but had changed in some way. He frowned and tried to decide what had happened. He looked wild-eyed, even reckless, which seemed somehow out of character. Did he really care so much about what the captured Englishman had said? Why, when he had brought them so far with unerring skill and cool judgement, had he allowed some clumsy insult to affect him?

Dehler drummed his fingers slowly on his knees, his small eyes frowning with concentration. He tried to listen to von Steiger's quiet voice and digest the information about coal consumption, food and fresh water, but all the time he could feel the rising edge of panic inside him, which made his body cold in spite of the sunlight which filled the small cabin. He kept seeing that implacable white smoke-cloud, and imagined the long, slender muzzles of the cruiser's guns as they lifted to maximum elevation before discharging a salvo at the vulnerable and slow-moving *Vulkan*. Twelve six-inch guns she had. Twelve great, armour-piercing shells in a single salvo! He felt the sweat gathering like ice-rime along the edge of his stiff collar.

Von Steiger moved to the chart and stared down at it. 'We will maintain this course and speed, and then tomorrow we will alter course to the south. If Fleiuss's information is reliable we will find no more warships in this vicinity, so, provided the *Waltham* maintains her present patrol, we shall get clear away into the South Atlantic once more. In four days there is a possible rendezvous with the collier, as you know, so we must be in position on time.' He tapped the chart thoughtfully. 'That will be here, two hundred miles east of Pernambuco. Well clear of the trade routes, and yet near enough to our last victims' port of departure to allay suspicion.'

Dehler licked his lips. 'Shall we take all the coal from the collier?'

'I hope so. Our stocks are getting low, and I feel that the pace is getting warmer. If possible, I should like to send the collier off again when we have milked her dry and let her do a dummy attack on a few ships herself.' He saw the uncertainty in their eyes. 'Just show the flag, I mean, and then sheer away on an opposite course to us. The ships she disturbs will be bound to call for assistance, and then we will have a better chance of closing with a worthwhile prize somewhere else!'

Heuss eyed him quietly. 'And the men on the collier, sir. What will happen to them?'

'They will be taken prisoner, I am afraid. But by the time that happens we will be striking a harder blow elsewhere!'

'It seems a bit hard on them. To get so far and then be put out as bait for the British.'

'Rubbish! There are plenty of men aboard who would welcome the chance of reasonable comfort and safety behind barbed wire for the rest of the war!' His eye passed quickly across Dehler's strained face. 'We will find no shortage of volunteers, I think. However, I shall leave that to you. One officer and ten men should do. Just enough to watch over the prisoners and work the ship.' Half to himself he added: 'Call me a pirate, do they? I'll make them wish they'd never thought of such a word!'

Heuss said slowly, 'When shall we turn for home, sir?'

'Home? I cannot answer that yet, Heuss. There is so much to do. We must keep going while we can and while the ship is in good running order. If the ship fails we all fail, for, as you have seen, we have no friends any more.'

Heuss thought of his conversation with Damrosch. 'Why is that? We were feared and respected by so many before; now Germany is alone.'

Von Steiger smiled sadly. 'The Chinese have an interesting answer to that. "An empty hand is not licked!" I fear that we have nothing left to give anyone.'

315

Dehler spoke at last. 'The cruiser, sir. How long will it be before it comes after us again?' He did not seem to have been listening, and von Steiger shrugged with sudden impatience.

'Those lifeboats will reach the Brazilian coast tomorrow perhaps, or the next day. They might even be sighted by a coaster before that. When that happens the hunt will be speeded up, but by that time we can be several hundred miles away.'

Heuss smiled grimly. 'It is quite a thought, really. We see so little and yet it requires no imagination to visualize the havoc we have caused to the enemy. Ships sunk here and there, convoys re-routed, sailings cancelled and no doubt warship reinforcements moved south when they can be ill spared at present. I expect every solitary ship that moves has been reported as a raider! The British must be thirsting for our blood!'

Von Steiger stared into the sunlight. 'I shall try to postpone that privilege for them!'

Dehler stood up, his face working like a fractious child's. 'It's not fair!' He ignored Heuss's warning glance and the frozen stare which von Steiger turned on him. He could feel the cabin walls closing in on him, and tore at his tunic collar as if suffocating. 'It was not meant to be like this! How much more strain can we take?' He peered blindly around him. 'We don't get a second's rest, and every day brings some new danger!'

'Control yourself, man!' The Captain's voice was sharp.

'Wildermuth is in the collier, Kohler is confined to his quarters and the rest of us are having to work twice as hard! It's not fair, I say!' He sat down suddenly, as if his legs had collapsed.

'Are you afraid, Dehler?' Von Steiger's tone was even. 'Is that what you want me to believe?'

Dehler looked at his knotted fingers and nodded dumbly. 'I didn't bargain for all this, sir. I've always had a rotten life, and I thought this would be a chance to make some good out of the years I'm wasting in this damned war!' He looked up and glared at his captain. 'I can't go on, sir! I'm beaten, finished!' He dropped his head, and his fat shoulders shook convulsively.

Heuss held his breath and waited for von Steiger to explode. Instead, he said quietly: 'Go to your cabin, Dehler. Lieutenant Heuss will take over your duties as First Lieutenant completely, and you must make a final effort to control yourself. We all have our fears, one way or another. Pieck was afraid to ask his own officers for help, and that was as great a fear as yours. You are afraid of death, Dehler, and yet that is the only thing we can all be sure of.' He watched Dehler's blank face and saw him suddenly as a tired, frightened old man. 'Go below, Dehler. You are on the First Watch, I think?' He added gently: 'You have served the *Vulkan* before any of us. It would be a pity for you to fail her now.'

Dehler moved to the door, his face crumpled. 'Yes, sir! That's true enough!' He wiped his eyes vaguely with his sleeve. 'She was a good ship, too, even for a poor mate!' He was still mumbling to himself as the door closed.

Heuss watched von Steiger and breathed out slowly. 'You were very kind to him, sir.'

'Maybe. I think perhaps I have done him more harm than good, but we shall see. Now, attend to your duties, Heuss. Keep the men occupied, and as happy as you can. We shall be crossing the Equator tomorrow, so that will give them something to celebrate.' His eyes were dreamy as he stared down at the dazzling water. 'It seems a lifetime since I crossed the line for the first time.'

Heuss picked up his cap and stood up. 'Are *you* afraid of anything, sir?'

Von Steiger eyed him soberly. 'You are impertinent, Heuss, but I like you for it. Since you wish to know, I can tell you that my only fear at present is that of failure.'

He stared hard at Heuss, who was shaken by the intensity of those gold eyes.

'By God, Heuss! They think I am a butcher, a pirate, eh? Well, we shall see. Dehler thinks I am just driving this ship because I want more glory for myself! Well, perhaps that was once true of me, too. But now I want something much more priceless. If we fail now and allow our name to be slandered and beaten into the mud, it will not only mean ignominy and disgrace for Germany, but for each one of us aboard this ship!'

He waited until the Lieutenant had gone and then rested his head against the warm brass rim of the scuttle. He felt spent, and yet was unwilling to accept the advice he had given to Dehler. There was so much to do. So many preparations which had to be made.

317

I must see Kohler again, he thought. Any more of his behaviour and I will put him under close arrest, no matter how shorthanded we are. He watched with sudden excitement as Caryl Brett moved along the sheltered side of the boatdeck.

Her hair shone in the sunlight, and the grace of her movements was accentuated rather than spoiled by the shabbiness of her torn skirt and stained blouse. Reeder had told him that the girl had apparently recovered from her rough handling on the hillside, but no longer smiled, and showed no inclination to make use of her freedom to move about the upper deck. He had also told him that the other prisoners had turned their backs on her when she had passed, and the man Gelb had called something after her, which had made her cheeks burn with either anger or humiliation.

Von Steiger watched her thoughtfully. When I took her from the sea I did her more harm than I realized. And by her own humanity she has added to her discomfort and uncertainty. Even her fellow prisoners hate her because of their own fear, and because she alone has retained her personality. They call me a criminal because I do not fight according to their rules.

He strained his neck round the scuttle to watch the slim figure pass out of sight, and then turned back to the cabin.

They lie, he thought with sudden bitterness. The only crime we have committed is that we are on the losing side!

He felt the blood throbbing in his temples and was conscious of the ache in his wound. He sat down heavily and pushed the chart and the vital logbooks on to the deck.

Reeder opened the door and peered anxiously at his master. 'You rang, sir?'

'Yes. Bring me a bottle of schnapps and a clean glass!' He smiled at the dismay on Reeder's colourless face. 'Quickly, man! The war can wait for a while, but I suddenly find that I cannot!'

17

A T NOON the following day, as the ship cruised steadily and smoothly through a deep-purple sea, von Steiger, dressed in a fresh white drill tunic and ceremonial sword, stood stiffly below the fo'c'sle ladder to welcome King Neptune aboard.

Seaman Schiller made a magnificent monarch; with his long beard and wig made of ropeyarn and a crown of painted cardboard, he carried an enormous trident, which he now pointed imperiously at the waiting Captain.

'What ship is this?' His booming voice, slightly slurred with a generous measure of schnapps, echoed around the crowded foredeck and brought a roar of laughter from the older seamen and uncomfortable titters from the waiting 'victims'.

Von Steiger saluted. '*Vulkan*, your Majesty! We crave pardon for entering your Kingdom and trust you will give our voyage your blessing!'

The King scowled and prodded the neat Captain with his trident. 'Have *you* passed this way before? I do not recall that face!'

Von Steiger grinned in spite of his thoughts and pretended to falter. It was like being an onlooker, he thought. As if I were watching my other self perform. 'I have! Many times.'

The Queen, Seaman Schoningen, wearing a long robe of signalflags, and coyly peering at von Steiger over a painted fan made of seagull feathers, nudged her monarch. 'Bit stiff-necked, isn't he? Give him another jab with the trident!'

There was another great roll of laughter, and then, followed by their 'Court', the two royal figures led the way down to the hastily erected dais which was rigged in front of the first hold. A large canvas pool had been constructed with a slung tarpaulin, around which the Court assembled to await their victims.

319

Sub-Lieutenant Damrosch was the first. Grinning with embarrassment, he was slung into a rickety chair and dutifully lathered by the Court Barber and his assistants. He choked and spluttered as he swallowed some of the vile mixture of soap, vinegar and cooking-fat, and stared with apprehension at the huge cardboard razor which moved none too kindly across his streaming face. The chair tipped backwards, and his half-naked body vanished amongst the waiting bears and ship's policemen, who liberally ducked him, to the approval and final reproof of King Neptune.

Von Steiger had returned to the bridge, and leaned on his elbows to watch the surging, colourful ceremony below him. For a few moments at least his men could forget their fears and enjoy the age-old custom of Crossing the Line, backed up with extra schnapps and salt pork for all hands.

Heuss joined him on the bridge, grinning broadly, his face smeared with grease and soap. 'The rough devils!' He groped blindly for a towel he had placed in readiness and wiped his sore face. 'They had it in for me, all right!'

Von Steiger smiled. 'You took a risk, going down with that great bruise on your skull! Especially as you've been across the line before!'

'I could not let poor Max take all the punishment on behalf of the wardroom, sir! It was the least I could do!'

He squinted up at a small, slow-moving range of clouds. 'Rain-squall?'

Von Steiger nodded. 'We shall pass right through it. They come and go like lightning down here, but it will do the decks some good, they are as dry as tinder!'

The squall did indeed descend with a suddenness which left them gasping, and scattered the remainder of King Neptune's Court like so many skittles. It moved across the water in a thick, hissing wall, so that when it struck the ship the vibration made the parched decks quiver and flaked some of the cracked paintwork right down to the bare metal. Some of the seamen cheered and ran drunkenly about in the torrential downpour, their mouths open to catch the warm, heavy drops. Others hurried for clothes which needed washing, and Schiller, his wig in scattered remnants, shook his trident at the sky as if to challenge its right of intrusion.

Von Steiger said suddenly: 'Take over the ship, Heuss. I am going to my quarters for a while.'

Heuss stopped towelling his face and stared at him curiously. 'Your quarters? But have you forgotten, Captain? The woman is there!'

'I have not forgotten.' He glanced briefly around the bridge. 'Call me if you want me. But we are away from the trade route for a while, and I think things will be quiet for a little longer.' He saw Heuss follow his gaze around the bridge and smiled with amusement. 'As you see, Heuss, there is no escape for you from responsibility! You have been promoted already, and now you are in sole command until I return!'

Heuss watched him move on to the open bridge-wing and saw his shoulders quiver beneath the savage onslaught of the rain. He stood still for a moment in the downpour and allowed it to bounce off his back and stream down his face and beard. Then with a little secret shrug of his shoulders he vanished down the ladder.

Heuss sighed. The Captain was a strange one, true enough. He groped for his old pipe and groaned when he found that the pipe-stem had snapped during his rough handling from the Court Barber. He leaned on the streaming glass window and watched the distorted shapes beyond. Instead of being cooler, the rain seemed to have shut out the remaining air, so that the ship felt humid and devoid of energy.

It was right what von Steiger had said, he considered ruefully. In spite of all my ideas and self-styled defences, I have been unable to avoid my responsibilities. Dehler wanted power so badly that his breakdown had been all the more devastating when he had realized his inadequacy. I have always shied away from it, and have sneered at those who thought promotion and rank were the ladder to heaven. Perhaps we were all right in part, but von Steiger has shown me what really matters. He has shown me how to discriminate between loyalty and duty, between personal honour and self-respect.

· · · · · · ·

Von Steiger passed the pantry where Reeder snored behind a locked door, and walked along the dim passageway towards the armed sentry and his own quarters. He nodded as the man banged his rifle-butt sharply on the deck and pulled in his stomach. His features were rigid and expressionless, but as the Captain opened the door by his side, his eyes blinked in surprise. The man had hardly ever seen his captain away from the bridge at sea. It was almost like seeing a complete stranger, he thought.

Von Steiger knocked at the inner door and coughed loudly. The driving force which had suddenly decided him to act and come to see Caryl Brett lost some of its compulsion, and he again felt unsure of himself. He caught sight of his reflection in a narrow bulkhead mirror, and paused to consider what he saw. A too-serious face, he thought. His uniform, freshly laundered, was mottled with rain, and the dress sword at his side looked rather theatrical. He started as she called, 'Is that you, Lieutenant?' He pushed aside the curtain and stepped into the wide cabin.

She was sitting on the arm of the big chair, and had apparently been watching the long fingers of rain against the sealed scuttle. She was wearing the long dressing-gown which Reeder always carried for him aboard every ship, and beneath its heavy skirt he could see her small feet, bare on the carpet. Her hair was loose and flowed down across her shoulders, rich and dark against her pale features. Her eyes seemed to fill her face as she stared across at him with surprise.

He grinned awkwardly. 'I am sorry, perhaps I should have warned you.' He glanced quickly around the cabin. 'I just wanted to make sure that you are all right.'

She still seemed unable to realize that he was there in the cabin, and one of her hands moved nervously to her hair. 'I was surprised to see you, Captain. But now that you are here, please be seated.'

Von Steiger remained standing. 'I have been so busy. I should have come earlier.' He played vaguely with the tassel on his sword. 'I will fetch another officer, if you wish.'

Her face relaxed slightly, and her steady eyes seemed to twinkle with amusement. 'You are very formal, Captain! I think that with you a chaperon is unnecessary!'

Von Steiger felt some of the tension draining out of him. He even laughed as he unclipped the irritating sword and threw it down on a chair. He moved slowly across the cabin, conscious of her eyes following his nervous movements.

'I hear that some of the prisoners have been trying to insult you.' He spoke casually, but noticed her sharp intake of breath. He continued evenly: 'That is very stupid of them. I shall see that you are not disturbed again. Believe me, there is no need for you to worry. When you are free of this ship you will be a heroine if you so choose, and can tell your friends how you alone had the nerve and the strength to stand up to your captors!'

'Are you laughing at me, Captain?'

He swung round, his face immediately concerned. 'I am sorry if I gave you that impression! I would not hurt you any more for the whole world. You have suffered too much because of me, and yet I am selfish enough to thank God for your presence here!' He broke off, aware of her wide eyes and the slight quiver of her lower lip. He shrugged helplessly. 'You see? I cannot even explain that properly!'

'You have been very considerate, Captain,' she answered him quietly, as if afraid to break the spell.

Von Steiger forced himself to sit down opposite her. 'That affair in Corata, for instance. It was my fault. I should have guessed that something like that would happen.'

She smiled sadly. 'You could not have known that my own country-men would take me as a hostage against their enemy!'

'You must not think that way. That man Gelb would take his own mother hostage if he could further his own ends. It was a moment of madness, and I am grateful that nobody was seriously hurt.'

She said, half to herself: 'They tied me up. Like a common thief, or a traitor!'

She moved her hands, and von Steiger saw the red marks on her wrists. He stood up and moved to her chair.

'Show me.'

Like a child she held out her arms, and he took her wrists in his hands. They were slender and very smooth, and he was painfully aware of her nearness as he examined the bruises with great concentration.

I must leave here immediately. It was sheer madness to come. Another voice said: They have called you a pirate, why not act like one? Show her that you can do anything you like!

She sat tensed like a spring on the arm of the chair, watching his bowed head and trying to control the thoughts which raced across her mind. She had to press her knees together to control their trembling, and the heat in the cabin seemed to be choking her. His hands felt strong and hard, but his grip was gentle.

All her stored emotions, the strain which she had endured since her rescue from the lifeboat and even before that, surged through her like a great flood. *If I fall on his shoulder and let the tears follow, he will despise me. That is not the way. I must resist. Resist.* She bit her lip until the pain made her eyes sting, but she could not move.

Von Steiger lifted his eyes and watched her face. 'As we are the two loneliest people on board, I suppose this was inevitable?' He tried to smile, but she could sense the strain behind his words.

She felt the trembling grow stronger in her limbs, and she was almost afraid to speak in case he should see her thoughts and desires laid bare.

'Inevitable?' Her voice was small and faint. 'You think of me now like those others do?'

The grip on her wrists tightened. 'Never! You must not torture yourself with such ideas!' *We are just saying senseless things,* he thought dazedly, *anything to control our reason.* His voice was level, almost grave, as he added: 'We will not have long together now. I have a feeling that this cruise is almost done.' He shook his head as she opened her mouth to question him. 'Maybe it is for the best. We are living here in an unreal existence. We do not know what the next hour may bring.' He smiled suddenly, his face boyish. 'But I will not speak of that now. I came to you because I need you. I cannot tell you why, and I do not know how it is that I am sure of you. You might have laughed at me, cursed me or rekindled your hatred which you once had of me. I would not have blamed you for any of these things. But I *had* to know!'

There was a long silence, and somewhere in the ship a bell chimed the half-hour. The rain had passed on, but the air was still heavy and damp.

As von Steiger stood holding the girl's wrists he could feel the yearning in her body as much as his own, and saw the desperate, half-drugged expression in her eyes.

He released her hands and stood up. His throat was completely dry. 'I must go. There are several things which must be done before nightfall.'

She stood up also and watched him move reluctantly to the door. When she spoke it was with a breathless rush, as if she was afraid that strength would be denied to her if she waited longer.

'I shall be waiting for you!'

They both stood quite still, listening to the echo of her promise.

He reached for the door, hating the world beyond it. 'I shall come,' he answered simply.

.   .   .   .   .

Before the friendly darkness had time to cover the ship the masthead lookout reported another vessel, dead on the raider's port beam. The minutes dragged by, and after several more reports, each more definite than the last, von Steiger was left in no doubt. The other ship was a warship. As the *Vulkan* altered course away from the newcomer he moved to the chart which quivered on the table like a live thing as the ship increased speed.

Heuss watched his face and the deft movements of the parallel rulers.

'We shall have to make quite a detour, Heuss,' he said at length. 'That fellow is too close for my liking!'

'I don't understand, sir. How could that cruiser have worked round us like that?'

'It did not. That is another cruiser, Heuss!' He watched the grim tightening of the man's mouth. 'It may be only a coincidence, but I do not like it.'

Heuss adjusted himself to the new situation and said thoughtfully: 'That would explain some of the wireless signals we have picked up. There must be two or more ships patrolling this area in a long line. Each in touch with the other by short, coded signals, and all able to congregate at a given place should one of their number make a sighting report!' He gave a forced grin. 'That makes me feel quite important!'

Von Steiger nodded absently. 'So it should!' He still stared at the chart, but seemed to have difficulty in concentrating. 'I only hope that we can get to the collier in comfort.'

Heuss peered over his shoulder. 'Amazing, isn't it? All that ocean, thousands of square miles of nothing, and yet ships are drawn together like magnets!'

'Send Damrosch around the lookouts and tell him to check that they all realize their importance at this time. Double them, treble them, if you think fit. During the daylight hours things might be very

325

dangerous for us. I do not want to miss a target, but at the same time I want to be sure we do not become one ourselves!'

'I shall warn the engine-room, too, sir. It is a pity we do not have some more powerful form of propulsion!'

Von Steiger smiled grimly. 'Fear is the best encouragement for them!'

He glanced across the screen towards the darkening water and thought of the girl. How could she fit in with all this? he wondered. As he stared at the watchful lookouts, and listened to the powerful thunder of the engine, he wondered indeed if he had ever left the bridge at all. Perhaps it had been a dream, a culmination of all his tortured thoughts.

I shall not go to her. I cannot throw away my principles and my reserve merely to satisfy a need.

Dehler appeared at the top of the ladder, his face empty of expression. He waited until they had reduced speed and von Steiger had walked to the wing of the bridge before accepting the watch from Heuss. 'I relieve you, Lieutenant,' he said formally, and marched to the centre of the wheelhouse, his chin sunk on his chest. He seemed indifferent to the bustle of men changing their watch and the metallic reports passing down the voice-pipes around him.

Heuss said quietly, 'Feel better now?'

Dehler answered stiffly: 'I feel like hell! But you had your chance to save yourself and the ship. You turned it down just for the chance of getting my job!' He waved his beefy hand resignedly. 'That's all right by me! I would have probably done the same, in your shoes! But you'll be sorry, my fine friend!'

Heuss sighed. 'Don't be such a fool!' Then as he stared at Dehler's brooding face: 'Oh, what is the use! You're as twisted as a corkscrew inside, you can no longer see anything but the grave!'

He slammed away down the ladder, his mind turning reluctantly to the duties he had to attend to before he could at last sit down.

.   .   .   .   .

Schiller sat on the damp planking outside the sick-bay door, his head resting on the cooling metal plates. He was drowsy and content, and listened with one ear to the small group which lounged around the open door.

326

Erhard, serious as ever, rolled himself a crude cigarette, his sour face filled with concentration. 'Another ship then, eh? A man-o'-war, too!' He shook his head and licked the edge of the paper. 'It is time we were getting away from here!'

Hellwege straightened his back and grinned towards the boy on the bunk. 'Hear that, Willi? Our religious comrade has doubts!'

Pieck grinned happily, easily able to ignore the pain in his ribs and enjoy the casual banter of the men around him. He had strained his ears to listen to the Crossing-the-Line ceremony while Steuer, the Swiss, had relayed reports of what was happening outside.

He had lain back exhausted and had stared emptily at the deckhead as the downpour had sluiced across the ship. Then, in twos and threes, the men from his mess had lounged into the sick-bay. Tough, casual and apparently there by accident. But he had known that it was no accident. When Schiller had staggered drunkenly through the door, his cardboard crown flattened by the rain, and had pointed his trident at him with a bellow of rage, his joy had been complete.

Schiller had bawled: 'How did this little runt escape me, eh? Skulking in the sick-bay to avoid his just deserts, is he!'

They had lathered his face in the bunk and shaved him with grinning indifference to Steuer's protests. When the Swiss had protested about their behaviour and the mess they were making, they had cheerfully strapped him to a stretcher and lain him carefully on the rain-swept deck.

Pieck relived each precious moment, and turned his head to watch Alder, who squatted quietly on another bunk, his face peaceful and blank. It was all too good to believe. His pain was worth it all. He could forget even the undreamed-of Iron Cross and the friendly touch of the Captain's hand. This was more important than all those wonderful things. He was accepted at last. He was one of the crowd who now grumbled and cursed with easy satisfaction by his bunk. He blinked his eyes rapidly and wanted to shout for sheer joy.

Gottlieb breathed in and tugged a pack of cards from his belt. His china-blue eyes roved across their faces and he ruffled the cards with practised ease. 'Any takers?'

Schoningen grunted and wiped some pork-fat from his mouth with his wrist. 'I'm on!'

Schwartz tilted back his cap and plucked at the ends of his ragged beard. 'Not for matches again, surely?'

Hellwege belched. 'Watch that beard of yours, friend! It's taken long enough to grow, so you don't want to talk too much, it might fall off!'

'That's enough, children!' Schiller rolled a stub of cigar around his mouth and pushed the cardboard crown jauntily over one eye. 'You deal, Gottlieb, we will play for our first week's pay when we get home!'

'Home? Some hopes you've got!' Hellwege was scornful. 'On and on for ever, that's us!'

Schwartz grabbed his cards eagerly. 'Well, and why not? What is there at home for us, eh? It's just a pipe-dream which all you barrack-room sailors carry around with you!'

Schiller threw down a tattered card, his eyes on the others. 'Quite right, mate! Rationing, moaning civilians and damned military police! That's home for you!'

Lukaschek cradled his stubbly chin on his knees and watched the players with fixed attention. 'When the war is over, things will be different, eh?'

Schiller eyed him with disdain. 'Yeh, a home fit for heroes to live in! With luck you might get work selling matches! And when Lieutenant cocky Kohler passes you in his carriage on his way to the Emperor's banquet you will raise your stinking cap, and he *might*, he just might, throw you a cigar-butt in memory of your faithful service!'

Hellwege frowned. 'I wonder what *will* happen? We can't go on fighting for ever!'

'*You* can't!' Schwartz glared contemptuously. 'But the admirals can! So could I if I had a nice big desk and a fat mistress waiting upstairs!'

'That is dangerous talk!' Gottlieb coloured as he remembered what had happened when he had voiced those sentiments before. He hurried on, 'I mean, some of our lads mutinied at Kiel, and where did it get them?'

Schiller threw back his head and roared, so that a sentry by the poop looked up from his drowsy vigil with alarm. 'They got careless, that's what! Poor goddamned Bolsheviks! Still, they had the right idea; after all, champagne tastes just as good from a cracked cup as it does from a crystal glass!'

Dehler walked to the wing of the bridge and peered down into the velvet shadows which moved inwards across the ship. The laughter unnerved him, but he felt incapable of action and could not bring his mind to concentrate on such matters of discipline. Every sound jarred his mind like a saw, and several times he had snatched up his binoculars to investigate a shadow on the horizon which he had been sure was a ship overlooked by every lookout in the watch. He scowled angrily as Lieutenant Kohler's tall figure moved restlessly back and forth across the maindeck. Von Steiger had released him from his cabin, and he paced the deck as if nothing had happened. If only I could be like him, he thought suddenly. To be sure of something once more; to have faith, even in the ship.

Kohler was oblivious to the scrutiny from the bridge, and watched his own neat feet as he paced restlessly on the rain-dampened planks. Von Steiger had left him in little doubt of his opinion of him. His interview had been short and sharp.

'I need officers badly, Kohler. But not that badly! I blame myself for not guessing what you are, so I shall not punish you further at this point!' He had paused, his eyes cold and merciless. 'But if you forget once more that you are wearing the uniform of an officer I will have you killed!'

Kohler flinched at the memory. Not shot, or punished, but killed! It sounded like slaughtering a pig the way the Captain had spat it out.

Kohler drew himself up and stared out at the dark water. A few stars twinkled through the parting clouds, and astern he could see the long unbroken line of the ship's wake. He smiled. He needs me, that is why he threatens me. His smile broadened to a maniac grin. The whole ship needs me, because without my iron self-discipline, without my watching eye, they are all frail and empty!

He cocked his arrogant head to listen to the coarse laughter from the sick-bay. I have not finished with you, Willi. You cannot hide in the sick-bay and behind your Iron Cross for ever. His grin faded and two small tears of frustration pinched from the corners of his pale eyes. After all, where would you be without me?

The ship glided into the empty sea, her stem thrusting to meet the brightening stars and invisible horizon.

．　　　．　　　．　　　．　　　．

But for the shaded light from a small reading lamp, the cabin was in darkness. He closed the door quietly behind him. She sat on the arm of the big chair, and as he stared at her shadowy outline he thought it was as if she had not moved since his last visit. He was conscious of the stillness in the cabin and the pounding of his heart.

As he crossed the space between them he could see the pale shapes of her feet beneath the dressing-gown and of her hands as they clasped the arm of the chair. She looked as if she were holding on with all her strength, but she did not lift her head until he placed his fingers beneath her chin and gently tilted her face towards him.

As he touched her hair he felt a great shiver move through her body, and as if mesmerized she rose to her feet and stood looking up at him, her eyes dark in her pale face.

'I kept my word, you see.' He tried to smile, but his voice sounded strained and unsteady. 'Are you afraid?'

She shook her head so that the loose hair swung across her neck, the movement bringing a stab of pain to his heart.

He was conscious of her warmth and the soft smell of her body. He wanted each moment to last for ever, and yet he was afraid to wait. Her lips parted in a soft moan as he pulled the cord free from her waist and allowed the dressing-gown to fall to the floor. In the gentle light her slender body gleamed like gold, and seemed to sway as he pulled her towards him. His voice was muffled as he spoke into her hair, and her violent trembling seemed to quiet as he ran his hand around her waist and upwards until it encircled the rich fullness of her breast.

She could not feel her limbs, and was aware only that he had carried her to the wide bunk where she had so often thought of this moment.

The hands moved caressingly across her body until she could stand the agony no longer. Her groping fingers dug into his shoulders and she pulled him desperately towards her.

'Be gentle with me! It has been so long . . .' She felt the weight of his body upon hers, and as he covered her mouth with his she drew him to her, her breathing stifled by the pain of exquisite longing.

18

BENEATH the merciless glare of the sun the sea was almost motionless, the motion so small and laboured that it seemed as if it was stifled and could no longer breathe. There was a fine haze across the horizon and the glittering, undulating blue water shimmered like a distorted mirror.

At slow speed the *Vulkan* moved across this empty and unprotected desert, the screw throwing up a small wake of churned foam and disordered bubbles, which faded after a few yards as the sea closed in once more to cover her painful progress. On deck nobody moved, and the slowly turning head and shoulders of the masthead lookout and the glint of sunlight on his binoculars was the only sign of life. The decks were dry and cracked, and from the superstructure great flakes of paint had drifted away, and the pitch in the seams bubbled and glowed like black wax.

There was no air, no breeze and the ship was stifled. On the bridge the still figures stood at their usual stations, but any movement was laboured and any new sound brought a furrowed frown or a fresh stream of sweat down their strained faces.

Dehler moved his sodden jacket against his body in weary flapping movements, his eyes squinting as he peered across the helmsman's slack shoulder towards the gently pirouetting water. Damrosch held both hands on the flag-locker, his chest moving as if he were taking deep-breathing exercises. His white tunic was dark with sweat-stains and his face glowed with heat and the salt-aided burns. He found his head drooping, his chin rasping against his high collar, and each time it became harder to jerk himself out of it, more difficult to fight back.

He made a great effort as the door of the Captain's sea cabin banged open and von Steiger walked to the chart-table. He watched the neat bowed head, the calm eyes and the hand that moved like a pointer across the chart. He blinked away some of his fatigue as the Captain said: 'Bring her round to the south-east, Dehler. We will do one more leg and then lay off a fresh course.'

Von Steiger watched the dumb bitterness in Dehler's eyes as he rapped out his orders. The wheel went over, and labouring heavily the ship swung on to her new course. There was nothing on von Steiger's face to show his gnawing anxiety, and his eyes were controlled to hide the agony he was inwardly suffering. For over twelve hours the ship had patrolled a giant rectangle, first in the dusk, then in the cool of the night and now in this blazing heat. Over twelve hours of waiting and watching, every telescope and glass trained and ready to welcome the first sight of the old collier. But the sea was empty, and even the most hopeful heart on board was heavy and dulled.

He leaned his back against the wheelhouse door and stared hard at the shimmering sea. The heat enclosed him like a warm blanket after hours on watch, and as such tempted him to fall asleep in a split second. Three days of steaming, three days of hoping and planning. Now there was no collier and the *Vulkan* moved buoyantly on her empty holds.

He closed his eyes and felt the sun drying the moisture on his tight lips. He shut out the sounds of the bridge, the occasional creak of the wheel, the heavy breathing of the two lookouts at his side and the mocking grumble of the engine. It all faded, and he was back again in the girl's cabin.

He could still feel the smoothness of her limbs and the urgent movements of her body. They had made love with a wild fierceness which only their kind of desperation could bring. Afterwards they had lain quite still, searching for the right words, words which would neither soil nor destroy the perfection of their union. He had waited until she had fallen asleep and had gently moved from her side. For another long moment he had stared down at her in the yellow light of the one small lamp. It was as if she was sleeping for the first time in freedom and security, and there was a small desperate smile on her parted lips. He had pulled the sheet over her naked body, and switched out the light. At the door he had faltered again. The door, through which lay that other world. He had been almost frightened to step on to the deck beyond, and try as he might he could no longer remember his journey to the bridge. He could recall only her perfect beauty in the cabin and the uneasy silence which greeted him on the bridge.

He felt the door cutting into his shoulders, but was too weary to move. For three days he had driven himself and the ship unmercifully, so that in his mind the collier had become a sort of desperate pilgrimage. It was as if he had told himself that he had been guilty of more than just moral weakness. He felt that he had failed the ship in some terrible way, which only a fresh sign of success would erase.

The telephone buzzed, and he felt the sweat coursing down his legs as he levered himself from the door.

Damrosch nodded into the mouthpiece and looked towards him. 'Masthead reports a ship, sir! Dead ahead!'

The agony of waiting was replaced by one of cold fury. That fool Wildermuth! I should never have given him such a responsibility! He should have been able to make a perfect rendezvous and not keep the raider steaming round in helpless and vulnerable circles.

'Call Lieutenant Heuss! Break open the holds and prepare the ship for coaling! It will be easier to get alongside in this weather, but speed is essential!'

He walked to the wing of the bridge and the sun smote at his back like an open furnace-door. He shied away from the thought which had grown steadily in his mind since he had been with Caryl Brett. He stopped in his tracks, as if to face the thought again like an adversary. After all, why not? They had made their gesture, and perhaps more could be gained by turning back to Germany now, before it was too late. He clenched his fists with excitement. They could break the British blockade yet again and steam into Kiel as he had done before. Surely that would dispel the lies and accusations. The return of a victorious *Vulkan* would be more than enough for Britain *and* Germany.

He examined his other plan carefully. They could go back again through the Denmark Strait and make their way to Norwegian waters. His friends he still had in Norway would always help him, would not question his reasons for sending them an English girl to look after and protect until the finale of this bloody war. She had become an outcast of her own country, and there would be little room for such as himself in Germany after their final defeat. He tried to picture what would happen when the Emperor was forced to admit defeat. Peace with honour? He frowned at the water. It would not help the millions of killed and mutilated men, whatever the outcome.

In the sun-baked crow's-nest Seaman Hauptmann mopped the sweat from his deep-set eyes and raised his binoculars yet again. At the first sign of the telltale smudge of smoke he had peered fixedly through the glass until his eyes felt red raw, but as soon as he was sure that no tripod mast was lifting through the haze, no sleek grey cruiser was tearing into the silent world of his powerful lenses, he sighed and passed his report to the bridge below him. Thank God it has happened while I am on watch, he thought. It is even better up here than coaling ship in this weather. It will be like ten ovens down in those gaping holds! He peered downwards at the white-capped officers on the port wing and sneered. *They* would be pleased, too! The damned officers were always glad to get a chance to shout orders to the poor seamen! Perhaps after this we will cross the sea to the African coast. A man could get ashore there, and get a woman maybe. He remembered the girl's face in the swaying whaleboat as he had moved down its length towards her. But for that oaf Schiller, I would have had her there and then. Well there's still time, even though they do keep her cool for the damned officers. Perhaps when the collier comes alongside . . . He lifted his glasses and peered with bewilderment at the distant ship. He licked his lips with sudden apprehension. This was no collier. She was a big ship, a cargo liner by the look of her upperworks. With mounting dread he groped for the telephone.

Von Steiger listened to the new report, his hand halted in mid air as he reached for a cheroot. 'Cargo liner? Is he sure?' He could sense the shock and disappointment even in his own voice. 'Damrosch, get up there yourself, at the double!' He turned as Heuss appeared on the bridge, his jacket loose across his chest.

'Trouble, sir?'

Von Steiger did not hear him, he was standing with the brass handset against his ear, watching the vision of snow-capped Norwegian mountains fade into the shimmering heat-haze which still hid the approaching ship from his empty eyes. A cargo liner. Too big to be any use as a prize, but too dangerous to ignore. At any moment she might send frantic wireless signals for the world to hear. I must frighten her away so that I can find the collier. Destroy her wireless and perhaps get some information from her. In his ear Damrosch's distorted voice said, 'Cargo liner, sir, British without a doubt.'

Von Steiger slowly replaced the hand-set. 'Send the hands to quarters, Heuss. Stand by to engage this ship!' He walked away from the other officer as the alarm bells rang shrilly throughout the slumbering raider. Please God this British captain will not do anything reckless!

.   .   .   .   .

The S.S. *Fiji Star*, of seven thousand tons, pushed her great bulk steadily and unerringly towards the smaller vessel, which moved with deceptive slowness from the low haze. The holds were crammed almost to overflowing with good Argentine beef carcasses and great areas of sugar, while on her spacious decks were lashed some twenty fighter aircraft, being despatched to the Western Front for the use of the Brazilian Air Force. Passengers and crew flocked to the rails and stared at the strange ship, enjoying the sight of anything which might help to break the boredom of the passage to England.

They saw the signal-light flashing, and a murmur of excited conversation broke out as an officer blew his whistle and a group of seamen ran with unusual alacrity along the upper deck. On her high bridge the old Welsh captain had just ordered his wireless operator to send the urgent S O S, and, with the wheel hard over, the proud ship heeled slightly as she turned away from her distant challenger.

From behind his screen Lieutenant Kohler licked his lips and peered across his sighting-bar at the lengthening shape of the other vessel, his pale eyes watering with concentration. His petty officer, Weiss, stood straddle-legged behind the inert torpedo-tubes, his fingers locked as if in prayer, his tiny eyes on his superior.

A forward gun barked out with sudden anger, and a tall column of white water rose within yards of the great ship's swinging bows and glistened like snow in the bright sunlight before falling back into the calm sea.

Von Steiger snapped his fingers. 'The wireless! Shoot down the wireless!' He was only half aware of the chattering Morse which had started to pour loudly from the wireless-room, and the urgent chant of orders through the maze of voice-pipes nearby. Another shot, but with the sun practically in their eyes the gunners were shooting wild. The frantic Morse bored through the cordite-tinted air like a drill, and von Steiger peered through his glasses at the rapidly turning ship with growing despair.

Heuss was again at his side, his voice tight but controlled. 'That S O S will be heard for miles, Captain! Shall I give the order to give her a full broadside?'

Von Steiger shook his head. 'Look, Heuss! Her decks are crammed with passengers! After getting this far, do you want me to fire on helpless women and children?'

In a corner of the wheelhouse Dehler heard them talking and dug his fingers into a voice-pipe to stop himself from screaming. His whole frame shivered uncontrollably and he thought his head would split apart from the staccato squeak and stutter of the Morse which poured from the wireless receivers. He glared with wild eyes at the two officers he hated most, terrified by their calm-sounding voices and their steady hands as they turned their glasses on the British ship.

They are raving mad! They are inviting death because of their stupid pride. They don't understand war, they only play at it like all these professionals! To them it is an annoying interlude, a game which allows the poor fools like me and the civilian sailors to get slaughtered by the thousand while they stand and watch and fire criticism at us at every move. His neck swelled inside his collar and the wheelhouse seemed to swim in a red mist before his eyes. He was vaguely aware of a disembodied voice coming to him from the voice-pipe which he held for support.

'Torpedo officer here! What orders?' Kohler sounded sharp and querulous.

Dehler stared at the bell-mouthed tube which he held in his hands like a precious flower. His voice shook with thankful emotion, and in a strange, cracked voice he muttered, 'Fire when your sights bear!'

Von Steiger tore his eyes from the ship as the thick voice penetrated his racing thoughts. In two strides he was across the wheelhouse, his swinging fist pushing Dehler's fat bulk clear, so that the man fell like a rag doll on the trembling deck.

'Captain here! Kohler, do *not* fire!' He stared with desperate disbelief at the brass tube as the dull thud of the firing charge echoed up into the wheelhouse.

Kohler's voice sounded very close, excited and defiant. 'Torpedo running, sir! I obeyed and carried out my orders!'

Von Steiger turned without a word and ran back to the wing of the bridge. Perhaps it was a poor shot, and in his eagerness to fire Kohler

336

might have misjudged the range and angle. He stared at the thin white line which ran as straight as an arrow for the distant ship. He forced himself to watch it, punishing himself when his whole body felt twisted with revulsion and horror.

Heuss whispered: 'My God! She doesn't stand a chance!'

The explosion was strangely subdued, but the great orange curtain of fire which flowered from the ship's side seemed to dim the sun, and the towering whirlwind of black smoke and falling wreckage blotted out the stricken ship like a solid wall.

They saw the tall funnels dip towards them as the hull rolled over slowly on to its beam ends, and imagined they could see the tiny figures of the trapped and terrified passengers who, minutes before, had pointed at, and even waved towards, the *Vulkan*.

Von Steiger concentrated his stricken gaze upon one single figure. A man was wriggling through a scuttle which had been high up on the superstructure. He held his breath, willing the tiny figure to get free of the ship before it rolled over completely and engulfed him. A drifting bank of smoke covered the scene, and he heard himself say: 'Lower the boats! Try to find if there are any survivors!'

Heuss thought of the S O S and the terrible danger they risked by staying in this place. He looked at von Steiger's face and forgot the danger immediately. As soon as he had stopped the engine and signalled to the waiting boats' crews, he said hoarsely, 'I do not think there will be a single survivor, Captain.'

Von Steiger walked silently to the centre of the bridge and stood looking down at the kneeling figure of Lieutenant Dehler. His lip was hanging loosely and his small eyes were watching him like a triumphant maniac.

Dehler rested on his hands, oblivious of the watching seamen and the white face of Lehr, the Coxswain. He could see only von Steiger's pain-filled eyes and the slackness of his shoulders as he stared down at him.

'You made me do it! You were prepared to sacrifice the ship because of an outdated idea! But I saved all of you!' He laughed, the sound loud and obscene in the silent wheelhouse. 'What will you tell the world now, eh? Who will believe *you* did not give the order? All your precious admirers will think again now!'

Von Steiger did not take his eyes from the cringing, blustering figure.

He held out his hand to the bridge at large. 'Give me a pistol! Now, at once!'

Heuss stepped forward, his hand on the Captain's sleeve. 'Let me put him in a cell, sir! He has done his worst! He can be given a proper court martial!'

Von Steiger glanced at him almost disinterestedly, his eyes distant. 'He has done more than his worst, Heuss! Do not get led astray by your ideals again! Forget the trite phrases and the words of consolation!' His fingers closed over the butt of a Luger, still warm from the Coxswain's holster.

'Get up, Dehler! Get out on the port wing!'

Dehler backed into the sunlight, his eyes mesmerized by the gun. He dragged his stare from the unwavering muzzle and peered at the silent men. He raised his voice to a shout: 'Are you fools going to stand for this? Don't you see I've done it for *you*! For Germany!'

Nobody moved. The eyes of the men were cold and empty, like the condemned men they now were.

Von Steiger halted and gestured with the Luger. 'Look in the water, Dehler!'

In spite of his mounting terror Dehler lowered his eyes to the friendly sea which lapped against the raider's rough plating.

The two whaleboats idled nearby, their silent crews resting on their oars. He could see Damrosch at the tiller of one, but already he looked like a stranger. Then he saw what von Steiger wanted him to see.

Around the gently wallowing hull floated the pathetic remains of the *Fiji Star*'s passengers. Like newly gutted fish they floated amongst the fresh flotsam and drifted aimlessly in a bloody tangle of arms, legs and distorted faces. One, he saw, was a woman, her clothes blasted from her by the torpedo, her legs severed neatly from the trunk as if by a cheese-wire. Her hair floated on the water like a pale halo around her contorted features.

'Take a good look, Dehler!' The voice came across his quivering shoulder. 'See what you have done for Germany! For us whom you leave behind! Do you still think mine was an outdated idea?'

He did not wait for an answer, but squeezed the trigger and saw the fat shoulders jump beneath the impact of the bullet. Dehler screamed and pitched over the bridge rail, his clumsy body falling with a great splash beside the dead woman. Von Steiger leaned right over the rail, the Luger jerking in his hand as he emptied the magazine into the slowly turning body of Lieutenant Dehler.

Heuss took the empty pistol from the Captain's unresisting hand and turned heavily towards the Coxswain. 'Recall the boats. We will get under way immediately.'

He threw the Luger on the chart-table and walked back to the hunched figure by the bridge-wing. 'Shall I call your steward, Captain? I think you should rest for a while.'

The answer was muffled, and when Heuss lowered his head to hear, he saw that von Steiger's eyes were rimmed with tears.

'I was going to tell you that we are going home, Heuss. Back to Germany!' His body shook uncontrollably. 'How can we go back now? What is there left?'

Heuss thought of the U-boat attacking the lifeboats and the countless other atrocities committed by both sides through fear and ruthless determination. But again he looked at von Steiger and knew that this kind of reasoning would sound empty and foul to such a man.

He said quietly, 'After this we shall need you more than ever, Captain!'

Von Steiger stood up and removed his cap as the screw began to turn once more. 'Whom do you mean by "we", Heuss?'

'The ship, sir. Whatever the rest of the world may say, we know we have done our duty as we see it.' He watched his words change the dullness in the gold-flecked eyes and added: 'We can still go home, Captain. There is not a man alive who can dispute your leadership and courage!'

Von Steiger watched the pathetic remnants drift astern of the *Vulkan* and craned his head to follow them into the path of the sun. He could still see the white patch of Dehler's uniform and the bobbing pieces of broken woodwork. He replaced his cap and pulled down the front of his jacket.

'Increase speed, and steer to the east as arranged. There is still a chance we may come upon the collier.'

Heuss watched him with cautious admiration. He could see the torment in von Steiger's mind fighting against the cool, trained power of his judgement. Heuss swallowed hard and saluted. He saw the surprise in von Steiger's eyes at the unnecessary salute, but he did not care. If he had not made some gesture he knew he, too, would have given way to his emotions, and at that moment he would have died rather than that.

.   .   .   .   .

A golden glow from the setting sun filtered through the open scuttles of the wardroom, and as the ship rolled easily on the gentle swell the officers seated at the mahogany table caught regular glimpses of the deep-blue horizon.

Damrosch stared moodily at the table as a messman reached over his shoulder to remove his half-empty plate. He watched the man's thick wrist and the incongruous white glove which covered a hand more used to handling ropes and wires. The evening meal had passed in almost complete silence, so that the shipboard noises intruded into this normally cheerful place, and Damrosch could hear the steady hiss of leaky hoses across the upper decks as pumps sprayed salt-water on to the dry planks to soften them and make them more resistant to shock and sudden vibration. It was a sinister sound, he thought, like the uncovering of guns or the blare of a bugle summoning the men to quarters. On a quiet empty sea, as the ship moved smoothly to the south-east, the Duty Watch made final preparations for any sort of engagement. Apart from the treatment of the decks, a precaution which cut down the risk of flying and murderous splinters, doors were being unscrewed, spare glass taken below and watertight compartments were getting another check.

He lifted his eyes slightly and watched Heuss's face as he sat at the head of the table. He had still not got over the shock of seeing Dehler's body fall horribly into the water, and the fact that Heuss now sat in his place at the table seemed to accentuate his loss from their company. Niklas sat at the other end, his unhealthy skin pale beside Ebert's, who moodily cracked a ship's biscuit into minute pieces and then arranged them on the table in a neat pattern.

Damrosch thought back to the first days in this very wardroom. There were always arguments and disagreements, officers forming private groups and then re-forming with new loyalties as some fresh incident or disaster disrupted their tiny world. Wildermuth was somewhere on the collier. God alone knew what had kept him from the rendezvous, or even if he was still alive. Dehler was dead. Dehler, the coarse, overbearing ex-mate, who prided himself on his seamanship and toughness, and yet had hidden the greatest weakness of them all. Schuman, Seebohm and Kohler were on watch, and the four around the table could find nothing to say.

He started as the hand came round his shoulder and filled his chipped coffee-cup. We four, he thought, have probably been closer than any. He felt a tinge of remorse and shame as he studied the three set, engrossed faces. Each man was head of his own department. Each was thinking of his own vital problems and shortcomings. And I, he thought, can only whimper because of my own bruised mind.

He cleared his throat and turned towards Heuss. His voice was unnaturally bright. 'What do you think has happened to the collier, Emil?'

Heuss blinked and looked up at him, as if emerging from a deep sleep. 'Lost, maybe. Or perhaps she has been chased away.' He sounded vague, even dispirited.

'I don't like it!' Niklas banged his cup down noisily. 'We sit here like old women! It's unhealthy!'

Damrosch answered: 'I expect we were thinking of Lieutenant Dehler. I feel as if he is still going to come in through that door and start complaining because I have forgotten to do some duty or other!'

'Forget him!' Heuss's voice was sharp. 'We never speak of a man who has been killed. Your thoughts are your own, but keep them to yourself.'

Niklas looked to make sure that the messmen had left. 'It is not as if he *was* killed in the normal sense.' His voice was bitter. 'He did wrong, but he deserved a better death.'

'Did he?' Heuss asked evenly. 'I wonder. He tried to save himself, but went a long way to making our destruction inevitable.'

'But you tried to stop the Captain!' Niklas cut in, his lined face angry.

'I was wrong. Dehler deserved to die, I see that now, and it was better that he should die in anger, knowing that his blood was being spilled in the same heat with which he destroyed those others!'

Ebert, who had been silently watching, said mildly, 'You have changed, Emil!'

'I know. I no longer have any false illusions, and whether I like it or not, I am being made to take the responsibility I have always avoided.' He glanced at the others sadly. 'I know what you thought. When I sat

341

in his place at the table you were secretly outraged—am I right? You imagined that I had after all been waiting to step into his shoes, and this was the final move.' He shrugged. 'Imagine it being any different. If I had left the chair empty we would have had not only a spectre in our midst, but a stupid sense of guilt also.'

Ebert nodded. 'I understand. The Captain has had a hard time and it is not for us to question him. I have learned to obey orders well,' he glanced directly at Heuss, 'perhaps because I came from the lower deck, but I am not stupid enough to think I could do what von Steiger has done. Sometimes I thought he was wrong to place the value of honour too high in a war where such ideals are as dead as armoured knights, but after today I shall never think so again. He feels guilty, because the ship has fallen below his standard!'

Damrosch frowned. 'But even he is not responsible for the whole ship, surely?'

Heuss smiled across at Ebert. 'But von Steiger *is* the ship! So he feels guilty, and, for that matter, so do I!'

Niklas snorted and wiped his stained hands on his jacket. 'You damned hypocrites! You should be made to serve in the engine-room for a bit! There results are measured in precision and performance, not by stupid, muddling idiots!'

Heuss laughed. 'Hark at the sage! By God, he has more cracked ideas than the rest of us together! Years of steam have sweated away his intellect!' He pressed the bell and embraced them all in a boyish smile. 'I am going to order some wine, gentlemen! I know it is not usual, but I feel this is an occasion!'

Niklas shook his head, but his eyes twinkled with sad amusement. 'I apologize! I should not have said stupid, muddling idiots. I should have said *sincere*, muddling idiots!'

Their brittle laughter filtered through to the pantry, where the messmen were washing the dishes.

'Listen to them!' said one of them. 'Laughing at a time like this! The heartless bastards!'

The other dusted a bottle of wine and groped for a corkscrew. 'Dead or alive, *all* officers are bastards!' He straightened his face and carried the officers' wine into the wardroom, which was large enough to make the group at the table seem small and lonely.

. . . . .

Steuer straightened his back as a shadow fell across the sick-bay door. His frown faded as he saw the girl's slim body silhouetted against the darkening water. He spread his hands and said cheerfully: 'Welcome! Have you come to visit us again?'

She stepped inside the cool cabin and glanced over her shoulder at the red rim of the setting sun. There was a wide, shimmering path of deep gold which spread over the lip of the horizon like a rich cloak. She leaned back against the door, her hands behind her, and Steuer saw the gentle movements of her breasts beneath the white drill naval jacket she was wearing over her blue skirt. He marvelled at her serene expression and the deep tint in her hair which seemed to blend with the sunset. It was pulled into the nape of her neck by a black cap-ribbon, and in the high-necked tunic Steuer was reminded of a Russian dancer he had once seen in a circus.

'I never fail to be moved by the sea's beauty,' she said, and again he was surprised by even her voice. All the day the ship had been agog with fear and apprehension, heightened by the shadow of the First Lieutenant's death, and made complete by the preparations for possible action. He had not seen the girl for some time, and when last she had visited him he had been concerned to see the pain in her eyes, an aloof defiance which surrounded her in a protective barrier. Now she was relaxed, indifferent to all else but her thoughts.

She pushed herself from the door and crossed to a nearby cot. Pieck peered at her from over his blanket and smiled shyly. She smiled back at him and said to Steuer, 'How is he getting on?'

'Well enough. He needs professional care, but if he gets no worse I shall be satisfied.'

She watched the sun slowly dip over the edge of the sea, and shivered. Beneath the white jacket her naked body moved with sensuous pleasure, and she was still surprised to find that she had no regrets, no aftermath of shame or guilt. She had not seen the destruction of the cargo liner, but had covered her ears to shut out the rumbling explosion and the echo of rending metal as the great ship had rolled on to her side. She had sensed the change in the *Vulkan*. The faces of the seamen she had seen were sunken and lined, and more than one had looked at the placid sea with a hunted expression, or one of bitterness.

She glanced at the neat rolls of dressings and gleaming instruments which Steuer had been checking. 'So you expect the worst, too?'

He looked surprised. 'What else is there? We cannot sail unchallenged for ever!'

'It will be a mere incident one day.' She folded her arms and tried to ignore the feeling of alarm which tried to intrude upon her secret thoughts. 'The *Vulkan* will be captured, the prisoners will become heroes and history will not even mention any of us!'

'You may be right. But of one thing I *am* sure, the *Vulkan* will never surrender!'

She looked at him with sudden fear. 'But surely if he meets the Royal Navy . . . ?'

He shrugged. 'Have no fear. You and the others will be safe. I understand he has made arrangements——'

But she interrupted him with an impatient gesture. 'I am not thinking of myself!'

He stared at her, seeing her secret laid bare for the first time. So it was true, she had become a mistress to her captor. The quiet, frightened girl had at last become a woman. He struggled with his feeling of envy and despair. 'Who are you thinking of?'

But a shrill whistle interrupted her answer, if answer there was, and a figure bounded past the open door.

Steuer called out sharply, 'What is happening?'

The running seaman halted, his face excited. 'The collier! They have sighted the collier!'

  •   •   •   •   •

Von Steiger traced an imaginery design with his finger on the varnished woodwork and pressed the telephone to his ear with the other hand. The bridge was shrouded in deepening shadows, but the sky was still tinged with red and gold, as if unwilling to surrender to the night.

'Are you quite sure, Damrosch?' He waited, imagining the breathless officer clinging to the crow's-nest and trying to level his glasses on the tiny image of the collier.

'No doubt about it, sir!' His voice was excited and far away. 'I can see that peculiar foremast and the extra derrick she mounted!'

Von Steiger stared hard at the heaving water which glided towards the *Vulkan*'s bows and parted in two strips of silver spray. Wildermuth

344

had managed to survive, after all. Somehow he had kept away from the sea lanes and had made his rendezvous. He was late, but where time was measured in tides and winds, and distance by thousands of square miles of unpredictable ocean, it was still a small miracle. Von Steiger felt the excitement around him and listened to some of the seamen shouting the news to their comrades below. It had been a very close thing, he thought bleakly. With the memory of that S O S message still hanging in the air, the future was threatening enough. Without fuel, and room to manœuvre, it was hopeless.

'Stay where you are, Damrosch! Pass all bearings directly to the officer-of-the-watch! I shall signal the collier as soon as we can draw nearer to her!'

He passed the hand-set to Lieutenant Ebert and walked slowly to the bridge-wing. He forced himself to ignore the freshly scrubbed deck and the low rail where Dehler had plunged to his death. The air was cool but heavy, and he took several deep breaths as the ship came alive beneath him.

But the vision of the *Vulkan's* torpedo was still clear in his mind, and as he relived the agonizing moment of impact, the suddenness of the cargo liner's destruction, he could feel the tightening in his throat like that of a man facing his own death. He clenched his fists and stared straight ahead at the heaving, silent water, and prayed for strength.

'Shall we try to coal tonight, Captain?'

He spun round and peered at Heuss's shadowed face. 'Yes. Yes, we will!'

He saw the quiet watchfulness in the other man's face and cursed himself for being caught off guard. When the voice had intruded on his brooding thoughts he had been startled. He had turned as if expecting to see Dehler's angry face once more. Dehler, with his perpetual bitterness, the nagging resentment which all through his life had deprived him of personal satisfaction, or even happiness. Now he is dead. I killed him as I have killed before. Anyone who comes near me is in danger of losing his life, it is as if I have some hideous disease.

He shook himself abruptly. 'Yes, Heuss, I will take what coal I can. It may be a long while before we sight another ship which can be kind to us.'

'Will we still be going home?'

He nodded absently. 'I will try to take her back to Kiel.' He shrugged. 'Fetch Captain Mason.'

He waited, his arms resting on the smooth rail, his thoughts excluding Heuss and his perplexed expression.

A clatter of feet sounded on the ladder and Captain Mason, dishevelled and unshaven, appeared on the bridge, an armed petty officer at his back.

Von Steiger turned to face him, his elbows propped on the rail. 'Captain Mason, your ship has just been sighted!' He watched the hard eyes flicker with interest and surprise. 'In an hour we shall be alongside her and taking on coal.'

Mason eyed him with guarded caution. 'Are you trying to humiliate me? Do you want to see me break down and weep?' His face trembled with anger. 'You will never see that! Not you nor any other bloody German!'

'Hold your tongue!' Heuss stepped forward, but von Steiger waved him aside.

'No, Captain, I have not sent for you for that reason. I intend to give you back the *Nemesis*.' He let the words sink in. 'You will be allowed to sail where you will, without wireless of course, but free! You will be given all the prisoners, and you can land them in Brazil if you wish!'

Mason swallowed hard, his eyes searching the German's set face. 'I don't understand. Why are you doing this?'

'Why? Because I am tired of carrying you about with me. When you meet with your friends you can tell them what has happened, what has *really* happened in this ship! About your own daring escape attempt, and of how you planned to pass the rendezvous position to the British warships through any wounded man whom I chose to put ashore!' He nodded as he saw the surprise on Mason's face. 'Oh yes! I knew all about your little scheme, Mason! I am a dirty ruthless pirate. But when I risked my ship and men to save the agony of the wounded, it was you and your friend Gelb who acted as men of little charity!'

Mason shook his head dazedly. 'You knew? The woman must have told you.'

He laughed shortly. 'No, my friend, she did not! When you came aboard my ship as a prisoner, a defeated enemy, I offered to shake your hand. You thought you would withhold that privilege. You imagined

346

that you might be showing weakness, eh?' The gold eyes were hard and unwavering. 'Do not delude yourself any further! I was not chosen for this task because I am a fool, or because I am a stupid sentimentalist! When you are safe once more on your own ship, Captain, just think on these things, and thank God that I am not half the swine you have imagined!'

Mason blinked and looked at Heuss. 'I shall never understand you Germans!'

Von Steiger signalled to the guard. 'Captain Mason, let me give you a word of advice. Try to learn something from all this. If you can survive a world war and still learn nothing, there is indeed no hope for mankind!' In a calmer voice he finished, 'Take him below!'

Heuss waited, watching the darkening sea and the gentle corkscrewing of the black bows. 'Will it make any difference, Captain? Will your gesture count to the enemy?'

Von Steiger sighed. 'It was no gesture. I just want to be rid of them. To get this ship as it was. I shall not put Frau Brett aboard the collier.' He was going to add 'of course', but without looking at Heuss he knew such an addition was unnecessary.

Ebert appeared at the wheelhouse door and von Steiger glanced at him. 'Is she near enough to signal? Well, spit it out, man! What's the trouble?'

Ebert looked puzzled, unable to grasp the enormity of his knowledge. 'The collier, sir! Damrosch reports that she is settling down!' His face paled. 'Captain, she's sinking!'

Heuss stepped towards the telephone, his eyes angry. 'That's impossible! He must be mistaken.'

Von Steiger looked as if he had received a blow in the face, but recovered instantly. 'Not impossible, Heuss. Wildermuth had my orders to scuttle the ship under certain circumstances.'

Heuss stared at the unruffled face. 'But only if he was stopped by a British warship, sir!'

Von Steiger smiled. 'Exactly!'

Several seconds passed, and then von Steiger added, 'Bring her about, Heuss, steer north-east and increase to fourteen knots!'

He turned away as Heuss ran to carry out his orders, and lifted his glasses to the horizon. It was dim and almost lost in the dusk of the night sky. But not too dark for him to find the tiny black shape, the

347

merest smudge against the encroaching sky. A small, sinking ship, already worthless, and soon to be forgotten.

But as he swung his glasses to hold the collier's image against the swinging turn of his own ship, he knew that it was an irreparable loss for him.

19

EXTRACT from von Steiger's report:

February 15th, 1918.

Since my failure to rendezvous with the collier Nemesis, and the subsequent avoiding action needed to outdistance whatever ship caused her to scuttle, I have tried to steer a course which would eventually bring me into a favourable position from which I could break northwards and recross the Equator. In five days we have steamed one thousand, six hundred and eighty miles, but at Noon today our estimated position was four hundred and fifty miles south of Cape Palmas on the African mainland. Repeatedly I have endeavoured to turn on a more northerly course, but on five occasions have been forced to steer an almost parallel one with the Equator, which still lies to the north. Five times we have sighted separate ships which were, without doubt, large war vessels. It would appear that a line of enemy steel extends across the Atlantic both to the north and the south of me, so that despite every manœuvre I am being forced into the Gulf of Guinea. Whether this is by accident or design I do not know, but the large extent of coded wireless signals which we have intercepted seems to show the enemy's overwhelming pressure and eagerness to make contact with us.

It is bitter to realize that only nine hundred miles to the north-east lies Togoland, once a proud colony of the Fatherland and now being exploited by the Allies. Even Kamerun to the east has surrendered to the enemy. There is no escape for us but to the north. But for the shortage of fuel I would be prepared to bide my time and make a wider detour. The sinking of the cargo liner Fiji Star has made such a luxury impossible, and I can only maintain my present plan and take every advantage of the night with its brief cover and protection.

The weather has done little to help, and for days we have cruised in extreme and oppressive heat. There is no wind, and my men fall about like

349

dead men, or creep into the shadows without a song or even a complaint to ease their wretchedness.

Food is, of course, severely rationed, and consists of a meat diet, salt pork or some British tinned beef. Two ship's biscuits a day and half a pint of fresh water for each man aboard.

I have no regrets at the death of Lieutenant Dehler, which I have already explained, but only that I could not have foreseen his actions and thereby prevented them. Because of that, I blame myself for the events which followed and the increased pressure of the enemy. To sink a passenger vessel in these circumstances can only be compared to kicking a sleeping lion.

Since leaving Kiel we have logged nearly eleven thousand miles, and maybe we must steam the same again if we are to see Germany in this ship. But without coal we will be lucky even to cross the Equator, unless I can find a break in the enemy's line. . . .

.   .   .   .   .

Von Steiger placed the pen on the vibrating table and leaned far back in his chair. The air was stifling in the small cabin, and he was tempted to switch off the light and open the scuttle to the night with its velvet sky and haze-covered stars. He could feel the heavy, labouring rolls of the ship below him and tried to drag his mind back to the empty holds and fast-diminishing stocks.

His eye fell on his empty coffee-cup and he felt the immediate longing for a fresh supply. Because of the water shortage, however, the coffee for the whole ship's company was made only twice a day, the amount measured like gold-dust by the watchful cooks. Wine, then? He shook his head, angry with himself for being tempted. In a modern age, it somehow proved the inability of man to produce sufficient water for a ship at sea, when there was more than enough wine and spirits for every man aboard.

The telephone above his head buzzed in its leather case and he lifted it quickly to his ear. He thought momentarily of its long wire, which now connected him with that other world of terrible heat, pounding pistons and back-breaking work at the hungry furnaces.

The voice said, 'Chief Engineer speaking, Captain!'

'Late for you, Niklas! It is nearly midnight!' He waited, sensing some new disaster.

Niklas coughed. 'I want to shut down one of the boilers, sir. It's urgent, I am afraid!'

Von Steiger tensed on the edge of his chair, trying to calculate what it might mean. 'How bad is it?'

'It is leaking very badly. Tube-plates damaged by the constant high speed!' He sounded irritable, even accusing. 'I shall have to draw the fire in it.'

'How long?' Von Steiger tried to control the anxiety in his voice.

'Four or five hours maybe. It depends. No man can work inside the boiler for more than five minutes at a time, maybe less after what they have had to suffer.'

Von Steiger tried to visualize the luckless stoker being thrust into the still smouldering ashes of the furnace, protected only by a stretcher of dampened timber and thick clothing, and fumbling with his tools to expand the faulty tubes, or as many as he could, before the intense and suffocating heat overcame him. What it was like to work under those conditions, with the furnace door shut behind him to prevent a flash-back, von Steiger could only imagine, but he forced himself to concentrate on the real problem and ignore the personal discomforts of Niklas's men.

'You want to reduce speed, then? What is the maximum you can give me?'

'Steerage way only. Or perhaps five knots for varying periods.' Final, definite, no room for compromise.

'I see. Very well, Niklas, but for God's sake make haste! We must be ready for instant speed!'

'Don't tell me, Captain! Tell the fool who suggested a ship like this for cruiser warfare! They never ask an engineer anything until it's too late and everyone else has failed. Then it's "More speed!" or "We must go faster!" I know, I've seen it all before.'

Von Steiger knew it was useless to argue and it would only waste time. With a sigh he hung up the hand-set so that Niklas could make his point with the officer-of-the-watch. After a few minutes he heard the telegraph ring twice and then the steady, pulsating beat of the engine died away to the merest tremble, which oddly enough increased the vibration and nerve-jarring rattle of every loose fitting throughout the bridge.

He rang for his messenger and sat staring at the man's nervous face

351

and red-rimmed eyes. They are cracking, he thought bitterly. They did not mind the idea of danger, because they thought they would be able to see and recognize it. But there is nothing to see. Only the threat and the constant fear of sudden destruction from an invisible enemy.

'My compliments to the officer-of-the-watch, and tell him to pass the word to the watch on deck the reason for our reduced speed. I do not want them to think we are in trouble. That is all.'

He watched the man's lips moving silently as he scurried away on his errand. Probably a farm boy or a clerk in civilian life. Now a seaman in a hunted ship. He sighed again. Well, he was not alone in his misfortune.

.   .   .   .   .

Heuss blinked several times to stop his eyelids from drooping, and finished writing up the First Watch log. The small light which cast a circular yellow glow across the chart-table defied his efforts to concentrate, and he skimmed briefly through the coldly worded phrases which had filled a million logbooks. He creased his eyes and frowned. What was the use of estimating the wind and describing the state of the weather? It was all non-existent. He grinned crookedly. There *was* no weather. Nothing but darkness, a blessed cooling of the air and a brief escape from the heat and eye-burning glare off the empty sea. His ear was constantly drawn to the mumbling sound of the engine. It seemed so weak and trivial after its steady thunder, which had been a constant companion for so many thousands of miles. He wondered if Niklas had started to draw the fire yet, and whether they drew lots for the task of working inside that metal hell.

Damrosch moved quietly into the wheelhouse and stood beside him. His jacket was open to the waist and Heuss could see his skin gleaming in the pale light from the chart-table.

'Enjoying the night air, Max?'

Damrosch nodded. It was so much more pleasant to share the watch with Heuss than with Dehler that he felt guilty for enjoying it as much as he did. For the five days following Dehler's death he had thrown himself into his duties with such grim determination that Heuss had had to warn him. Damrosch had discovered that there was yet another side to Heuss. As an executive officer he was a pleasure to watch, and, in his own small experience, he was also unique. He never seemed to get irritable or give way to the tiredness which was so apparent in his face. He was cheerful with the men, and yet seemed so sure that his friendliness would not be abused.

'It was good out on the wing,' he answered quietly. 'Nothing but the stars and darkness.'

'I should hope so! I'd hate to think of a British ship creeping up on us right now. Barely making steerage way, one boiler out of action and coal at a minimum! I wish the Captain would have another of his intuitions about meeting a collier!'

'It's funny, Emil, but I did not think you cared about anything before. You've changed, you know.'

'Bilge! It's just that I've had no time for things which really matter.'

'Seriously, Emil, you remember when you came to my cabin, after you captured the collier? When we got drunk on White Horse?'

Heuss sighed. 'A long time ago it seems. Yes, I remember.'

'You told me about the girl, Frau Brett. Do you remember what you told me?' He stumbled over his words, not sure of himself or Heuss's reaction. 'Have you got over it yet?'

Heuss shrugged. 'I do not think I can answer that yet. Perhaps next month, or next year. Maybe I shall never know. I suppose in my heart I knew she was made for von Steiger! It just had to be this way.'

Damrosch swallowed hard. 'You are not serious, surely? He would not behave like that with a prisoner?'

Heuss patted his arm affectionately. 'You are a gem, Max! The last of the gentlemen! Von Steiger is very human in one way, we know that now. Caryl Brett is no ordinary woman, and she is not just a *prisoner*. She came from the sea. She came from amongst the dead. Perhaps he saw her as retribution, or as a chance to clear his soul. Whatever it was at the beginning, it has taken them both by storm. I will go further, Max. If it had not been for her presence, I think he would have surrendered long ago.'

'Surrender?' His voice rose to an incredulous whisper. 'Never!'

'Hold on, Max! I mean it, but not to the enemy. If he could not have shown himself and his soul to someone whom he could trust, someone who had no hold over him, he would have given in to a greater foe than the British! Himself!'

A messenger scurried into the wheelhouse, peering around for an officer. 'Lieutenant! The prisoners' sentry has reported a fire in Number Two!' He stood gasping as his words electrified the bridge.

Damrosch reached for a telephone, his mouth drier than before. 'I will call out the fire party!'

Heuss shook his head. 'Never! If it is spontaneous combustion water is the last thing we want! Call the Captain!'

Heuss walked to the open bridge-wing, his tired eyes searching the darkened foredeck. Against the pale decks he could see the black rectangles of the two holds and the imitation deck cargo which hid two of the five-point-nines. He sniffed the heavy air. No doubt about it. Quite different from the acrid funnel-fumes which occasionally invaded the bridge. This was the scent of real smouldering.

Von Steiger was suddenly by his side. 'Number Two, is it?' He sounded wide awake. 'It *would* be!' The main bulk of the untouched coal lay in that hold, and all the bitterness and disappointment showed momentarily in his quiet voice.

'Right, Heuss, close every ventilator and seal every grating! The only way to stop it bursting into open fire is to cut off the air!'

'But the coal, sir! We need every piece!'

'You can forget that particular hold, Heuss. For a while yet it will just be so much ballast.' He banged his hand viciously on the rail. 'Probably some of the coal we took off that drifting freighter. Too wet to be safe.' He turned, his teeth white in the darkness. 'Too late to complain now, eh?'

Heuss shouted his orders to the waiting petty officers and watched them double towards the smoking hold. Von Steiger is calm but resigned, he thought.

'Perhaps we shall come across another collier, sir.'

'Perhaps. We can only hope.'

.   .   .   .   .

'Number Two hold sealed off, Captain!' Heuss mounted the ladder, his limbs feeling like lead.

Von Steiger nodded curtly and turned to the relieving officer-of-the-watch. 'Keep a sentry posted there, Ebert, and leave word for your relief. It should be safe enough, but you can never be sure.'

He turned his head. 'Singing, Heuss? Who is singing down there?'

'The prisoners, sir. They are making a terrible row, and our men are getting annoyed. They have been laughing and singing since we sealed off that coal! Shall I go and shut them up?'

'Let them sing. If it makes our people angry, so much the better! I would rather have them that way than dispirited and indifferent!'

Heuss frowned. 'What has got into those prisoners?'

'News travels faster than fire in a ship like this. They put two and two together and imagine that we are in dire straits! It is only natural.'

Heuss grinned wearily. 'They are singing "I want to go home!". They have even forgotten to sleep.'

'I suppose that is how we all feel now.'

Ebert opened the wheelhouse door. 'Port lookout reports a red glow on the port quarter, Captain! He can't make it out, and neither can I!'

They ran on to the small crowded wing and levelled their glasses into the night.

Heuss settled his binoculars carefully against a stanchion and stared hard at the dim orange glare. No, there were three or four tiny lights, close together and apparently shimmering like a regimented column of comets.

Von Steiger watched them also, his ears deaf to the murmurs and guesses of those around him. It was a long way away, but there was no mistaking that unearthly fire.

'Thank God we reduced speed, Heuss, whatever our reason! That fellow will eventually overtake us and cross our bows. But for our miserable progress, we should have met!'

Ebert lowered his glasses. 'I don't understand, sir.'

Von Steiger smiled grimly. 'Those four little lights are the funnel-tops of a warship! They must be driving her like hell to make such an inferno!'

Heuss chilled and turned back to watch the distant lights. He even imagined that he could see the four tall funnels, the rakish hull beneath and the long guns pointing into the darkness like rows of teeth. He thought of the Captain's matter-of-fact explanation, his quick summing-up of the danger, the action to be taken. How could any of us replace him? he wondered. It is not training we lack. It is experience.

Von Steiger yawned. 'I am going to walk round the ship, Heuss. You had better turn in.'

355

Heuss grinned uncomfortably. His mind and body screamed out for rest, but he felt unable to free himself from the new force within him. 'I think I will stay on the bridge, sir.'

'As you wish. Make use of my sea cabin. I shall not sleep tonight.'

He walked from the bridge, his hands thrust into his pockets. I cannot sleep tonight, nor any other night, he thought. He could feel the ship calling to him as he walked the deserted decks and ducked beneath the swinging derricks and canvas dodgers. He paused beneath the high poop and leaned over the bulwark to watch the minute wake. The sea bubbled and slapped against the worn plates, and as he turned his back on it he could see the heavy masts and rigging made delicate against the stars. He tried to relax his mind and shake himself free of the fantasy that this was the last peace he would know. He felt as he imagined Heinz must have felt so many times before the dawn. Waiting in the mud, or crouched on a crumbling fire-step to await the first light. Then the urgent whistles, the blind, scrambling dash over the edge of the trench and into the dawn. Into the merciless wire, the chattering machine guns, into nothing.

As he sat against the bulwarks he could hear the ship talking, as every ship talked in the night. It was ridiculous, of course, but it happened. The faint, unmistakable murmur of sound. It was the metal expanding and contracting, loose wires, straining deck-beams and countless other normal and explainable reactions. And yet, as he listened, he could identify none of these things. Just a quiet, incessant murmur.

He paused by the sick-bay and stood just inside the open door. He could see Steuer's white jacket swinging from a door and hear the painful breathing of Pieck, the boy in the cot. Another figure sat behind the table, his face lowered, his eyes staring at his hands. He did not look up as von Steiger passed, but the Captain heard the weary, dispirited voice say: 'My name is Emil Alder. My name is Emil Alder.'

The night fire party sat back to back in a solid block of human statuary, their feet sticking out like the spokes of a broken wheel, their heads lolling in time to the rolling ship.

In the galley the duty cook tended his fire and whistled softly as he groped in the darkness for his favourite pipe and the remains of his tobacco.

The boatdeck, damp but humid, and the lookouts swinging their long telescopes like guns over the low rails. He spoke to them,

356

although he did not know what he said, but was aware of their dark anonymous faces split by white grins and embarrassed pleasure.

Nobody in the engine-room saw him looking from the high catwalk, but von Steiger stood for several minutes watching the gleaming, orderly world, where results did not rest or depend upon the strength of mere men.

Out on the deck again, he shivered and glanced upwards to the square outline of the bridge. It was strange how the threat of failure and defeat had succeeded in drawing them all together at last. Had it been so from the start would things have altered? he wondered. Or would such buoyant team-spirit have driven them to destruction in those first days? In the Denmark Strait perhaps, or earlier when Dehler had wanted to break out into the Atlantic. He thought again of that bitter, misguided man. He had, at least, loved this ship. If he had achieved nothing more in life, he had succeeded in knowing the ship.

He quickened his pace towards the officers' quarters, his boots quiet on the damp planking.

．　　　．　　　．　　　．　　　．

The girl opened her eyes and stared upwards into the darkness. She did not know what had awakened her, but as sounds arranged themselves for her ears she noticed the slow pace of the engine and deep, uneasy roll of the bunk beneath her. Her limbs were hot and damp, and as she moved her hand across her naked body she could feel the skin soft with perspiration. There was little air in the cabin, and she was conscious of the loud beating of her heart. She no longer awakened from sleep in a panic, with a silent scream on her lips or struggling to free herself from the blankets. She was able to shut her mind to the reality of the outside world and find comfort again from her thoughts.

There was a click in the darkness, and she sat bolt upright on the bunk. 'Who is that? What do you want?' She stared into the darkness, the rough blanket pulled up to her chin.

The yellow light from the small reading-lamp suddenly enfolded her in a small frame of colour, and she saw von Steiger looking down at her, his eyes steady and calm.

Without speaking, he sat on the edge of the bunk and pushed her

357

gently back on to the pillow. He smiled as if to reassure her, and brushed a strand of hair from her cheek.

'I make no apologies,' he said, 'for I have no excuse for my behaviour!'

'Is anything happening? You know I do not mind you coming to me. I have waited so long to see you again!'

He took the blanket from her unresisting fingers and pulled it down to her thighs. For a long while he looked at her body, and then ran his hand gently across her shoulder and around her breasts. She trembled, but did not speak. She watched his face as if mesmerized, while his hand explored her body with such gentle power.

'I cannot stay long.' He seemed to have difficulty in saying the words. 'But tomorrow will be difficult for all of us, and I must speak to you before then. I am going to try to steer north, to make a final break through the British squadron. If I succeed I will try to get some more coal. If I fail I shall have to think again.'

Her lips moved slowly. 'When you get back to Germany you will forget me!'

'You know that is not true. We cannot help ourselves. It is fate. I will put you ashore, not with those others from the British ships, but alone, with sufficient information and money for you to get back to safety. When the war is over, perhaps you will still think of me as you do now?'

'It will be over soon! It must be! But I shall be an ordinary girl again, while you will be back with your traditions and your own way of life. You will not be able to share it with me.'

The hand stopped moving, and she could feel the pain of longing like fire.

'That sort of life is over after this. A whole new world will be waiting for those who are strong enough to take it!' His eyes blazed in the light. 'I will put you somewhere in safety before I return to Germany. You belong with your own people now. Do not worry about what has happened between us, nothing can destroy that. Whatever you hear said of me you can ignore and keep your own judgement for yourself. I have done my duty, as you would have done yours.'

He made as if to move, but her hands closed over his wrist. He could see the tears on her cheeks as she cried: 'Not yet! There is so little time!'

He smiled sadly. 'Yes, I have much to do. When the engine-room have completed the repairs I will be permanently on the bridge.'

He listened to her quickening breathing, and remembered the sounds he had heard on deck. This was the moment of peace. He could not turn his back on it. He dare not.

She pulled him down to her, feeling his defences crumble. Later, as her body gave a long shudder and the fierceness of their passion had been replaced by a feeling of great calm, von Steiger looked down at her relaxed, childlike face and prayed that he could protect her at least from disillusionment and misery.

20

THE murmur of voices died away as von Steiger stepped on to the hold-cover and stood for a moment looking down and around at his ship's company. In response to the urgent twitter of bosun's pipes the seamen had thronged aft, and now in the blazing sunlight they stood, packed shoulder to shoulder or clinging to stays and rigging, to watch the slight, white-clad figure of their captain.

Von Steiger saw the lean, sunburned faces, the dispirited, even sullen, expressions, and felt strangely moved. He wondered if this time his words would be enough. They looked too weary and beaten to be receptive to mere oratory.

When he spoke his voice was confident yet quiet, so that those men who were farthest away had to lean forward, their strained faces tense with concentration.

Unexpectedly he said: 'In a few moments I am sending you to breakfast! After you have eaten you are going to work even harder than you have already, and the first job you must do is to broach Number Two hold!'

A ripple of uneasiness and resentment transmitted itself through the packed ranks, and Heuss, who was watching with the other officers, felt a pang of alarm. This time von Steiger was asking too much. The men were tired, and they were without hope. It would need more than mere words to bind them together again.

Von Steiger continued: 'I want the coal from that hold for a very good reason. I want to fill the bunkers at once, and in addition I want every unnecessary piece of woodwork stripped from the ship and sent to the stokehold: lockers, bunks, doors . . . everything! The petty officers have lists of gear to be chopped down, and you will, I know, do the rest!'

He paused, and ran his eye over the slowly labouring ship. Since dawn the men had been painting canvas and disguising the ship once again. Deckhouses had been altered, and a false deck cargo had sprung up aft of the bridge. He stared at the empty sea, glittering with a million mirrors, and at the placid sky. So quiet, yet so full of menace.

He faced his crew once more, picking out individual faces which had come to mean so much to him.

'Men, we are going home, back to Germany!'

There was an electric silence as the faces changed from shocked incredulity to dumb amazement. Then the ship rang with fierce, crazed cheers and wild, even hysterical, cries of delight. Von Steiger raised a hand, and the silence fell instantly.

'You may know that a British cruiser passed us during the night. I believe she was going to answer an S O S given by a Greek steamer. The cruiser probably thought that the *Vulkan* was attacking the Greek and wanted to be in at the kill. Whatever the reason, the warship went to her assistance.' He paused, sensing the anxious faces about him. 'And that could mean that for a while at least the British steel ring is broken! Give me the coal and the wood, and I will increase speed at once! If required I will drive this ship to the depths! If we return to the Fatherland now, I am sure that no one can speak against us——'

He got no further, his voice was drowned by their excited cheering.

He watched them disperse before the petty officers, and walked slowly towards the bridge. He smiled as men reached out to touch him as he passed, but as he reached the foot of the steel ladder he faltered, and Heuss saw the emotion laid bare on his worn face. He had never seen von Steiger so moved or so defenceless, and turned away with something like guilt. As if he had intruded on something private.

.   .   .   .   .

Von Steiger watched the vapour-trail thicken as it billowed over the edge of the stained funnel. Below, the stokers were pouring on the precious coal, mixed with hastily lashed bundles of chopped wood. He could feel the ship shaking with renewed life as the revolutions mounted and the sharp stem flung itself into the lazy water. He felt slightly light-headed, like a reckless gambler who has thrown his last coin on the

361

table. It was all a matter of speed and distance now. Once clear of this closely combed area there was a chance. As a last resort he might touch the African coast and cut more timber for the boilers from some secluded forest-land. And there was always the chance of meeting another collier. He frowned, distrusting his unusual optimism. He was glad that the seamen had burst into a fit of shouting and cheering. The trusting, hopeful faces turned upwards towards him had almost been too much for his reserve, and only those standing near him could have heard the tremor in his voice.

They gave me the sweepings of the fleet and the barracks. The Admiral thought that a gesture did not need trained, hand-picked men like von Spee, Count zu Dohna-Schlodien or Karl Nerger had commanded on *their* victorious sorties into the enemy's territory. Perhaps he was right. Maybe only the captain *did* count in the long run. But I would not change these men of mine for the pick of the Imperial Navy now.

He listened to the clatter of shovels and walked to the forepart of the bridge to watch the working party which had been detailed for Number Two hold. He could see the shimmering haze from the coal as it was plucked from the narrow hatchway at the rear of the hold and bundled towards the bunkers. Wet, dangerous and every bag spelling disaster. But the risk was worth while just so long as the work was handled with great care, and he was thankful to see Niklas's grey head bobbing amongst the crowded figures.

Von Steiger lifted his cup to his lips, savouring the dregs of the coffee. In spite of his regulated, wire-taut mind, he found himself thinking of the girl and what she had done for him.

I have changed beyond all recognition, he thought. Now I want to live, to return home, even if only for my men. There has to be some sort of future. Without hope I had nothing, but she has opened another door for me.

He rubbed his sore eyes and watched the helmsman as he steadied the wheel against the thrust of the madly thrashing screw. I have spent all my life in the Navy, and yet my true memories started to form only with the war. Now they are compressed even further. There is nothing I can recall beyond this ship, this mad, all-demanding search.

He seated himself carefully in the tall chair and allowed his head to nod forward. He could feel the trembling vibration of the hull like the pounding of life-blood, and to its tune fell into the first real sleep he had enjoyed since he had taken command.

Lieutenant Kohler watched him for a few moments and then walked slowly to the wing of the bridge. The sun was hot across his face, but he hardly noticed it. Already his mind was busy with possibilities and plans for his return to Germany. It was not quite as he had hoped, but there was still a chance really to distinguish himself, he considered. After all, when they got to Kiel it was almost certain that the officers would be decorated. That honour, plus a few useful introductions, could assure him of a command of his own. He licked his lips at the bright prospect. A command of his own. Where every man would behave and act in the proper manner, as would befit the crew of his own ship.

High in his sun-baked pod, the masthead lookout peered steadily through his powerful glasses. Port to starboard, and back again. Hellwege, the poop gunlayer, had managed to take over the important position temporarily, after promising some tobacco to Petty Officer Eucken. He grinned to himself and rested the glasses against the lip of the crow's-nest. Anything was better than humping coal or breaking up woodwork. He blinked as a shaft of sunlight lanced through the lenses and dazzled his eyes. The sea looked very beautiful, he thought. It would be something to talk to Erhard about. I shall ask him again about God. How can we be sure that God really made the sea? He grinned at the prospect of goading that dour bible-scourer.

The light glared through his glasses again, and he cursed angrily. Then he stiffened. Why should the light be reflected from that quarter? He held his breath and levelled the glasses on the purple horizon. Flash. There it was again. A bright flash through the haze, like the sunlight reflected against glass. Against glass. . . . The plate-glass of a high bridge, for instance.

Hellwege, the stocky, amiable gunlayer, whose only serious thought in life had been about the reality of God, had never tried for the rewards of promotion or fame. He had been content to be a good gunner, and to make the most of the friendship offered by the lower deck. He was unimaginative, even a little stupid, but as he lifted the telephone his voice did not hesitate, nor did it falter.

With his eyes on the horizon he reported: 'Officer-of-the-watch? Enemy in sight, sir!'

.   .   .   .   .

Heuss reached the bridge, panting and breathless. The shrill alarm bells, coupled with the urgent twitter of bosun's pipes, had come with such suddenness that he could hardly remember his wild dash up the ladders from the wardroom, his journey obstructed by careering figures, cursing seamen and vague impressions of startled eyes and tight mouths.

Lieutenant Kohler greeted him bleakly. 'Enemy in sight. Bearing red four-five. Range about twelve miles.'

Heuss glanced at the compass and then looked around the bridge, which was rapidly filling with men. Extra signal ratings, messengers, machine gunners and all the rest of the attack team. The Coxswain's giant body momentarily blotted out the sunlight as he made for the wheel and took the spokes, with hardly a glance at the officers. Petty Officer Heiser opened his telescope with a squeaking sound and calmly examined the horizon.

Kohler said: 'I am going below to my tubes. There will be work for them again!'

Heuss halted him with a raised hand. 'But the Captain? Where is he?'

'He has been, and gone! He said to tell you he would be a few minutes.'

Heuss watched the other officer go and half listened to the crackle and bark of voice-pipes and telephones around him.

'Close all watertight doors and scuttles! Down all deadlights!' The orders were followed by the dull thuds of steel barriers being dropped to seal the ship into separate sections. The men in each compartment prayed that those in the next would be the ones to be trapped and drowned, not themselves.

'Main armament closed up!'

'Twenty-two pounder closed up!'

'Damage control party closed up!'

Heuss saw Damrosch moving quickly about the bridge, answering the reports and passing the set orders to every corner of the racing ship. And racing she was. The hull shivered from truck to keel, and without checking he knew that she was trying to exceed even her other dangerous record.

A door clicked behind him, and he turned to salute automatically as von Steiger crossed to the front of the bridge. His hand faltered, and then he said quickly: 'Ship at Action Stations, Captain! Course north twenty west. Maximum revolutions!'

He forced out the report, his face impassive, yet he could only stare at the Captain. At first he had been unable to understand what was different about him, but now, as he watched the trim figure outlined against the open windows, he saw quite clearly. Von Steiger had changed into a freshly laundered white uniform, and in front of the dull varnish and smoke-stained paintwork he seemed to gleam with an unnatural light. The trousers were knife-edged, the cap-cover starched and on his breast and about his neck he was wearing his full decorations.

Von Steiger moved to the engine-room voice-pipe. 'More speed, Niklas! This is the real thing this time!'

From far below, the tired voice, 'How can you ask for more speed? We are up to the red now!'

Von Steiger gave a brief smile. 'I am not asking, Chief! I am giving you an order!' He snapped down the cover, dismissing Niklas and the whole of his straining department.

'Warship is definitely a cruiser, sir! Turning towards us now, bearing constant!'

Von Steiger felt relaxed, even relieved. Hopes, fears and uncertainty had vanished with the appearance of the enemy ship. His training and experience had taken over his body and mind, as he had taken over the ship and its crew, from Heuss to the engine-room staff, and he could throw himself completely and without reservation into the complicated picture as he now saw it.

'Port twenty! Steer north ten east, Heuss!' He slung his glasses around his neck and walked on to the open wing to watch the sudden curve in the *Vulkan*'s frothy wake. No longer creeping stealthily and guiltily across the enemy's seas, she was tearing through the water like a destroyer, a thoroughbred.

He lifted his glasses again. The haze was still quite thick, but he could clearly see the darker shadow etched into the horizon like a gun-sight. Black tripod mast outlined by a rank of slender grey funnels. That was all there was to see at present, but she would be working up to her maximum speed, too. He calculated calmly. Say twenty-three knots minus sixteen. That meant she would overhaul the *Vulkan* at a steady seven knots. Within random shooting in thirty minutes and accurate range in another fifteen. If the haze clears it will be rapid fire in half that time, he concluded grimly.

The decks both forward and aft looked unnaturally deserted. He could see a few heads showing from behind the screen around the poop gun, but the big five-point-nines and their crews were still hidden by their false deck cargo and the neatly piled sandbags. The hoses sprayed across the empty decks, the water making queer patterns across the planking before gurgling into the scuppers. No flags flew from the yard or staff, and only the canvas screens remained to remind him of the disguises he had used in the past.

The cruiser was dead astern now, and as she ploughed into a low-lying bank of surface haze it looked as if her mast and upperworks were floating disembodied in the air. She was making smoke too, he noticed. No longer the need for stealth or pretence. The cards were down, and the English stokers would be sweating every bit as much as the Germans.

Heuss stood in the wheelhouse doorway. 'The cruiser is using her transmitter, Captain! Code, of course, but I imagine she is calling up the pack.'

'Never mind the rest of them, Heuss! We will have enough to keep us occupied here. If we can hold her off until nightfall we will have a good chance.'

'That is another nine hours at least, sir!'

'I know.' He pulled the slender gold watch from his breast pocket. 'It is now thirteen hundred exactly. But the visibility is not too good, and things might be worse. Do you know, Heuss, that on an Admiralty chart of the Atlantic a pin's head represents the complete vision of a ship at sea?'

He could see Heuss trying to concentrate on his casual words and not to be affected by the bark of reports from the voice-pipes behind him.

'Relax, Heuss. There is quite a wait yet!'

Heuss said quietly: 'We cannot outdistance her! We can only shoot with the poop gun, and that is a pea-shooter by comparison! What will you do, Captain?'

'I will explain. When action is joined, I will go about and engage her with torpedoes. While she takes avoiding action, I hope that Ebert will score a few good hits. I am depending on that to cool the Englishman down a little!'

366

Heuss peered back at the faint shadow astern. 'You will turn towards her? But, Captain, we cannot match points with a man-o'-war!'

'We must, Heuss. We have no choice. If we let her overhaul us, she will pound us to pieces at leisure. We cannot even mark her paint if she stays out of range of the twenty-two pounder, as you have observed. We must turn and show our teeth. There is only one other alternative.' He watched Heuss's eyes. 'Scuttle and surrender!' He saw the anguish working on the Lieutenant's face and waited.

'Surrender or die? Is that all we can choose?'

'Fight, or give the world the news it wants to hear, Heuss! That the cowardly German raider has given in like the treacherous dog it is! Has struck her flag to a warship, when she has slain and destroyed the innocent and weak without quarter!' His eyes wrinkled without humour. 'Is that what we want to allow, my friend?'

Heuss shrugged. 'My God, I believe you have been waiting for this!'

'Not waiting, Heuss, merely anticipating!'

·   ·   ·   ·   ·

The foremost gun of the starboard battery was situated below the fo'c'sle deck and snugly concealed behind one of the steel doors which had been cut into the raider's side. In the semi-darkness, and enclosed by the sun-heated metal, the atmosphere was stifling and tense. The bolts which secured the shutter were already withdrawn, and as the ship rolled it swung slightly away from the hull, revealing momentarily the sunlit water and the crisp, high wave creaming back from the bow.

Schiller stood at the rear of the long gun, his gloved hand resting on the smooth brass handle which secured the breech. His thick body swayed easily to the ship's urgent motion and his bare back sweated steadily as the long minutes dragged past. His eyes flickered to the hunched backs of the gunlayer and the trainer who sat on their little stools on either side of the gun, fiddling with their blind telescopes or scratching their sweat-tormented bodies. Behind Schiller the loader sat, collapsed on the steel deck, his arms wrapped round his bony knees, his eyes closed as if in prayer. The ammunition ratings moved restlessly around the oval hatch which connected them with the deep magazine below the waterline. Lukaschek, the loader, opened his small eyes and blinked upwards at Schiller. He had never forgiven Schiller for deposing him as senior man of the mess that first day he had joined the ship. He remembered the humiliation and fear when this great brute had thrown his blankets on to the deck and had made the other men laugh at him. Now he stood there, stolid and unshaken. While I, he thought, am almost afraid to stand.

Aloud he said: 'How much longer? I can't stand this waiting!'

Schiller looked down at him, his eyes still and lazy. 'Shut up, earwig! Your whining makes me puke!'

Petty Officer Elmke peered crossly into the gloom, his piggy face nervous. 'Silence! I am trying to listen!'

Schiller gripped the breech-handle and swore silently. Fools. Snivelling, gutless fools! If they try to run away from the gun I'll smash their skulls in! He thought of Willi Pieck in the sick-bay. I wish he was here with me, and Alder, too. Just like it was in the old days. Even Hahn would be more use than Lukaschek, at least *he* had guts. The gunlayer turned his head and looked at him. It was Schwartz, lanky, dour and impassive as usual. It cheered Schiller to see his miserable face.

'I wonder where the damned Tommy is, eh, Gustav?' Schwartz bared his uneven teeth to clear away a shred of tobacco. 'Christ, what wouldn't I give for a glass of beer!'

'A glass, you bastard? A barrel *I* want!'

Elmke hissed fiercely: 'Silence! I shall not tell you again! I must listen!'

Schwartz grinned. 'What for?' He whispered across the great shining breech, 'A message from the Pope, perhaps?'

A figure sitting apart from the rest of the gun's crew, his narrow head deformed by a giant pair of headphones, jerked upright as if he had received an electric shock.

'Attention!' His voice was loud and unnecessarily harsh. 'From Director, all guns load! Armour-piercing shell!'

Schiller drew a deep breath and pulled back on the brass lever. Like a great oven door the breech swung open. He watched as the long black shell was man-handled into the gaping hole and thrust into position by the rammer. His eyes watched the fat charge as it followed like an evil servant. He slammed the breech and stood clear, listening with half an ear to the gunlayer and trainer chanting to each other, and the communications rating reporting back to the gunnery officer. 'Number One loaded!'

·   ·   ·   ·   ·

Damrosch jumped as von Steiger brushed against his sleeve. The Captain hardly seemed to see him as he recrossed the bridge, his glasses swinging from his neck.

Damrosch tried to concentrate on his duties. In his mind he had laid out his plans like playing cards, allowing for every eventuality. He knew it was useless, because he had often heard that real action had no use for plans—it allowed only for the moment, a case of moral courage versus brute force. He told himself over and over again, like a child repeating a prayer, This is what I have been trained for!

There was an echoing rumble, like thunder across distant hills, and he felt the vomit hard against his tongue. He waited, staring down at the chart, counting seconds. There was a subdued explosion, something like a deep sigh, and he heard a rating report, 'Two cables short, sir!'

Damrosch felt the sweat like ice on his neck, and remembered Dehler's terror-stricken face. He thought furiously, They must be mistaken! Only two cables short with the first salvo. It was impossible, and yet . . . He stiffened as von Steiger moved to his side and picked up a freshly sharpened pencil. He felt his eyes drawn to the neat, firm writing as it moved across the log.

At thirteen-fifteen the enemy opened fire. That was all. No dramatics. Just a statement of fact which perhaps no one would ever read. He felt the edge of panic once again, and found that the Captain was watching him.

'That was a salvo, Damrosch,' he said calmly. 'They are not deceived. They are out for a kill.'

'Yes, sir. It was very close.' His voice sounded unsteady.

'Not bad shooting, but still out of range, I think.' He walked to the open shutter and looked at the bare masts.

'Petty Officer Heiser! Hoist battle-ensigns!'

Damrosch pulled himself away from the table and followed von Steiger to the shuttered door. Through the observation-slit he could see the giant naval ensigns climbing the foremast simultaneously with

369

the gaff. Against the blue sky the great black cross and spread eagle looked indestructible and arrogant.

Von Steiger called: 'See that they stay there, Heiser! Have your men ready with replacements if necessary!' To Damrosch he added: 'I expect that surprised the cruiser! They probably anticipated a white flag!'

Damrosch followed him with his eyes. How can he joke like this? How does he do it?

Another rumble cut his thoughts short, and he listened to the reverberating thunder as the shells ploughed harmlessly into the sea.

'Clear for action, Seebohm!'

Sub-Lieutenant Seebohm, short and fat, scurried to a telephone like an untidy spider. Within seconds of the order they heard the steel shutters fall, while from the poop came the impatient rattle of metal as the gun trained aft towards the enemy.

Damrosch glanced at the still damp paintwork and false fittings. In the harsh sunlight, and beneath the German ensigns, the wasted deception seemed to mock all of them.

. . . . . .

Heuss halted beneath the boatdeck and glanced quickly at the sky overhead. It was clear and bright, and no longer seemed part of the life which existed below it. He listened to the occasional thunder of gunfire from the pursuing cruiser, and found himself trying to calculate the range and estimate the nearness of those eager muzzles.

Against the sky the poop looked high and black, and he could see the white caps of the gunners as they crouched impotently around the weapon. He walked aft towards the poop, conscious of the deserted decks, of the great white wash which surged past him on either side of the hull and the shaking exertions of the engine. He walked into a twisting patch of shadow and glanced upwards at the great flapping ensign. He remembered the brave flags at Jutland, and felt his heart sink. There it had been so different. Surrounded by friendly ships, and within steaming distance of home, the battle had been fought in a daze of excitement and amateurish heroics. The flag which streamed from the gaff above his head seemed to emphasize their loneliness now and lay bare their weakness.

He reached the foot of the poop ladder and mounted the trembling rungs with quick, nervous steps. If only they could fire back. And yet the thought of what was to come when von Steiger turned the ship to face the cruiser made his brain reel.

Hellwege peered down at him, his face taut. 'When can we open fire, sir?'

Eucken, the petty officer, snorted. 'What the hell good would that do?'

Heuss peered over their heads and saw the fall of the last British salvo. The water fell in a great white curtain, very slowly, as if reluctant to reveal once again the plunging shape of the cruiser.

A bell jangled from the ammunition hatch, and Eucken banged the gunlayer on the arm. 'Right! Open fire when your sights bear!' He watched as the men leaned on their polished wheels and then looked towards Heuss. He shook his head briefly, as if to indicate that it was useless.

The twenty-two pounder hurled itself back on its mounting and simultaneously belched a long tongue of fire and smoke towards the cruiser. Through his glasses Heuss saw the single waterspout rise like a feather in line with the cruiser's haze-shrouded stem. Far, far too short, but it gave the gunners something to do, he thought.

The rating wearing headphones turned towards them, his eyes wild. 'Director reports we are going about! One hundred and eighty degrees!' He sounded as if he could not believe it.

Heuss threw himself down the ladder. When the *Vulkan* made her turn, she would momentarily expose her full length to the enemy. As he was now in charge of the damage control parties, he would have to be ready. He reached the boatdeck, and then felt his feet begin to slide. Cursing, he grasped a wire stay and hung on desperately as the ship's four and a half thousand tons careered round in a tight turn, the rudder hard over and every plate and rivet protesting at the violent manœuvre. He found that he was hanging on to the mast-stay and staring down across the lee rail as the surging water reached up towards the deck and the ship began to lean over at a fantastic angle. He set his teeth as the world exploded about him and a great hot breath seemed to suck the air from his lungs. The sea boiled and then shot skywards in two mountainous cones, while from somewhere forward he heard the splintering crash of a shell-burst, followed immediately by the uneven clatter of falling wreckage. He groped for his whistle, his eyes smarting with cordite smoke. He blew three short blasts, and yelled at the cringing shapes of the nearest party of men.

The ship had heaved herself upright once more, and even as Heuss ran towards the bridge he saw the brief flash of silver as Kohler fired his last two torpedoes over the rail. He did not wait to see where they had gone, but ran on through the splintered deck-planking, past a great smoking crater by the bridge, to Number Two hold which belched black smoke in a great twisting coil from the shattered tangle which had once been the cover and coaming.

'Come on there! At the double! Get those hatches replaced! Petty Officer, take your party below and tackle the fire from that angle!'

He reeled through the smoke as his men vanished like rabbits into the smouldering crater. He tried to guess what had happened. The ship must have been straddled by a full salvo, and struck by at least two shells. All around him he could hear shouted orders, faint cries and the hiss of water being poured on to the hungry flames. He turned to look at the bridge, and saw the levelled binoculars above the scarred plating and punctured woodwork. He followed the direction of their glasses and saw the cruiser, stark and suddenly close as it swung away from the two racing torpedoes. It had been a fantastic turn. The sharply curved wake still showed astern, clearly etched on the placid blue water, and instead of a dim shadow beyond the poop gun, the British ship now stood clear and grey on the *Vulkan*'s port bow.

As he stared, the cruiser's shape lengthened, her side still flashing with gunfire as her full battery came to bear. But this time her momentary exposure gave Ebert's gunners their chance. The big five-point-nines roared out their defiance, and almost immediately a bright orange mushroom burst from the cruiser's lean side, while close alongside another shell exploded dead on her spray-lashed waterline.

Heuss gulped with amazement as the guns fired again, and yet again. The shells screamed across the shortening range, and another hit was scored even as the cruiser twisted out of her turn and swung away from the torpedoes. Her slender maintopmast staggered, and then pitched over the side to drag alongside in a mass of aerials and loose rigging.

It was incredible. Von Steiger had made a great gamble, but had known that the enemy would hardly expect him to turn and fight.

They had hit the cruiser at least three times, and a fire was raging fiercely around one of her guns.

A ripple of cheers ran along the *Vulkan*'s guns, cut short immediately by Lieutenant Ebert's harsh orders from the Director.

A messenger groped his way through the smoke. 'Fire under control, sir!'

'Very good!' Heuss wiped his face with a filthy rag. 'Pass the word for more timber for this hold!'

He saw the man's tense expression alter to a mask of pain as a shell exploded on the foredeck. Before he was hurled from his feet, Heuss saw the man's chest open like a ghastly scarlet flower.

He struggled to his feet, shaking his head and trying to restore his hearing. The white-hot shell-splinter must have missed him by inches. He stepped over the lifeless corpse and ran towards the upper bridge. He could see the gaping holes punched along the front of the steel plates, and heard the crackle of burning woodwork from the exposed wheelhouse. As his feet slithered on the rungs of the ladder he felt his clothes pulled against his limbs as another great blast surged along the decks, followed by the tearing crash of crumbling metal.

He paused on the ladder, his forehead resting on a rung. He tried to control his shaking limbs and the fear which moved in his mind like a mad thing.

A voice, disembodied and unearthly, floated from the smoke. 'Stretcher-bearer! Stretcher-bearer! Quick, for God's sake!'

He bit his lip and half ran up the remainder of the ladder. The bridge was a shambles. Hardly a square foot of the place seemed to be unharmed, and the deck was littered with wood splinters, pieces of torn metal and, he saw with horror, a bunched, headless figure which crouched in the middle of the chaos like a hideous monster.

Von Steiger lowered his glasses and looked at Heuss with surprise. 'I am glad you came, Heuss! It is warm work here!'

Heuss moved round the corpse and noticed the flecks of blood which had splashed across von Steiger's white trousers. The air was acrid with cordite, and everything seemed to be covered with flaked paintwork and tiny particles of wood.

'Direct hit, Captain!' a messenger reported. 'One hit below her bridge!'

'Good work, eh, Heuss?' He turned towards the Coxswain, who

373

clung to the wheel, his eyes dark and unmoving. 'Hard a-starboard!'
He watched the spinning spokes and listened to a salvo as it roared
overhead. The shock-wave of its passing seemed to press down on the
bridge like a giant hand. 'Midships! Steer north ten west!' His orders
were quite clear and level, and Heuss blinked at him with surprise.

Von Steiger frowned as a great mountain of water rose close alongside where the ship would have been but for his helm order. 'Too
close, Heuss!'

Damrosch emerged from the wireless-room, wiping his hands on
his tunic. He saw Heuss and tried to smile, but his lips seemed to be
frozen.

Sub-Lieutenant Seebohm was shouting into a voice-pipe, his voice
rising to a scream as another set of shells plummeted around the rocking
ship. 'Gunnery officer reports seven casualties up forward, Captain!'
Seebohm seemed unable to let go of the voice-pipe. 'He wants
replacements!'

'Very well. Go up there yourself and see to it. Clear the poop gun
if necessary!'

Seebohm sobbed as a shell struck the bulwark and ricocheted along
the foredeck without exploding. It passed cleanly through a group of
seamen who were carrying a wounded comrade to safety. One man
was left whole. The others were scattered across the torn planking in a
writhing, scarlet tangle.

Von Steiger saw the look of terror on Seebohm's face. 'Go on, man!
It is no use looking at it!'

Seebohm ran from the bridge, and Heuss took his place by the voice-
pipes. He felt calmer now, hemmed in by noise and destruction. Deaf,
numb and helpless.

Damrosch turned his face away as a small shell struck the hull like
a fiery hammer and threw a few splinters over the bulwark. He saw
Seebohm falter, his hands pawing at the air, and then, as he half turned
towards the bridge, saw the great splash of colour across his chest.
Then he was down on the deck. Damrosch shook himself and stared
hard at von Steiger. It was useless to think of the dead. They were
already forgotten, ugly and without human form.

Von Steiger heard Damrosch vomiting, and walked to the rear of
the bridge. The cruiser was hidden beneath a pall of smoke, but was
firing with rapid, if haphazard, vigour.

He heard Heuss say: 'How bad is it, sir? Can we shake her off?'

'I think we have hit her badly. With luck we might——' His words were silenced by the single shell which struck the top of the bridge and blasted the Director to fragments. Splinters whined and clattered through the wheelhouse, and Lehr, the giant Berliner, fell like a tree, his thick fingers slipping from the varnished wheel as the life ebbed from his huge body.

Even as he rolled across the grating, another man was in his place and the spokes were harnessed once more.

Heuss found that he was sitting on the deck, his ears singing with a noise like rushing water. He watched dazedly as feet and legs rushed past him, and he had an unreal picture of mouths moving with silent commands, terrified eyes and limp bodies being pulled from the wheelhouse like slaughtered pigs.

Something moved in the wheelhouse door, and he could only sit and stare at it. He could hear nothing, and the blast had numbed his legs and made any decision impossible. Yet he still stared at Lieutenant Ebert. Karl Ebert, his friend. Ebert, the one cool-headed and dedicated man he met when he had first joined the ship. He crouched like a beaten animal in the shattered doorway, his uniform in shreds, his hands moving across the deck like claws. He had no face, just two wild eyes above a bubbling mess of blood and torn muscle.

Ebert had lost control of his beloved guns, but even at the end had wanted to report to his captain. Heuss saw all this and wanted to go to his aid. But even as the feeling returned to his legs and his ears restored the sounds of horror and death from all sides, Ebert pitched forward at von Steiger's feet.

Heuss pulled himself upright and looked at his captain. There was no pity, no remorse, to be seen. Von Steiger's features were composed, almost relaxed, as if he was praying.

'For God's sake, what are you trying to prove?' Heuss swayed on his feet and realized vaguely that the ship was beginning another sharp turn. 'What do you think this ship can take?' His voice was wild, on the verge of hysteria, but he could no longer control it.

The bridge seemed isolated in a great billowing pall of dense smoke, which repeatedly changed colour as the forward guns continued to fire at the cruiser and as fresh flames leapt freely from some new explosion below. The air was full of noise and flying shapes. Voices cried out from every side. Imploring, cursing, screaming and demanding. Around the foot of the boatdeck dark pain-racked shapes pulled themselves along the splintered planking, each move adding to their agony, but every inch bringing them nearer to the illusion of safety beneath the bridge.

Von Steiger lifted his eyes and stared at him coldly. 'Don't be a fool, Heuss! We are committed now! There is no turning back, there never was!'

He watched his words leave their mark on Heuss's white face and turned sharply to Damrosch who clung stiffly to a buckled voice-pipe. 'Get below, Damrosch! Get the prisoners mustered and ready to leave the ship. When you are ready, lower the boats to the deck level and report to me! Lieutenant Kohler has gone forward to supervise the guns personally, so he can probably cope with the fires there. But see that the petty officers are dealing with the other damage!' He halted Damrosch as he started to run for the ladder. 'Do not run! Remember that our people will be looking to you!' He held Damrosch's eyes with his own, compelling him. 'You are doing well! I am proud of you!'

Petty Officer Weiss appeared through the smoke, his beak of a nose pale against his blackened face. He glanced momentarily at Ebert's body and then stepped over it without a word. He took Damrosch's place and began to relay commands through the incessantly chattering voice-pipes.

A shell struck the tall foremast and exploded with a bright-orange flash. The mast reeled drunkenly, temporarily suspended by its rigging and stays; as they parted it staggered across the port rail and carried its great ensign after it.

Heuss lifted his head as the last of the splinters sang through the air or tore into the plating, and took a deep breath. The smoke rolled clear from the fo'c'sle head, and he saw the distant shape of the cruiser. Still firing, still attacking. He turned quickly to von Steiger as his numbed mind recorded that the *Vulkan* was not making another turn to avoid the next salvo. The Captain was gripping the edge of the screen, his head thrown back as he took great gulps of air. Heuss stared with horror at the steadily widening patch of scarlet across the right breast of the white tunic. He caught von Steiger as his fingers slipped from the screen and held him protectively below the rim of the plating. He heard himself say quickly: 'Hard a-port! Quickly, man!'

The ship heeled readily to the rudder as another great explosion rocked the hull. He fumbled with the buttons, his fingers reluctant to reveal what he knew would be there.

Von Steiger's gold-flecked eyes watched him, assessing his own wound from what he saw in Heuss's face. 'Lift me up, Heuss!' He struggled with sudden desperation, his hands reaching out for the rail. 'Lift me up, damn you!'

Heuss gritted his teeth and took a shell-dressing from Petty Officer Weiss. As he applied it to the great throbbing wound von Steiger twisted in his grip, his features contorted with sudden anxiety.

'Bring her about, Heuss! Our second gun is out of action! Bring the other battery to bear!' He coughed and clutched the front of his tunic to his chest in a bright-red ball.

Heuss tore his eyes away, and shouted fresh orders to the misty figures around him. It was madness to fight on, and he knew it. He could feel the ship reeling and shivering like a tortured beast, and on every side the air was filled with screams and distorted commands.

The voice-pipes kept up their cries of disaster and death.

'Poop's ablaze, sir!'

'Eighteen casualties aft!'

Heuss shook himself as von Steiger clutched his arm. 'The ensign, Heuss! The foremost flag has gone!' With a flash of his old power he shouted: 'I ordered Heiser to keep it flying at all costs!'

'Heiser is dead, Captain!' Heuss saw von Steiger slump back in his chair.

'All dead,' he said in a small voice. 'Wildermuth, Dehler, Seebohm and Ebert! I have done for them all!'

He would have fallen, but Heuss encircled his shoulders with his arm, cradling him against the shock and the savage thunder of the guns.

Von Steiger said suddenly: 'It is your responsibility now, Heuss! Will you strike your flag, or fight on?'

Heuss saw the agony on von Steiger's face, and looked around at the carnage. A great pall of smoke enveloped the ship, yet overhead the watery sun still shone. How can that be? he thought.

He felt von Steiger flinch as another shell plummeted on to the maindeck and hurled a giant winch into the air like paper. A derrick crashed on to the torn poop and cleaved down the struggling fire party. On the bridge, the remaining men still stood facing the enemy, their boots planted alongside their fallen comrades. A new ensign flapped from the mast-stump.

Von Steiger struggled upright in the chair. 'You won't let them surrender will you, Heuss? Not without honour?' His eyes shone like fire in his pale face, and Heuss felt the resistance draining from his screaming nerves.

How can I fight a man like this? Aloud he said, as if in reply: 'Starboard twenty! Steer due north!' The ship heeled, and Heuss stared down at the man in his arms. 'She is sinking, Captain! It is not long now!'

Von Steiger fought the nausea which threatened to engulf him with each movement. He listened to Heuss's clear voice, and watched the great black clouds of smoke which closed in on the wheelhouse. Heuss understood, and that was all that mattered.

As Heuss glanced down at the Captain he saw with amazement that he was smiling. Through his teeth he said: 'Close the range, Heuss! Close the range!'

Heuss shouted above the terrible chorus of death, 'The enemy have ceased fire!' He felt the hysteria in his own voice. 'They have ceased fire!' Below him, the *Vulkan* began to reel slowly towards the smoke-shrouded water.

·   ·   ·   ·   ·

Schiller slammed the breech shut and jumped clear, his streaming eyes already peering round for the next shell. The gun bellowed again, and hurled itself back on its recoil springs. Automatically he pulled back the breech lever, and coughed thickly to clear the fumes from his lungs. The ship was turning, and for a while his gun would no longer bear on the enemy. He watched the next shell being pushed home, and tried to remember how many they had fired. The confined space was filled with fumes, and the gun-barrel seemed to glow with the heat of battle.

Schwartz looked back at him, his face old and lined with fatigue. 'Poop gun's gone!' he shouted hoarsely above the roar of the other battery. 'Poor bastards were wiped out!'

Schiller spat, and leaned heavily on the lever. Hellwege, Schoningen and the fat ex-shoemaker, Gottlieb. Wiped away like steam from a pork-shop window.

Lieutenant Kohler thrust his way through the waiting figures, his chin jutting forward. 'Stand by there! Prepare to reopen fire!'

Petty Officer Elmke whispered from the rear of the gun mounting: 'They're pounding us to pieces! Why don't we surrender?'

'Keep quiet, you pig!' Kohler snarled through the dense smoke. 'One more word like that and I'll shoot you down!'

Schiller did not hear the shell which fell on top of the fo'c'sle, but was clearly aware of the great five-point-nine gun rising up in front of him, the steel bright where the mounting had burst in two. The gun lurched past him and fell back into a great jagged hole in the deck. He found he was looking straight down into the glittering water through shattered plates, the edges of which curved towards him like wet cardboard.

He shook himself and gave a low moan. He was alive, and, but for a long gash in his arm, unmarked. He saw the petty officer crawling round in a small circle, like a blinded animal. Schwartz had been cut down by splinters, and was smashed into a pulp against the steel bulkhead. The other gunners were lying in a tangled heap, and, as he watched dazedly, Lukaschek staggered free from their dead embraces and ran towards the rear door. Schiller watched him go, his ears closed to his shrill screams. Without arms, he thought, he cannot get very far.

Another sound made him walk unsteadily to the edge of the crater behind the mounting. Lieutenant Kohler lay on his back, the full weight of a steel girder resting across his legs. It was part of the support built beneath the gun, yet it had been blasted apart as cleanly as a carrot. Schiller watched as Kohler tried to pull himself clear, and noticed that the lower half of his trapped body remained motionless, as if he had been cut in half by the girder. Beyond him he could also see the gleaming surface of trapped water. God, he thought wearily, we are going down.

'Don't leave me!' The voice cut into his shocked thoughts like a knife. 'Get help! I am trapped!' Kohler's arms thrashed about, and reminded Schiller of a pinioned insect.

Schiller glanced at the dead gunners, and then spat. 'Go to hell!' he shouted. 'Better men than you have died today!'

He walked out into the smoke-clouds of the upper deck with Kohler's screams and curses still ringing in his ears. He saw the big ensign, torn by splinters, flapping gaily from the stump of foremast.

379

Great tongues of flame billowed from Number Two hold, where the coal had finally been fired by an exploding shell. He watched the line of prisoners being hurried to the boatdeck, and saw Damrosch, hatless and wild-eyed, as he pushed the last of the stumbling figures past the roaring flames.

Another shell burst alongside, and even as the spray hissed on the fires a seaman at Damrosch's side spun round and fell quietly on the deck. Schiller was bending over him as Damrosch returned.

'Is he dead, Schiller?' His voice was taut and brittle.

Schiller nodded, and stood up. It was Erhard. His sad face strangely composed in death.

'What is that in his hand?' Damrosch leaned against the deckhouse as Schiller prised it from the man's fist.

Schiller looked at the small, tattered bible in his hand and sent it spinning over the rail. To Damrosch he said: 'She's going down, sir! We'd better get to the boats!' He saw the indecision and anguish on the young officer's face and added, 'Come on, sir, I'll help you with the others!'

Schiller stopped and gaped at the two figures which reeled through the smoke, a third propped between them. Pieck and Alder were carrying a wounded petty officer, and also halted to peer with disbelief at the others.

'Hallo, Willi!' Schiller grinned with sudden abandon. 'Here, give me that one! You're too much of a shrimp for men's work!'

Pieck faltered as Damrosch and Alder hurried towards the boatdeck. 'Where's Lieutenant Kohler?' Pieck asked.

Schiller picked up the wounded man and said, 'Up forward!'

Another explosion sent them reeling, and when the smoke had cleared Pieck had gone, limping towards the fo'c'sle. Schiller shrugged wearily and shambled towards the boatdeck, unaware that the man he was carrying was now dead.

Pieck groped his way into the smashed gun-compartment, his boots skidding on the broken bodies and hot metal. He felt the pain in his broken ribs tearing him apart, but he ignored it, and followed the incessant stream of abuse, curses and sobs until he was down in the crater beside Kohler. It should have been his most triumphant moment, but the childlike gratitude in Kohler's terrified eyes robbed him of everything but pity.

Another shell ripped into the fo'c'sle and sent the broken gun rolling from its smashed mounting. Like a giant gate it crashed across the mouth of the crater and sealed the two occupants below.

Pieck felt the water cold about his feet, and looked upwards towards the tiny crack of filtered daylight. The water seemed to have reached his shins, and he was tempted to run screaming against the impenetrable barrier of steel. He felt a groping hand feeling frantically for him in the darkness, and with sudden determination he grasped it with his own. Then, in silence, they both waited.

. . . . .

Damrosch pushed a seaman away from the swaying whaleboat as it hung alongside the boatdeck. 'Get back there! Put these men aboard!'

He saw the dory and another whaleboat idling clear from the ship as it reduced speed, crammed with men, prisoners and hastily gathered wounded. Other heads bobbed in the smoke-covered water and then vanished astern; friend or foe he could not tell, nor did he care.

He realized suddenly that he had fallen to the deck and sat almost on the edge, his shocked eyes staring at the blood which seeped steadily down his leg.

A man seized him and bundled him into the boat, and then he was dropping down the ship's listing side. He was aware that the girl was crouched with him, and that a great silence had fallen. He lay back and stared at the blue sky beyond the smoke. I am alive, he thought. I am still alive.

. . . . .

Schiller scrambled up the port bridge ladder and pushed his way into the listing wheelhouse. He did not know why he had come, but felt a strange relief as he saw Lieutenant Heuss and the huddled figure of the Captain.

Schiller gathered von Steiger into his arms and staggered down the steep slope of the deck. 'I have him, sir! Come on, Lieutenant! There's nothing more you can do!'

Heuss paused in the canting doorway and peered back through the smoke. The wheelhouse was already lifeless and dead, like the men who were sprawled across its splintered deck.

381

With a sigh he followed the big seaman, and scrambled down the ladder to the deserted deck. It was barely feet above the hungry water, and he saw with dulled amazement that a boat was still hooked on and hands were already helping Schiller and von Steiger over the gunwale.

The boat pulled clear, and even the wounded seamen were silenced as a great shadow loomed across the calm water and blotted out the sun.

Von Steiger struggled weakly. 'Help me up! Quickly!'

He felt himself lifted above the gunwale so that he, too, was beneath the great shadow. Above him the *Vulkan* loomed like a black pinnacle of rock as she slowly lifted her stern towards the sky. Von Steiger raised his fingers to the peak of his cap.

With a great roar of inrushing water the *Vulkan* dived, as if eager to be gone from pain and humiliation.

Von Steiger watched the swirling whirlpool and said, 'Was the flag still there, Heuss?'

Heuss stared across his head at the girl, who held von Steiger's shoulders against her breast, her eyes brimming with tears. Behind them the British cruiser moved slowly towards the drifting boats, and the sound of their cheering drifted across the quiet water.

Heuss wiped his blackened face, the strength coursing back to his limbs. 'Listen, Captain! There is your answer. They are cheering *you*!'

Von Steiger smiled, and allowed his head to fall back. Poor *Vulkan*, he thought wearily. Together, we became the last raider.